LUCA²
ANNIVERSARY EDITION

GREYHUFFINGTON

TRIGGER WARNING

PLEASE READ THIS SECTION!

Seeing this note means the book that you are about to read could contain triggering situations or actions. This book is subject to one or more of the triggers listed below. **Please note that this a universal trigger warning page that is included in Grey Huffington books and is not specified for any paticular set of characters, book, couple, etc. This book does not contain all the warnings listed. It is simply a way to warn you that this particular book contains things/a thing that may be triggering for some.** This is simply my way of recognizing the reality and life experiences of my tribe and making sure that I properly prepare you for what is to unfold within the pages of this book.

violence
sexual assualt
drug addiction
suicide
homicide
miscarriage/child loss
child abuse
emotional abuse

PAPERBACKS
HARDCOVERS
SHORT STORIES
AUDIOBOOKS
MERCH
AND MORE...

Copyright 2023 Grey Huffington
All rights reserved.

The content of this book must not be reproduced, duplicated or shared in any manner without written permission of the author except for the use of brief quotations or samples in a book review, blog, podcast, or social media post without harmful or infringement intent.

In the event that this work of fiction contains similarities to real locations, people, events, or situations, it is unintentional unless otherwise expressed by the author.

instagram.com/greyhuffington

To my dearest Luca.

Thank you for one year of greatness. You were just the beginning.

G

LUCA²
ANNIVERSARY EDITION

GREYHUFFINGTON

PROLOGUE

EVER

THE SOUND of the garage lowering alarmed me. My eyes popped open as I lie in bed, listening for the engine of Dewayne's Corvette to sound in the distance. The roaring confirmed my suspicions. He had taken off for the night.

I sprang up despite the achiness in my body. From the very top of my head to the bottom of my feet, I experienced unfathomable pain from constant blows to the body. Suffering through the agony, I pushed through the bedroom we shared, headed for the closet. Inside, I stretched to reach the suitcases at the very top of it.

"Urgh!" Groaning, I folded from discomfort.

My rib cage felt as if it had been set ablaze. Lifting

my shirt, I examined the discoloration. With flared nostrils, I mustered the strength to push through.

"I'm sorry," I admitted, remembering to show myself the grace I deserved. Beating myself down wouldn't rectify the situation, building myself up would.

My spiked adrenaline forced me to continue moving instead of dwelling on the results of Dewayne's latest episode. I jumped once, and then again, finally catching the suitcase handle and dragging it down with me. Pain soared through my body as I repeated my actions, pulling down the second suitcase. The third was in the room just down the hall where my children slept peacefully.

I unzipped the largest suitcase and began stuffing it with the necessities, leaving anything that wasn't of value to me or my children where it was. Within three minutes, the suitcase was filled to the brim with undergarments, the twenty-five pairs of leggings I owned, a few pairs of jeans, all the t-shirts that would fit, two shirts suitable for interviews, a few dresses, a pair of tennis shoes, sandals, and the large envelope that housed all the important documents for the girls and I.

Feeling accomplished, I plopped down on the suitcase and ran the zipper from one side to the other. Simultaneously, my cellphone buzzed on the floor next to me. My breathing halted as I leaned over, prayerful Dewayne's number wasn't displayed on the screen. Lyric's contact replacing the image of his allowed me to continue breathing without flaw.

"Hello?" I answered.

"Hey. Just calling back to check on you and see if you made your final decision."

"I'm tired, Lyric. It's as final now as it was when I said it earlier. I'm exhausted," I choked, trying my hardest not to crack. There was work to be done.

"Say no more. How can I help?"

"Just be waiting for the girls and I when we get there. Lyric, I have nothing."

"You have your girls, Ever. You have everything you need. Don't let that stop you."

"I promise... It won't."

"Good."

"What time will you arrive?"

"Around eight, possibly earlier."

"You already have the tickets?"

"Yes. I got them about twenty minutes ago."

"OK. I won't hold you up. Do you need a Carriage or anything to get you to the station?"

"Yes. Please. We can be ready in ten minutes but I really want to waste as little time as possible. I won't have time to call you back."

"I got it, babe. Ten minutes, the car will be waiting."

"Lyric."

"Yes?"

"Thank you."

"Don't mention it. I'll see you when you arrive."

"OK."

I ended the call, popping right up and heading for the girls' room, lugging the suitcases behind me. Before exiting the bedroom, I made sure to grab my cell charger, the iPads, and the chargers they'd been on all night in preparation for this moment. The strength of a mother was the only justifiable explanation for the power to push through the achiness throughout my frame. Every step I made was harder than the one before.

Nevertheless, I made it to the bedroom and popped the light on in the closet, trying my hardest not to wake the girls until necessary. Kneeled in their closet with the door shut behind me, I stuffed the medium-sized suitcase with my oldest's clothes, making sure I didn't leave any of her favorites or anything she'd be needing for school. When the door popped open and in walked a half-asleep Essence, my heart plummeted out of my chest and onto the floor.

"Essence?"

"Mommy?" She yawned, rubbing sleep from her eyes. "Are you OK?"

As I recovered, I pushed the tears that were threatening to fall back. I nodded, dramatically, trying to convince us both that I was, although it was a lie from the pit of hell. I hated the thought of lying to Essence, so I compromised.

"I will be."

"What are you doing? Can I help?"

Inhaling, I counted quickly in my head in an attempt to keep from falling apart. Managing my emotions at the moment felt almost impossible but it was necessary.

"Can you help me get all of your favorite things that you need and that make you feel comfortable inside of the suitcase?"

I dropped my head, unable to look my child in the eyes and admit that I was disrupting our home and moving us six hours away to save us all from the turmoil we were in. I couldn't quite admit, yet, that I was ripping her away from her financial stability for uncertainty. I couldn't.

"Okay. But, why, Mommy?"

Taking a second to consider my next words, I quickly understood that there was no way for me to avoid the truth. Essence deserved that. Both of my girls did.

"Be-because," I stuttered. "I have to get us out of here, Essence."

I'd never talked to my children about the abuse that I endured in our home but I didn't have to. They witnessed it as often as it happened. Their father cared nothing about their presence when he raged.

"I have to go," I cried. "I can't stay here anymore, baby. I have to save myself, Es. I'm sorry. I have to—we have to get out of here. I'm sorry."

With both hands, she cupped the sides of my face and lowered her tiny frame onto the ground until we were both kneeling. I watched the glossiness of her eyes transform into full tears.

"I'm sorry, too." She cried.

"You're sorry?"

"I'm sorry Daddy hurts you."

"Don't be, Essence. Last time was the last time, OK?"

"OK."

"He can't hurt me anymore."

"Thank you, Mommy." She nodded as I wiped her tears away.

"For what, baby?"

"Saving us."

Pulling her into my chest, I buried her head and wrapped my arms around her. Her fragile frame shivered, confirming the accuracy of my decision. My trauma was her trauma and neither of us deserved any of it.

"We have to hurry," I announced, snapping out of the emotional rut and cleaning both of our faces. "We have about five minutes to get downstairs and out of the door. Finish packing your things and I'll pack Em's, OK?"

"Yes. Five minutes."

I used my cellphone to set a timer. Our arms didn't stop until it sounded. I rushed out of the closet and into the bedroom. Without waking Emorey, I pulled her into my arms and ran her down the stairs before coming back up for the two larger suitcases while Essence managed the small one with her sister's belongings inside. Just as the Carriage was pulling up, the girls and I were walking out, dressed in our nightly attire, ready for whatever the journey had in store for us.

LUCA·EVER

"WATCH YOUR STEP, ESSENCE," I whispered, rocking a sleeping Emorey in my arms.

My heart drummed against my chest as she reached the top step. I was next. My height increased immediately, making me bigger than I actually felt. Heck, small wasn't even the correct word to describe my feelings exactly.

Maybe it was *microscopic*. Maybe it was *inadequate*. Maybe it was *meager*. Maybe it was *insignificant*. Or, maybe it was *invisible*. It couldn't have been because I felt very visible. Exposed, even. Vulnerable to the highest degree. Which was why I peeped over my shoulder and out of the small windows that we passed each time I lifted and lowered my feet to the floor.

"Right here, Mom?" Essence stopped at one of the first empty seats she saw, drawing my attention to her thin frame, again.

"Uh. No, baby. Keep going," I instructed her, giving her back a gentle push so that she wouldn't hold up the people in line behind us.

We passed the seats two by two, a full year seeming to pass before we reached our designated seats. They weren't at the very back, but they weren't nearly as close to the center as I would've preferred in the event of an emergency. But for the task ahead, any seat would do.

"Here, Essence."

Because there were three of us, I'd purchased three seats. Only two of them were near one another. The other *was* at the very back of the bus, but I refused to even waste my time finding it. With children the ages of five and three, we'd have to make it work with the two seats that were next to each other on the same row. There was no way we were parting for the six-hour ride to Channing.

"Right here, Mom?" Essence pointed toward our seats to confirm.

"Yes, baby. Go ahead and take a seat near the window."

My arms were screaming for relief. Emorey felt like a sack of potatoes resting in them. Though she was a very petite girl, after over an hour of holding her, she seemed to have gained the weight that her doctor had been trying to get her to since she was born.

Essence obeyed, taking the seat closest to the window. I slowly laid Emorey in the seat I planned to occupy to relieve my arms of the pressure her little frame had put on them. Once she was settled, I began removing the bags and backpacks I'd brought along for the journey.

Last, my saving grace fell from my arm and to the ground in front of me. Not wanting to cause a delay in seating, I hurriedly snatched the stroller up and slid back into our row. The line continued to move, getting shorter each time someone found their seat.

There was just enough room between us and the seat in front of us for the small, emergency stroller I kept for Emorey. Sometimes, it proved to be the best fifteen dollars I'd ever spent. Though it was cheaply built with only bones and absolutely no support or padding, it got the job done in a crunch. Tonight was definitely one of those moments. I unfolded it while still standing in the aisle and pushed it between our row and the one in front of us. Once I realized there wouldn't be any leg room for me, I pushed it closer to Essence's end to create space.

I placed a sleeping Emorey inside, never disturbing

her beauty rest. She was a hard sleeper, just like her sister. The two of them didn't hear anything once they closed their eyes. The world could be ending and they wouldn't know until they woke up in the afterlife.

After getting her squared away, I pushed the bags that I'd brought onboard underneath the seats in front of us so that they wouldn't be in our way. They were filled with snacks, juices, and small games that didn't require too much space but would keep the children entertained if necessary. I hoped that the late trip would help them rest, but one never knew with children. A trip with them could be a dream or it could be a disaster.

"Hhhhhhhh." I sighed loudly as I sat down, finally.

"Mom, I'm tired." Essence yawned. "Can I go to sleep with you?"

"Of course, love."

She placed her feet near the window as she maneuvered until her head was in my lap. I could feel her little breath tickling the thin strands of hair on my legs as she sighed, too. My heart ached for her, *for us*. She, too, was feeling the effects of our sudden relocation. My babies deserved to be home sleeping in their beds, but things beyond my control had led us here with the three of us crammed into a space designed for two.

"I love you, kid," I reminded her, smoothing her frazzled curls back into the low ponytail she'd attempted to keep her long, sandy hair out of her face.

"I love you, too."

Exhaustion had worn my baby down, and I wanted nothing more than for her to rest well and get comfortable, even if it made me uncomfortable. I was willing to suffer if it meant she wouldn't. There wasn't a question about it.

The chattering of the passengers picked up slightly after everyone was seated near or next to their loved ones. Each time a deep, unfiltered baritone sifted its way through the crowd, my head darted in its direction – needing a face put to it immediately. My anxiety wasn't any good for situations as such, but I had to survive it. This was the only option left.

The bus driver made the final call for boarding as he prepared to close the doors for our trip to begin. I pressed the side button on my phone to light the screen. It was nearly one-thirty, our official departure time.

A sense of relief washed over me, allowing me to finally breathe once the doors closed and the bus proceeded from the gate. For the first time since I'd packed as much of the girls' and my things that would fit into the three large suitcases three hours ago, I could close my eyes.

Dewayne had put his hands on me for the last time, and instead of retaliating or physically harming him as payback, I chose my sanity and safety. Because mentally and emotionally, I'd left him two years ago. I was just waiting for the physical aspect to follow. My only fear was the lack of financial resources that I had for myself and children, but after so long, being broke wasn't the worst of my fears. Staying committed to failure was.

Starting from ground zero had never sounded better. With only four hundred dollars to my name, I bought my children and I tickets to Channing, leaving me with only two hundred dollars. With a place to stay already lined up when we touched down, I knew I could figure the rest out when it was time.

Lyric was a godsend. When I called her asking to crash in her spare bedroom with the girls for six months, she agreed without hesitation. Neither did she hesitate to tell me she'd been waiting for us to make the move. Her joy for the decision I'd finally decided to make spoke volumes because she'd never truly voiced her opinion about my predicament. She simply listened when I needed an ear.

"I couldn't force you to be ready. When you were, I knew you'd leave and never look back," she told me as we cried on the phone together. They weren't tears of sadness, but of happiness and joy. I'd finally put myself first and that was worth the tears.

The same tears that I'd cried on the phone with her, I felt dropping from my eyes as I closed them. We'd hardly made it out of the station, but the freedom I felt was indescribable, so instead of attempting to place or describe the feeling, I allowed myself to just feel. That's all I wanted and needed. To feel.

It had been a day from hell, but my girls and I were safe and headed to our new home. It was only temporary, but there we didn't have to worry about their father's temper, distaste for anything remotely close to living the life that a real man was supposed to, random fights, or long nights.

Unlike Dewayne, Lyric was predictable. She went to

work, came home, loved on her family, and repeated the process, again. I knew because I'd been her friend for the last ten years and that's how it had been since we had gotten close. We met at my cousin's wedding over eight years ago and fell into a friendship. It was one that I never knew I needed but definitely did.

That was before I'd gotten accepted into a culinary school for my degree and moved six hours from Channing. That was before I met Dewayne and put my dreams on pause, quitting school mere months before I was set to graduate.

It was before Essence and even Emorey. It was even before I'd discovered my pregnancy with Dylan and lost him. She'd been by my side through it all, making trips to see me as often as I needed her presence. This time wasn't any different. When I called, she was to my rescue.

Though I'd closed my eyes briefly, rest was truly impossible. My thoughts were all over the place. They all screamed at once, demanding my time and attention. There was only one that caused my eyes to pop open only fifteen minutes into our trip.

I need employment... and fast. With only about two hundred dollars to my name, I knew I was walking a fine line and would soon have nothing. I hadn't been broke since I'd gotten my first apartment and lost my job right after. It was the year before throwing caution to the wind and moving away. That year had been tough but this year was even tougher.

I unlocked my phone using face recognition and

opened the Safari browser. Google had gotten me very far in the past, and I was hoping it did me justice once more. In the search bar, I began describing my needs.

On-the-spot hiring in Channing City, I typed. Instantly hundreds of results popped up, but there was one that stood out to me a little more than the others. I clicked the title and it took me to a gorgeously designed website for a popular eatery in the city.

I'd heard great things about it, but I'd never gone myself. It was partially because I no longer lived in Channing, but also because I was always in and out when I did visit. They weren't frequent, and they were never pleasure trips. I always came for a reason and left within forty-eight hours of my arrival. There wasn't time to do much of anything.

Baisleigh's House. The brunch house was hiring for a new waitress and special events coordinator. The roles were intertwined and after a quick glance at the base pay, my interest was piqued.

According to the listing, the special events coordinator was paid thirty dollars per hour for the coordination of large party brunches, birthday brunches, corporate brunches, and more. Outside of coordinating events, waitressing was the chance to make money when an event wasn't being planned or hosted. The base pay was twelve dollars in addition to 100 percent of the tips received daily.

Coordinating was only part-time. Waitressing was daily guaranteed income. That's exactly what I desired. I didn't have three to five weeks to wait for a check from a nine-to-five. I needed money to be flowing through my hand from the time I walked through the door until I walked out.

Without hesitation, I clicked the link that led me to the simple application. The questions were straightforward, occupying my thoughts and helping me think of something other than my current situation for once. I scrolled, tapped fill blanks, and uploaded documents stored in my files before submitting the application for consideration.

As I shut off the light from my cell, I rested my head on the seat and reclined it approximately three inches. It was as far back as the seat would go, but for now that would be enough. Sleep wouldn't find me. I knew that for a fact. Rest wasn't my goal – not until the girls and I were safe and with Lyric.

The silence of the bus as the passengers settled and dozed off lulled me into a state of calm and quiet that not even my thoughts could interfere with. Though I wasn't at peace, the moment was peaceful. The creaking of the bus as it trudged down the highway, mile after mile, remedied my soul.

Almost, I reminded myself. Almost out of the city that had caused me more pain than it had brought me progress. Almost away from the man who'd cornered me with his financial, physical, emotional, and mental abuse. Almost back where I started. Almost where I belonged and where I could thrive. Almost home.

I peered at a sleeping Emorey in the stroller in front of me. She seemed miles away. With Essence sound asleep in my lap, I strategized how I could retrieve Emorey and have the two remain comfortable in their sleep. Every solution ended with the realization that any arrangement other than the one we had would be uncomfortable for my girls, except one that would result in tired arms and possibly a stiff back for me. For the tranquility they both brought me, I was willing to sacrifice it.

Leaning forward, I pulled my sleeping child from her stroller and placed her head on my shoulder. Her legs dangled near Essence's head as her butt hung slightly over my right arm. She adjusted to her new position, still sleeping as she made herself comfortable. I rested my back on the seat, once more, sighing as I settled into the quietude that our new arrangement offered my soul.

My heart rejoiced as I laid my left arm on Essence's back. At that very moment, my entire world was in my palms. The two humans I'd given birth to mean everything to me and it was because of them I had muscled the strength to finally hit the ground running – with nothing to my name.

I love them so much, my God. The prickling of my eyes and slowness of the ache in my chest accompanied my thoughts. Willing myself not to cry, I inhaled deeply and exhaled dramatically until I had counted down from twenty.

Everything will work itself out – even if it doesn't look like it right now. I had nothing to worry about because as long as I had my girls at my side, I knew I could overcome any obstacle put in front of me. I owed them a good life, and I wasn't going to stop until I gave it to them. I turned my head, watching the white stakes of the highway as we passed them by. After fixating my sight on the road, I became rooted in a comfortable restfulness where sleep wasn't necessary or welcomed.

LUCA-EVER

WITH TIRED EYES from staring in the darkness for hours on end, I used the edges of my hands to clear the blurriness as we approached the well-lit rest stop. According to the itinerary, it meant that we were halfway through our trip with only three hours left to reach our destination. As the bus came to a stop and the lights throughout glowed, Essence began to come to. Rubbing her eyes, she lifted her head, bumping up against Emorey's house shoes.

"Ouch," she whimpered.

"Are you okay, baby?"

The force from the blow made her rub her head and made Emorey stir in her sleep. Paired with our voices in the distance and she, too, was popping her little head up to see exactly what was happening around her. Her onesie clung to her body as she slid down my arm and into my lap where Essence once was.

"Mommy, I so tired," Emorey told me as she laid her head on my chest.

"I know, Em. Mommy is too, but the good thing is you can go to sleep again. I'll hold you in my arms until you do."

"Good evening, ladies and gentleman, we're officially

halfway there. This stop is for anyone needing to stretch their legs, take a cigarette break, use the restroom, freshen up, or grab something from the store. Meet me back here in thirty minutes. We're pulling off with or without you, unfortunately," the driver announced.

Simultaneously, my phone began buzzing in my hand. I checked the screen, noticing another blocked call trying to get through. It didn't take a genius to know who was behind the blocked calls. Dewayne had finally gotten home and noticed we weren't there waiting for him.

In a panic, I was certain he'd tried my cell only to discover he'd been blocked. Now he was shielding his number to try to get through to me. It wouldn't work. Not this time. It was too late for the apology that he mustered after each fight. It was too late for the shopping spree or the trip or the new car.

For once, I was giving myself the apology I desperately needed and it had nothing to do with words. Changed behavior was the only apology I was accepting, now, from myself or anyone else. I deserved that. I owed it to the future me.

I silenced the call and placed Emorey on her feet in front of me. She didn't understand what was going on and her confusion brought a smile to my face. She was the cutest, tiniest thing with the biggest personality.

Just like Essence, she shared my hazel eyes and sandy brown hair. Both of them had skin that mimicked the color of mine. Brown sugar. It was the only thing that came to mind when trying to describe our shade. My genetics seemed to be the only ones that showed up to the party when my girls were created. Years apart, and they were still mini versions of me, twinning to the fullest.

"Do you have to potty, Em?"

"Yes, Mommy," Emorey yawned, again.

"What about you, Essence?" I turned to her and asked.

"Yes, ma'am. I need to pee," Essence said, stretching her arms as she watched me stand and join Emorey.

Because the stroller was stopping her from sliding out of her seat, she slid across the row until she was able to stand with us. The other passengers were preparing to exit as well, causing a line to form to get down the stairs to the first level and then outside.

My girls practiced patience as we waited. Once we were outside, I pulled Emorey's tiny frame into my arms with the knowledge that she was extremely tired and wasn't up for much of anything. The heavy breath she exhaled confirmed my suspicions. She was grateful that I'd taken the task off her plate.

"Come on, Es," I demanded, gently, while reaching for my daughter's hand.

Once our palms connected, I picked up the pace and headed straight for the gas station's doors. If I could, I wanted to be one of the first in the girls' room. With Emorey's impatient bladder, it was best if I got her in and out.

"Thank you." Appreciating the kindness of the stranger holding the door open for us all, I thanked them.

The store's bell chimed as we entered the store. Emorey's head popped up as I felt Essence's grip on my hand loosen. Both of their eyes blossomed as we passed the selection of goodies on the way to the restroom.

Thankfully, there wasn't a long line at the door. The restroom was large, allowing up to twenty-five people to enter a stall at a time. We entered the family stall that was equipped with two toilets, standing room, and a changing table for the babies. There were also two sinks, one smaller for the children to wash their hands. We were in and out in under six minutes.

When I bent to pick Emorey up again, she swatted my hand away. Much more alert, she made her way through the store, lacing her hands into Essence's. When the two of them stopped near the front of the store where the snacks were located, I gnawed on the inner corner of my lip, trying to find the words to tell my children that we had to get going and couldn't stop for snacks. It would be a lie, something I'd prided myself on never telling them, but as I stood watching them browse the selections, the words failed me.

My stomach knotted at the realization that it was the first time in the girls' lives that I'd be telling them I wouldn't be buying them anything. And for the first time, it wasn't because they already had too much or had just bought other things. It was because I couldn't afford it.

The fact nearly brought me to both of my knees as I stared at a browsing Emorey and Essence. Turning in the opposite direction, I smeared the tears threatening me with sorrow with the end of my shirt. Coughing, I concealed the heart-aching whimper that my body fought to release.

While I wasn't a stranger to struggle, my children hadn't seen anything remotely close. They'd been blessed with the best of everything, except a healthy relationship with their father and a balanced two-parent household. Anything else, they were privy to. Leaving their father meant leaving it all behind – for now. Soon, we'd be up, but for the moment we weren't.

"One thing, girls," I caved, unable to deny them of their instant gratification.

"Okay, Mommy," Essence called out, taking a look over her shoulder to let me know she understood. I melted three times over. She couldn't comprehend the situation fully, but she was aware that things had immediately changed for us without much explanation, and I was thankful for her maturity – even at her tiny age.

"Only one, Em. Choose one and put the other one back," she explained to her little sister so that I wouldn't have to. She was willing to be the villain in Emorey's story for the moment, freeing my conscious and lifting my spirit.

"Come on, girls," I requested. "We don't have much longer before we have to get back on the road. Hurry with your selections."

After a bit more debating on Emorey's end, she decided on a Push-Pop, and Essence went with a bag of tropical Skittles. The four-dollar total was a breath of fresh air to my account, especially knowing I didn't recall a time that the girls and I didn't spend at least eighty dollars at the gas station when including gas for my Mercedes.

We returned to the bus with a few minutes to spare. Because both of the girls were awake, I pulled their iPads from their bags to keep them occupied. For more legroom, I folded the stroller. Both of the girls fit comfortably in the second seat of our row. Emorey laid against me with her iPad in my lap. Essence propped hers up on the small tray that flipped down in front of her. With her Skittles in her hand, she zoned out, headphones in as she watched Disney+.

As we settled in, the bus pulled away from the curb and onto the roadway. My cell stirred in my lap, vibrating shortly. The rhythm let me know it was a text instead of a call, and I simply prayed Dewayne hadn't found a new way to contact me.

Dee called me. He wants to know if I know where you are. It was my mother. Obviously, he'd taken desperate measures and reached out to her at ungodly hours.

What did you tell him? I wanted to know, praying she hadn't slipped up in any way and let him know we were on the way to Channing. It was unlike her, but I had to hear it from her mouth.

Nothing, of course.

Good. Answer if you feel inclined, but you don't have to if he calls back. Just make sure you continue to remind him that you have no idea where we are and haven't spoken to me.

I don't plan on telling him anything.

How far are you guys? My mom double texted.

waiting for the girls and me and that was all we needed. The rest would figure itself out. I wasn't afraid to get it out of the mud. I just wanted a little help while I did so. I couldn't do it on my own, not with the girls. My mother and Lyric were more than enough to help me establish my foundation.

Anxiety swelled in my chest, feeling as if someone had my heart in their palms, squeezing it, but for the first time since packing our bags and getting to the bus station, it wasn't embedded in mind-numbing fear. It was the kind of fear that changed your future that had me breathing deeply and counting down from twenty in my head as we turned the corners of downtown Channing. Fear of just how great things could get, that's what had me in a chokehold.

As we pulled into the station's gates, I noticed Lyric's matte Rubicon near the entrance. She stood outside of it with her suburban girl persona on full display. Even at six in the morning, she was the definition of Black girl luxury. There was so much I'd learned about being a woman – a softer version of one – in the last decade of knowing her, and I couldn't wait to soak up so much more. Because I was always in survival mode or on defense, I didn't have the privilege of softness or vulnerability.

That's what made it so hard for me all these years with Dewayne, but it was time to stand for who I truly was and wanted to be. I was ready to let my guard down and if that meant never letting a man get close to me again to stop from getting taken advantage of, then so be it. I didn't mind being single until I was buried if it meant protecting my softness and fragility.

When the bus came to a complete stop and the doors opened, those without bags were the first off and located their loved ones if there were any waiting. The girls and I were among the last to exit and grab our luggage from the area designated for the undercarriage.

Lyric was falling over laughing as she watched Emorey's little legs moving so swiftly as she wheeled her luggage in the suitcase that was bigger than her. Essence struggled with the large hard-shell suitcase I'd tasked her with but was relieved by Lyric once she noticed the challenge.

"Hi." Lyric leaned forward and greeted Emorey once we were all at the curb waiting to put the bags in the back of the Jeep.

"TT Lyric?" Emorey finally realized who'd been waiting for us.

She had been so focused on the task at hand that nothing else mattered, but as soon as she noticed Lyric, she dropped the ball. Her suitcase fell to the ground as she let the handle go and ran toward Lyric, who was kneeled and waiting to embrace her. The two loved each other dearly. They'd formed a bond that I never saw coming, but was beautiful to watch.

"Hey, Es," she called out to Essence after she'd scooped Emorey into her arms. It would be hell getting her to let Lyric go, but I wouldn't complain. It would be great to have a break from the little one.

"Hey, Auntie Lyric." Essence blushed. She, too, was fond of Lyric.

"Come on. You kids look like you could use some breakfast and a bed. Let's get you guys settled in. Get in. I've got the bags."

"I can't let you do that alone," I told Lyric, heading for the tail of her truck.

"You're not letting me, Ever. I'm demanding. Now, get in the truck. You've done enough, love. Your hardship ends here. It's time to relax," Lyric emphasized.

Silence sat between us as emotions flooded me at once. Deciding against challenging her, I followed directions and headed toward the passenger side. Essence and Emorey followed me. I put them both in the backseat and strapped them down, already cringing at the missing money from my account that a new car seat for Emorey hadn't even taken yet.

Once the girls were settled, I slid into the passenger seat. I wasn't sure how, but Lyric had beat me. She was already seated when I pulled my seatbelt over my waist. When we didn't pull into traffic immediately, I turned to her to see what the issue was.

"What?" I asked, noticing she was staring at me.

"Here," she responded without answering my question.

My eyes fell, finding and then following her hands as they sat neatly banded and stacked bills in my lap. Each band had a $1000 label on it. With furrowed brows and an aching chest, I turned a bit more in my seat and begged for an explanation from Lyric.

"That nigga not stopping shit for you, Ever. I've just been waiting on you to make the call. You don't owe me anything. Get on your feet. Don't rush into getting a place to stay. Stack your money at my place. You can stay as long as you'd like. It's big enough for us all. That's eight thousand dollars. I've already gotten Emorey into my mother's school, so don't worry about that. I can take her once she wakes up. She can do a half-day today.

"That'll give you time to get Essence prepared for tomorrow. You've already filled out the necessary paperwork. We can stop by once Emorey is at school to finalize things. Look in the glove compartment. There's a printout from one of my brother's good friends who owns a cash car lot. Find one you think you'll love that's within your budget, and we can pick it up tomorrow when the girls are away."

"Lyric." I couldn't gather anything else. That was all I had. That was all that would come out. "I have to pay you back. I promise I will."

"Win, Ever. That's how you can pay me back," she responded, finally putting her truck into gear and pulling out of the parking spot she'd been occupying.

LUCA²
ANNIVERSARY EDITION

GREYHUFFINGTON

ONE

EVER

THREE WEEKS LATER...

SUNDAYS WERE ALWAYS the busiest and for them, I was so grateful. I'd worked three Sundays in a row and hadn't gone home with less than three hundred dollars in tips. Though I wished I was at church worshipping with my babies, I knew there would be a time for it. Right now wasn't it. The thought saddened me as I stared blankly at nothing in particular.

Each Saturday night, I dropped the girls off at my mom's in preparation for an early morning shift that didn't end until after four. I didn't mind the long hours because it gave me more time to wait on more tables, which resulted in more tips.

Only a few hours after I'd submitted my application, I received a call from Baisleigh, my boss, and the owner of Baisleigh's House. She scheduled an after-hours interview for me the same day after explaining to her that it was my first day back in town, and I needed to get my girls into school before stopping by.

At seven-twenty that evening, I was signing the employee documents, getting a code for the register, and having my schedule printed at once. Baisleigh had hired me on the spot, willing to take a chance on someone who was willing to take a chance on themselves. My transparency sat well with her. She, too, had once experienced a narcissistic partner.

The following day, after driving off the lot with the Avalon that had cost me five-thousand dollars, I headed straight to work. It was a day of training and one that had overwhelmed me to the point of tears once I made it home to my children. Since Essence was discovered in my womb, I'd been a stay-at-home mom, afraid of losing her like I'd lost Dylan. Dewayne supported us, so working wasn't on my agenda. My job was to take care of our home, and I did it well.

"Ever!" Baisleigh yelled, startling me as I stared out the window at the blazing sun.

"Hmm?" I snapped my neck in her direction. From the tone in her voice, it was obvious that it wasn't her first time calling my name. So lost in my thoughts, I hadn't heard a word she'd said.

"Are you OK?" she asked, concern etched in her forehead lines.

She was darling; beautiful inside and out. With her, everyone was on the same playing field, from the janitors to the managers. She made working in hospitality simple and so did her customers. They were the most respectful bunch of people I'd ever met and from all walks of life as well. I hadn't had a bad encounter with anyone yet and according to the staff, I probably wouldn't. It was highly unlikely. Just as Baisleigh was a respectable boss, her customers respected her and her place of business.

"Yeah." I sighed. "Just thinking about my girls and dreading getting out in this Channing heat. It's brutal."

"It is. I'm having the landscaper come out next week to plant more trees. That'll offer us all a little relief from the sun, especially our cars. Getting inside your vehicle mid-day is torture."

"Exactly. That's why my car is cooling off while I watch from the window," I agreed.

"But seriously, are you OK?" She stopped wiping the table that she'd been cleaning and closed the gap between us somewhat.

"Are you adjusting well? Do you or the girls need anything? I'm always here to help in any way that I can."

"It's a huge adjustment, but it's going well. The girls are getting acclimated with their new schools. Emorey, my youngest, had never been to school prior to us moving so it's been somewhat of a challenge for her. She's never been away from me so much or for so many hours a day."

"And how are you feeling about it?"

"A little guilty because I enjoy the break. Even though I'm only at work when she's away, it's still the break I didn't know I needed from motherhood."

"I'm not a mom yet, but I promise I get it. We all need a break sometimes."

"We do."

Baisleigh didn't pry, but she made it a priority to check on every staff member to make sure that we were all taken care of. I appreciated that. I appreciated her.

The Channing sun beamed on me relentlessly as I pulled the shade from my car's windshield. It was nearing five, and with the girls at my mom's for a few more hours, I had time for a much-needed nap. Making it to Lyric's was the only thing on my agenda.

Thank God. I sighed as I got comfortable in my seat, taking in the coolness of the AC. It was one of my favorite aspects of my car. Though it was an older model, the air conditioner performed exceptionally well.

My cell had always automatically connected to Bluetooth when I was close enough to any of the cars I'd had in the last decade, but my 2007 Avalon was a bit different. The USB cord was my only hope, being that there was a technical issue stopping my phone from connecting to the system on its own. When I found the time, I planned to have it checked out or a new stereo installed completely, but the USB cable would do for the time being.

SZA's "Miles" began to play as soon as the cable was inserted into the charger port of my phone. My journey began shortly after with me pulling out of the parking lot and merging onto the expressway almost immediately after. I still knew the Channing streets well. Since I'd been home, I had yet to need the GPS as long as I knew the area of the location I was headed to.

And why can't I be like everyone else?

Losin' my mind, think I look good when I'm really just high.

Scared of my life, can a bitch get by?

Sick of listening to everyone else.

Sick of my pride.

Sick of saying shit just to be nice.

"Ohhhhh," I sang with SZA, feeling like she had a microscope, peering into my life when she wrote most of her songs.

I wasn't sure how, but she just got me. She understood. She knew. Or, maybe she was just like me in so many ways that our lives entwined in her song. Whatever the case, the combination of her voice and lyrics were exactly what my heart and soul were always missing.

"Miles runnin' wild in my head," I continued along until the short piece ended a few seconds later.

When I arrived at Lyric's four-bedroom home twenty minutes later, I wasn't surprised to see her truck in the driveway. Like me, she was a homebody. If we weren't coming out for work or the girls, we were locked away in our rooms without guilt or shame.

I unlocked the door with one of the three keys that Lyric had given me once the girls and I woke from a much-needed nap the morning we'd made it to Channing. As I stepped inside, I noticed two bags stacked on top of each other beside the door. Lyric hadn't mentioned going on a trip, but it was obvious that she was going somewhere for at least the next two or three days.

"Lyric," I called out as I searched the common areas for her.

When I discovered she wasn't in the kitchen, dining rooms, living room, or theater, I headed for her bedroom. It could only mean that she was buried in her closet or inside of her bathroom. Those were the only two places she could be that she couldn't hear me calling her name.

Her home was immaculate, and I'd tried my hardest not to let the girls wreck the place. Every time I got onto them, Lyric would get onto me about being so hard on them assuming that they were ruining the place when they were simply being children. She'd even forbade me from picking up after the two of them each time they put something down. Now, I waited until they were sound asleep and done destroying the place before I moved a muscle.

I stepped into her bedroom, admiring the spaciousness and earthy decor as if it was my first time seeing it. The neutral tones made the space feel airy and light. It was the same theme that traveled throughout her home, even in the girls' room, which she'd totally transformed since we'd arrived. What was once a bland guest suite, she converted into a haven for the girls, completed with bunk beds and large toy chests for each of them.

"Good, you're home." Lyric appeared from her bathroom just as I approached the door.

"I am. Were you so bored without me in the next room being bored, too?" I asked her.

"No. I'm just glad you're here so that we can hit the road. My brother, Laike, was supposed to be picking up my oldest brother in the morning, but he can't make it. Something has come up so he's asked me to. I figured we could turn this into a mini vacation. You know? A girls' night out in another city? It's only one night, so that it's not overwhelming for either of us. You need a little fun for once, Ever."

"I don't know, Lyric. The girls have school in the morning. My mom might have something to do tomorrow." I tried talking my way out of the impromptu trip, though I knew it was pointless. Lyric had made her mind up *and* packed our bags. There wasn't any talking myself out of this one.

I've already called your mom to see if it's OK for the girls to stay until we get back tomorrow evening. She said she'd take them to school in the morning. By the time they're out, we will have been back for at least a few hours. He will be released at eight in the morning. Possibly earlier."

"Released?" I could feel my brows center on my forehead as I asked.

"Yes. Released. He's been gone for eight years. I've mentioned this one to you before, Ever. Don't get slow on me now. We need to get going."

"Okay," I agreed, still trying to recall a time when she'd mentioned anyone but her brother, Laike, whom I'd yet to meet. He seemed busy enough and hardly ever sat still long enough, but I was sure it would happen with time.

"So, you're in?" Lyric smiled.

"I don't think I have much of a choice and maybe you're right. I could use a real break that isn't Baisleigh's House."

"Now you're talking," Lyric sang. "I've already booked our room and packed our bags. Just hop in the truck. We have four hours until we're there."

"Where is there?"

"Cadet."

"In Azul?"

"Yes, in Azul. Not very far. I'll drive the entire way. You focus on getting some rest because we're going outside tonight. Maybe you'll meet one of them Cadet men. I heard their pockets hang low and not just from their pistols. From their paper, too."

"Hooray, good for them. I'm not interested. Dewayne was the first and last of that kind I'll ever deal with. Give me a square. The one not everyone wants and the one that can treat me like I need to be treated."

"The way Dewayne treated you had nothing to do with his occupation, unfortunately. He's just a shitty person. He could've been selling insurance, and I promise he would've been the same asshole. It's embedded in him. He's wired that way."

"Maybe you're right, but I'm not going to try to find out. Aside from how he treated me, the lifestyle itself is just scary. Living in constant fear just isn't my cup of tea anymore."

"I get it, Ever, and I don't blame you."

"Let me slip into something a little more comfortable and then I'll be ready. It'll only take a few minutes," I said to Lyric as I looked down at the Baisleigh's House uniform I still wore.

"Of course. Meet me outside. I'm going to load up the truck and wait for you out there."

"Wait. I don't have anything in my closet that seems suitable for a night out so what did you pack exactly?"

"I didn't even check because I figured there wouldn't be anything. After I got the call from Laike this morning, I visited the shopping centers and got everything we'd be needing for the trips so we're both good."

Lyric was a dream. She always took matters into her own hands when it came to taking good care of the people she loved. She wasn't overbearing and neither was she nonchalant about anything when it came to her circle of friends and family. I just prayed that I'd one day be in the same predicament so that I could be the blessing she'd been to me.

"Thanks, darling."

Before leaving her room, I leaned forward and kissed her red cheek. Her high yellow skin was smooth like a baby's bottom because she took care of it like it was one. Each night, she was painting a mask on her face or exfoliating. She'd even gotten Essence into a small skin care routine that she followed faithfully each morning.

"Don't mention it."

LUCA-EVER

"I SHOULD'VE LIED. I should've done it. I should've given away all my love."

"Or maybe I... I should've played you because you don't appreciate me, no," I sang along to Keyshia Cole's track with Lyric as we crossed Azul's state line.

With Cadet being on the edge, it was the first city we entered. Lyric had cut the four-hour trip down by thirty-five minutes with her heavy foot. She'd gone one hundred miles an hour the entire way when the speed limit was only seventy. What was supposed to be a chance to rest for me became a bonding experience for her and I.

It was our first road trip together, and I didn't want to waste it on sleep I could get back home. We only had a few hours to make the trip count and that started the second I got into her truck back at home.

Darkness surrounded us as we pulled into the roundabout in front of our hotel. Valet rushed toward the truck and began opening the doors straight away. I stepped out with only my purse in my hand. Lyric was right behind me with her purse strapped across her body.

"I've already checked in on the app. The key is digital so we don't have to go to the front desk," she informed me as we watched the valet attendants get our bags from the back.

"We can carry them up ourselves," she told them, grabbing one and handing it to me while she kept the other.

I assumed it was my bag that she'd given me. I wasn't sure because I'd never seen either of the Michael Kors weekenders. Both beautiful, they were in different colors. Mine was eggshell and brown. Lyric's was black all over with speckles of gray here and there.

"Are we in a rush?" I asked in my attempt to keep up with her pace as we headed for the elevators.

"Not really. I'd like to be out by eleven and back by three. We have a forty-minute drive to my brother, so we need to check out by six-thirty." She pushed the button and an elevator pinged instantly.

"Gotcha. Where are we heading?" I stepped on before her.

"I hate clubs, and I know that you'll agree with me on that so I was thinking of a lounge that stays open until the wee hours of the morning." Lyric pushed the button that displayed the number thirty as the doors closed behind us.

"I'm loving that idea," I chimed in, holding onto the rail as the elevator ascended.

Lyric and I were much the same. We loved the same things, had the same taste, and preferred peace over chaos. The only difference between us was she'd never let a man tear her confidence and sanity to shreds.

That's why we bonded so well. She was exactly who I would've become had Dewayne not entered my life. She mirrored the me I was desperate to be, which was why I loved and respected her so much. A lounge was right up our alley.

"I figured you would."

We stepped off the elevator and walked a short distance to our room. There were over fifty floors in the boutique style hotel. I didn't even want to calculate the numbers in my head as they pertained to how much Lyric had possibly paid for the room, so I simply asked.

"How much is this hotel a night?" From the thick carpet underneath our shoes to the wallpaper on the walls, it was spectacular.

"Right at five hundred. Laike's treat, not mine. He's funding the trip since he got us out here. So, don't hold back. Everything is on his tab and his pockets aren't shallow. Have the time of your life because I plan to." She tittered.

"That would sound like music to my ears if I didn't have a two-drink alcohol tolerance and preferred clubs over lounges. There won't be a light show, bottle show, insane entry prices, or unlimited shots. I can't hang. Maybe I'm getting old."

"Lies. Because I can't hang either, and I'm not old. We're the same age. That just isn't our thing. Never has been, or at least since I've known you. If it's chill, we want in. That's it. That's all."

"The lounge life is my type of life," I concluded.

"I made a tiny list of some near, but it's one in particular that I've heard good things about," Lyric shared as we stepped into our hotel suite.

It was stunning. The double beds were both queen-sized with thick linen and a gift bag on each. For once, something at a hotel was actually complementary. Inside the bags were body washes, toothbrushes, mouthwash, body scrubs, and a small Bluetooth speaker.

"I'm going to shower before I even sit on these sheets," I told Lyric who was digging through her bag of goodies as well.

"Me too," she looked up and replied.

The suite was equipped with two bathrooms, one on each side and near each bed. I chose the one closest to the full-length, floor-to-ceiling windows. The small sign that was attached to the corner of the shower, which also had a full-length window inside, assured me that no one could see my privates through the glass.

We're thirty plus floors up with one-way views. Your secrets are safe here.

I could see outside, but no one could see inside of the glass. With that notion, I stripped down to my bare skin instantaneously. The shower automatically started when I stepped in, allowing me to change the temperature with the small dial that was near the door.

LUCA·EVER

"AND TWO DISARONNO SOURS, PLEASE," I requested from the waitress after ordering a serving of Cajun pasta and garlic knots.

"For you?" she turned to Lyric and asked.

"I'll have the same, minus the drinks. She was ordering for us both," Lyric responded.

The crushed velvet booths and marble tabletops were direct indicators of the lounge's customer aesthetic. Their inventions were to attract the middle to upper class African Americans who enjoyed a good time in a clean, luxe environment. It was designed with women in mind, the plush swings instead of chairs at the bar were proof.

"Ever, I'm no genius, but I'm not a dummy by far," Lyric started, picking up the drink menu that we'd been given.

"Where is this going?" I inquired, preparing myself for whatever shenanigans Lyric had up her sleeve.

"Since we walked up, there's been a particular set of eyes on you. And I don't want you to look now, but that same set is staring in your direction right now."

"Lyric, you're seeing things because I haven't felt or seen anyone staring at me. I can pick up on those things easily. Always have."

"Then, let me just say you're a little out of whack tonight because those eyes are headed in our direction, and I'm almost certain they'll stop at you."

I began to heat all over. Instead of looking up to see if what Lyric was saying was true, I began asking myself a million questions in my head. *Do I look fat in this?* was the first that came to mind, followed by, *am I slouched? How is my posture? Why is he looking at me and not Lyric? Don't everyone know I just got out of a relationship?*

I was flooded with questions that didn't have answers as I straightened my posture and took a good look at the black pants and black cropped button down that hugged my abdomen area.

"Told you," Lyric squealed on the low.

When I looked up to gauge the distance between the man she'd sworn had been staring and I, I was surprised to see that there wasn't much – *if any*. His hand extended as he lent me his palm to meet.

"Hi. I'm Cedric. And you are?"

His smile was inviting, showcasing a set of perfect teeth that were pearly white. Either he'd visited the dentist faithfully since a kid or he had gotten the most natural set of veneers available. Whatever the case, his smile was beautiful.

"I'm Eve," I half-lied. Eve was part of my name, so it wasn't an awful fib.

Lyric's sniggering nearly caused me to break the seriousness of my gaze, but I remained straight-faced as I accepted his hand in mine. The softness of his skin reminded me of my own. Except he was darker and aged a bit more. Looking at his handsome face, I'd give him about seven or eight years my senior. So, approximately thirty-eight.

"Nice to meet you. Mind if I buy you a drink?"

"Only if it doesn't come with your company. As much as I'd love to hang another time, tonight is special to my friend and me. I'm not looking for a third wheel, tonight," I explained, happily speaking up for myself for once.

Those days of not saying exactly what was on my mind, setting clear boundaries, and telling them what I wanted when it came to a man were over. Dewayne had ruined me for the rest of them. From day one, I wanted to be as assertive as my thoughts and heart required to save myself from heartache and pain in the end.

"That's cool. I'm not trying to stop your shine, love. I just wanted to make sure we connected before either of us got on our level. But since we're cutting straight to the chase, do you mind if we keep in contact?"

"I don't," I admitted, admiring him from my chair.

The dark denim and tee to match were suiting. The clear glasses with the gold rim revealed the truth. They were part of his attire. He didn't need them to see. They were cute, in general and on his face.

"Then lock your number in, and I'll leave you two ladies to your fun," he told me as he handed me his phone.

"I'm Ever, by the way," I folded, unable to keep the lie going.

I didn't have it in me to do so. Lyric would clown me for it later, but I could stand the heat. Lying had always been hard for me, which is why I preferred not to if I could help it. Even harmless lies got my panties in a bunch.

"DAMN, you hit me with the fake name." Cedric chuckled as he dropped his head to count the money he'd pulled from his pocket.

"Kind of, but I mean, my name does have Eve *in* it."

I shrugged while returning his phone. Simultaneously, he was handing me two crisp hundred-dollar bills. I wasn't sure why, so I looked to him for an explanation.

"Tonight is on me. If you guys need more, just holler at me. I'm in the section near the bar. You can't miss me."

When I looked in the direction where he was pointing, I nodded. He was right. I couldn't miss him. He was in the section that wrapped around the corner. It was the largest of the few the lounge offered. Lyric and I had only grabbed a small booth for seventy-five. Anyone that wasn't in a booth or section were left to stand in the free space throughout the lounge. There was a lot of it, leaving it spacious without feeling overcrowded.

"You don't have—" I started but felt Lyric kick me underneath the table. "Thank you, Cedric."

"No problem, Ever."

He left our booth without more being said. I didn't even care to look in Lyric's direction because I knew she was wearing a dirty little smirk. After staring ahead and the smile bursting from my seams, I snapped my neck in her direction.

"What?" I knew she was staring at me.

"Okaaaaaay! I see you!" she chanted. "Just make sure you never turn down a man's offer to give you free money while you're in front of me."

"Coming from a relationship where a man controlled you with this very thing..." I held up the money for emphasis before continuing. "You're pretty hesitant to accept it, knowing how much pain and time it cost you."

Lyric didn't respond. She simply nodded her head to let me know she understood. Dewayne had used my lack of finances and his abundance of cash to keep me gagged and bound to our relationship. It was the sole reason I'd stayed as long as I had. I didn't have anything. Barely a dime to my name. He only gave me enough money to pay bills, and he knew how much each of them cost. Whenever anything more was needed in our home, he made me use his debit card.

In a full year, I'd only been able to save four hundred dollars and that was not from his pockets. It was from birthday gifts that I'd returned and small amounts of cash that fell from birthday cards for the girls' birthdays. Technically, not even that money was mine. It was theirs. We didn't want for anything, but Dewayne never gave a red cent extra when paying.

The night continued without flaw. My two-drink limit was increased substantially, being the reason I handed the waitress the two hundred dollars with wobbly hands when it was time to pay our tab. Three drinks, two shots, and a hookah, which neither me nor Lyric had ever smoked in our lives.

Cedric had sent it over shortly after our food arrived after first offering marijuana to smoke. We politely declined but accepted the hookah after the waitress demonstrated how it was to be used.

"We don't need any change," I told her.

"It's literally more than two hundred dollars, Ever. Ain't no change." Lyric laughed hysterically.

Trying to catch my breath, I zeroed in on the ticket and realized the tab was two hundred and twenty-four dollars. Not only was there not any change, but I hadn't given her enough. My eyes darted around the lounge in search of Cedric, but his handsome face had disappeared from the section he'd been in all night.

"He told me he'll handle the rest," the waitress informed me as she placed a hand on my shoulder to calm my racing heart.

Sighing with relief, I looked at her and nodded. "Thanks. Make sure that he tips you well."

"He will," she stated as a matter of fact, letting me know she knew something about Cedric that I didn't.

"You ready?" Lyric asked, still sniggering.

"I'm ready. Are you sober enough to drive?"

"When I get behind the wheel, I'm about as sober as sober gets. I don't play with my life. I can't. My brothers would kill me again if I killed myself and broke their hearts like that."

Hearing Lyric mention her brothers made my heart warm. She was the youngest of her siblings and though she hardly talked about them, I knew she loved them and vice versa. As I thought more about their closeness, I realized why I'd never heard anything about her oldest brother. He wasn't around so there wasn't anything to say about him.

"And, my babies wouldn't let me rest in peace, so get us to the room safely!"

My phone displayed four missed calls from a blocked number once I tapped the screen to see what time it was. Dewayne had yet to get the point and was still trying to figure out where I'd gone with the girls. I made a mental note to change my cell number as soon as I got the chance. I had yet to, but I would. I'd had the same number for so many years, it would be hard letting it go, but I knew it was necessary.

"We were supposed to be back by two," I reminded Lyric. "It's almost four in the morning, Lyric."

"Time flies when you're having fun," she responded with a shrug as we got situated in her truck.

"It does," I agreed, resting my head on the passenger seat.

TWO

EVER

"EVER."

I could hear Lyric's voice in the distance.

"Ever!"

It got a bit closer.

"Ever!" Panic stricken, she yelled my name as she shook my body.

For once, I felt like Essence and Emorey – a bump on a log. Lyric had obviously been calling my name for some time, but I was too tired to even hear her. That was happening a lot lately. I can't remember sleeping as hard as I had been since moving back to Channing. Or maybe it was the fact that I didn't have to look over my shoulder or worry about Dewayne coming home on his bullshit, *if he came home at all*. The peace the move offered me had me sleeping like a baby. Like my babies.

"Yeah?" I groaned, eyes still closed because I wasn't ready to wake, yet.

"It's right at seven. We overslept. He'll be released in the next hour. We have to get going," she rushed out, shaking my arm to wake me completely.

Finally, I sprang up and out of bed. I knew how important it was to Lyric to be at the gates when her brother exited them and the last thing I wanted to do was hold her up. I could sleep in the car, on the way to the prison and back to Channing. For the moment, I had to muster the strength to get packed up and down to the truck.

"OK. OK. I'm up. I just need like five minutes to get myself together, and I'll be ready."

"Same. I need five, too," an obviously exhausted Lyric agreed.

I'd never seen my friend look so pathetic. After the lounge, we'd ended up grabbing more food from the twenty-four-hour burger spot on the way. Our plan was to stay awake and leave at six. That way, we could drive to the parking lot of the federal facility and fall asleep there waiting for her brother, but it didn't happen that way. Around five, we both crashed. Lyric had set her alarm, but apparently we'd both slept right through it.

God, maybe my children got it from me, I thought as I made my way to the bathroom to quickly freshen up. My clothes were already out and waiting to be put on, but I needed to run a wet, soapy towel over my body before anything fresh touched my body.

That was a peeve of mine, putting fresh clothes on a dirty body. Technically, mine wasn't filthy, being that I'd showered before we went out, but it was dirty enough. I tiptoed on the cold floor, cringing as I made it to the sink and turned on the water. I quickly re-entered the room and grabbed the slippers Lyric had bought and packed for me along with new panties and a bra.

The temperature of the water was perfect when I touched it with my hand. I grabbed the thick, costly towel from the towel dispenser that was on the wall. There were three of them. One for face towels, one for hand towels, and one for bath towels. When they ran low, the housekeeping staff was automatically notified and brought fresh ones to the door.

Lyric and I had discovered this on our way out of the door last night. She'd used all the hand towels. Before she could fix her mouth to ask for one of mine, there was a housekeeper at the door handing her more.

I soaped the towel with the Dove face wash Lyric loved so much. After scrubbing my skin until it tingled, I added a quarter-sized amount of body wash onto the same towel and began scrubbing my entire body. The task of cleansing and rinsing the soap off only took two minutes. When I was done, I patted myself dry with one of the bath towels from the dispenser.

Feeling much better and a bit more alert, I stepped into my panties and then hooked my bra. I oiled my skin, skipping the parts that weren't necessary to coat or wouldn't be visible. Time wasn't on my side, so I had to take a few shortcuts. When I completed that, I pulled my toothbrush from the holder on the wall. I honestly didn't think that there was anything the designers of the hotel experience hadn't considered when creating it.

The gray shirt, gray leggings, and comfortable slides that Lyric had chosen for us both felt like butter on my body. The jersey knit fabric was pillow soft and fit like a glove. I dressed in haste, getting myself together in the five-minute timeframe I'd promised Lyric.

She was still in the bathroom by the time I'd finished. Her clothes had disappeared from the bed, which let me know she was getting dressed as well and would be out shortly. I utilized the extra time to pack both of our bags and sit them by the door. Lyric's was left open in case she needed to put anything else inside.

While waiting, I did a once-over in the room to make sure that I hadn't missed anything. The coast was clear. As I ended the search, Lyric popped out of the bathroom wearing a tee and leggings that were almost identical to mine, only hers was a much darker gray and her shirt was cropped. The material and maker were the same.

"You ready, love?" I asked as I watched her stuff a few pieces into her bag.

"Yeah. I won't forgive myself if I get there, and he's already outside."

"Should we stop for gas, first?" I hoped we could make it. That would only put us behind schedule even more.

"No. We can stop on the way back. There's enough to get us to him and then some."

"Alright. Well, I'm ready. We can head downstairs."

My head was throbbing, and I wanted nothing more than to close my eyes and rest. Lyric looked like she could use some more shut eye, too. Though she looked a lot better than when we'd awakened, she still looked shot. I did, too.

Lyric's perfectly sculpted, braided ponytail that had hung past her waist was now wrapped, creating a bun of sorts. On her face, she opted for shades to cover the redness of her eyes. I didn't have any, so I had to muster the courage to face the harsh light as we made our way to the elevator.

Still hungover, silence was the only thing either of us wanted to hear. It hurt too much to talk or think, so words weren't a preference, either. All we could hear as we descended was the pinging of the elevator with each floor that it passed. When we made it to the lobby, Lyric stepped off first with the valet ticket in her hand. She handed it off to the attendant before we made it out of the door so the car could be pulled around.

The bench that was reserved for waiting guests seemed to have been calling my name from the time I noticed it until I sat on it. Lyric flopped down beside me, close enough to rest her head on my shoulder as I got comfortable. The whimper that followed was hilarious, causing me to laugh out loud.

"Shut up," she warned me. "I couldn't help it. I feel like I've been hit by three trucks."

"Can't be, because then you wouldn't feel a thing. You'd be dead, babe."

"You're right. Maybe a half of a truck, then," she corrected, causing me to chuckle.

"Our ride is here," I told her as I watched her truck roll around the roundabout.

"Already?" she groaned.

"Already." Confirming, I patted her leg for a bit of comfort. It was all I could offer at the moment. We needed to hit the road, and we needed to hit it immediately.

"He's driving back to Channing. I'm taking a big, fat nap as soon as he takes the wheel."

She sprang from the bench and stomped outside like a toddler who couldn't have their way. I wanted to, but I knew that both of us acting like brats wouldn't change the situation. One of us had to keep a leveled head. I assumed that would be me.

"He. He. He. My brother. My oldest brother. The one that's in jail. That's all I keep hearing. What's your older brother's name, Lyric?" I probed as we neared the truck.

"Luca," Lyric stopped in her tracks and revealed.

Luca, I repeated to myself.

LUCA-EVER

AS I GOT SITUATED in the passenger seat, my thoughts led me back to Channing where my children were getting up and getting ready for school. I searched my purse for my cell phone, only to notice it was dead when I located it.

"Do you have some juice?" I asked Lyric as I held the charger cord up.

Although I wanted to call my children before they were off to school, I knew Lyric needed her phone more than I did at the moment. She needed it for the GPS as well as any communication between her and her brother. We were running behind, so just in case he called, I wanted her to be able to answer instead of him being sent to voicemail. That would make anyone worry.

"Yes, ma'am. I somehow managed to get mine on the charger last night. I literally don't remember doing so, but I have a full battery," she explained.

"Well, at least one of us was thinking somewhat clearly."

I'd never consumed as much alcohol in my life as I had at the lounge. I wanted so badly to chastise myself or feel anything remotely close to guilt, but I felt nothing. It was a good time and one I needed. I didn't plan on having so much to drink, again, but I didn't regret the ones I had. Even the hangover and throbbing headache wasn't enough to make me reconsider anything. I'd enjoyed every minute of my time out and that was the end of the story.

I pushed the end of the power cord into my cell and laid it on my lap to wait for it to restart. My eyes closed involuntarily as I sighed deeply in an attempt to relax my body. Between the rising morning sun and the bumps we hit in the road, I didn't think it was possible. Not with my head aching and my body punishing me at the same time.

"You alright over there?" Lyric muttered.

"Are you alright?" She was in much worse shape than me.

"No. The only thing that's keeping me together is knowing it's only a forty-five-minute drive and then I can lay the fuck out. I literally halfway want to cry, but I had too much fun to be a bitch this morning. I'll save all my tears for when I see my main man. I've missed him so much."

"I bet. I don't have any siblings, but if you ever went away for all those years, I'd be sick to my stomach daily."

"So, imagine my pain. We haven't even known each other for a decade yet. This man knew me before I even knew myself. That's why I never even mention his name. They broke my heart when they gave him that time. It hurts to even think about it or him."

"What did he do?"

"Killed my ex-boyfriend."

"I'm sorry, what?" I sat up in my seat, trying to gather my thoughts.

"I caught him cheating, and being the narcissist he was, he got mad at me for something he'd done and getting caught. I left him, but he wasn't having it. A week after I called it quits, he showed up at my apartment. It was late at night, and I didn't even notice him. Usually, I'm a little more aware of my surroundings. My brothers have always taught me to be. He caught me off guard. I feel like he would've killed me had Luca not pulled up. He was coming over for a plate that I'd put up for him. I'd cooked dinner, but he wasn't able to make it. I ran to the gas station to get him some wraps because he loves to smoke before he eats, and I wanted him to be comfortable. When I got back is when Chauncey attacked me. Anyway, long story short, he had a white judge and prosecutor who refused to give him manslaughter because he had a prior gun charge on his record. He wasn't supposed to be around any weapons. He was given a sentence of ten years. He's done eight and is coming home."

"Lyric, you've never..." I started, but she interrupted me.

"Ever, there's a lot that I've never told you. Not because I didn't want to, but because telling you one thing would require me to tell you why that thing is or how it came to be. Luca is one of those things. My past relationship, one of those things. I was with Chauncey from seventeen until I was twenty. My brother was sentenced the week before I turned twenty-two. I met you a few months later."

"I had no idea."

"I lost two men I loved that night. Though Luca didn't physically leave me until he was sentenced, I knew it was coming and no matter how strong he wanted me to be, I couldn't prepare myself not to see him for so long. I felt like it was my fault, too. That's why I understand and have never judged your situation at all. I know what love feels like, and I know what redemption feels like too. I want that for you, so I've stayed out of the way until you was ready for it."

"Did he pull up while he was still there?"

"Luca pulled up while he was outside dragging me like a dog. He'd never fought me so hard. We'd had little fights, but never on that level. I should've left then, though, when the little fights began. I thought it was just how relationships worked, but I know better now. If a nigga has to put his hands on me, he can't have me. That's it."

"And, that's why – that's why you haven't been in a relationship since," I repeated the words I recalled her saying.

"Since my ex. That's why I'm always saying that. I cannot put my people's lives and freedom on the line again for the sake of love. It's not worth it. The minute I feel myself falling, I'm out." Lyric chuckled though I could hear the pain she was trying to disguise. She was only laughing to keep from crying.

"Before meeting you, I was a mess. Not the way I moved or anything like that, but my life. My brother had gone to jail, my ex was dead, my mother was diagnosed with breast cancer, and my other brother was wilding. He was lashing out about Luca's situation and it wasn't pretty. For the first time, money couldn't even dictate his outcome. They were out for his life, and they got a big chunk of it."

I listened as Lyric revealed things she'd kept buried inside. She didn't mention her life before we met that much. She only spoke about life after, but I always figured it was because that's when life really started for her. At twenty-two that's when it really started for me and that's all she ever really heard about on my end, too, but hearing her explain her reasons made all the sense. She'd blocked it all out because it was too painful.

Ping.

Ping.

My phone's screen lit up as notifications came flying in. I wasn't familiar with the number they'd come from, so I bypassed them to get to my call log. My mom was the first number on the list. I tapped the screen and dialed her up.

"It's your mommy, Em," my mother said to Emorey, who I assumed was near.

After a bit of ruffling and heavy breathing, her little voice boomed through the phone.

"Mommy?" Emorey answered the phone.

"Hi, baby. What are you doing?" I could feel my smile as it pushed my cheeks further into the sky. As tired and unwell as I was, my girls always brought a smile to my face.

"Nothing," she responded. "Where are you?"

"Mommy is taking care of something really important and will be back in time to pick you up from school, OK?"

"OK."

"Are you being good for your grams?"

"Yes," she answered, nodding her head.

"What about Essence? Where is she?"

"Her in there. Her still sleeping."

"Mom!" I started.

"I was on my way to get her up when you called.

She's already dressed. She wanted to lie down until I got Emorey together and it was time to go."

"Well, it's about time for you guys to leave out."

"Ummm hmmmm. I got this. I don't need a manager or a monitor," my mother sassed.

"Alright, now, your mouth getting a little too sassy. How old do you think you are, honey? I will take out my belt," jokingly, I warned.

"Goodbye, Ever. I'll beat your ass before you can beat mine."

"And she's using profanity. Wow."

My mother ended the call, not up for my crap so early in the morning. I wasn't sure how I'd gotten the energy to even give her all that I did. Because, as soon as I ended the call, I was slumped in my seat with my head in my hand again.

Oh yeah, I thought, remembering the notifications that were sitting in my message thread. I unlocked my phone again and opened the new, unread messages from the number that was unfamiliar to me.

Hope you got home safely. -C

Good morning. Can I interest you in a conversation over breakfast? -C

"He texted," I spoke my mind, though I hadn't meant to.

"Who? The guy from last night?" Lyric wanted to know.

"Yeah. Cedric, I think his name was."

"That's it." She nodded. "I like him. He's not overbearing and he's not in Channing. Honey, that's good money, seems like good dick, and some distance. It's just what you need right now. Nothing serious."

"Right. Nothing serious. I'm not even looking to have sex right now. I just want to give my little coochie a break. She gets me caught up. I can't trust her."

"OK then, good coochie. Must be nice," Lyric sang.

"Shut up. I guess I should decline this breakfast invitation and let this man know that I do not live in Cadet or nowhere near. I was only stopping by."

"Ummm. Hmmm. But let him know that he's invited to Channing, though."

"Not really, but whatever." I shrugged.

Hi. I wish, but I was only stopping through Cadet for the night. I'm on my way back home now. Maybe another time?

Where you live?

Channing.

You right up the street.

If you say so.

I know so. What you getting into this weekend?

I'm working this weekend and every weekend up until the 29th.

Well, it seems like I'll be seeing you on the 29th, he responded, unfazed by the distance.

The screen on my phone seemed so small or maybe it was only because my eyes were hurting. Words were tinier than usual and it was taking me a bit longer to read the messages that appeared on the screen. I decided to give it a rest and close my eyes for a brief moment.

"You got anything in particular you want to hear?" Lyric nudged me to ask.

"Silence." I tittered.

"Come on, Ever. I need something to keep me up until I get there," she whined.

"OK. OK." I grabbed her phone and unlocked it. Her music app was already open. I searched for some goodies and began compiling a playlist for us.

Though exhausted, sleep didn't come easily. Too worried about Lyric's driving capabilities under the circumstances, I couldn't rest. So, instead, I played the DJ as we continued the forty-five-minute drive.

"If his status ain't hood, I ain't checking for him," Lyric sang while I stayed quiet. For once, those were lyrics I could no longer relate to.

"Got to be street if he looking at me, I need a soldier," I joined, knowing that no matter what type of man I met and married in the future, I wanted him to be familiar with my urban world.

That part would never change. No matter his profession, I wanted him to know what it looked and felt like to grow up in a Black neighborhood. That was a box he had to check or he couldn't check for me. It was simple.

LUCA·EVER

THE SUN HAD SETTLED in its position, which happened to be in the parking lot of the prison where there wasn't a tree in sight for shade. The wait for Lyric's brother had officially commenced, which meant that it was safe for me to rest my tired eyes and body, but the sun's brightness was unbearable, forcing me to climb to the back where our bags were to grab something to help shield my eyes. I found the shirt that I'd worn to Cadet the day prior. Black, it was the perfect shield. Before I was able to climb back up, Lyric had the back door open as she adjusted the seat cover to her liking.

"Ma'am, what are you doing?" I chuckled.

"I'm about to lay the hell out as soon as he gets in. I want to have my bed prepared."

"If you're back here, then where the heck will I sleep?"

"Shit, either on top of me or in the front seat. You can sleep sitting up. I can't to save my life. I have to be laying down."

She was right. I could sleep upright if necessary. Her passenger seat reclined enough so that I didn't have to, though. If I let it back far enough, it touched the back row, nearly lying flat. I didn't even put up a fight when I thought about it.

"You're right," I admitted, climbing back into the passenger seat where I began to get comfortable. Sleep was waiting impatiently for me. With heavy eyes, I knew it wouldn't be long before I was out completely.

Bzzzzzz.

Bzzzzzz.

Bzzzzzz.

"Can you hand me that?" Lyric asked me as she

pointed toward her phone, which had stopped playing music to alert her of an incoming call.

"Sure." I removed the phone from the cup holder and laid it in her palm.

She slid her perfectly manicured nails across the screen before saying, "Hey, what's up?"

"You made it?" The sonorous baritone consumed me, demanding my full attention.

"Good morning to you, too, Laike."

Her brother, I concluded once she revealed the name.

"Yeah, all that," he calmly, collectively responded.

"Yes. We've made it."

"Aight. They'll release him around nine."

"Nine? I thought it was eight?"

"Na. I told you that so you'd be there on time. I know how you like to get your beauty rest and shit."

"Laike, are you serious? We're here an entire hour early. What do you expect me to do in a parking lot for an entire hour?"

"Get some sleep. Seems as if you could use some. Have you seen yourself?"

"Shut up. I had a long night."

"That goes without saying. Get yourself together before he exit those gates. He's already been worried about you."

"Why?" Her brows furrowed as she frowned.

"Because that's what big brothers do, Lyric. Just pull yourself together, love. Have that nigga to call me when he touches down. Get some rest."

"Wait."

"What's up, baby girl?"

"I love you," she rushed out.

"Always," he responded.

My heart swelled listening to the exchange. The love was in Lyric's eyes as she stared into her phone at her brother. They ended the call shortly after.

"He hates talking on the phone," she shared with me. "But he also hates he couldn't be here. I can imagine that won't be the only call from him. I'm sure he will call me more today than he does in a month."

It wasn't until she mentioned it that I realized in the three weeks I'd been at her home, I'd never heard them on a call. Given our schedules didn't always align and we were often in our respectable corners, but I'd never heard a peep from him. If I had, I would've remembered. That voice wasn't easily forgotten.

"Awwwww, Baby Lyric."

"Shut up."

I was so accustomed to the strong-willed and fierce woman that had become my best friend from a distance that it was hard recognizing Lyric, the little sister, but since I'd gotten home from work, she'd been right in front of me. I could see that her brothers were her safe places. With them, she could peel back her layers of protection and remove the shields. In their worlds, she could be vulnerable. She could be the softest version of herself, and the thought of having someone be to her what she was for me made me utterly satisfied.

"I'm about to get some rest for this hour. Don't wake me up until we're leaving. As a matter of fact, don't even wake me up then. Wake me up in Channing. I plan to sleep the entire ride there." I got comfortable in the passenger seat, placing the black top over my entire face. The sun was brutal with its rays.

"Hard as you sleep, it's possible."

"Well, in this case, that's a great thing."

THREE

LUCA

8 *YEARS.* **4** *MONTHS.*

Each day, a new strike was marked in my memory, ensuring I'd never forget how much of my time I'd given to the system. As much as I wished it could all be erased the second I pushed the large green door open and was met with sunlight, I knew it was impossible.

Every day that I'd spent behind the wall was a necessary part of my journey that I didn't regret. I'd do it again and then once more if it still meant protecting my gem. It was whatever when it came to Lyric. Always was and always would be. She was the only person I'd lose my cool over, and I'd done exactly that the night I shot her ex down in the middle of the pavement like the dog he was.

Ennnnn. The gate ahead of me buzzed as I neared it. Every few feet was another obstacle that made it harder for prisoners to escape their reality. Niggas were inside fighting for their freedom and it was only a few taps of a motherboard away. Some would never see the day while those who did would never leave the same person they'd come.

Ennnnn. A second gate opened as I stepped closer. It was the only thing standing between me and the rest of my life. Once I was from behind it, they'd never get me behind another. That was, without a doubt, and the one thing I was certain of.

The air on the other side of the gates was different. As I inhaled and welcomed my freedom, it became a bit more obvious. The contaminated, depressive oxygen they were feeding us inside was more apparent. I pushed it from my lungs and invited the freshness to enter.

"LUCA!" I heard in the distance.

The voice was a familiar one, one that made my heart burst at the sound of it. Though it had matured after so many years of not communicating vocally, its peculiar notes were still recognizable. No matter how much time got between us, her entirety would always be etched on the inside of me. I knew her by heart and that was putting it lightly.

During my stay, I'd decided to avoid unnecessary contact with the outside world. It only made time harder. Aside from a letter to Lyric every six months to let her know I was well and thinking of her, we'd only spoken four times over the last eight years.

One was when our mother beat cancer. Another was when our grandfather passed away. The third call was for a wellness check that Laike forced out of me because Lyric was taking my absence and silence hard at one point. The final call was to congratulate her on getting her real estate license.

She could do anything she put her mind to as far as I was concerned, but I still wanted her to know how proud of her I was. Since, she'd been making moves and building her portfolio. Laike's knucklehead ass wasn't having my silence. He'd managed to find a way to get in contact with every cellmate that I'd ever had and get them a cell smuggled inside. There wasn't a moment he needed me I wasn't a call away. The only stipulation was never mentioning it to anyone in our family that we were in constant contact.

"LUCA!" she screamed, headed in my direction.

My Lyric. She was a pleasant surprise. With Laike being the only one who was supposed to have knowledge of my release, I was excited just considering the look on her face when I popped up on her in Channing. Hers and my parents, but that nigga had obviously flipped the coin and it was me who had been set up.

As she obliterated the space between us, my heart rate sped as my head began to throb from the rapidness of my thoughts while trying to comprehend the moment. Seeing Lyric made it real. Lyric running in my direction meant that shit was behind me.

"Luca!" The tears that streamed down her face were

visible as she jumped into my open arms, wrapping her legs around me.

"Luca." Lyric cried. "Luca. You're home."

"I'm home," I assured her, still not believing it myself.

She was light as a feather in my arms, squeezing my neck as if I'd disappear at any minute. Her wetness stained my cheeks as she wept into my shoulder. Allowing her the moment, I stood in place swaying her from one side to the other. Even at thirty, she was still my baby girl. It wouldn't ever change.

"I missed you so much." She clung to me.

"I missed you, too, Lyric."

"OK. Let me down so that I can get you as far away from this place as possible," she demanded.

I obliged, lowering her tiny frame to the ground. She utilized her skin as a napkin to clear her face of her tears of joy. When she felt like she'd gotten herself together, she grabbed my hand and intertwined our fingers together then pulled me closer to her ride.

"I hope you don't mind. I brought my friend along for the ride," she revealed as we reached the Rubicon that I was certain Laike had everything to do with.

"Nah. It's cool. I'm just glad you didn't have to make the drive alone."

"We came last night and stayed about forty minutes away. We had a very long night, and she's fallen asleep. She needs the rest, so please don't make too much noise."

"Didn't plan on it," I confirmed.

"And I need some rest, too, so you're the driver."

"Aight," I agreed, knowing that would be the case anyway when I saw her running from a distance.

"We need gas, too, so stop whenever you're ready. Laike sent a bag for you. It's in the back."

"Aight. I'll get it once we stop. Get in so you can get some rest, Lyric. You look like shit, baby girl."

"Rudeness!" she shrieked, rolling her eyes as she opened the back door.

She turned back with a finger over her mouth as if to remind me to keep quiet. My memory was sharp, so there was no way I was forgetting something she'd told me just a few seconds ago. Without verbally responding, I nodded as I opened the driver's door. I wasn't prepared for what was waiting for me on the other side of the vehicle.

Like a sleeping beauty, Lyric's friend rested comfortably in the passenger seat. There was a black cloth of some kind partially covering her eyes but leaving the rest of her face exposed. Even with a quarter of her face restricted, the beauty was unmatched. I turned toward Lyric to inquire about the woman next to me, but she'd already laid down and closed her eyes – giving me time to linger on my passenger a bit longer.

With pecan-colored skin and full, brown lips to match, her features were perfectly designed by the man above. From the small opening of her mouth, I saw the pearly whites that were waiting for display.

I gathered myself and discontinued my lingering gaze to give Lyric's friend the privacy she thought the black piece of clothing would. To help her cause, I pulled the sun visor down and extended it on the side, hoping it would add relief for her. I adjusted the seat for comfort during the ride and checked the three mirrors I'd be needing before tapping the buttons on Lyric's stereo to find a decent station.

Before pulling off, I found myself giving my passenger another once-over. *She's a hard sleeper,* I noted. It was the only way to explain her complete oblivion as life around her continued. Nevertheless, I knew she must've needed the sleep that she was getting, so I was satisfied knowing that she'd been able to sleep right through my entry.

I pulled from the space that Lyric occupied with some shit that I was unfamiliar with playing on the radio. Though I didn't know the song, it had a nice vibe to it. With both of the women in the car attempting to get some shuteye, the calmness of it was perfect for the occasion.

Though I was in foreign territory, the direction I was headed in was obvious. To the right were only more federal holding buildings while there was an open road to the left. I made the left without thinking twice and headed for the nearest gas station. Before we got on the road, we needed to fill the tank.

It was damn near too easy to succumb to the tranquil ambiance. It wasn't a cumbersome task at all. Mainly because it allowed me to acknowledge my thoughts, ones of freedom, future, and rehabilitation. I'd prided myself on not falling victim to the joint and becoming institutionalized. Though my body was locked behind the fence, my mind wasn't. My time was spent in the books, heavily, to escape the reality of it all. The last thing I wanted to do was be set free physically while still being shackled and bound mentally.

Two gas stations sat across from one another, forcing me to choose between them. Because it was more convenient to choose the one on the right, I did. There were available pumps and a huge storefront for the girls to have their way if that's what they wanted.

I rolled down the window to make sure that I was pulling up to the pump on the right side. The arrow on the tank displayed it, but I wanted to double-check. After confirming I'd pulled up on the correct side, I switched the gear to park. The shade provided that was courtesy of the gas station forced my eyes in her direction again.

And there she was. The serenity that was plastered on her now fully exposed face was priceless. What I'd learned was a shirt she'd been using to block out the sun had fallen from her eyes shortly after I'd pulled off the lot of Cadet Federal Institution.

I stepped out of the truck in the gray sweats and gray tee that was one of many I'd purchased while behind the wall. As I caught a glimpse of my reflection on the paint of Lyric's truck, I considered stopping for a change of clothes before we hit Channing, but quickly dismissed the thought. I'd rather wait until I showered, rested, and went for a haircut before stepping into anything remotely close to my preference in clothing.

The back door swung open as Lyric stepped out. She stretched her long, slim arms until she couldn't anymore.

She stepped aside and slowly, carefully closed the door behind her.

"I'm going to go pay. Do you want anything out of here?" she asked, yawning.

"A bottle of water, two bottles of Pedialyte if they sell it, and a Twix."

"Weird combination, but OK." She turned her nose up at me.

"Document each expense, Lyric. I got you as soon as I get home."

"Luca, I'm offended, but I won't turn down any money."

"That must mean Laike paying you already?"

"He's not paying me per se. He's just funding the trip."

"Then consider it double the money for your time and energy. I'm going to toss ole girl something too for riding with ya," I told her as I nodded toward the woman in her passenger seat.

"Just give her whatever you were planning to give me. Laike already has me covered."

"Aight. Who is she anyway?" I probed.

With a shake of the head, Lyric shrugged. "I don't know. Why don't you ask her yourself."

She was on to me and it was a damn shame how quickly she'd caught on.

"Na. I'm good. Just asking a question." I tried covering up the lapse in judgment. Asking Lyric was the wrong route to take.

"Ummmm hmmmm," she responded with a roll of

her eyes. "I'll be back. You can start pumping in a bit. I'll pay for the gas first."

"Aight."

After Lyric had disappeared in the store, I rested my elbows on the door, leaning my body slightly into the truck as I waited. Again, my sight wandered in her direction. She continued to sleep, unaware, unfazed, and unbothered. Whatever peace she was experiencing, I wished for. It had to have felt so fucking good.

Respectfully, I desired one thing at the moment and that was to know if she was OK. *Like...* Was the temperature alright? Did she need more leg room? If she preferred the radio or silence. If she was resting well.

And as if she read my mind, she maneuvered in the seat. She twisted her body in my direction. My breath hiked in my chest, but I remained calm as I waited for her to open her eyes.

Come on, I silently encouraged. *Wake up.*

Her eyes popped open, slowly and bashfully, as she began trying to figure out where she was at and what was going on around her. Once. Twice. Three times, she batted her eyes in an attempt to adjust and rid them of the sleepiness. When she finally looked up, she met my gaze. I witnessed the large sum of air that she'd inhaled around her get caught in her chest.

She hadn't even opened her mouth yet I was interested in everything that she had to say. Maybe it was nothing. But, maybe... maybe it was something. Hoping for the latter, I remained quiet and waited for her to speak. However, my eyes never left hers and vice versa.

"Hi," she said, releasing me from the dungeon where I'd been captured while waiting for her awakening.

What's good? I responded, *in my head*, but the words didn't quite see the light.

Ping.

The cell in her lap sounded. Neither of our eyes faltered. Locked in on one another, I waited for her to break contact. It wasn't until her phone chimed a second time that her gaze fell, and she looked at the screen of it.

Ping.

And *the smile*, the smile that etched away at her cheeks when she opened her cell made my chest burn. *Who the fuck is that?* I wanted to know immediately.

"Luca!" Lyric screamed from afar.

Turning toward her, I waited for more to come from her mouth.

"You can pump, now."

I fought the urge to inquire about anything concerning the beauty in the front seat and decided to let her be. 93, I assumed Lyric used if she was anything like Laike and me. It was the only thing that touched the engine of our vehicles.

Forcefully, I removed the pump from the hook and unscrewed the gas cap with my freehand. I inserted it and began filling the gas guzzling truck with premium fuel. I could feel my right eye begin to twitch as I swiftly became aggravated with every single thing around me.

Except her. Whom eyes I met as I stared through the back window into the front seat. I felt her rounds on me, causing me to glare in her direction and return the favor.

Once I did, she snapped her neck and fed me the back of her head the duration of my time alone outside.

After pumping ninety dollars' worth of gas, I slid back into the driver's seat. Instead of waiting for Lyric where we were, I proceeded to pull into one of the empty spots near the door. The truck had barely stopped before she opened the door and fled.

Her body was as beautiful as her face. With bowed legs and brown skin, I knew my ass was in trouble. Though I'd try to keep my distance for the sake of it being Lyric's homegirl, I couldn't keep any promises – especially not with the way my mind was already recalculating the time I'd promised to spend alone before jumping into anything serious once I got home.

Both girls returned in less than ten minutes. I assumed they'd relieved their bladders and did a bit more browsing in the massive store. They were both carrying bags when they re-entered the truck.

"Lyric, you sure you don't want to sit up front?" she asked Lyric as she slid into the passenger seat.

The delicacy of her voice was addictive. I wanted to hear more of it.

"No ma'am. I need to stretch out and get some shuteye."

"Not before you drink some of that Pedialyte," I interrupted.

"That's why you wanted Pedialyte?" Lyric finally realized.

"You too." I turned in her direction, admiring her side profile for a brief moment before she turned to face me.

"We will be fine, Luca. We're not even all that hungover." Lyric sniggered with a slight groan that told me everything I needed to know.

"Drink it. Both of you, before we pull off."

There wasn't any use of going back and forth between the two of them. They were shit-faced and needed the electrolytes to recoup. The naps would help, but they wouldn't cure them. Their bodies needed to be replenished.

"I forgot how annoying you are," Lyric whined.

"Good thing you remember now," I finalized.

"Here, Ever. This man isn't going to stop tripping until we drink this shit."

Ever. As the thought crossed my mind, her eyes found mine.

Ever. It suited her.

She accepted the orange Pedialyte that Lyric was handing her without fuss. I watched as she unscrewed the top, removed the seal, and turned it up. She consumed a decent amount before that familiar sound demanded her attention again.

Ping.

She lowered the juice and reached for her device. The same smile she wore the last time she took a look at the screen returned. This time, I didn't even wonder about who the fuck was on her line because now that I was in her mix it didn't matter.

Quickly as it had come, all the shit about her being Lyric's best friend had gone out the window. As she pecked away at her phone, it took everything in me not to gently slide it from her fingers and toss it out the window along with it. I would've gotten her a new one when I made it back to the city, but I didn't have grounds to do so, not yet.

I straightened my line of vision and pulled from the spot that we'd been occupying. Gratitude heavy on my heart, I prepared to hit the road and put the last eight years of my life behind me. I had so much more to look forward to and so much I was ready to accomplish. There was one mission in particular that I was exceptionally open to the idea of. It was *Ever*.

FOUR

EVER

EVEN WITH THE MUSIC PLAYING, all I heard was silence. That was the only way to explain how my heart's throbbing was the loudest thing in my ear. Loudly and dramatically, it galloped in my chest.

She could've warned me, was my only thought. It replayed over and over in my head. There wasn't a single picture in her home of her family members. There wasn't a single jailhouse picture in a tiny frame on her nightstand near her bed. There was literally no trace of family throughout her living quarters. Not even her parents graced the walls.

Lyric's home was full of abstract art, which puzzled me because the man who sat beside me was the epitome of art – *real art*. From his obviously brown hair to his thick, fit frame. He weighed no less than two hundred and twenty-eight pounds that was perfectly dispersed over approximately six feet and four inches, give or take one inch.

His brown skin hadn't seen much of the sun. Eight years behind bars, and I was sure that he'd darken in no time when it came to the Channing sun. Nevertheless, his brown skin was perfect. It matched his brown eyes and warm aura.

Each time I found myself gazing in his direction, it was either because his eyes were already on mine or because I wanted them to be. His side profile was spectacular, each of his features forming curves of their own, which made for the perfect silhouette. This man was beautiful. Ravishing. Blemish-free.

Needing to disperse my attention so that he didn't consume it all, I turned toward a sleeping Lyric. *Just as beautiful*, I reasoned. How I'd expected anything different of her brother was foolishness. I only had myself to blame.

Her arms were tucked underneath her as she laid out flat on her stomach. I smiled as I watched her for a brief moment, her mouth hanging open as her back rose and fell with each breath she took. She was in a deep slumber, and I loved that for her. After the night we'd had, I wanted nothing more than to join her, but I was too afraid that I'd also be snoring with my mouth hanging open. Had it only been us two in the truck, it would have been fine. Now, we had a guest, and I just couldn't see myself going out like that.

I'd grabbed a blanket from the store just in case I did manage to get some shuteye. I wanted my entire face concealed so that I wasn't worried about how crazy I looked when in a deep, uninterrupted sleep. I knew that wouldn't be an issue, now, because suddenly sleep wasn't a desire of mine. So, instead, I pulled the tags from the blanket and unfolded it before unbuckling my seatbelt to lay it over Lyric's body.

Once she was fully covered, I settled in my seat. The chill bumps on my arms that pierced the air the moment I re-entered the truck were evidence that it might be a bit too cool, anyway. So, I knew the blue blanket would bring Lyric comfort. As for me, closed vents and lowered AC would do the trick.

As I leaned forward to twist the circle that closed the vent that was aimed in my direction, so did he. His hand rested on top of mine without moving in a haste. The somberness of my world was lifted briefly and replaced with unforgettable rays of sunshine and unique rainbows. But when he pulled back, it returned full throttle.

"Sorry," I murmured.

He said nothing. In fact, he hadn't said anything to me in particular since I'd awakened. Hadn't it been for his conversation with Lyric, I would've sworn he was mute, but I knew that wasn't the case.

Ping.

I smiled inwardly at the mere thought of the text I'd

been sent. Cedric wasn't as easy to get rid of as I'd thought. Me living in Channing didn't seem to faze him. It was four hours away, which was a lot for me. Too much, even.

Did you enjoy yourself? It looked like you did.

I did.

Why didn't you say bye?

When I looked over in your section, you'd disappeared.

I was looking forward to seeing you off.

I would've liked that.

I need to handle something in a sec. Make sure you're by your phone around eight tonight. I'm going to hit you up.

OK. Talk to you then.

Holler at ya.

Just by the conversation and endless funds he seemed to have, I knew his occupation. Although I wanted to block him because of it, the distance between us was enough to keep me from pursuing anything serious with him so it didn't matter. The most Cedric would ever get out of me was a little conversation. I'd experienced his type, and they weren't it for me anymore.

8! Cedric reiterated in a final text.

8, I responded, chuckling.

With rosy cheeks, I closed my eyes and tried resting them without inducing sleep. My rest would have to wait. After several seconds, I found myself staring at the road again. That wouldn't work, either.

The wheels of Lyric's truck etched away at the distance between us and Channing with Luca at the wheel. Luca. I unlocked my phone and opened the Safari application. In the Google search bar that popped up, I inquired about the man beside me.

What's the meaning of Luca? I typed.

"Bringer of light," his voice radiated, drowning out the music with its rasp.

My eyes bulged and breath got caught in my throat. The world must've stopped because I felt like time stood still as shame rained down on me from the clouds. My trembling hands hovered over the search results, but I dared to tap one.

Shit. He'd caught me red-handed. Though I felt the need to apologize, I wouldn't. I genuinely wanted to know a bit more about him and that started with his name. It was a sure way to learn a bit more about a person who left you clueless. For me, Luca was one of them.

Fitting, I concluded, shutting my phone down completely. It was obvious that I wasn't the only one who had eyes for it. Luca's perfect vision and curiosity had entered spaces they weren't invited to.

LUCA-EVER

THREE HOURS, a bag of almonds, and an entire jug of Pedialyte later, and I was still fighting my sleep while staring ahead at the road. I'd fallen into a comfortable silence that allowed me to think about everything that had happened in my life over the last three weeks.

They'd been a rollercoaster, but one that I was grateful to be on.

Emorey loved her new school though it was a challenge getting her accustomed to being away from me for so many hours a day. Mrs. Laura, Lyric's mother, told me every day how much of a joy she was to have around. Since day one, Emorey had become her little helper. Because she had a hard time getting acclimated with the structure of the classroom and being around so many children at once, Mrs. Laura pulled her out of the class as often as she could to help and spend some one-on-one time together.

Essence's year was drawing to a close, although she'd just started her new school. There were only two weeks left before she would be going to the same school as Emorey. The end of the year had approached and when the new school year rolled around, she'd be a first grader. I wasn't ready. My little baby was growing too fast. I wanted her to slow down.

"How much longer do we have?" Lyric groaned near my ear, still half-asleep.

"Maybe an hour or less," I responded.

"Good, because I need to pee."

I shrieked on the inside as I looked to Luca for a response. He didn't give one. He simply continued driving, seemingly lost in thought, too.

Lyric reached forward and turned the volume of the music down. She faced Luca, who hadn't taken his eyes off the road, and smiled. The admiration in her eyes was adorable.

"So, how does it feel to be home?" She yawned.

"I don't know yet. I'll tell you when I get there."

"Such an arrogant asshole." Lyric scoffed.

Luca didn't respond, not verbally anyway, but the smirk that peeled his features back was close enough. I drained my lungs of oxygen in an attempt to recover from the lethal blow to the chest. *My GOD.*

Lyric leaned forward again and pumped the volume up again. I was thankful because if I could hear my heart's rapid beating, I was almost certain he could. The last thing I wanted was him knowing the effect he was having on me though he'd barely even said a word to me. I could count on one hand how many he had sent in my direction.

My cell vibrated in my lap, the ping replaced with the standard iPhone sound. When I checked the number to see who was calling, I wasn't surprised to see that it was restricted. For the one hundredth time, I made a mental note to get my number changed. But this time, I went a step further and blocked out thirty minutes of my day on my phone's calendar to do so once I was settled and had a nap.

Mondays and Wednesdays were the only two days of the week that I had off, and I tried utilizing them to take care of myself and my business. I'd already gotten a mail transfer so there wasn't any mail going to my old residence. Instead, it had been transferred to a P.O. Box that I had purchased for six months at the post office. The girls and I all had new physicians that we'd seen since being in Channing.

There were other small tasks that I managed on those days unless it was rest I needed to prioritize, but the final piece to the puzzle was getting a new cell number so Dewayne could no longer bother me. Sometimes, he'd go days without calling. Sometimes, he'd only call once a day. Other times, he laid on the call button it seemed.

I silenced the call and my phone as well, knowing that it might be the beginning of Dewayne's wrath. He could go on for hours, a few calls here and there until he realized I had no intentions of picking up. It was pathetic to watch.

IN UNDER AN HOUR, we were crossing over into Channing. I rejoiced inside knowing that the trip was almost complete. I'd never felt as bound in my entire life. What was so shameful about the entire ordeal is that it was by a man who'd barely even open his mouth.

"Finally!" Lyric cheered from the backseat as we pulled onto a secluded street that seemed to go on forever.

As we ascended the back road, I realized we were deep in The Hills, where the wealthy slept peacefully at night with their doors unlocked and windows open. In The Hills, the only true threat was financial loss. Money solved their problems for the most part, and silver spoons were frowned upon. It was diamond-encrusted spoons that the children were fed from and without shame.

"45336," Lyric called out as we pulled up to a gated home that seemed to go on for miles and miles.

Its beauty was striking. Obviously, a new build, there was grass still being laid around the property. The sleek design was an architectural masterpiece. But even with all its beauty, it looked so cold. That warmth I was accustomed to seeing on older modeled homes was missing. The windows were large, reminding me of the hotel we'd stayed at. Each bend, fold, corner, or top was squared perfectly, without a single round edge in sight.

Luca pulled close enough to the box near the gate and punched in the numbers that Lyric had given him. Seconds later, the gates parted, giving us access to the wide path that led to the home. Up close, it was even more breathtaking.

"Okay, now, how does it feel to be home?" Lyric questioned as Luca parked near the back of the gorgeous home.

From where we'd ended on the curvaceous path, I could see the large, very blue swimming pool that lapped the back of the home. It was just off a gazebo that stopped only a few feet away from the concrete that led to it. There were four cut-outs that offered a bit of privacy and lots of shade. They reminded me of small sections at rooftop parties that were dug out for guests to feel a bit more exclusive than the other partygoers who were either standing around or burning in the scorching sun at an uncovered table.

The smell of fresh soil lingered in the air, slapping me across the face the second Luca opened his door and exited the truck. He then opened Lyric's door, too, and waited for her to slide out of the back seat. I watched as the two of them embraced before Luca stepped back.

"It feels good, kid," he finally answered her question.

"I love you," Lyric uttered, barely audible because her face was planted in her brother's chest. Her 5'6 frame had no chance with the meaty giant that had pulled her in for a hug.

"Always," he enunciated before letting her go.

"The bag from Laike is in the back."

"Yeah. Grabbing it now," Luca assured Lyric with a nod.

I hadn't realized just how long I'd been waiting for his eyes to discover mine again or that I was waiting at all until I was able to exhale the breath I'd been holding when his rounds appeared in my line of vision. The glance ended as quickly as it had started, leaving me breathless for the hundredth time.

With flushed cheeks and prickly skin, I snapped my head in the other direction toward the massive pool and state-of-the-art gazebo. They didn't look as half as good as the man who'd held my thoughts and body captive over the last four hours, but anything to keep my orbs off him would do.

"Ever," Lyric beckoned for me. I turned to see what would fall from her lips next.

"I'm going to go take a leak really quickly," she announced, bouncing toward the house.

And for the first time, I wasn't opposed to the idea of Lyric leaving us alone. Luca was a drug that I'd rapidly become addicted to in only a four-hour time span. I wanted to be the center of his attention even if it was only for a minute or two. Solidarity with my narcotic of choice didn't seem like too much to crave.

Head forward and chest out, I swept the air for confidence that I wasn't even sure I could possess as I listened to the rummaging he was doing in the back of Lyric's truck. When he slammed the tailgate, I waited with bated breath for him to say something – anything to me. I could hear his footsteps as they got closer and closer, but I never expected him to open the door that I was behind.

My chest deflated instantly as my head dropped a few inches. My shoulders were no longer squared and that confidence I'd found was replaced by intimidation. He was so close and so calm. I, on the other hand, was melting down internally.

"Ever," he started, saying my name as if he was the only person in the world with the privilege. "Nice meeting you."

I held my breath, waiting for him to continue. I'd reprogrammed my cell number in my head just so that I could be prepared for this moment. Because from the obvious chemistry that we shared, him asking for my contact information had to be next. Otherwise, he wouldn't have bothered me and gone into the house.

Right? I questioned myself.

I watched as he extended his free hand until it was underneath my chin. He then lifted slightly until our skin touched. I couldn't bear the task of looking into his brown eyes, so I closed mine. He lifted my chin slightly and demanded my attention with his words.

"Look at me," he challenged, ever so softly.

I obliged, parting my eyelids to see his handsome face. It was faultless. He was flawless, physically. From his kissable lips to his large arms that I wanted him to pick me up with and spin me around as if I, too, had been waiting for his return all these years. I hadn't, but I wanted to be treated as such.

"You should keep your head up." Luca pored over my features and said to me, "You're prettier that way."

After he'd dropped his hand, my head remained high. I took his advice to heart as I deepened the breath that I inhaled. I wanted to consume as much of his air as possible. With those parting words, he disappeared behind the double doors that led to his home.

Immobile, I remained fixated on the double doors as if he'd reappear from behind them. When I finally came to and gathered myself, I slammed the door of the truck and released a sigh. As astonishing as the man that was just before me was, he didn't see me. He saw my pain and that within itself said so much about my trauma. At that moment, I made it a priority to let go of whatever hurt Dewayne had put on me because it would only keep my head down and shoulders slumped.

My cell buzzed as my thoughts bounced around in my head. It was my mother calling.

"Hello?" I answered while reclining the seat.

"Hey, Ever. You made it back yet?" she wanted to know.

"Yes. We just got back so I'll be able to pick up the girls for sure."

"That's what I was calling about. James and I really enjoy having them over. I was thinking we could keep them for the week to give you a break. I can get them to and from school and have them back after church on Sunday. If that's OK with you," she emphasized, making sure she wasn't overstepping boundaries.

"This is the most time they've ever spent away from me." I was saddened, realizing just how much I missed them already.

"I know. It's just a thought, baby. You can decline if you're not up for it and maybe we can get them for a full week during the summer."

"No. No. It's fine. They can stay. I'm just trying to wrap my head around the fact that I've never spent more than a day away from them," I explained.

"Well, now that you're around family you can expect to spend more time without them. And, I don't want you feeling guilty about it either. Allow your village to help."

"I know."

"So, is that a yes?" I could hear the excitement in her voice.

"Yes."

"Good. OK. I'll let you go now. Don't be calling all day every day, either. Give yourself time to breathe."

"I won't make any promises."

"Alright. Go on about your day. Enjoy your time off."

"I'll try."

As the call ended, Lyric hopped up into the truck.

"You ready?"

"My mom is keeping the girls until Sunday," I revealed.

"Then why the fuck you looking all sad?" she sneered.

"Because I miss them already and was looking forward to picking them up."

"Ever, baby, let your hair down or get your pussy sucked for once. Tell Cedric to bring his ass to Channing if he really wants to show you how much of a good time he is."

Or maybe Luca could, I thought, but refused to acknowledge the tiny crush I had on her brother. It all seemed so silly and immature.

"I don't think I'm ready for that yet, Lyric. Maybe in a few weeks."

"Alright. It's your call. Meanwhile, I'm going to see what we can get ourselves into this week since you're free."

"Who are you fooling? Both of us will be under the biggest blanket in the house, praying no one bothers either of us."

"Well, at least it sounded good," Lyric agreed.

We arrived at Lyric's house in no time being that she lived on the cusp of The Hills in Edgewood where the only difference between the residents was an additional zero on their bank statements. Her home was immaculate, too, with enough room for a family of six to eight.

Neither of us bothered with the bags that were in the trunk. We scurried to the door where we stood until

Lyric unlocked it. The cold, crisp air from inside welcomed us with open arms.

My extroverted battery had died the moment we'd left the lounge, but I hadn't had the proper amount of sleep to recharge it. That was all about to change. The minute my head hit the pillow, I wanted to sleep until I heard the birds the next morning. But, first, I needed a long, relaxing bath. They always put me right to sleep, but it wasn't often that I was able to indulge because I was almost always in a rush.

"See you later, girlfriend," I sang, dismissing Lyric, who simply waved her hand as she closed her bedroom door.

The stairs threatened to take me out as I climbed them slowly, praying that each one was the last one but I knew better. Once I made it to my bedroom, I peeled the clothes from my body one piece at a time until I was standing in the nude and pulling the door of my bedroom that led to the hallway bathroom open.

I admired myself as I took a few steps, closing the door in the hallway for the bathroom. Though it was only Lyric and I home, I didn't want to leave the door open while I bathed. Privacy was preferred.

For a mother who'd breastfed, my boobs still had volume and were slightly perky. Aside from the barely noticeable pudge at the bottom of my belly, one wouldn't know I'd carried three children, two of them to full term. There wasn't a part of my physical appearance that I wasn't in love with. It was the mental and emotional aspects that I was ready to get a grip on and after spending the night away, I knew that was coming soon.

I searched underneath the cabinet for the large bottle of bubble bath I used for Emorey and Essence three times a week. It wasn't hard to find. Before starting the water, I poured one-fourth a cup at the bottom, right underneath the faucet.

The water splashed as it met the bottom of the tub, immediately forming fluffy, white bubbles that continued to grow as the tub filled. I stepped inside after a short wait, knowing that the water needed time to warm. I pulled my hair into a loose bun with the hair tie that was wrapped around my wrist, which allowed me to slide deeper in until my shoulders touched the backrest at the rear of the tub.

"Hmmmmmmm," I moaned, closing my eyes as my body began to relax.

Look at me. His voice rang in my ears.

Keep your head up. Visions of Luca appeared behind my lids.

You look prettier. Snippets of the few words he'd said to me haunted me.

Bringer of light. His haughtiness aroused me.

"Ummm." I squeezed my lids tighter, hoping he'd go away, but he wouldn't.

Ever. I wanted my name to fall from no other man's lips after it had come from his. It belonged there.

My eyes popped open after I'd had enough of his sultriness in my head. The water sounded as I rushed forward and grabbed the faucet to keep from swaying along with it. Once it stabilized, I reached for the plug and removed it completely. The water pouring from the faucet was much too hot, prompting me to turn the nozzle until it was a more appropriate temperature, a much cooler one.

"Ahhhh," I hummed, lowly, as I positioned myself right underneath it.

The running water tapped against my clitoris relentlessly. The pressure was perfect, sending me spiraling fast. As I closed my eyes, he reappeared.

His brown, slightly reddish hair.
His brown skin that reminded me of a paper sack.
His perfect build.
His perfect height.
His voice, the deepest rasp I'd ever heard in my life.
His eyes, the big, round circles I wanted on me all the time. Every time.

I'd never met a man like Luca and though I'd only been in his presence for a few hours, discernment was a gift of mine. When I met Dewayne, so many alarms went off in my head that I ignored for the sake of having a good time. I'd imagined we would be cutty buddies at the most, but that quickly turned into a full-fledged relationship the minute I discovered my pregnancy with Dylan. So overcome with grief from the loss of my pregnancy, I desperately wanted to carry a child to term to unbreak my broken heart and fill the void that my loss had left me with.

Years later, I looked up and too much of my time had been wasted with him. In reality, he didn't deserve the first year I'd given him, so I didn't understand how I'd stayed around seven more. But, I'd finally awakened and there was no more going back.

Luca. Luca was in an entirely different realm. His aura was one of a kind. Effects of his presence loitered long after he'd disappeared. Without being overbearing or unnecessarily rude, he left a memorable impression – one that was so astounding that I was impatiently waiting for the next time I'd laid eyes on him.

Big, *very big*, dick energy seeped from his pores. It was apparent in the way he walked. It was apparent in the way he talked. It was apparent in his silence. I'd bet my last dollar that he was holding something vicious between his thighs and after so many years in prison, I was hoping to be the first meal on his menu. I wanted him to split me in two and suck on my private parts like oysters during fine dining.

He wasn't a man that obeyed rules or acknowledged certain boundaries. Just like Lyric, he was accustomed to having his way, and with me, he could. I encouraged him to, whenever he was ready.

"Fuck." I felt my peak building from my toes.

FIVE

LUCA

"SHIT," I groaned, massaging my rigidness to rid myself of the semen that had been resting in my sack.

Closing my eyes, I tossed my head back and allowed the pleasure to consume me, just like thoughts of her did. There hadn't been too many times in my life that I could admit to being unprepared, but to see such a gorgeous face with a spirit to match minutes after being set free was one of them.

Ever's beauty was unhinged. It was the kind that one remembered seeing in the early 2000s videos, back when everything on a woman's body was real and not up for questioning. She was the girl next door type of pretty, the one whose mother never let her come outside to play with the neighborhood kids because they'd turn her into a hot girl. But ultimately, she ended up with a block boy, anyway.

That's how Ever's epilogue would end her story with me being her love interest, but I was far from a fucking block boy. I was more of a sit at the head of the table and call the shots type of nigga. The type that didn't have to get his hands dirty because he had a hundred niggas willing to. One that paid niggas not to throw their lives away while giving the FEDs a few years of mine. Her story wouldn't end with a block boy. It would end with a boss.

Hi. I recalled her voice, still projecting even though timid.

She had absolutely nothing to be afraid of. Until I was ready for what I knew she had to offer, I wouldn't touch her because hurting her wasn't even in my deck of cards. I wouldn't hear the end of Lyric's fucking mouth.

Bringer of light, I'd told her as I peeped the search she had started on my name. Anything she needed to know about me, I wanted her to ask me herself. She'd get the exact answers she was looking for, no gimmicks.

"Fuck."

I quickened the pace, making sure that my palm brushed over the head of my dick with each stroke. Nut oozed from the tip slowly at first, but shifted gears as I continued to massage myself. Ending with theatrics, it splattered the shower wall I was standing in front of.

"Uhhhh, shit."

My knees weakened as I leaned up against the railing beside me for support.

"Fuck."

What I thought was the last of my semen wasn't. It continued to trickle from my dick and hit the tiles beneath me as I watched it spit up from above. Once I was certain that there wasn't a drop left, I released my tool and leaned my head against the wall. My limbs felt like spaghetti noodles.

Whenever I got a hold of Ever, she was in trouble, but before I conquered her body, I wanted to conquer her mind. It was the true treasure, and I was after it. All else would follow.

LUCA·EVER

LAIKE HAD DONE his best shit with my crib, putting his architectural hobby to good use. He designed good shit when he *felt* like it. My new home looked like it was fresh out of a real estate magazine, interior and exterior. There wasn't a detail that he hadn't included in the build. He'd considered shit that I hadn't even thought about, but was quite satisfied with having.

I descended the right wing of the staircase, leading me to the common areas that were all fully furnished and untouched. My first stop was the fully stocked fridge that resembled a walk-in closet. Inside the cool, well-lit space were shelves full of food. I snagged two mangos and a bottle of water, opting to get out and eat a little later.

Standing at the stainless steel sink, I rinsed my fruit and

removed the stickers off them before peeling back the skin of the largest one with my two front teeth. For the second one, I grabbed a large bowl and began my tour around my new home. The kitchen was impeccable. Its openness and plethora of counter space had me ready to bust out the pots and pans. Beside the kitchen was a large mudroom that was attached to an even larger outdoor activities room that was screened in. From there, I could see the dual-level pool house that was next to the in-law suite that was equipped with two full bedrooms and two full baths, one of each on each level.

I backpedaled and made my way around one of the two islands in the kitchen, still ravishing the mango in my palm, and headed deeper into my home. There were two living rooms, one with a fireplace that wrapped around the corner and the other with a couch that was big enough to fit a family of twelve.

Good shit, my boy. I nodded as I thought about what Laike had done there. He was aware that I wanted a big family and right in this home was where they'd be raised. So, the couch meant a bit more than it probably should've.

There was a great room and a dining room, a poker and pool room, a man cave on the basement level, seven bedrooms, two offices, a full laundry room, a playroom, a theater, and a pet room that was underneath the left wing of the stairwell. There was a small library under the right wing.

Laike had successfully built a multi-million dollar home for under four hundred thousand dollars and if that wasn't talent then I wasn't sure what the fuck was. I tossed the seed of the first mango into the bowl and started on the second as I sat on the cloudy couch that would one day sit my entire family at once.

On the table in the center of the sectional that nearly formed a full rectangle were a few necessities, two of which were phones. The others were a passport, driver's license, a Glock, and fifty-thousand dollars in cash. I wouldn't even question how he'd managed to get the license or passport. Because at the end of the day, money talked and we had plenty to spare.

I picked up the iPhone, leaving the rest of the table's contents where they were. There wasn't a lock code on it, giving me immediate access to the contact list. Only a few names had been stored.

Ken.
Laike.
Lyric.
Mom.
Pops.

There was a missing link to the family tree, but I'd add it sooner rather than later. Ever's name belonged at the top being that everyone was in alphabetical order. If it was the last thing I did, I'd make sure she was added to the list before anyone else's number made the cut.

"Ahhhh. That boy is home," Laike chanted in the phone as he answered it.

"Something of the sorts," I responded. "Nigga, you played no fucking games on the pad, I see."

"You deserved that. I had to make sure I set you up nicely to give your ass a reason to stay in that bitch."

"As long as niggas keep their hands to themselves, you ain't got to worry."

"Then I ain't got to worry."

"Where you at, nigga? My stomach touching my back, and I need to see Whiteboy to get a real fucking fade."

"I'm at yo' door. You slacking."

Barely a full second after he revealed his location, my doorbell sounded. Instinctively, I grabbed the loaded Glock from the table and took it for a walk with me. The path wasn't a short one. It took me a second to reach the door, but when I pulled it open I wasn't surprised to see Laike on the other side with a bottle of Ace in his hand that he popped the top on as soon as he laid eyes on me.

"Welcome the fuck home, my nigga!"

The bubbly splattered all over my fresh white tee. With a shake of the head, I left my annoying ass brother on the porch with the stupid ass bottle he was still piercing the air with while getting champagne all over my fucking floor. Some shit never changed.

"You still an old grouchy ass nigga, huh?" Laike finally joined me as I searched for something to clean up his mess with.

"Nah. I'm just not feeling niggas fucking up my floors or getting champagne on my tee."

"Nigga, we can buy you a hundred thousand new tees and get a bitch with a big booty and OCD to come clean the floors in nothing but a thong. Just say the word."

"Get out." I pointed toward the door.

"Not that word, short-tempered ass nigga." Laike chuckled.

"Bring your aggravating ass here, boy," I sneered, pulling Laike in for a brotherly embrace.

He annoyed the shit out of me half the time, but he meant well. He'd always been the pesky little brother, just like Lyric had been the pesky little sister, but I imagined it came with the territory. Our chests collided as I cupped the back of his head in my hands.

"I missed you, big dawg." He softened.

"I missed you, too, kid."

Laike was only two years my junior. We were so close in age and looked so much alike that it was hard for some to tell us apart. We even shared the same height. Both standing 6'4. The only difference was our frame. He was thin as the wind. Me, on the other hand, I had some meat on my bones.

"So, what's the plan? Food, barbershop? Then what?" Laike quizzed.

"I ain't got no plans, really. When do the parents get back in town again?"

"Wednesday."

"Bet. Seeing them is the only thing on my agenda this week," I told him.

"Aw, yeah. Getting pussy ain't?" Laike sneered, "'Cause if I was down for eight, I'd be whipping my dick out on any bitch that crossed my path."

"I've waited this long, shit, what's the rush?"

"Ummmmm," he responded with a clever smirk on

his face. "I know what the fuck that mean, nigga, don't try to stunt."

"I'm not." I shrugged, leading him into the family room where I'd just left.

"Who is she?" Laike insisted as soon as our asses hit the cushion.

"I was planning on asking you the same 'cause I don't have a fucking clue. I only got her name."

"What is it? Maybe I can have my people look into her."

Forever ready to put some people on it, Laike hadn't changed a bit. This wasn't the case though. I'd be the only one snooping around when it came to this one. Someway somehow, I knew she wasn't a threat to my livelihood, so it wouldn't be necessary.

"I doubt if all that's necessary. She's around."

"Then what's her name, nigga?" he probed, scrunching his face as if I was getting on his nerves, but he was the one on my fucking nerves.

"Ever," I revealed.

"Ole girl that's staying with Lyric? You seen her? Ahhhh. Shit, she did ride down with Lyric to get you." He slapped his leg as he recalled.

She had indeed ridden with Lyric to scoop me up, and I was glad that arrangement had come about. Hearing Laike mention her living situation had my interest piqued. Lyric didn't allow anyone into her personal space. She was introverted, a loner, especially since everything had gone down with that nigga, Chauncey. Since, she didn't trust a soul, always assuming the worst of a situation because she'd seen just how deadly it could become in a matter of seconds.

"Yeah. You seen her?"

If this nigga had seen her, then my chances of locking her in had possibly slimmed down to none. He couldn't keep his dick in his pants if he tried. He was a lover boy. There was no questions about it.

"Nah. I ain't. Not yet, but now I'm pissed 'cause nigga you just touched down and you're already trying to keep her to yourself."

I hadn't realized I'd been holding my breath, but I exhaled after he'd given his answer. Laike having not seen Ever meant that I was free to push forward. If he'd tapped that, I'd have to hang my pursuit up early. I didn't want to, but it was part of the game. I didn't fuck after Laike and vice versa.

"Nah, you definitely haven't seen her. I don't even know why I asked."

"Why you say that?"

"'Cause you'd be trying to keep her to your-fucking-self, too."

He would've. Ever was just one of those that you want to hold on to. Her essence was not only attractive, but it was magnetic, too. Since I'd left her presence, I'd been trying to figure out how I'd insert myself into her world without overwhelming her. She seemed like that type that was easily overwhelmed but accommodating because she was generally a hospitable person.

"It's like that?" Laike's brows raised.

"Just like that. And, you said she's staying with Lyric?"

I wanted to know more about their living arrangements and why she was living with my sister. The odds of that were very slim so to hear of it actually happening was interesting to me.

"Yeah. She's got two jits. One of them goes to the daycare. Em or some shit Momma calls her. She's her fucking shadow. Moms can't make a move without her little pretty brown eyes following her."

She's got them, too, I thought, imagining how pretty her children must've been if they looked anything like Ever. Learning that she had two children was understandable. Any nigga who'd crossed her path was right for attempting to hold her ass down. She was a treasure, but whoever that nigga was had better made plans to scoot his bitch ass out of the way. Because now that she was in my line of vision, I wouldn't stop until she was rocking my last name and sporting marks from a few of my seeds growing in her womb. She already had two. That was a great head start for me.

"You trying to be a stepdaddy, nigga?"

Yeah, I thought, but didn't have to verbalize. Laike already knew what was up with me. If I wanted you, I wanted everything that came with you. And when you became mine, what was once yours was now both of ours – *kids especially*. Liam, our father, made fatherhood look so fucking pleasing that I couldn't wait for my chance at it. Just like him, I knew I'd be damn good.

"What's her deal?" I ignored Laike's question and posed one of my own.

"Anything I haven't already told you, I don't know," he finalized, turning the bottle in his hand up and sipping from it.

"Aight. Let me pour myself a real drink and then we can head out of the door. You can sip on that shit you popped by yourself."

"Whatever, nigga."

We stepped out of the house ten minutes later, only for me to realize I didn't have a house key. I patted my pockets before remembering keys weren't among the contents of the table where Laike had left everything I'd be needing. I didn't recall Lyric handing me a key or using a key to let herself in when we arrived, either.

"What?" I turned back to get a good view of Laike, who seemed to think something was hysterical.

"Ain't no key, nigga. It's a smart home. Lyric and I are scanned in. Once we leave, the doors automatically lock. When we approach, the doors unlock, unless our head is down. For security purposes, the doors will remain locked if we approach without our faces showing or with an elevated heart rate. It scans the body for any signs of distress before unlocking. We need to get you scanned in."

"But what about if a nigga just left the gym or having a bad day or some shit?"

"Just look up when you step up or use the app on your phone to unlock it manually. It won't lock you out of your own shit, nigga, not unless there's a power outage. And, at that point, there is an emergency."

"Then where it's at?" I needed to know.

"In there," Laike pointed toward the black King Ranch Super Dually on Forgiatos.

The F-350 was sweet. I was almost certain that it took over two hundred dollars to fill the tank, but I also knew that trucks as such were meant for the open road so they were great on gas. A full tank could hold you over for at least 600 miles.

"I see ya, nigga," I complimented, loving the muscle sitting in my yard.

I couldn't conceal the pleasure on my face even if I wanted to. Laike had been making me proud since I stepped foot in the joint. He'd taken on my roll with an iron fist and doubled my predicted profit over the ten-year span I expected to be down. I received time served and came home in a little over eight. Now that I was home, I was wondering if I even wanted to dabble. He was getting the fucking job done with no questions asked, but I knew he wouldn't let me sit it out. He'd been waiting for me to return so that we could stand side-by-side and really run up a check. Both of our heads were better than one.

"That's all you, bro."

"All who?" I snapped my neck in his direction, peeling it from the designer shoes on the super truck.

"All you. That motherfucker too slow for me, man. That's more of your speed. I need something that can get me out of there in ten seconds flat. That ain't it."

"Appreciate that," I responded, pushing Laike across freshly laid grass.

"Keep your hands to yourself, Luca. I've put niggas in the ground for less."

Laike dusted off his shirt as if I'd gotten him dirty. Stepping closer, I pushed him again as I headed to the truck. Knowing that it was mine made it even sweeter. When I opened the door, the step descended so I was able to step inside. There was a massive gap between the truck and the concrete, so it was necessary.

I stepped on it and then into the truck, admiring the interior, too. When I started the engine and heard the roaring, a smile tugged at my lips. Laike had truly outdone himself. He'd spent at least the last six months putting together my welcome home kit, and I was nearly certain he wasn't finished yet.

LUCA·EVER

"I KNOW a spot where we can chill and kick shit at tonight. Nothing major, just good vibes and plenty of bad bitches."

"If you've planned a coming home party, please cancel it now. I'm not showing up to that motherfucker," I warned before piercing my salmon burger again.

We'd stopped by Manuel's to grab a plate before heading to Channing Galleria. I needed to holler at Rico, my jeweler, about upgrading the pieces I'd left with him before going in. The salmon burger with dirty rice was the perfect meal to welcome me home. I'd eaten bullshit for the last eight years, which included far too many noodles and snacks from the commissary.

"Then good, 'cause I haven't planned one. I knew better than to organize a gathering for the Grinch."

"Yeah, aight." I shrugged, not giving a damn what he was calling me nowadays. It wasn't anything new. He'd sworn I was the uptight one since we were children.

"It's a spot out here. A restaurant with a stupid ass bar in the back for the guests who aren't quite ready to leave after dinner and for guests who prefer the bar opposed to fine dining."

"I'm with it."

"Then call your sister and try to convince her to come outside. I hardly even see her ass unless it's at the house," Laike complained, referring to our parents' home as ours.

"If I tell her to come, she's coming. I'm not begging her little stubborn ass to do shit. I'd be better off physically removing her from her pad instead."

"You know I'm with that, too."

Of course he was. Laike was with anything that included physical force or violence. It was a form of therapy for him. My parents assumed it would be him behind bars long before I pled guilty, but to their surprise I was the one spending nearly a decade behind the wall.

"Unfortunately," I responded, placing my sandwich on the extra wide arm rest and grabbed my phone as we stopped at the red light.

"Facetime Lyric," I instructed Siri.

The music paused as the call was initiated. Seconds later, I saw Lyric's pretty face on the screen. She finally looked like she'd gotten some sleep and had pulled herself together.

"What's up, baby girl?"

"It feels like a dream, seeing you so clearly and whenever I want. Is this really real?"

"I'm happy to know you want to see your big bro or whatever. That means I won't get no back talk when I tell you to come chill with me tonight, right?"

"None at all. Where are we going and who all is going to be there?"

"Me and Laike. You and your homegirl," I insisted, not wanting to leave Ever out of the circle. She was officially part of the crew.

"You like her, huh, Luca?" Lyric smiled.

"Mind your business."

"She's good for you, so I don't mind."

"What's her deal?"

"She's fragile, fresh out of a relationship with a man who should've never gotten the time of day, but that's the past."

"Sure the fuck is as long as I got something to say about it."

"They have two children, so not exactly. Although he doesn't seem to give a damn about them, that fact still remains."

"Sounds like I've got two children, then," I coerced.

"They're the sweetest. She's determined to get some rest tonight, so I don't know if she'll be joining me."

"Lyric," I called her name.

"Yeah?"

"Don't dot the door without her," I warned her with raised brows.

"Laike, I know you're in the truck with this man."

"I am, sis, and I'm sitting here trying to figure out how he can get you out of the house and I can't," Laike sneered.

"You're just going to let him threaten me like that?" she sassed, ignoring Laike's apparent jealousy.

"That nigga ain't 'bout to do shit. He just acts like it sometimes. But don't leave your homegirl. I want to see what got this nigga asking questions. This nigga never asks questions."

"Right!" Lyric screamed in agreement.

"You don't need to see shit," I interjected. "You really don't even have to go."

"Nigga, I invited you."

"I uninvited you."

"Delusional!" Lyric yelled.

"Man, I don't understand how you deal with this shit." Laike shook his head. "I literally said I just want to see the damn girl. You acting like I said I'd shoot my shot."

"You will!" Lyric and I said simultaneously.

"Yeah. I'ma just shut up 'cause y'all right."

"Exactly." Lyric was tickled as she responded. "Anyway, Luca, we will be there. What time? Laike send me the location. It can't be too late. She works in the morning."

"Around eight."

"OK. I guess I'll see you two then. Where are you guys headed, anyway?"

"To see Rico."

"Pick me up something while you're at it," Lyric joked but those were my intentions anyway.

I wasn't feeling the last picture Laike had sent me of her. Her wrists were empty, aside from the iced watch and the chain she wore on her neck looked like it needed a bit of an upgrade. A bracelet or two would get her right.

"I plan to."

"Seriously?"

"Seriously. Your wrists look a little scarce, baby girl. Laike got you out here looking like the help."

"I got her out here looking like– What I got to do with this shit?"

"You supposed to look out for her while I'm away."

"Leave my name out yo' fucking mouth, Luca. I ain't got shit to do with what you want her to have on her wrists. If she wanted some new shit, she has my number, nigga."

"You know he's sensitive, Luca. Don't even play with him like that. Next thing you know, he's not answering the phone for either of us for a week."

"Fuck you both," Laike challenged.

"See you later, Lyric. Eight. This crybaby is about to send you the location."

"See you at eight. I love both of you."

"Always." Laike got out of his feelings long enough to recite along with me.

"Did you hit Whiteboy up?" I asked as soon as my call with Lyric ended.

"Na. Whoever is in the chair when we touch down has to get up."

"Say no more."

I picked my sandwich up and bit into it again. Not much of Channing had changed. Nearly everything seemed the same as I rode through Dooley on the way to the Galleria. Not quite ready to make my presence known, I kept my distance and allowed the tinted windows to shield my identity. When I got to the mall, it would be impossible to avoid the people of my city, but I'd tackle the task when I came upon it.

For the first time in a while, I felt comfortable. I was in my city, with my people, pockets loaded, and ready to spend some money. It felt like ages had passed since I was given the freedom to do or see either. The only piece to the small puzzle missing was Ken.

He was the only man who could ever honestly say that he was a friend of mine. I'd had a few associates through the years, but Ken was part of the circle. He ate Sunday dinner when we ate at the crib. He was in church falling asleep just like Laike and I during worship. He wanted all the church girls just like we did that came for vacation Bible school.

When I lost my virginity, so did he in the next room. When I shot my pistol, so did he. When I was at a nigga's neck, so was he. It had been eight years and four months since I'd seen his face or heard his voice. He didn't have to answer a single call from me when I was down because

I never made one to him, but we were still locked in. He didn't have to visit even once for me to know that he was missing a nigga. He knew Laike was taking care of the books, so I was good.

All I needed was for him to be around when I came home and that was enough for me. So many of our people had lost their lives to the streets or the police while I was away. My only wish was to be able to see him in the flesh when I did hit the pavement.

"Ken up in The Heights. By the time we leave the mall, that nigga will have word that you've already touched down."

"I was just thinking about him. When he hits my line, I'll pull up on him. I'm not reuniting over the phone. I'm home now."

SIX

EVER

THE BEAM of light that shined through my darkened bedroom awakened me. It was as if someone had turned on the light. With the girls away, there was only one person to blame.

"Ever," Lyric called out to me.

"Hm?"

My eyes bounced around the room as I tried comprehending what was happening, what time it was, and how long I'd been sleeping. Still in a very tranquil state, my arms remained stretched out on top of the cover while my head rested on the pillow beneath me. The sleep I'd gotten, however long my nap had been, was everything I'd needed.

"It's a little after six," she revealed, helping me understand the world around me a bit more.

"I slept the day away." I yawned, finally able to lay eyes on her.

The pillow felt a bit softer, and my bed felt a bit cozier with every second that passed. When Lyric finished her wellness check, I had every intention of revisiting the faraway place that I had in my dreams. I could sleep another few hours if she'd let me.

"You did, but you needed it. My brothers have invited us out to celebrate Luca's homecoming," she stated, standing against the door with her right hand clutching the edge.

"Maybe that's something you guys want to celebrate among each other?" I wondered aloud.

"You're a part of the crew, now, so you're one of us by default. If you're not there, he's going to take it very personally."

"It wouldn't be the first time a man has taken something personally," I reminded her with a shrug.

"Okay, maybe you have a point, but it's too much testosterone when it's just them and I. If you're there, it'll even the score. Even if it's not to celebrate Luca's homecoming, just come for me. We won't be all night, either. I'll have you back by eleven."

"I've heard something like that before. Next thing you know, I'm hungover and praying for some shuteye."

I stretched my limbs but refused to get up yet. The comfort I'd been laced with was hard to let go of. I wanted to lie in bed all day and night, but it didn't seem like Lyric wanted to hear that.

"Right again, but this time I promise. I won't even go past the two-drink limit. We'll both keep it cute. Please."

"Alright, Lyric. But if we're out past eleven, you owe me."

"Anything you want."

"You'll have to pick up the girls every day for a week straight."

"I'd do that anyway, so it looks like midnight it is then."

"Lyric." I closed my eyes as I yawned again.

"Just kidding," she rushed out.

"What time are we leaving?"

"Eight. And what about the girls?"

"My mom asked if she could keep them for a full week and have them back Sunday. I think I'll go get them after work tomorrow, though."

"No, you won't, Ever. Let them stay. You haven't had any time to yourself in six years. They can handle a week, and so can you."

"I wish I had as much faith in myself as you, Lyric, but I don't. When it comes to my children, everything is baby steps. Everything," honestly, I admitted.

"It makes sense, Ever, but take this time. It'll get easier."

"I have nothing to wear. It's really about time for me to grab a few decent pieces from the store, especially if you're going to be dragging me out of the house every chance you get."

I wouldn't admit it, but I was happy to be dragged out of the house for once. Seeing Luca a second time in the same day was as close as I'd get to winning the lottery. Lyric didn't have to convince me. When she mentioned his name, I knew I'd be in attendance.

"You definitely didn't go through your entire overnight bag, huh?"

"No, I just picked up what was on top, really."

"I know, because otherwise, you would've seen that there were three options. One of which you can wear tonight. The little black dress seems suiting. We're going to Oat + Olive."

"Never heard of it," I shared with her, finally lifting the top half of my body from the bed. I missed the pillow the second my head left it.

"You'll love it."

"Sounds gorgeous. I'm sure I will."

"If you need shoes, just holler or look in my closet. I have plenty, but the ones you wore last night match as well."

"Eight?" I asked to be sure.

"Yes, which means we need to leave by seven-fifty. The spot is in The Hills."

"Fancy," I joked.

"Whatever. Just get your fancy ass up and start getting dressed."

Lyric exited, taking the beam of light from the hallway with her. In the dark again, I plopped back down and rested my head on the pillow. This time, with my phone in my hand. There were several notifications, but before acknowledging them, I unlocked my cell and dialed my mother's number.

"I was just about to call you," my mother said when she answered the phone.

"Why? Is everything OK? Where are the girls?" Panic stricken, I jumped up from the bed completely, waiting to hear the delivery of bad news so that I could beat myself up over the decision to let the girls out of my sight for more than a few hours.

"Nothing is wrong, Ever. I told you the girls will be fine. You have nothing to worry about."

"Then why were you about to call me?"

"To tell you that ole boy texted my phone today, asking if I'd heard anything from you yet."

"And what did you tell him?"

"That you'd called me from a restricted line to tell me you and the girls were OK but you'd left him. I also told him that was about a week ago, and I hadn't heard anything since."

"Did he buy it?"

"Yeah. He told me he might've really fucked up this time and all I could do was agree. I also told him I'd appreciate it if he didn't contact me anymore now that he knew that you guys were alright. That's the only reason I made up the lie in the first place. He needs to stop calling me. I googled how to use that block feature, and I managed to block his number."

"Good. He'll call you restricted. Just don't answer," I instructed.

"Oh, I won't."

"You think I should come get the girls just in case?"

"Noooo. Nooooo. No. The girls are fine, and James is on alert. Dewayne shows up and he'd better hope the police can get to him in time after James puts one of those bullets in his ass."

Chuckling, I couldn't help but think of how ridiculous my mother sounded. James, my stepfather, was the perfect match for her. Aside from their cuteness, he kept her safe and took good care of her. He was the reason I decided not to stay with them. I didn't want to put him in any unnecessary danger. Dewayne had no idea where Lyric lived or anything about her beyond the fact that we talked occasionally.

He was clueless to the fact that she had become my best friend and the first place I'd run to when I left him. That's how I'd made sure it was kept in the event of an emergency, and I wanted to truly disappear. My mother's house was the first house he'd suspect. That's why I wasn't there and was leery about the kids being there.

"I'm going to think about it, mom. I promised Lyric I'd get out with her this evening, but if I start to feel too uneasy about the entire situation, I'm going to come get them. It has nothing to do with me not thinking you guys will protect them but everything to do with the lengths that Dewayne is willing to go to cause me pain. We both know that he cares very little about our girls, but he's going to try to use the fact that he's their parent too against me. I'm just trying to keep them close because he is unpredictable."

"I understand, Ever. But, I'd rather them be here,

honestly. At least until you get yourself a gun or something. Not to sound insensitive, but he can overpower you, baby. We've seen it time after time. He can't do that shit to a real man."

"I'm not offended, mom. You're just telling the truth and maybe you're right."

"They'll be fine. He won't come to my house and not be sent away on a stretcher. James has made that very clear."

"Tell him I said thanks."

"No need. He knows you're appreciative, and he wants to do anything he can to help."

"I'm going to go, mom. I need to start getting dressed."

"Alright."

"Tell the girls I love them and call me if you need me."

"I will. Enjoy your night and pay attention to your surroundings."

"OK."

I ended the call with a sigh. My mother was a godsend, just like Lyric. I wasn't sure why it had taken me so long to come back home. When it came to me, they'd both move mountains to make sure that I was taken care of.

My text thread had a few unread messages. One being from Cedric, which I was anxious to open. The other was from Pam, an extension of Dewayne that made my ass itch at the thought of. She was the woman who'd birthed him but didn't deserve to be called mother.

So, you just take my grandchildren away from their father without an explanation. And, over what? A few love licks? You don't work or do shit. My son handles everything. You should be more grateful. There will be times when y'all fight and go through shit but to leave? That's a weak ass move.

As much as I wanted to give her the satisfaction of responding, my energy wasn't set up that way. I couldn't and had never gone back and forth with her or anybody else. It was always pointless to me and always would be because they'd still have their beliefs and I'd have mine. It was the main reason Dewayne thought that he'd won every argument that we'd ever had. The truth was, I was hoping he'd hear himself talk long enough to shut up and understand that I didn't have the capacity for meaningless words with fools. It would only make me look and feel foolish.

Instead of responding, I edited her contact. She would no longer be able to send pesky texts because she'd been blocked. I found it amusing that she'd even found the time to send such a distasteful message because whenever I needed her to get the girls for a few, she claimed to be too busy. She hadn't helped with them once since they were born, so her input on the situation was irrelevant in my eyes.

I moved on to the more lighthearted and anticipated message of the thread. It was from Cedric. He was a frequent communicator. I liked that about him. His message had come right on time and was enough to help me forget the one I'd read prior.

Thinking of you.

His short, straight to the point message made my cheeks redden and rise. Not feeling the need for words, I simply sent a smiling emoji. I watched as the gray bubble appeared and then disappeared. He didn't have anything to say either. Sometimes, it was like that. Words weren't needed. Just feels.

I stood from the bed for the second time and stretched for what seemed like the hundredth time. The nap had really done a number on my body. I felt well rested and ready to conquer the world – or Luca in my case.

Just the thought of seeing him again had me bright-eyed and jittery. I bounced toward the restroom where I planned to take care of my hygiene for the night out. I wanted to brush my teeth again and slather deodorant under my arms and in between the creases of my thighs where I tended to sweat a bit too much.

The smile that reached my eyes at the thought of the knight in near sandy hair and brown eyes, startled me as I walked past the mirror. Taking a few steps back, I centered myself. My reflection was as flawless as I remembered it being but there were so many scars within that, I could hardly recognize myself three weeks ago when I stood in front of the same mirror. Now I could see exactly who I was.

"Okaaaaay!" I hyped, snapping my neck until my head tilted to the far right.

My brown hair and hazel eyes glistened as if they'd gotten a refresh simultaneously. The dark circles that had formed underneath my eyes from stress and worry had disappeared. The bruises from Dewayne's physical assault were no longer visible on my chest, arms, and neck areas. Aside from the few pounds I'd gained during my pregnancies, I resembled the old me – the Ever I was before I allowed a man to destroy me. That, for me, was a victory.

LUCA·EVER

I EXAMINED my wrinkly skin as I sat in the tub. I'd warmed the water three times and still wasn't quite ready to get out. The mound of candles around me as Sade's music serenaded my alone time had me wanting to soak the rest of the night. I couldn't though. Lyric was expecting me at the door before the clock struck eight.

Leaning forward, I pulled the stopper up to allow the water to drain. My bubbles had dispersed and popped for the most part. They'd added a nice touch to the soak, leaving me feeling as rich as they were when my bath started.

I stepped out and grabbed the fluffy drying towel that had been hanging from the hook on the wall. It was my second bath of the day, but it didn't threaten to put me under like the last. It woke me right up. The grogginess that lingered after such a long nap had disappeared.

Mascara.

Gloss.

Bronzer.
Ponytail with bun.

I ran down the plan for my look. I'd yet to go into my bag, but Lyric had mentioned a black dress and that was enough information for me. I wanted to make things as simple as possible and that started with a simplified look. What I had in mind wouldn't take a full thirty minutes. I had forty to spare. The other ten would be spent on body moisturizer and pouring a glass of wine from Lyric's impeccable stash.

When I reached my bedroom, I noticed the MK bag that I'd left in the back of Lyric's truck on my bed. I'd forgotten it was out there until it was in my face. That could only mean that Lyric had been nice enough to grab it for me.

"Thank you!" I screamed, hoping she was close enough to hear me.

Her room was downstairs, but she somehow managed to hear me every once in a while. When I didn't get a response, I figured she hadn't. She knew my heart, so I wasn't going to sweat it. I'd just be sure to tell her when we met downstairs.

I dug through the bag and found two more pieces. One was a black dress, just as Lyric had mentioned. The other was a black romper that was a soft cotton material. I laid them both on the bed trying to figure out which would match my vibe. It didn't take long for me to choose the romper that was short-sleeved with a fitted pant.

The top of it was perfect, obviously designed to reveal a little side boob which I'd always found sexy. I'd never worn a piece that offered that bit of detail, but I'd admired women who I'd seen in one. To have one of my own, finally, had me doing a bit of a victory dance as I tucked the dress in a nearby drawer.

I used a body oil and lotion mix to coat my brown skin. From my forehead to the bottom of my feet, I moisturized every inch of visible skin. Even my freshly Naired vagina was part of the action. Once I was satisfied with my sleekness, I pulled on the seamless thong and bra to match. I had always been a sucker for a good panty and bra set. Half of my suitcase was filled with my favorites. I refused to leave them behind. Good bras had cost me anywhere from seventy to one-hundred dollars. I simply couldn't let them go. Not yet, anyway.

I wanted my skin to soak up the moisture, so I gave it time while I ran over my curls with the flat iron and pulled my hair into a high ponytail. My goal wasn't to get it bone straight, so I worked in huge sections to get through the thickness in twenty minutes. I parted my sides, leaving a piece of hair on each to frame my face and slightly mask the large, dangling set of earrings I'd chosen. I was usually a stud or small gold hoop kind of girl, but I couldn't find any of my favorites, and with the simplicity of the romper, I needed my accessories to pop.

Minutes after applying three coats of mascara and bronzer to my cheeks and the tip of my nose, I was sliding into my romper. It fit like a glove, cinching my waistline and giving me the perfect amount of support for my breasts. I didn't even consider a bra because it had my girls sitting perfectly.

I slid into the sandals that Lyric had gotten me for our trip. The thick strap across the top was clear and the heel was a chunky black one – a really nice addition. It was gorgeous. I slid on the gold watch that I had no idea was still in my suitcase before I packed for Channing. I'd discovered it while unpacking after we'd gotten to Lyric's place. It was perfect for the night.

Just after seven thirty-five, I was descending the stairs and headed for the kitchen. I could hear the handling of glassware in the distance, which only meant one thing. Lyric had already beat me to her stash. When I stepped into the kitchen where she was, she was holding a glass out for me to grab.

"Let's go. I made us a little something, something for the road."

"Thanks. I was on my way to grab something myself."

"You went with the romper. Good fucking decision, friend. Wow."

Lyric circled me as she sipped the crimson colored concoction from her glass. She was stunning herself, dressed in black as well. She was wearing a pair of black denim with a black top to match, showing off her curves even though she'd probably tried to conceal them. Her brown skin was flawless with the full face, natural glam she'd applied.

"Yeah. I thought it fit my mood a bit more than the dress tonight. I'm feeling really chill."

"Well, you look really fucking hot, so I wouldn't say that much."

"Shut up," I sniggered.

"Stand back a little," Lyric instructed as she held her phone up to snap a picture.

Putting on my poker face, I straightened my posture and positioned my drink so that my body wasn't blocked in the shots. I'd disabled my Facebook and Instagram accounts, but Lyric's impromptu shoot had me wanting to create a new Instagram page that I'd make private from the beginning so that I could screen everyone who requested a follow.

"You have to post this one," Lyric squealed, rushing to show me the pictures she'd taken.

"I don't have my Instagram account anymore, but I'm thinking about creating a new one tonight. One that doesn't use my actual name, but something fun and witty."

"Do that and make sure it's private."

"I love this one. Send them all to me."

"I will."

"You ready?"

"Ready as I'll ever be. Keys right here."

Lyric dug into her small Chanel crossbody and presented her keys. She was the most stylish person I knew. Everything about her wardrobe, I obsessed over. From the designer threads to the basics, she could pull off anything. She doubled as an accountant and a real estate agent. Her jobs paid well but after meeting her brothers, I understood that they probably paid better. There didn't seem to be a thing that Lyric could ever want that they wouldn't make possible.

After we were both out of the house, Lyric locked up,

and we headed for the truck. I climbed in first with her sliding in right after. When I noticed the top was off, I thanked God for the bun that I'd decided on. It was only a ten-minute drive according to Lyric, but any other style, except my natural curls, wouldn't have survived the wind.

"I'm happy you decided on a ponytail. I meant to tell you I took the top off when I got our bags out of the back."

"It's fine. I was just thinking the same thing."

The Bluetooth connected as soon as Lyric started the engine. She didn't back out of the driveway until she found the perfect song. I wasn't mad at her for going with the Summer Walker album. There wasn't a skip on it.

Hands swaying, lips moving, and vocals projecting, we made our way through Channing and to Oat + Olive. Word for word, I matched Summer's energy on "Circus". It was one of my favorites and one of the most underrated tracks on the entire album. I loved everything about it.

Three songs later, and we were pulling up to the busy spot to meet Lyric's brothers. As we pulled up to the valet booth, my palms suddenly grew sweaty as my mouth began to produce an insane amount of saliva over and over. From one side of the parking lot to the other, my eyes darted, wondering where he was and if his eyes had found me before I could find him.

"Ever. Get out, babe," Lyric beckoned for my attention while standing at the small booth.

I was so tied up with my discovery of seemingly nothing and no one that I hadn't noticed she'd already exited the truck. I followed suit, stepping out and meeting her at the booth. Twice in under twenty seconds, I smoothed the front of my romper down to make sure that it was presentable.

"You ready, boo?" she asked after handing the attendant a twenty-dollar bill.

"Uh, yeah." My words fought to surface as my chest tightened and limbs began to feel looser – almost too loose.

Please don't let me fall, God, I silently prayed. Though I had complete control in the heels I had on, my legs felt like spaghetti noodles.

"Well, we're definitely not standing in that line," Lyric announced as we rounded the corner and headed toward the door with the huge BAR sign over it. There was another entrance in the front, but it seemed to only be for the reserved restaurant guests.

She dug into her small purse and retrieved her phone. I watched as she placed a call and put the phone up to her ear. Seconds later, she got an answer.

"Laike, can you guys come out to get us? There's a line, and I'm not standing in it."

There was a brief silence before she continued.

"It's Ever and I. We're at the bar entrance. You'll see us as soon as you step out."

She ended the call right after, then shoved her phone back into her bag. Gnawing at the inside of my lip, I fixed my eyes on the door ahead. When the realization that Luca would in fact be exiting it soon hit me like a sack of bricks, I quickly turned in the opposite direction. I wasn't ready. It didn't matter how much I'd tried to prepare myself to see his handsome face again, I wasn't ready. If I wasn't aware that running away with my arms piercing the air as I squealed would make me look as immature and stupid as I did in my head, I would already be headed in the other direction doing that exact thing.

Collapsing my hand on my chest, I tried slowing my heart rate and gaining control of my sketchy breathing. I transferred my weight from one foot to the other as I watched Lyric's face light up from my peripheral vision. I swallowed deeply before closing my eyes and bracing myself for what was to come. Bracing myself for him. For Luca. He was a lot. Possibly without intention, he was so much. Too much, almost.

"Laike, this is my friend, Ever," Lyric said as she pulled at my arm, forcing me to turn around.

Face to face with the man she was introducing as Laike, my breath hiked in my chest. *My God*, I cringed. I didn't understand how it was even possible for two men to be equally fine. Though slimmer, Laike was the spitting image of his older brother.

"I'm Laike," he said, extending a hand for me to shake.

Though he stood front and center, my eyes drifted over his shoulder where the man of the hour stood with his eyes trained on me. I could feel my body's temperature spike as our orbs stalked the air, hungry for one another.

"Ever. Nice to meet you," I introduced myself, absentmindedly shaking his hand. My eyes and attention were elsewhere. Not too far, but definitely not where they were supposed to be at the moment.

Turning slightly, Laike followed my line of vision. I bit into the side of my jaw as I realized I hadn't been as discreet as I'd imagined. His handsome face turned toward me again as he snickered.

"Y'all ready?" he asked, finally letting my hand go.

"We are," Lyric answered for us both. I wanted to thank her because I wasn't capable.

We followed Laike up the walkway, forcing me to encounter Luca on the way up. He stood with his shoulders squared, consuming the attention of so many around him. His presence was so demanding, even without a word ever leaving his lips.

As I neared him, he lowered his head, stuck the toothpick from his hand into his mouth, pulled the right corner of his lips into a smirk, as if he was pleased with what he saw. With the way that my romper was hugging curves I didn't even know existed, I didn't blame him a bit. I felt his eyes on my backside as he fell back, choosing to walk behind us all.

I could smell the zestiness of his cologne as we passed the line to gain entry into the bar without incident. As we stepped inside, I understood why the line was as long as it was and no one seemed to have an issue standing in it. Well, except Lyric, of course. The place was impeccable.

The bar wrapped around the entire space. There were high top tables, bar seating, and carved areas with rope that reserved space for those who belonged in the cubbies that seated at least six. Laike led us behind the ropes of one and to our seats.

Laike. Lyric. Me. Luca. The order was chaotic. Just as I considered the empty chairs on the opposite site of the table, Luca stood and decided to take one of them. I sighed but my victory was short-lived when I realized he was now seated across from me. All night, I'd be forced to refrain from staring at his unique, strikingly beautiful features.

As he made himself comfortable, I tried focusing on something else, anything else. But every few seconds, my eyes ended in the same direction – his. I wasn't sure how I'd get through the night without revealing my fondness for Luca, but I prayed I managed.

"What y'all drinking?" he asked Lyric and I, yet his eyes were trained on me as if there was no one else in the room and he hadn't just addressed more than one person.

You, I wanted to respond, but refrained. Instead, I met his question with my silence. I was drawing blanks with him gazing at me, unwaveringly.

SEVEN

LUCA

"I WANT HENNESSY AND CRANBERRY JUICE," Lyric told me.

Though I'd heard her, it wasn't her response that I was waiting for. I could've guessed her drink of choice on my own. It was Ever's request that I was waiting on. When she didn't respond, I lifted a finger to press the button on the table that would alert our hostess. Her service had been purchased with our reservation.

While we waited to be serviced, I removed the two cases from the empty seat between Laike and me I'd brought inside earlier and sat them on the table. I watched as Lyric's eyes bulged and her hands went over her mouth. Seeing her happy never got old. I loved that shit.

"You really grabbed me something from Rico?"

"I told you I would." I'd always been a man of my word. I wouldn't stop being that, either.

I slid one of the black velvet cases in front of Lyric and the other in front of Ever. Her eyes bloomed, never leaving mine. Lyric looked from Ever's case to me to see if I'd meant to slide the case in her friend's direction. I had. If she was going to be in my presence, I wanted her to look the part.

"I can't." Ever finally spoke as she pushed it back in my direction.

"I insist," I told her, pushing it back toward her.

"Really. I can't."

I witnessed the sadness in her eyes as she looked from the case to me and then back again. The shift in her mood made me cringe inwardly, but I didn't falter.

"Let me ask you something," I started, sitting up straight and fixing my posture.

"Um hm?" She gave me permission to continue.

"Why can't you?"

"When you're accustomed to being controlled by material possessions and monetary donations, you tend to stray away from them," she explained.

Nodding, I noted her underlying message. Her ex was a pussy. I'd summed it up quite quickly and easily.

"You're a grown ass, free ass woman, Ever. The only person here that will ever try to control you is you. I'm not that nigga, whoever the bitch may be. Laike ain't that nigga, either. Anything that comes from us comes from here." I pointed at my chest.

Reaching forward, I pulled the case closer to me, but was halted by long, trembling fingers. My chest tightened at the realization that her trauma ran deeper than my eyes could see. From the outside looking in, she appeared to be unblemished. But as I looked into her glossy rounds, I knew it wasn't her case.

"Thank you," she pushed out as she slid the case toward her again.

Lyric had already popped hers open and was forcing Laike to wrap the two bracelets around her wrist. They complemented her AP so well. A bigger chain was all she needed to complete her set.

"Oh, wow." Ever examined the two bracelets in her box. They were nearly identical to Lyric's.

I waited for her to ask for my help, but she managed to get them on her wrist alone. I watched in awe, feeling a sense of relief as her smile concealed the silent tears that baby girl was crying. For the first time, she'd been gifted from the heart, a milestone that I felt like any and everybody should experience from the opposite sex.

"Take the watch off," I instructed.

"Huh?"

"The watch you're wearing. Take it off. It's depreciating the value of your ice. Trash it," I suggested.

"Let me see," Lyric interrupted, demanding she see the new ice that was on Ever's wrist.

The two pieces immediately amplified her entire appearance. She was easily the baddest in the room already. Now, she looked like she belonged with the steppers that she had come with. That was my goal.

"Didn't think love would come so easily so soon but here we are," Ever joked with Lyric as she held her arm out.

"How can I help you?" the waitress finally appeared and asked.

"A bottle of Hennessy and a tube of cranberry juice. Get us a round of shots, too. Hennessy."

"Coming right up," she responded before disappearing again.

Small talk began around the table, mostly involving Laike and Lyric as Ever and I played the background because we were too invested in the frequent gawking in one another's direction. Every so often, we'd lend a few choice words or include our honest opinions. I witnessed the sadness disappear from her eyes with each second that she spent in my line of vision. Admittedly, it was a beautiful sight. I wanted her comfortable. I wanted her open. I wanted her.

Our drinks were brought to the table shortly after they'd been ordered. With a shot of Hennessy in front of us all, we looked to each other to see who'd set it off. Laike took the initiative.

"To my motherfucking nigga. My right hand. My crutch. My brother from the same fucking Momma and Pops. Welcome home, nigga. Shit ain't been the same without you out here. Happy to have you back."

"Welcome home," Lyric chanted.

"Nice meeting you," Ever concluded, shrugging as her eyes left mine.

We all lifted our clear glasses in the air before hitting them against each other and then the table. Laike and I finished off ours first. Lyric was next. After Ever revealed her glass when she sat it back on the table, everyone burst into laughter.

"Na. Gone finish that shit off!" Laike commanded.

"OK. OK. Give me a chance, gee! I'm new to all of this. It's been a while since I've been outside."

"About seven years, to be exact," Lyric blurted out.

"But who's counting, right?" Ever asked before tossing the rest of the shot back.

I could see her soften and become undone as the contents flowed down her throat. The uptight, timid woman that I'd met hours prior was on her way out of the door, and I couldn't wait to meet whoever was at the end of that shot glass.

"One more," I suggested as I smashed the button again.

"One more." Ever shrugged, surprisingly the first one to speak.

She was accepting the challenge, which meant more to me than getting her wasted. Not only did I want her to enjoy herself, but I wanted her to unwind, too. Tonight would be the last night she ever thought about that nigga willingly. I wanted to swipe her memory with my words and reprogram it with my actions.

"One more," Laike and Lyric followed up with.

"In the meantime, I'm about to pour me a drink,"

Lyric announced as she picked up the bottle of Hennessy.

LUCA-EVER

TWO SHOTS and a cup of Hen heavily diluted with cranberry juice, and the girls were on the floor grinding their hips on one another. Laike and I stayed seated, choosing to watch from afar rather than join the action. Prolonged glances from Ever kept me thoroughly entertained as I sipped from my cup.

"You ain't been out twenty-four hours and you're already tricking, fam," Laike joked.

"I'm still waiting for you to make your point," I responded, unbothered by his observation.

"That's the fucking point, nigga."

"Oh," I replied, unamused and unmoved. With a shrug, I shifted in my seat.

"This nigga whipped and ain't even got the pussy yet, only the print in that tight ass romper."

"Sounds like you looking too fucking hard."

"Have you seen her? Who the fuck wouldn't look that hard?" Laike babbled, pushing out air as if I was on some bullshit.

Nodding, I agreed.

"I like that ice, though. She likes them motherfuckers, too."

"She needs a watch," I disclosed, staring across the table at the one she'd taken off after I'd asked. She'd put it in the back of her purse that she'd sat on the table. Taking it upon myself, I reached forward and slid it out.

When I laid eyes on Ever again, she was no longer dancing. Instead, she was smiling in a nigga's face while bouncing one foot on the floor as she nodded over and over. My nostrils flared as I gnawed on the inside of my bottom lip, drawing blood. My eyes never left her frame as she openly showed interest for the man who'd stopped her little innocent whine.

"Whew. My feet hurt. So Kates should really be discontinued. There's nothing comfortable about these fucking shoes," Lyric complained as she plopped down in her seat.

I'd heard every word she'd spoken, but I didn't have the capacity to respond and keep my focus intact. Ever was my main concern at the moment and if she didn't return to the table soon enough, I'd usher her over myself. I forced my limbs to relax for the second time in about a minute as I homed in on the subject at hand.

Ever's alluring spirit was so rare and magnetic that I wasn't surprised by the attention she was getting, neither did I blame the nigga. She'd sucked me into her web, too. But the thing is, she was mine. It didn't matter if I hadn't made it official yet. I'd staked my claim the moment I saw her. He was on my turf, and I needed him off before I began a riot in this bitch.

As if she felt me watching her, Ever looked up and then at me. My brows hiked in question as I circled my cup to move the ice around in my drink. Nervously, she smiled at me, but I didn't see a damn thing to be happy about. In fact, I was the exact opposite.

When I saw her hand slide across her screen after her phone had appeared out of thin air, all the moisture drained from my mouth. I sipped from my cup again to re-wet the dryness. An impatient snort fell from my lips, pushing a massive breath from my nose as I turned my cup up again. I hadn't realized my fingers were gripping my jeans until I began smoothing my left hand down my leg – up and down to wean myself of the foreign feeling I was suffering from.

I watched as Ever ended the conversation with the bald, suited guy and headed toward our table. The restraint I practiced could've won me an Oscar because I wanted nothing more than to demand her silence when it came to another nigga. Besides, when it was me showing interest, I wanted her mute when a nigga approached her.

"I need to go to the ladies' room," Ever stuttered nervously as her eyes danced around the room. She looked everywhere but to me.

"I need like two minutes, Ever. My feet are killing me. If I stand up now, I'm certain I'm going to end up on my ass," Lyric proclaimed.

"Come on," I interjected, standing from my seat with my cup in tow.

Before she could object, I was grabbing her hand and leading her in the opposite direction. Like a rag doll, I pulled her through the crowd and toward the restrooms. When we finally made it to the hallway where they were located and out of plain sight, I gently pushed her back against the wall right behind the other women, waiting to get into the restroom as well. I could hear the gasp as it came from between those thick, glossy lips of hers that I wanted wrapped around my dick on a daily.

"Unlock your phone," I demanded.

"Huh?" she asked, truly baffled.

To help her understand better, I explained, "Erase that nigga's number you just put in your phone, Ever. Don't play stupid."

As harsh as my words may have sounded, I meant well. I just couldn't conceal my selfishness if I tried. I wanted Ever all to myself but with niggas in her mix that couldn't happen.

"Don't talk to me like that, Luca," Ever expressed. The same sadness I'd witnessed cross her eyes at the table reappeared, etching away at my heart.

My chest tightened as I closed my eyes to regain my composure. *She's fragile. What the fuck are you doing, nigga?* I chastised myself.

"Erase the number, *please*." I softened as much as I could while still demanding she put an end to the shit before it even started.

"Why?"

"Because you know why," I countered.

"I can't read your mind, Luca." She sighed, our eyes never leaving each other.

"Because I'm ready to be the only nigga with the number, Ever." I made shit plain and simple for her.

The look of contentment appeared in her eyes and left as quickly as it had come.

"Then what took you so long to tell me?"

"I'm sorry," I admitted.

"For what?"

"Speaking to you that way and not making my interest obvious a little sooner."

"I'm not ready," she responded, tightening my chest with each word she spoke. "I'm not ready for you. I'm still trying to find me."

Soundlessly, I nodded to show her I understood.

"Don't you have anything to say?" she wondered aloud.

"I don't."

"Why not?"

"If you're expecting me to beg you to fuck with me, I'm not," I assured her.

"That's not what I expected, Luca!" she exclaimed.

"Then what else we got to talk about?"

The line moved as she dropped her head to unlock her phone. I watched silently as she did as she'd been asked far too late. She erased Dennis' number from her contacts along with someone by the name of Cedric. Though I wished it had felt as much like a victory to me as I'd expected, I felt somewhat defeated. However, I wouldn't let her in on that secret.

The line continued to move as we waited in silence. I could feel her staring at the side of my face waiting for me to return the gesture or acknowledge her at all.

Instead, I kept my eyes ahead and moved every time the line did until it was her turn.

Ever returned from the restroom minutes later. I'd finished my drink and was ready for another one. I considered going out to the car to retrieve the weed that we had left to come inside, but decided against it.

"Nah. I'm really on my level," Lyric slurred, whining in her chair.

It was good seeing her enjoying herself. She was a homebody and didn't get out nearly as much as women her age. It had always been that way but since I'd gone to prison, it had worsened. Baby girl was an introvert at heart. The more I was around Ever, I noticed she was, too. They were a match made in boredom.

"You're driving her home," I leaned over to Laike and said.

"Already on it." He nodded.

"But let her enjoy herself. We just have to watch them."

"Nigga, you been watching Ever like a fucking hawk, anyway. I'm sure that ain't no problem for you."

"It's not," I responded with a chuckle.

I witnessed Ever's entire demeanor change. Once we settled in from the restroom, her infectiousness was absorbed by the guilt that she felt for rejecting me. I wanted to let her know she had every right and that I wasn't fucked up about being turned down, but I was afraid that it might've made things between us even more awkward. So, to spare her the agony, I decided to dismiss myself from the table and go grab another drink from the bar.

I slid back in my seat with her eyes on me, stalking my every move. I left the white Styrofoam cup that I'd been sipping from on the table and nodded toward the bar to inform Laike it was my destination. When I stepped away from the crew, I sensed the regret that had settled into Ever's spirit.

"Cheer up," I told her as I leaned in her ear before tapping her on the shoulder.

She snapped her neck around in my direction but before she was able to say anything, I took off. Ever didn't owe me an explanation. It was her right to deny me access to her if she wasn't ready. I just needed her to stand on that and not back down because she thought I was indifferent about her choice. I wasn't. I respected it and wouldn't try swaying her in any way. If I wasn't the nigga for her, then life would continue. It wasn't the end of the world.

"Hi," the bartender greeted as I stood against the wooden bar.

"What's up? Let me get an Old Fashion."

"Sure, coming right up." She smiled at me, flashing her perfect teeth.

Her big, fake pornstar titties were the only thing I saw, though. *I'll pass.* There wasn't shit I could do with her. She returned with my drink a few seconds later.

"Here you go. I'm Amy. If there's anything else I can help you with just give me a holler."

"Bet." I nodded as I responded, ready for Amy to get the fuck out of my face.

Before she could, I felt a small hand on my back and smelled a fruity mix up my nostrils. The elegance of the voice that followed up piqued my interest.

"Can I have a shot of Jack, please," the woman beside me asked the bartender.

"Coming right up," Amy told her.

"Your momma never taught you to keep your hands off strangers?" I asked her, turning slightly to get a good look at her.

"She did, but when they're as handsome as you, I find it kind of hard."

"I'm Luca," I introduced myself.

"I'm Kasey," she revealed.

Her dark skin and perfect hair would do. She wasn't Ever, but she was close enough. From the smile on her face as she licked her lips, I could tell that she was into exactly what I was into.

"Lock me in."

"I was just about to ask." She chuckled, pulling out her cell and unlocking it.

I punched my new number in after opening my phone to retrieve it.

"You don't know your own number?" she teased.

"Just got it today."

"Hmmmm. Crazy ex?"

"Nah."

"Switched carriers?" She played the guessing game.

"Nah. Is you the FEDs or what, baby girl?"

"Hmmm. Fresh out?" she figured out.

"Something like that."

"OK. Fresh out dick always tastes better."

"When you trying to find out?" I challenged, not giving a damn who she was referring to or how many niggas were considered in her statement.

"Soon."

"That's good enough for me. Just hit my line whenever that may be."

"I will."

"Here you go," Amy said as she sat her shot on the counter.

"Ayo, grab her a bottle of that shit," I instructed. "Put it on my tab."

"Thanks, daddy," Kasey told me as she smiled.

"No problem."

I watched as she killed the shot, tossing it back like it was nothing. She sat in silence as she waited for Amy to bring a new bottle. When it was in her hand, she leaned forward and kissed my cheek.

"See you soon, stranger."

I didn't bother checking for her as she walked away, mainly because I felt like a fucking hypocrite. I didn't have to see Ever's face to feel the disappointment radiating from her. Neither did I have to turn around to know that she was watching me. Her energy was evident, encompassing me as I sipped from my glass. If she wasn't ready, that was cool. But there were a thousand bitches that were ready to hold it down until she was. Hopefully, no one compared because otherwise, the position I was trying to put her in would probably no longer be available by the time she was.

Two drinks and an order of traditional wings later, I was back at the table and chopping it up with my people. My stomach was touching my back, prompting me to dig into the platter the second our waitress put it down. Laike was right behind me, followed by Lyric and Ever.

I wasn't sure why, but seeing her dig in brought me joy. I'd been on a few dates in my lifetime and knew that there were women willing to starve than allow a man to see them actively eating on the first date. This wasn't a date for Ever and me, but the same sentiments existed.

"Mom and Dad are coming home tomorrow," Lyric shared, giggling for whatever reason she deemed suitable in her drunken state.

"I thought that was Wednesday."

"Tuesday. I told Laike Tuesday, Wednesday at the latest."

"One of them motherfuckers I remembered," Laike jabbered with a shrug.

"Aight. I'll pull up on them when they touch down."

"Mom will probably have dad take her straight to the center. You know how she is, acts like she can't stay away from them kids more than a day," Lyric reminded me.

"Wherever she is, I'm going to find her. She's going to be on my ass about not telling her I was coming home, but I'll take it."

"She is," Lyric agreed.

Ever's movements caught my attention again. She'd brought her wrist to her face a third time in the last few minutes, forgetting that she no longer had the watch on her arm. I'd tossed it on our way to the restroom. It was evident that she was trying to keep track of time because she'd lighten her cell screen right after.

"It's going on one. You got somewhere to be, Ever?" Laike asked, wondering the same thing I was.

"Work in the morning."

"Oh shit. That's right. I promised to have you back earlier. I'm so sorry," Lyric apologized as she began wiping her fingers with the wet wipe. Ever had already cleaned up and applied more gloss to her lips. She was ready to bounce.

"It's fine, but I'm ready when you are."

"Are you OK to drive?" Lyric asked.

"No," I interrupted, "Laike is taking you home. Ever can ride with me. Y'all both need to chill out."

"It's only a ten-minute drive," Lyric fussed.

"It only takes a second to get wrapped around a pole. Not up for debate. Clean yourself up and we're heading outside."

She knew she wouldn't win because whatever I wasn't willing to say, Laike would. If necessary, neither of us minded tossing her over our shoulder and carrying her out with her lips turned up in a pout. Her safety had always been and would forever be our highest priority. I'd did eight years to prove it. I refused to get out and let her kill herself on some drunk shit. My job was to protect her from everyone, even herself at times.

We filed out of the bar with me on the tail end. The slight breeze that welcomed us when we hit the door was appreciated. We all made our way to the valet booth, both Ever and Lyric barely able to walk straight as their giggles pierced the air.

"Oh my God." Lyric realized just how fucked up she'd gotten. "Yeah. Nah. No driving for me."

"You ain't have to tell us that," Laike assured her. "We knew that shit two hours ago."

"We meet again, stranger." I felt a hand on my back as Kasey rounded my body.

She smelled just as good as she had back at the bar.

"Somehow you don't feel so much like a stranger now," she joked.

"Yeah?"

"Um. Hm. What are you about to get into?" she asked as I threw my arm on her shoulder.

"Bed."

"Can I join you?"

"If that's what you want to do, then I won't stop you. This my ride. Hit me up," I told her as I stepped away. "Come on," I turned to Ever and commanded. Drunk and giddy, she leaped off the curb and toward my truck. I walked her around and helped her inside, afraid that she'd fall on her ass if I didn't.

Once inside, I handed her the bottle of water that I'd been sipping from earlier without hesitation. She needed to be hydrated to combat the liquor she'd consumed. Ever turned the bottle up without question, although it had obviously been opened.

"God. I can't believe I drank so much again tonight," she fussed.

It was obvious that she wasn't used to being so far off her rocker. Neither was Lyric, but when with us, they were cool. I wanted them to drink as much as they could tolerate because we'd always make sure they were good.

I remained silent, watching the road. Lyric's place wasn't very far, but she'd have enough time to begin to sober up. The water, in addition to the wings she'd eaten would soak a bit of the liquor up. She'd sleep really well and wake up refreshed the next morning.

Neither of us indulged in conversation, instead opting to allow the music to lead us. Laike drove like a fresh graduate of driving school to ensure our sister's safety, forcing me to fall in line. When we approached her street, I breathed a sigh of relief. Ever noticed we'd reached our destination and leaned up to lower the volume on Meek Mill's album.

"Can we talk?" she asked as we pulled up to Lyric's home.

She'd been saving her words for this very moment. I'd caught her orbs a few times in the ten minutes we'd traveled to my sister's place. Ever wouldn't let things go so easily, I could tell by the look on her face when she turned to face me.

"What we talking about, Ever?"

I shifted the gear, placing the truck in park. Laike had left the remainder of the weed we had smoked in the cupholder on the armrest. I removed the clear bag and the grinder that was next to it. As I waited for Ever to give me a straight answer, I filled the grinder and sealed the bag of weed up again.

"I feel like you're upset with me," she admitted.

"You shouldn't feel that way because I'm not."

"Then why aren't you talking to me?"

"What do you call this?" I pointed between the two of us as I picked the grinder up and began twisting it.

"You know what I mean!" she fussed.

"I don't. Enlighten me."

"Your attention is elsewhere," she explained as she removed the grinder from my hand and sat it back in the cupholder.

"You want my undivided attention, Ever? Is that why you're suddenly in a panic?"

"I'm not in a panic."

"When I explained to you it was only you I wanted to give my undivided attention to, what did you tell me?"

"I'm not ready."

"Then why don't we leave it at that?"

"Because you've been upset ever since."

"I'm not."

"Then why haven't you said anything to me?"

"Before I told you that, had I said much to you?"

"No."

"So, what's your point, again?"

"Luca," she called my name, waking my dick up.

"Don't do that," I warned.

"I don't understand." She sighed.

"You do understand, Ever. You like the idea of a nigga but like you said, you're not ready."

"Is she coming to your house tonight?"

"Who?"

"The girl you met at the bar."

"Maybe." I shrugged, knowing that I wouldn't be having company until I secured a second spot, somewhere that I could entertain others. Not everyone would come to my home.

"She gets an invite before me?"

"She's ready, Ever. Ready to get fucked and if that's all you want, you don't have to get out. Laike will find his way home. It's been eight years since I slid into anything. I got a lot of dick to give you tonight if that's what you looking for but if not, then I suggest you go in the house. Because if you go with me, then I'm treating you just like I plan to treat her. You'll be reduced to a bird, and I'll only feed you enough crumbs to keep you around until I stop benefiting from your presence. I'm not getting my feelings involved knowing you're not ready. I'm a grown ass man without the time or energy for the games you want to play."

Her silence infuriated me.

With a snort, I concluded, "Imagine me offering you the world but you'd rather have crumbs because another bird has access. You really not ready."

Ever had said nothing. She, instead, opened her door and climbed out of the truck. I watched as she walked up the driveway and into Lyric's home. It wasn't until I reached for the grinder again that I noticed the bracelets I'd given her laying across the armrest. I didn't bother picking them up. For the effects of Ever to wear off, I'd need another blunt or two. She was a fucking problem, and she didn't even have a clue.

EIGHT

EVER

DREAMING WITH A BROKEN HEART. I'd done it countless times while in a relationship with Dewayne, so I was unsure of why this one felt so differently. As I sat wrapped in my towel reading the time displayed on the nightstand clock, I released a long, necessary breath. 6:34 a.m. I'd been up since 5:55 a.m. with the inevitable on my mind.

The thought of Luca's hands and mouth on someone other than me had me tight in the chest. Images of him penetrating the girl he'd met at the bar had awakened me from my sleep. *I'm not ready*, I'd told him. I didn't think I was, but I couldn't explain why I wished it was his bed that I'd awakened in and not my own.

My mind raced back to the valet booth where he wrapped his arms around the beautiful girl with the long, voluminous weave and sickening shape. There was no denying her of anything. She was the full package. From afar, she looked so well put together, and I didn't miss the Mercedes that she hopped into right after we'd settled into our vehicles.

She had her shit together. So did Luca. I could tell from the home he had built from the ground up, the community he lived in, and the lack of stress being released had caused him. I wasn't sure how he'd made it happen, but he'd come home with seemingly as much as he'd gone in with. I wasn't a fool. I knew illegal activities were involved, and I'd promised myself I wouldn't date a man like that again but Luca was different. I could feel it. He was for me. Yet, I was sleeping in his sister's extra rooms, driving a used Avalon, and working as a waitress.

There was so much work that needed to be done on my end. I refused to sit at anyone's table empty-handed. I'd done that before and that's how I'd gotten abused financially for nearly a decade. That wouldn't happen to me again. Couldn't. If I ever decided to walk away from whatever it was that Luca and I built, I didn't want to walk away empty-handed, nor did I want to end up in his sister's spare bedroom.

Going back to sleep wasn't an option, so I decided to shower and rinse the remnants of the night off. The sun's ascend had begun, leaving a beautiful pinkish yellow hue across the sky. Sighing again, I lowered my back until I felt the pillow underneath me. As I stared at the ceiling, I discovered the feeling I'd been avoiding for the last forty-eight hours. *I miss my girls*, I thought. Going an entire week without seeing their faces was insanity, and I simply couldn't commit.

I didn't mind them staying over at their grandmother's, but I needed to see them, and I didn't mean later. I wanted to see them as soon as possible. There was no doubt in my mind that my mother was awake. She woke every morning around five. It was routine for her. That's why she was always napping by noon and back up around two-thirty in the evening.

I grabbed my phone and placed a call to her immediately. Before I left out, I wanted to make sure the girls didn't need anything from home. I was sure my mother and James had gotten them everything they needed and more, but I wanted to be certain.

"Hello?" she answered her cell.

"I'm going to take the girls to school this morning. I'll be there by seven-fifteen."

"Are you sure? You really don't have to."

"Yes. I miss seeing their little faces. You can pick them up this evening. I just want to drop them off."

"Alright. I'll see you in a bit, then."

"Do they need anything?"

"Yes. Emorey has been talking about her baby named Sky that she misses. If you could bring her, then that would be great."

"Yes. I can definitely bring Sky."

I smiled thinking of how much Emorey must've missed her favorite stuffy. She and Sky slept together every night. Emorey took Sky everywhere around the house with her except to the bathtub.

We ended the call, and just as I was about to begin getting ready, my phone pinged. It was a notification from an unknown number I'd never seen before. I opened the message that they'd sent and wasn't surprised to see that it was Dewayne.

Bring me my fucking kids, bitch! he'd sent. With a roll of my eyes, I deleted the message as soon as I'd read it completely.

"Yeah, I can't put this off any longer," I thought aloud.

Dewayne didn't give a damn about Emorey or Essence. I couldn't recall a single time he'd made either of them a priority, not even during their births. Because he swore that labor took far too long, he'd suggested I called him when I was almost ready to push. Foolish enough, I'd done so with Essence, but when Emorey came, I didn't even bother.

When my water broke, I drove myself to the hospital and called Lyric while I was on the way. She boarded the first flight she could find and made it to my hospital room an hour before I pushed Emorey out. Dewayne didn't return to the hospital until it was time for me to be discharged. He hardly even gave Emorey a second look and didn't keep Essence during my hospital stay – neither did Pam.

I was on my own, always had been when I was with Dewayne. Now that I was taking heed and really out of their hair, suddenly they found interest in my girls. It was ironic and borderline hilarious.

Responding wasn't even a thought of mine. I dialed the T-Mobile hotline instead. I couldn't put off changing my number any longer. It was time to revoke my ex's access to me completely. Luckily, we were on central time. It was already seven eastern time.

"Change my number," I spoke to the automated machine that asked my reason for calling.

Two minutes later, I was connected to a live representative.

"Thanks for calling T-Mobile. Can we start with the passcode on your account?"

LUCAEVER

I PULLED up to my mother's house to get the girls, feeling like a weight had been lifted off my shoulders. It was insane how much better a number change had me feeling. Before getting out, I was sure to text the new number to Lyric. Besides my mom, she was the only person who I wanted to have the new number. Everyone else could wait until I was ready.

When I stepped onto my mother's porch, I could hear Emorey's little voice as she tried convincing Essence to watch her. I was almost certain that she wasn't doing anything spectacular, but she was always wanting all the attention.

"Watch this, sister!" she yelled.

My mom had opened the storm door, allowing me to see through the glass door upon entry. Emorey bounced toward the door, not knowing I was behind it. When she finally realized I was watching her, she jetted for the door, running straight into the clean glass and hitting her face.

Ouch, I cringed as I sprang into action. Her whimpers began immediately as she stepped back and held her aching face. I opened the door and pulled her into my arms and allowed her to cry on my shoulder.

"It's OK. It's OK. Hi, Essence." I multitasked, bouncing Emorey in one hand while beckoning for Essence to come hug my leg.

She rushed over with the prettiest look of astonishment I'd ever seen. Maybe I was biased because she was mine, but no one could deny the twinkle in those hazel eyes as her dirty blonde curls bounced in my direction. My girls were perfect in every way. I couldn't have asked for a better bunch. The moment I was married, I would add to the crew but for now it was just us three.

"Mommy!" she squealed as Emorey continued to have a meltdown in my arms.

"Are you ready for school?" I asked.

"Yes."

"Good. Go get your backpack and come on. I'm taking you guys today, but Grams is still picking you up, OK?"

"Good morning, Ever," James said as he made his way downstairs and out of the front door.

"Morning!" I yelled behind me.

He was probably running behind. Otherwise, he'd stick around to talk a bit. Right after he left, my mother came down the stairs. Though in her late fifties, she didn't look a day over forty-five. I aspired to be just like her when I reached her age. She looked good.

"Hey. They're both ready to go. I've fed them eggs and bacon. The little one didn't eat much, but I packed her a Pop-Tart for the ride to school."

"OK. Essence is gone to grab her bag and then we're heading out. They haven't been too much trouble have they?"

"Honey, these are the most mild-mannered children I know. Most times I forget they're even here. Respectable and listen well. Sometimes I have to tell Emorey twice, but she gets the job done eventually."

"Yeah. She's a little firecracker."

"Spoiled is all. She reminds me a lot of you. She has a fire to her. Don't ever put that out. She's going to need it to face this big, bad world."

I wonder when my fire was smoldered, I thought. Maybe it was when Dewayne entered my life because prior to that, I remembered being this outgoing woman with a bright future ahead of her. From the moment he entered my life, insecurities crept in that led to me shying away from life and its beauty altogether. Before I knew it, I was a stay-at-home mom who hid herself from the big, bad world.

"I promise I won't," I agreed with my mother. "Come on, girls. Let's get going."

Emorey had finally calmed down enough to wave goodbye to my mother as she said her goodbyes to the girls.

"See you two this evening. It's popcorn and movie night."

"Caramel popcorn?" Essence probed.

"If that's what you prefer."

"Yup. I want caramel popcorn."

"Me too," Emorey chanted.

"Then caramel popcorn it is, ladies. I'll pick you both up, and we can come straight home and pop it. How does that sound?"

"Fantastic," Essence responded with a nod.

"Pantasic," Emorey tried, but fell a bit short.

"See you, Mom. Thanks again for getting the girls. Love you."

"Love you, back."

"Oh, I got a new cell number. I'll text it to you when I get in the car and get them strapped in."

"OK. That's good. I was wondering when you would. I might do the same. I'm about tired of the old thing I've got. Too many people still remember the number."

I knew she was only being nice. Dewayne had possibly reached out to her from another number, too.

"It's OK if you're changing it because of Dewayne, Mom. I'm sorry to put you in all of this."

"Dewayne and his stupidity doesn't bother me. I've seen his type. They're just a bunch of wasted energy. Too many people from my past have access to me. I'm ready to change that."

"Well, that makes sense."

"Changing yours just has me ready to do the same."

"OK. We're going to head out. I'll text you in a minute or two."

"Later." She followed me to the door, still giving the girls all of her love.

LUCA-EVER

EMOREY'S SCHOOL was only fifteen minutes away from Essence's, which made dropping them off at the same time so much more convenient for me – and my mother. As I pulled up to Eisenberg Smiles, I remembered the bet between Lyric and me. She'd kept me out much later than she was supposed to, which meant that once I did get the girls back next week, she'd be responsible for getting them from school. The thought of having two weeks free of pickups got me excited.

"Come on, Em. It's your turn," I cheered, reaching in the back of my car to unbuckle her car seat.

"I ready, Mommy."

She stood once she'd been unbuckled and climbed in the front so that I wouldn't have to walk around to her side. I pulled her into my arms and sat her on my hip while I closed the door and locked my car behind me. We caught a parent on her way out and gained access to the building. Otherwise, we would've needed a code to enter. Emorey's class was the fourth on the right, which we headed straight for. I'd clock her in after she was settled.

"Emorey!" Mrs. Eisenberg, the owner and Lyric, Laike, and Luca's mother, rushed out of her office to greet Emorey.

"Momma E!" she shouted, hands wailing as she reached for her.

Mrs. Eisenberg grabbed her from my arms and the two embraced as if they hadn't seen each other in weeks. It had only been Friday and Monday. I watched on, shaking my head at their dramatics. The two were inseparable and it was pathetic.

"If you keep babying her, she'll never get used to her classroom and playing with the others," I joked, knowing Mrs. Eisenberg didn't give a damn about any of that.

"Well, maybe she has a right. Children be knowing and not just when it comes to adults. When it comes to other children, too. It might be some bad spirits birthing in that room. I wouldn't want to be there, either. Little toddler demons everywhere she turns."

"That's just insane." I shook my head.

"It could be true, though."

"I have a new number. I wanted to change the one I have on file."

"No problem. Just write it down on a piece of paper in my office, and I'll have Shell to sort it out. Is everything OK?"

"Yes. Just tired of the restricted calls and such," I told her.

She was aware of my situation, so there was no need to hide anything from her. Lyric had already explained it somewhat, which was one of the reasons Emorey attended her center free of charge. She wanted to help me in any way that she could. Free childcare was more than enough.

"I bet you feel a lot better."

"I underestimated the power of something as simple as a number change. I feel twenty pounds lighter than I did when I woke up this morning."

Though my lifted burdens slightly had something to do with one of the men she'd given birth to, it was mostly due to the new number.

Luca. Even the thought of him was enough to get my panties in a bunch.

I wanted to ask how she'd made a human so perfect that it literally hurt to even think about, but I recalled him saying that he would come to see her. I didn't want to spoil his surprise, but I also wanted to know why no one had warned me. Not Lyric and not Mrs. Eisenberg. I'd been blindsided, and I was still trying to recover.

"I know the feeling. Before I got with my husband all those years ago, I was dating a man that called himself putting his hands on me. Let me tell you, that's exactly how I met Liam. He stepped in along with a few other patrons at the restaurant we were eating at. This man literally tossed my food on the floor and snatched me from my seat because I had caught him with another woman.

"All I'd come to do was have myself a salad. I didn't expect to find my man there with another woman. They hemmed that sucker up and that was the last I saw of him. Liam bought me another salad and ended up having lunch with me. We've been inseparable since."

"Maybe one day my knight will find me." I chuckled.

"Oh trust me, it's coming. I can feel it in my bones.

Your spirit is too mesmeric. Hell, I'm even drawn to you. It's going to happen and it's going to happen fast, darling. Probably when you least expect it, too. This time, though, you'll attract your forever. It won't be on that temporary stuff, so I hope you're ready."

I'm not ready. My words replayed in my head. I'd just told Luca that last night. To hear his mother speak the same words had me shaken to my core.

"I'm trying to get ready," I admitted with a sigh. "It's not easy coming from ground zero."

"But it'll be beautiful. Trust me. You'll look back at these moments and be filled with so much gratitude. These are your founding blocks. Your future starts now, not yesterday. So, just continue to make these days count and you'll have nothing to worry about. You hear?"

"Yes."

"Now, kiss the girl goodbye and go on about your day. She'll be fine. I wish y'all would stop picking her up so early. I could always drop her off to Lyric's when I leave."

"You've done enough," I assured her.

"Well, I want to do more, and I be bored when she leaves. Think about it and let me know."

"I will. See you later, Em." I leaned in and kissed her chubby cheeks.

Everyone pitching in to make my life easier had me full of emotions when I made it back to my car. I could feel the pricking of my eyes, but I willed myself not to cry. I'd waited so long to make the move back to Channing, afraid of the obstacles I'd be facing. Now that I was home, I hadn't stumbled upon one.

Lyric had made sure I was comfortable and wanted for nothing from the jump. She'd already set the girls up for success by the time we made it. The car that she'd practically given me by handing me so much cash was the reliable piece of transportation that I thought I wouldn't be able to afford for months.

I was ready to ride the bus with my girls every day if it was necessary, but it wasn't. Everything had worked itself out and was still working itself out. I had so much to be thankful for, and I prayed I showed just how thankful I was for the constant support I was getting.

Get it together, Ever. It was nearing the eight o'clock hour when I dropped both of the girls off. I had a twenty-minute drive, but with traffic it would be at least thirty minutes until I got to work. My shift started at 8:30, which was perfect. I had a thirty-minute meeting with Baisleigh about an upcoming event. One of our regulars wanted a birthday brunch for her and twelve friends.

It was my first event, and I couldn't wait to bring it to life. I wanted to get Baisleigh's permission to reach out and offer my cake making services to the birthday girl, Tamara. It was a hobby I'd picked up before leaving Channing, and still loved so much. I'd handmade all the girls' birthday cakes and even some for holidays like the Fourth of July.

I'd wanted to start a cake decorating business for years but hadn't had the time or energy because I was always taking care of the girls. With everyone in my corner and ready to step in, I knew it was finally time to put that business idea to the test. Being the event coordinator at Baisleigh's connected me with the very audience that I'd be serving. It was a win- win situation. Or, at least, that's how I saw it.

NINE

EVER

I MADE it to work with seven minutes to spare. Traffic was surprisingly light on the expressway. With the extra time on my hands, I downloaded the Instagram app to my phone again. The app appeared on my screen in a few seconds and was ready for use. I chose the option to create a new account and followed the prompts.

ESinclair, I thought for a username.

No. Too revealing. Anyone can find me like that.

ForEverSinclair. Still too close to my name.

SincerelyyEvv, I finalized. It was perfect and it was available.

When the new profile popped up, I immediately switched my settings to private and started my bio. I didn't mark my location or use my actual name. I stuck with Evv – Cake Creator for the identity line and kept things short. More than anything, I wanted a place to show more work than play. Heck, I hardly got out to play, excluding the last two nights.

I opened Lyric and I's text thread and downloaded the pictures she'd sent me. I chose my favorite and used it as my first post. My camera roll had many selfies that I wanted to consider as my profile picture, but I thought about how easily I'd be able to be identified. So, instead, I opted for a photo of me holding Emorey's cake for her third birthday. It covered almost my entire face.

My time ended before I was able to play around with the app, but before I exited my car, I found Lyric's profile and requested her. She immediately accepted, which let me know she was up on social media rather than doing any work. The green bubble on her stories appeared instantly, which let me know that she'd added me to her close friends list.

I played the stories she'd collected over the last twenty-four hours and gasped. She'd caught me on the dance floor at the bar, totally embarrassing myself while under the influence. I grinded against her body without a care in the world.

Though I thought I looked absolutely silly, I noticed one thing about that moment that I was thankful for. *My smile.* It was genuine because I was genuinely at a place of peace and finding happiness that I didn't know existed on the flip side of my breakup. I thought that I'd be sad and confused, trying to make it from day to day. But in three short weeks, I'd begun thriving much more than I ever had while with Dewayne. Money wasn't even an issue.

For once, my bank account had a healthy savings and some money in the checking account. I had adapted the 10 percent rule quickly when getting to Channing. I spent only 10 percent of my earnings and saved the rest. I didn't have any bills piling up. My only responsibility was gas, cell phone bill, and feeding my babies.

My tips were deposited into my account at the end of each week. I still had twenty-two hundred dollars of the money that Lyric had given me. The check that I received from Baisleigh's so far, I hardly saw because as soon as I received it, I snapped a picture and put it directly in the bank.

My smile. Even intoxicated, it was still evident that, in that moment, I was happy. The next few stories were simply about her getting her morning started, which she invited everyone to watch. The final one was heart-gripping, causing me to halt just before opening the door to my job.

"Look who just decided to pop up, unannounced!" she shared with only her close friends, eventually fanning the camera around to show both Laike and Luca. The pace of my breathing picked up slightly as I replayed the story over and then over again. It wasn't until the third time that I realized she had two tags on the bottom, one belonging to Laike and the other to Luca.

@TheLaikeShow

@NoIGLuca

I clicked the one that was obviously attached to Luca but found it to be private. Not thinking twice, I requested to follow him. Laike's page was public, allowing me to follow him without a request. However, he only had a total of six pictures posted, the last one dating back two years. If it was his case, then I knew that Luca's feed was either empty or had pictures dating back eight years before he went to prison.

Before stepping into Baisleigh's House, I took a deep breath. In an attempt to gather myself, I counted down from five. Knowing that I'd missed Luca by an hour was bittersweet. It also meant that the chances of him giving his dick to the girl from the bar was less likely. He was up and out way too early with a fresh fit and a fresh face. More than likely, he and Laike had slept at the same location and gone to visit Lyric before getting their day started.

Did he expect me to be home? I wondered as I pushed forward to begin my workday. It was past eight-thirty now. I still needed to clock in and meet Baisleigh in her office. The thought of hosting my first event had my cheeks flushed and my eyes bright with curiosity. I had no idea what the planning consisted of, but I'd managed two children and all of their events alone for the last six years. If I could do that, I could probably do anything, event coordination for adult parties included.

"Good morning," I said as I walked through the door of Baisleigh's office after clocking in and putting my belongings away. Her face was planted in her phone just like mine had been a few minutes ago.

"Hey. Close the door," she insisted, shutting down her screen and pulling her chair closer to her desk.

I closed the door behind me and took a seat on the other side of her desk in one of the two chairs that was in front of it. She clicked around on the computer for a while before she turned to me and began.

"So, the guest of honor's name is Tamara. She's turning twenty-nine and wants to reserve the left wing of the building for three hours to cater to her friends and family. There will be twenty-nine guests. How ironic. She will be paying a deposit to rent the area for three hours, but the guests will pay for their plates on her end.

"She will just pay us what she's arranged for them to pay for a full-course brunch experience. This includes a regular beverage and an alcoholic beverage. A medium bacon or sausage quiche patty as the appetizer, the Baisleigh special as the meal with a meat of their choice, and pancakes of their choice for dessert. That's it."

"Got it."

"What I need from you is to keep in contact with her and get everything lined up. There is a spreadsheet for you to keep track of everything that I'm going to email you. Also, you're in charge of decorations and making her day special."

"About that. I was going to ask if I could offer my cake decorating services to her."

"You decorate cakes?"

"I do."

"And, why haven't you been said that? I have a very big, very close family and it's somebody's birthday every month, most times a few people. We need a loyal cake lady because we are tired of the disappointment. Send me some of your work. My aunt needs a cake for her party in two weeks."

"I will email them to you. So, it's OK to offer that to her?"

"Yes. Of course it is. Hell, make some business cards, and we will pass them out to the guests until you run out. My job is not to keep you here. It's to lift you higher. Anything I can do to help you reach your full potential, I'm with it. That goes for every one of my employees. I wish I'd known, honey. You came right on time, though."

"Is that all?"

"Yes, ma'am."

"I'm going to go out here and get started, then. I saw that Ria and Isis were the only ones on the floor right now and we're probably about to get that morning rush."

"Yeah. They already have enough tables. The next four that come through the door are yours. You guys can figure it out from there."

"Thanks, Baisleigh."

"Of course."

I left her office while tying my apron around my waist. The beige fabric with Baisleigh's House written on it was so simple and so cute. The uniform was simple khaki pants and the tan shirts with a B on the upper right chest area.

As soon as I stepped onto the floor, the bell chimed,

letting me know we had new guests. I rushed to the hostess station to grab a few menus. When I lifted, so did my soul. The man whose Instagram I'd just attempted to stalk, who had me up in the early morning before my time, who'd consumed me wholly since seeing his face was standing before me.

"Wel-welcome to... uh, Welcome to Baisleigh's House," I stammered over my words.

I could feel my ears reddened as our eyes connected. As I grabbed the back of my neck and tried clearing my throat of the sudden debris, I adjusted my gaze so that he wasn't in the center of it. I was unable to look him square in the face this time. Pride wouldn't allow it. So, I deflected, dropping my head into the menus that I'd scooped up.

"What's up?" Laike smiled, stepping closer to the booth I was behind.

"Hi guys."

"You made it to work after all," Laike acknowledged.

"Fortunately. Just two?" I asked.

"Yeah," Luca answered. I could feel his eyes on me.

"This way."

I was so relieved to have given him my back to watch instead of staring daggers into the side of my face. Their table was only a short distance away, but it gave me time to compose myself, *somewhat*.

"Here we are, gentleman. What can I get you guys started with to drink?"

"Water," they both said simultaneously.

"Two waters coming right up," I told them as I sat their menus down, still avoiding eye contact with Luca.

I scurried across the floor and made my way behind the counter. Ria was making freshly squeezed orange juice when I pulled her to the side to give her the rundown.

"Hey. Can you take the table that just came in? I don't think I feel so well."

I didn't, so it wasn't a lie. Whenever Luca was involved, I felt foreign in my own skin. It was as if I was having an out-of-body experience. He ignited something within me that had never been discovered before – not by me or anyone else.

"OK. Sure. I've seen the thin one in here several times. He tips exceptionally well, so I'm down."

"Thanks. I'm going to take a second and sit in the waiting room in the restroom. If anyone needs me, tell them that's where I am."

"Of course."

Ria was an angel. She was about her money and didn't care about much else. She had three children at home counting on her to make it happen so that's exactly what she did on a daily basis. She was the only employee besides Baisleigh that worked six days a week.

Though I felt slightly guilty for handing Luca and Laike off to someone else, I didn't have the capacity to wait on them. To be honest, I didn't even want to see them. Not here. I loved my job, but it might not have looked so appealing to others.

As I pushed the door of the restroom open, my mind

returned to my night at the bar. Luca had draped his arms around the prettiest girl with the prettiest skin that drove an even prettier car. That wasn't me. My fresh start was a bit ugly. I'd chosen the first job that was hiring and where I could make the quickest, easiest money, never considering Luca into my plans. Now that he was here, I was wondering if I looked a bit different in his eyes.

I'll just stay here until they leave, I thought to myself, sitting in the large waiting room that was inside of the restroom. There were two velvety couches, two accent chairs, four floor mirrors that lined the longest wall, and small vanities in between each of them. Baisleigh had captured the powder room essence really well.

Making myself comfortable, I rested my head on the back of the couch. I was ready to wait out the duo for as long as it took. My sweaty palms rested against the couch's cushion, keeping them dry and keeping perspiration off my uniform. I closed my eyes and considered what I'd make us all for dinner. Lyric wasn't much of a cook prior to us joining her, but now we took turns cooking dinner. There was food on our table five to six out of seven days of the week. The other days we went with leftovers.

Five minutes into my stay, I heard the door open and a set of footsteps followed. I prayed Baisleigh hadn't come to see where I was and why I'd disappeared. Explaining my situation was not the easiest. And, frankly, I didn't want to. Not to my boss or anyone else.

"I thought we had this conversation, Ever." His voice

startled me. I looked up to find Luca standing before me with his hands clasped in front of him.

"Luca, what are you doing in here?" I looked around to see if I was the only one seeing this – seeing him. He wasn't supposed to be here.

"I thought I told you about that shit," coolly, he stated.

"You're not supposed to be in here," I rushed out, my eyes roaming the area as if someone was watching us.

"I'm supposed to be wherever the fuck I'm at. What's your issue?"

"I don't have one." I frowned, unsure of what he was referring to.

"Then why haven't I seen you since I sat down, and why the fuck did our waitress change?"

"Luca, she's great at her job. Even better than me."

"Nobody is better than you, Ever. And, fuck her. I want you."

His words gripped at my chest, squeezing my heart upon impact. I wanted to know how one could be so brutal and so enchanting at once. Luca was utterly and uncompromisingly both.

"I just need a minute," I explained to him with a sigh.

"For what?"

"Because I need a minute." He frustrated me with his persistence. It was as striking as he was, keeping me in a chokehold.

"To waddle in shame that is completely unnecessary?"

"It's not that simple, Luca."

"Listen, if you were sitting on your ass not doing shit, I still wouldn't look at you any differently because you'd deserve it. A nigga is supposed to make sure that you don't have to lift a finger. But since that isn't the case, you're hustling the clock, and I respect you even more for it. Money is money, no matter how you get it. That shame you're feeling right now, ball that shit up and toss it in the garbage because it ain't 'bout shit from my standpoint. If you like your job, then I love it. If you don't, then I got something else in mind for you. Just say the word."

"The word," I said without flinching.

"Giving me your undivided attention."

"What?"

"That's the job. And, it pays well. Starting bonus includes a fully furnished, fully paid for pad, a new whip, and unlimited credit card usage."

"I can't," I told Luca, lowering my head in my hands.

"Keep your head up, Ever. I've told you this already. And, why not?"

"Because my independence means more to me than you know right now. I just left a man who made it easy for me to be a stay-at-home mom and not have to work, but not working kept me tied down to him for so long. I just got my freedom and it includes being financially stable, without a man's help."

"I'm not that nigga, Ever."

"I know. Trust me, I know you aren't. I feel it. I just can't risk my sanity banking on a man again. I won't do it. I have children to consider and their happiness means the world to me."

"Let me help."

"By offering me money and worldly things? The best thing you can do for me, Luca, is have patience and understanding. I'm a mess right now, and I'm trying to clean myself up. I don't know what that looks like on a day to day, but I'm trying."

"Trying is enough."

"I thought about you fucking that girl all night and all morning. Did you?" I wasn't sure where the question had come from, but I needed to clear my conscience. So, he needed to answer me.

"I didn't."

"Why?"

"Because I'm waiting for you. You the only person I'm trying to fuck in the future."

With a chuckle, I responded, "Can you use another word? That sounds so, I don't know."

"Fuck, make love... same shit, Ever. I'm trying to slide up in you again and again and again. Is that better?"

"I don't know." I laughed, finally giving him my eyes.

"Be ready around seven, tonight. I'm taking you out."

"Are you asking me or telling me?"

"I'm telling you because I'm not giving you another chance to tell me you aren't ready. I know you are. Ready enough, at least."

Knock.

Knock.

Knock.

A knock on the door put a halt to my thoughts. My eyes darted between the door and Luca. Then again.

The smirk on his face told me everything I needed to know.

"Did you lock the door?"

"Yeah. I didn't need any interruptions."

"They're going to think we're in here screwing."

"I don't give a fuck what they think and if you want to make it happen so their chatter isn't in vain, we still have time."

"Goodbye, Luca." I tittered.

Stepping backward, he nodded. "Seven."

"Seven," I repeated.

I watched from afar as he put more and more distance between us. He was dressed in a pair of red Nike shorts with a white shirt to match. He wore a thick chain around his neck and a watch on his arm that looked like it cost a pretty penny. It reminded me of the bracelets I'd left with him after our night at the bar.

"Can I have my bracelets back?" I teased.

"When you bring your ass back out here and take my order."

"I'm coming," I assured him as he turned and unlocked the door.

I wasn't surprised to see that it was Baisleigh who'd come knocking to see if I was alright. She probably wasn't expecting to see Luca when the door finally opened, but when she did, I didn't miss the smile that followed.

"Luca! I didn't know you were home."

"Shit, not too many people do. I like ya spot. I'm 'bout to see what this food talking 'bout."

"It's so good to see you, and the food is everything

they've said it is. You'll love it. Tell your mother I said hello."

"I will. On the way to see her as soon as we leave here."

She moved out of the way so that Luca could exit while I considered the ways they might know each other. Before I could fix my mouth to ask, Baisleigh was standing in front of me.

"Everything alright?"

"Yes. He wanted to ask me on a date," I admitted, palming my face because I couldn't believe he'd come to my job. "Well, tell me he's taking me on a date."

"Go."

"Huh?" My head popped up as I questioned her.

"Go. He's one of the good ones, Ever, and you don't want to let him slip away. His brother, Laike, now that's a different story." She rolled her eyes as she said his name.

"You and Laike?" I chuckled, not believing my eyes.

"Um hmm. As teenagers, though. He was my first, honey. I don't regret it, but I'm so happy I have that out of my system. That dick was hard to let go of. I was still fiending for it and giving it up to him well into adulthood, but I've been delivered for the last six years, and I ain't going back."

"How do you guys know each other?"

"We lived on the same block. Our parents still do."

"It's such a small city."

"Very. Anyway, don't stand the man up. Make sure you enjoy yourself and spare no expense. His pockets can stand it."

"I know. He got me matching bracelets the first day I met him."

"Sounds like an Eisenberg boy." She giggled with a shake of the head.

"I gave them back."

"You what?"

"I gave them back after he was mean to me last night," I shared with her.

"Was he mean to you, or did he give you the honest, hard truth?"

"That one."

"Okay, because that doesn't even sound like Luca. He's brutally honest, but not mean. Not toward the people he cares about, at least. I can't speak for the rest of Channing."

"He told me he wanted to pursue me, and I turned him down. I told him I wasn't ready but when I saw him entertaining a girl he met at the bar we went to last night, I couldn't help but feel jealous. He picked up on it."

"And tore right into your ass, huh?"

"He did," I told her. *"Imagine me offering you the world but you'd rather have crumbs because another bird has access. You really not ready.* That's what he said to me."

"Sounds like Luca to me. Why don't you think you're ready? I've seen broken hearts, Ever, and you don't have one. Your heart is relieved, love. It's written all over your pretty face."

"I don't. I expected to feel like pieces of me were missing when I left, but I actually feel complete for once.

Me telling him I wasn't ready had nothing to with love but everything to do with me being able to stand on my own two feet before I get involved with anyone."

"You're standing, Ever. Trust me. If you're looking and comparing what you have to what they have, you'll probably never be ready. The Eisenbergs are no strangers to money. They've been the richest on the block since I can remember. The only reason they're still in Channing is because they love to be surrounded by Black folk. They have long, old money. The kind the hairy white men have and hate to see Black people with. That's whose level they're on. They stick around us common folk because it's us who they love and relate to most. Liam, their father, ask about him one day."

"I haven't met him yet. Only their mother."

"If you've never seen a drug lord in the flesh, that'll change when you meet him. The smartest criminal you'll ever encounter. The only reason I know his prior occupation is because I was screwing Laike for too many years not to. I'd overheard a conversation or two, but never had any concrete proof. No one did and the same goes for his sons. No one knows what they do, yet everyone knows what they do."

"And that's the other thing. I promised myself that I wouldn't go down that path again. My ex is into the streets."

"Your ex ain't an Eisenberg and the nigga sure isn't Luca. Don't even put the two in the same sentence. Now, get out of here and go get your money, Ever."

I stood from the comfortable bench in the waiting

room of the restroom and made my way to the sink to wash up, although I hadn't been in the stalls. I grabbed a paper towel to open the door after shaking my hands dry. Before stepping back out of the floor, I smoothed my clothes, making sure they were free of wrinkles. With my head held high, I stepped out – *in route to Luca's handsome face.*

TEN

LUCA

BABY, *you're the finest*
Pussy taste like diamonds
How'd you get so timeless?
Wanna get behind it, behind it
Remind ya, I know how to find it
Hit it how you like it

I SANG to the SiR track that I'd stumbled across during my shower after getting home last night. I'd never heard of the nigga before that and now he'd replaced my entire list of go-tos. I was getting on Laike's last nerve. I saw it on his face.

"I can't wait until you finally hit that shit because she got you smiling and singing and shit. I don't know who the fuck you are right now."

"You complain a nigga the Grinch. Then when I loosen up a bit, you don't know who I am? Pick a side."

"I'm on the other side because I'm 'bout tired of whoever this new motherfucker is."

"New? 'Cause I'm laying on a new sound?"

"And singing it and bobbing your head and yeah... that's just too much."

"Don't lie. He aight?" I asked, taking a quick second to glance in my little brother's direction.

"You going to turn this shit, or do I need to get in my own fucking whip? I'm not trying to hear this all day."

"Then get out and go pay for the gas. Give your ears a break," I suggested, pulling up to the pump.

I was on a quarter tank leaving Baisleigh's House and wanted to refill, even with over one hundred miles left on the dash. With a shake of his head, Laike opened the door and placed the Glock that had been resting in his lap into the back of his pants and pulled his shirt over it.

"And, I'm adding this high ass gas to your fucking tab."

"When I got in, this motherfucker should've been on full. You're just paying for the gas you burned before I got the chance to."

"That's OK. I know the account number."

"Then you should know that there isn't a man alive that can say they played with my paper. Do with that information as you please."

"There he goes!" Laike slapped the dashboard.

"Fuck you," I spat in his direction.

"The Grinch is back."

He hopped out of the truck and slammed the door before I could respond, leaving me with my thoughts as the music played in the background. Ever's pretty face came into full view as I drifted to a faraway place, one where her worries rested with me. She had no idea just how much I wanted to lift any and every burden from her small shoulders.

I saw the desire for more, for better in her eyes. Unlike the nigga she'd left, I only wanted to help her reach her full potential, never hindering or holding her back. It would take patience on my end, waiting to gain her trust, but I was willing to wait if it meant undoing the damage that he'd done.

For once, I wanted to save someone but to my surprise, she didn't want to be saved. Ever wanted to be her own knight in shining armor, and my heart tightened at the revelation. Baby had been damaged. The nigga who'd played with her had played her right into my arms, and I couldn't wait to show her what it felt like to fuck with and fuck on a real nigga.

Laike caught my attention from the second he exited the store, mainly because he wasn't alone. He had company. Squinting, I tried determining who was at his side while clutching the strap in my lap. As they got closer to the truck, the contorted facial expression dissolved as I relaxed my features. Before they reached the vehicle, I was out and headed in their direction.

"My nigga!" Ken shouted, spreading his arms and welcoming me into his personal space.

I accepted the invitation from my friend of over twenty years, patting his back forcefully to demonstrate my appreciation for his presence. There wasn't a doubt about it. I'd missed my nigga. Eight years of not seeing his face, hearing his voice, or kicking shit with him hadn't seemed like so much of a big deal until I was standing in front of him, again, dealing with my emotions.

"Wow. Eight fucking years, bro." I recalled my time away.

"Eight fucking years. You ate that shit, big dog. I thought my ears were deceiving me, hearing motherfuckers claim they'd run across you in passing. I'm like, not my nigga. I would've heard something by now. What's good?"

"I got home yesterday and had plans to pull up on you. A phone call wasn't gone do it for me, fam."

"Me, either," Ken agreed. "What's up? What you niggas about to get into?"

"Shit, pull up on Moms at the center."

"Aight. Aight. How the fam? How's Lyric? I ain't seen her in, man, shit... since you've been gone."

"Everybody straight, according to Laike. Lyric is the only family I've seen since I touched down. Mom and Pops been out of town."

"Word. Laike got the number. I've got to run, but hit me up. I don't give a fuck what I'm doing, I'm going to make time. Just give me the play and it's on."

"Aight. Here, program your shit in my phone. I'm about to text you the number now."

"Bet. Welcome home, nigga."

Ken dug into his pockets and emptied them in my hands, giving me every dollar that he had on him. I chuckled, happily accepting it because I knew he wouldn't allow me to leave if I didn't.

"Really?" I tilted my head and asked.

"What? You too good for blue faces, now?"

"Nah."

"Good then. You're going to need them for this fucking tank you're driving. Holler at me. I'm out."

I watched as he turned and jogged back to his ride. The black Mercedes was waiting for him a few pumps over. It had been parked when we pulled up. It had been the reason I hadn't seen him prior. He was already inside of the gas station when Laike entered.

"That nigga gets blacker each time I see him," Laike joked after climbing in the truck.

He'd pumped the gas while Ken and I caught up.

"I was thinking the same thing," I agreed, putting the truck in gear and pulling out.

Laike removed the cord from my cell as soon as I hit the road, replacing it with his own. I wasn't fucked up about it. I knew he was tired of listening to slow jams all morning. He replaced SiR with Jay. I couldn't be mad at him for that.

"'Cause when my backs against the wall, nigga I react. Secretly, though, I know you admire that. Wish you had the balls to fire back. Blat!" I sang along with my favorite few lines as I pushed through Channing with one person on my mind. My ole lady.

Twenty minutes later, and I was parked across two spots in her lot, sure that she was watching me on camera. I debated waiting her out and making her come outside to raise hell about someone being so crazily parked on her lot, but my heart wouldn't allow it. I was itching to get inside of her building and get her in my arms.

"You trying to start a war or what?" Laike asked when we stepped out of the truck.

He was so busy in his phone that he hadn't noticed my parking until we got out.

"If you know what's best for us, you'd walk a little faster so that she won't come out of that door," I warned, picking up my pace.

Shaking his head, Laike continued as if she wouldn't cuss his ass out too for allowing me to park that way. When I got to the door, I punched in the personal code I'd remembered since my mother had gotten the system installed a year before I went in. The sound of the lock retracting was like music to my ears. She hadn't switched up on me, either.

"Welcome to Eisenberg Smiles," the receptionist greeted me when I walked in. She was about to continue, but hushed as she saw Laike step in behind me. With his finger to his lips, he silenced her.

"Shhhhh. Where she at?"

"Office," the receptionist revealed.

"Appreciate you, Trina."

"No problem."

I led the way as Laike followed suit. Her office was just beside the main lobby. Her door was open, but instead of walking right in, I voiced my entrance.

"Knock. Knock," I pounded on the door and stepped inside at once.

Her head whipped around as she spun in her chair. The phone that she'd been holding in her hand fell to her desktop as her mouth slacked and eyes bulged from her sockets.

"Oh my goodness!" she exclaimed.

"What is it?" the tiny voice coming from the little girl in her lap asked.

When I saw the hazel eyes and dirty blonde hair, her origins weren't up for questioning. She belonged to the woman who had my head in the clouds and my heart in a headlock. There was no doubt in my mind that Ever would bear my children. Looking at the mini version of her, my future quickly flashed before my eyes with her at the forefront, surrounded by my blonde-haired and hazel-eyed offspring.

"LUCA."

"What's up, ole lady?"

"Luca." She said my name again as if she couldn't believe it. Her eyes closed and reopened twice. She wanted to make sure she wasn't seeing shit.

"You gone just sit there or what?"

"Luca! My God. My God!" She cried, tears staining her brown cheeks.

She stood while screaming, never dropping the little one in her hands or letting her little feet touch the ground. I met her at the edge of her desk and wrapped them both in my arms. My mother felt like home. Finally, I knew that this was real. Her essence proved it. I was really free.

"Wait. This has made my day! When did you get home? Does your father know? Oh my God."

"Yesterday. I've been waiting on y'all to get back."

"Our plane landed at seven this morning. I headed straight here."

"Yeah. Dad doesn't know. You were my first stop."

"Nah. Don't lie. She was not your first stop," Laike snitched as he rolled a toothpick between his fingers. He'd taken one of the seats in front of our mother's desk.

"Well, who was your first stop?" my mom asked, jealousy written all over her pretty face.

"Her mother," Laike butted in.

"Nigga!" I turned and slapped his chest.

Shrugging, he shook off the blow to his body and laughed.

"You know he can't keep his mouth shut, and why were you seeing Ever?"

"It wasn't intentional. I was only stopping for food, and she so worked at Baisleigh's House."

"But he's been checking for her since she rode to pick him up with Lyric on Monday. If you gone tell it, then tell it all, Luca. Ain't been home forty-eight hours and already in love."

"I'm not in love," I confessed.

"Then why have you been looking at this little girl

like she's the daughter you didn't know you'd conceived before you went in and this is y'all first time meeting?"

Silence.

My eyes hadn't left the sweetheart in my mother's arms. I wasn't sure if it was because she reminded me so much of her mother or because I wished she *was* mine. Nevertheless, Laike had called good money. I couldn't deny the accusations. They were true.

"Don't pay him any mind."

"I'm not."

"What's your name, sweetie?" I asked the mini version of Ever.

"Emorey," she responded clearly.

"Emorey. Pretty name."

"I'm not sure how true any of this is that Laike is talking about, but if there's any truth to it, then I'm not objecting. I like Ever. I do. There's this benevolence about her and her spirit that just makes me smile inside out."

"You sound like this nigga. He's been listening to R&B all morning because of her. I'm 'bout ready to cut my ears off and sell them to the highest bidder."

"Oh hush, Laike," our mother advised, drying the tears from her face with a napkin.

"I'm just trying to warn you. Your son is in love."

"I'm not," I corrected.

"Ever is going through a breakup," my mother told me. "And everything you need to know about her children's father is right in that file on my desk. She just changed her cell number on file, so it's still out from this morning. He's not allowed to pick up the children and we're not allowed to give out any information about them to anyone who calls. School lets out in about a week, and the second baby will be here then, too."

"There's two of these?" Laike chuckled.

"They look almost identical. Whoever he is didn't stand a chance in the gene pool. Ever won that battle."

I could see that without even seeing a picture of the nigga who'd knocked her up and left her to fend for herself.

"He doesn't know where she moved to. He's at least six hours away."

"Doesn't matter if he did now that I'm here."

"Luca," my mother warned, "just be careful."

"I'm not going back to jail, Ma. Let that be the least of my worries."

"OK. As long as that's not a possibility, I can breathe."

"Not even a possibility," I assured her.

I reached for the file on her desk and secured it between my index finger and thumb.

"I'm going to take this with me."

"Sure. What are you two about to get into?"

"Nothing. Going to see Pops and then dropping your aggravating a... your aggravating son off at the house."

"Where are you staying?" my mom inquired, shifting Emorey from one hip to the other.

She was obviously getting a bit heavy. However, I knew that my mother would not put her down. She had an attachment to children that people hardly understood.

I figured she was the reason I wanted so many – her and my father's love for fatherhood.

"Come here."

Reaching out for Emorey, I invited her into my arms. Surprisingly, her skinny arms extended as she climbed from my mother's arms and into mine. Visibly relieved, my mom waited for me to answer her question. It was obvious that Laike had actually managed to keep a secret. I was proud of him because if he revealed the home he was building for me, he would've had to explain why.

"The home Laike built for me over the last few months."

"Really?" Her brows hiked and stayed put as her eyes brightened with pride.

"Yeah. Maybe we can set up Sunday dinner or something soon. I'm still touring it myself. Once I've gotten acquainted with it, then I can show you around."

"Sounds beautiful."

"Sounds big." Laike tittered.

Turning in his direction, I shook my head.

"Because it is, nigga. It's twice the size we discussed."

I'd been meaning to tell him about himself. Though I was thankful for the space, as I continued to discover new territory in the home, I realized just how much of an overachiever my little brother was. He'd aced my vision and seemingly one of his own, too.

"Aye," he responded with a shrug. "What can I say? Got a little carried away."

"A little?"

"What's you name?" Emorey asked, pulling my face in her direction.

"Luca," I told her.

"I like you face."

"I like you face, too."

"You wan' stay wit' me?"

I turned to my mother for translation.

"No, Emorey. He can't stay, sweetie. He has to get going."

Soon, I thought.

"Why?" She saddened. "Why you not wan' stay wit' me?"

Her big, glossy eyes and upside down smile had me by the neck. There was nothing in the world that I wanted more at the moment than to see that smile of hers again. Shit had gone from sugar to shit quickly, and I wanted it to go back.

"This nigga is toast," Laike observed. Again, he was right.

"I do, Emorey. It's just that I have some things I need to do. I'll see you soon, though."

"Really?" She cheered up instantly.

"Yes. Really. I'll make sure of it, OK?"

"OK."

Her little arms wrapped around my neck as she rested her head on top of the right one. I wondered if my mother and Laike could see my heart as it melted in my chest. Wrapping my arms around her was inevitable as she continued to hug my neck.

"Come on, Emorey," my mother demanded, reaching out for her.

Reluctantly, she pulled her arms from around my shoulders and slid back into my mother's arms. I was sad to see her go. She felt like she belonged in my arms, like she belonged to me. I couldn't wait until she did. As an extension of her mother, she was technically already mine.

"We're going to head out. I'm going to try to catch Pops before he starts his day."

"He's golfing today. You'd better hope you haven't missed him already."

"I'm going to stop by and see. If I miss him and you see him before I do, don't tell him I'm home."

"That's asking a lot, Luca, so go try to catch him."

I didn't want to task her with keeping such a huge secret from my father, so I rushed out of the building with Laike in tow. We made it to my childhood home in the lower part of The Hills in only a few minutes. As I pulled my truck into the driveway, I watched my father descend the steps in front of our home with his hand on his hip. My old man hadn't lost it, and he refused to get caught slacking.

"Watch out there, old man!" I rolled down the window and yelled.

Dropping his golfing gear, he took off heading in our direction. I opened the door and jumped out of the truck. Both with our arms stretched wide, we embraced and began rocking from one side to the other.

"Goddamn, man," he kept repeating.

I heard the cracking of his voice as he continued to rock us both, not wanting to release me. It didn't matter how old I got, there was nothing like my father's embrace. For me, he meant security. For me, he meant love. For me, he meant stability.

When he pulled back, finally, I swiped the tears from his eyes, fighting those of my own.

"Don't go sucker on me," I teased. "What's good, man?"

"I love you, son. Let's start there. Shit, you 'bout to give your old man a fucking heart attack." He held his chest as he attempted to catch his breath.

"Headed golfing?"

"Fuck that. When did you get out? Why didn't anyone tell me?"

"'Cause then it wouldn't have been a surprise. I got out yesterday and was waiting for y'all to touch down."

"You seen your mom?"

"Just left her."

"Where are you staying? You need to hang out here until you get something situated?"

Of course he'd asked, too. My well-being was their top priority even though I was a thirty-six-year-old man.

"Nah. Laike set some shit up for me. A crib. Once I'm settled, you've got to come by. It's a big fucking deal."

"I bet. I wish this knucklehead would put his skills to use a little more often. Your mom and I are thinking about another vacation spot on the island. Something fresh."

"What's wrong with the one you have?"

"Nothing. I want to make room for my children and their children. You know."

"There's plenty of room in that house, Pops."

"Not enough for three kids that's fucking and their kids if they ever give us some."

"This nigga working on it, and he just got home," Laike told him as he rounded the truck.

"Well, at least someone is onboard. You've been home and ain't 'bout shit. Lyric won't even give a nigga a chance to even put her uterus to use. I'm hoping I can count on you, son."

"You can."

"Good. Now, it was nice seeing you, and I'm very happy you're home. Stay home, and I'll see you after you're settled. The guys are waiting on me. I'm on the board of the golf club we formed, and we're taking a vote today."

"They'd ban your ass if they knew who you really were," Laike mocked.

"I'm talking restraining orders and all," I added.

"Fuck you and fuck you, too," he fussed. "And if they knew who I was, then I promise they'd tread a little lighter and stop fucking testing me."

"Or what?" I challenged.

"Goodbye, I'm not about to fool around with you two. Call me. We can set up lunch or some shit. I've got to get going."

He hated tardiness and as much as he loved seeing me, I knew he didn't like that we'd set him back a few minutes.

"We love you, Pops!" I hollered behind him after I'd handed him the golf equipment he'd dropped.

"Always."

LUCA-EVER

THE PEACE my new home brought me was undeniable. Spending eight years in a cell had turned me into more of a loner than I'd already been. That's why it was so important to come to a tranquil dwelling when I touched down. Solitude, for many, was a dangerous place, but for me it was a place of accord. It was where I centered myself and my thoughts. For me, it was much more important than community – aside from those in my immediate circle.

For the first time since being released, I had an abundance of time to myself, and I was looking forward to it before I scooped Ever up at seven. With her file in front of me, I leaned against the larger island with a bowl of mixed fruit in front of me.

Ever Sinclair, I read the first line of the first page.

Ever Eisenberg, I corrected in my head. *Yeah. Fitting.*

I scanned page by page, getting a bit more acquainted with the family of three that I wanted to pursue. The final page was the one that I was most interested in. I'd find out all that I needed to know about Ever, Essence, and Emorey with time. Nothing that I actually cared to know could be explained on paper – only with time spent.

Dewayne Stark.

His mugshot was stapled to the file, something I was

sure my mother had added so that if she ever encountered him she'd know exactly who he was and who she was dealing with. His rap sheet was included along with his registration information and last known address. I snapped two pictures, one of his photo and the other of his information. I exited the camera app and opened my messages.

Send me Boo's contact, I texted Laike.

Without paying much attention to the number he'd sent, I simply tapped it and waited for the call to connect. Boo, the techie of our operation, was a trusted employee who could find out the last dish an opponent ate from if that's how far I wanted him to dig. He'd been on the team for over a decade and was easily one of the most useful.

"Yeah?" he answered his cell.

I could imagine him pushing his glasses up on his face as he always did. What was insane was the nigga didn't even need glasses. He just used them to lessen the damage from the computer's screen. He sat in front of it at least fourteen hours of each day.

"Boo, what's up?"

"Luca?" he exclaimed.

"Yeah. It's Luca, dog."

"When did you get home?" astounded, he questioned.

"Yesterday. Did you not see that coming?" It was hard to believe that he hadn't.

"I did," he admitted.

"Then why you acting dumb as fuck?"

"I'm alerted when any changes are made to your file,

but I thought the release was an error. I was expecting a new update soon. They're always fucking up the system and then fixing it a few days later. One time, they'd listed you as a handicapped inmate who needed to be transferred to a new unit," he explained.

"Alerted," I sneered. "You really need fucking help, bro. Anyway, I need you to find out everything you can on Dewayne Stark. Birthday December third."

"On it."

"Bet."

I ended the call and closed the file while making a mental note to return it to my mother's office when I got the chance. For the time being, it would be safe in my office. I headed in that direction with my bowl and cell. It didn't take long for me to get settled behind the mahogany desk. The cushion on the chair made it effortless.

An iMac sat on the desk in front of me. I powered it on and began following the prompts to get it set up. As I did so, my cell chimed, notifying me of a text. Laike's name appeared on the screen, lacing my movements with urgency.

There weren't any words in the thread, but he'd shared a picture with a link beneath it. The imagery that was attached to it stopped me in my tracks. Ever's famous black bodysuit from the night before hugged her body as she posed for the camera – Lyric's camera I could only assume. Without a second thought, I clicked it.

The image led me to the Safari browser where I was asked if I wanted to download the Instagram app. Hesitantly, I hovered over the colorful icon but eventually ended up clicking it. As the app began its install, I reopened my messages. I wasn't a fan of social media; the allure of Ever was a powerful drug.

How you work this Instagram shit? What's my password?

Eisenberg18. Download the app. Log in using NoIGLuca and the password. You can figure it out from there. It's simple, Lyric responded.

She'd made me a page a little before I'd gone in that I'd never signed into or cared anything about, but that was all changing. Not the shit that I didn't have to give for the platform – or any for the matter – but me signing in.

I did exactly as I'd been told and was logged in instantly. An orange tab appeared with the number seven beside a heart, the number two beside a chat bubble, and one hundred beside a contact icon. I tapped it and soon realized what the numbers meant. However, they were inaccurate. There were over one hundred requests for connections in my notifications, but there was one in particular that piqued my interest. It was the last one. It was *her*. My Ever.

SincerelyyEvv

I accepted the request she'd sent and left the others where they were. I clicked her picture and was led to her profile. Aside from the picture she'd posted a few hours ago, her feed was almost empty. She'd obviously created the profile recently. I quickly read her profile, learning that she was a baker. The image of her in the kitchen with desserts surrounding her in a chef's hat flashed in my head, bringing a smile to my face.

After staring at her perfect figure in the jumpsuit for an eternity, I finally double tapped it. Right underneath it was that bubble again. I pressed it and was led to the comment section.

Seven. There wasn't anything else to be said. I simply wanted to remind her of our plans.

I didn't wait for a response knowing that she was at work and probably not on her phone. When I got ready to shut off my cell phone's screen, another message from Laike appeared. I opened it and laughed out loud at his foolishness.

Seven. Nigga, you sound like a bitch.

Stay off her page, stalking ass nigga. I blackened the screen and tossed my cell aside to finish setting my new computer up.

An hour later, and I was still searching the web for the perfect gift for Ever. Time wasn't on my side, but I didn't want to show up empty-handed. My goal was to keep Ever smiling all day, long before I even showed up to the door.

Another hour passed, and I'd placed a rush order with a small embroidery company for one of the gifts I needed by seven. I searched the Farmer's Fresh website while configuring a thorough grocery list for everything I'd be needing to make dinner for the night. With lobster, steak, potatoes, and broccoli on the menu, I wouldn't be a full hour in the kitchen while Ever sipped wine and waited for dinner to be served. By eight-thirty, I wanted us seated and blessing our food.

During my browsing, I continued to run across the fifteen-dollar delivery option. After realizing how long a grocery store run would take, I dug a little deeper to find out exactly how delivery worked. In less than thirty minutes, I'd put in a full order and would have everything I was missing within two hours. It wasn't much. My fridge and cabinets were stocked, but there were a few things that I couldn't substitute – like fresh broccoli and fresh lobster.

ELEVEN

EVER

"HI, BABY. HOW WAS SCHOOL?" I smiled in the camera at an obviously exhausted Essence.

"Good," she told me as she yawned.

"Where's your sister?" Emorey was too quiet.

"She's sleeping."

"Already?"

"Yes. She said she didn't take a nap at school, so she's tired."

"Sounds accurate. You seem tired, too."

"I am tired," she admitted.

"Then just call me tomorrow, Es. I just wanted to see your face. I'm pulling up to the house now."

"OK."

Before I could get another word out, Essence ended the call. I winced at the internal infliction of her move. I'd never felt so neglected by my children in my life. In all honesty, I wanted them begging and crying to come home so that I could rush to get them, but they weren't thinking about me. I figured they'd needed the break as much as I did.

After the call ended, I decided to take a minute for myself. We'd had such a busy Tuesday at work, and my feet were killing me. I opened the Instagram app on my phone to see if Luca had accepted my request and to my surprise, he had. He'd also made his way to my notifications. Under the one photo that I'd posted, he had written *'seven'*, which was the time he was due at our doorstep.

My cheeks burned as they rose to form a smile. Instead of replying to the comment directly, I chose to message him instead. But before I hit the message tab, I checked out his profile. It wasn't lost upon me that it was empty, much like Laike's. He only had one photo, too. It was of a beautiful rottweiler with saggy cheeks and wet lips.

Rest easy, Major, a caption beneath it read. It was short and straight to the point. The picture was dated back four years prior, which only could have meant that his pet had died when he was in prison, and he wasn't the one who'd made the post.

Seven it is. I'm really looking forward to our time together. - Ever.

I sent the message and shut down my app completely. Knowing Luca, there wouldn't be a response. I'd see him when I saw him.

With Essence back at the forefront of my head, along with a heavy heart, I shut off my engine and grabbed my purse from the passenger seat. I locked my doors and headed up the driveway. When I made it near the door, I noticed the short, stubby man in white ringing our doorbell.

"Can I help you?" I asked as I got closer and closer.

"Yeah. I'm looking for Ever. Ever Sinclair?"

"That's me," I admitted, wondering who he was and what his presence meant.

"I have a delivery for you from Mr. Luca Eisenberg. If you'd do me a favor and sign for it, I can get out of your hair."

"Uh. Yeah. Uh. Sure." Baffled, I responded, still trying to figure out what was going on as he handed me the white box.

I held it in one hand as he handed me a pen and placed a notepad in front of me. I scribbled my name across the paper and seconds later, he vanished into thin air. He didn't give me much of a chance to ask any questions, but I figured I'd discover whatever answers I had once I opened the box he'd handed me.

I stumbled inside of the house, excited and nervous about opening the package at the same time. It was five o'clock, and I'd be seeing Luca in about two hours, so I didn't understand why the gift couldn't have waited. I assumed it was directly connected to the night we'd be having.

As I rushed past Lyric's room, I saw she was knee deep in her computer screen. She barely looked at me as she waved in my direction. I took the hint and continued down the hallway then up the stairs. When I made it to my bedroom, I slammed the door behind me with my foot and laid the box on the bed carefully, being that I wasn't sure what was inside of it. Whatever it was wasn't heavy at all.

I removed the tape from the sides and opened the flap in the front. The flood of emotions that followed the discovery of what was inside left my knees weak and my eyes moist. My heart swelled in my chest, beating slower and with so much more purpose.

A thoughtful man was one I'd always seen myself with. One that took the time to make life more meaningful, down to the last second of your day. One that didn't need to be told what you were into, loved, or wanted to tap into because they paid close enough attention. One that was out for your heart when it came to gifts, birthdays, holidays, and special occasions because it was their time to show just how much you meant to them. It was only day one and Luca had nailed the test.

I pulled out the chef's hat with Ever embroidered across the top in brown. I pulled it on my head and over my low bun. It was a perfect fit. Next, I pulled out the white coat to match. It, too, had Ever written on it with a three-tier cake above it. I brought it to my chest and wrapped my arms around my body for a hug. Even more than the diamond bracelets that he'd purchased for me, I loved this gift.

"Was that who was laying on the doorbell? A delivery guy?" Lyric stepped into my room and asked.

"Yes. Luca sent me this hat and chef's jacket. I never even mentioned being a cake maker."

"He's meticulous, Ever. You didn't have to. He pays attention to detail and your Instagram says you're the cake woman. Your profile image is also you and a cake."

"I guess I've just never had a man pay much attention to me," I admitted with a shrug. "This means so much."

"As it should, and you deserve it. I saw the little comment he posted under your picture. What's up with seven? Is there something you need to tell me?"

"Me, too. And, yes. There is something. He invited me on a date and promised to be here by seven."

"And you didn't feel the need to scream that when you walked through the door? Honey, we have to get you together."

"You were working."

"Ever, I'm an accountant for the Eisenbergs. All of them. From my father to my mother to my brothers. I could've stopped if I wanted to."

"What about your other accounting gig?"

"Two hours of work a day, and I'm literally done. They pay me well but my family pays me better. I can't give them all of my time like that."

I'd said the same thing. It was obvious that Lyric was the princess of the family and was compensated well. However, I imagined the bulk of her work was for the company that she'd been working for since I met her. Now, I understood it was her family's finances that got most of her time. It was as if I learned something new every day about my friend. Long distance friendship Lyric and local Lyric were two different people.

"Okay, that makes sense."

"Alright, let's get you to the store. We don't have long, girl."

We decided to take my car to the mall with Lyric at the wheel. She drove like a bat out of hell to get us there in under twenty minutes. Luckily, all the stores had mall entrances as well as outdoor entrances, which helped tremendously in our time crunch. We made it to Zara and walked right in from the parking lot.

"We should split up to cover more ground," I suggested.

"Yeah. If we haven't found anything in ten minutes, let's meet at the door that leads us to the mall. We can go by Nordstroms or Forever21."

"Forever21, but only because it's so much smaller. I'd rather not have so many options."

"Okay. I'll call you to the dressing room if I find anything."

As planned, we separated and began our searches. I combed through the pieces that were closer to the front while Lyric searched the area near the cash registers. Though I liked a few of the pieces they had to offer, I didn't love any of them. Nothing stood out to me and nothing seemed good enough for the date night with

Luca. Everything was mediocre. I wanted some sassiness going on.

"There you are." Lyric sighed when she found me at the mall entrance.

"Didn't find anything either?" I asked.

"Nothing worth taking a second look at. Let's head to Forever21. I'm sure they have something we can put together really quickly."

"If it ain't Lyric motherfucking Eisenberg in the flesh," a deep rasp blurted in the busy mall.

I looked up to find what was arguably the blackest man I'd ever seen walking in our direction. As much as I wanted to tear my eyes from him and look to Lyric for an explanation, I couldn't. His midnight black skin and gold teeth that shined as he showcased the dimpled smile was too commanding. I couldn't help but wonder where all of these men were when I was living in Channing my entire life before moving, searching for some decent material. There was none! Since I'd moved back, I'd run into four men who were breathtaking, two of them being the Eisenberg brothers.

"Ken," Lyric acknowledged the handsome specimen, opening her arms to embrace him.

"Long fucking time. I just ran into your hoe ass brother earlier. Nigga didn't plan on telling me he was out, I don't think," he fussed. His smile immediately turned into a smug expression as his brows furrowed on his face.

"You know that's not true. He's still processing it himself. Eight years is a long time, Ken."

"Don't I know," he replied, combing over Lyric's body with his eyes. Even in a simple pair of denim and a white cropped top, she was stunning. "That's how long it's been since I've run into you. Where you been hiding?"

"In the house. Staying out of the way. My ignorant choices led to my brother's incarceration. I had nothing to be happy about or outside for. I did his time with him if you ask me," Lyric answered, shifting her weight from one foot to the other. She continued to wipe her palms on her pants and fix her top, though nothing was wrong with it. I chuckled inside, knowing the motions she was going through all too well.

"I get it, but don't beat yourself up about that. If he hadn't ended that pussy's shit then I'd be looking at him a little differently. He did what was supposed to be done. I'm just pissed the nigga got caught. He's smarter than that."

"He lost his shit, Ken. I'd never seen him like that. He was so beastly." I cringed as I watched her blink for the hundredth time. Lyric was losing it inside, something I'd never seen her do.

"For good reason. I'm going to let you go. Y'all look like y'all in a rush or whatnot. Hit me up sometimes. Don't be a stranger."

"I don't have your number, Ken."

"Get it from one of your brothers," he told her as he began stepping away.

"But you're literally right here," she whispered so low that I knew he couldn't hear her.

When he disappeared, we both gave each other

knowing glares that ended in laughter after nearly twenty seconds had passed. Lyric knew I'd called her bluff. My cheeks hurt from the smile that tore through my features as I nodded my head knowingly.

"Um. Hm," I mocked.

"Shut up!" she whined, storming in the opposite direction.

"I ain't said nothing."

"But that look on your face."

"I've been there. Just saying," I explained.

We filed into Forever21 and before we could even split up, we discovered the prettiest, sleekest black bodysuit that dipped in the front and gave your boobs a nice lift. I paired it with a black, curve-caressing skirt that stopped below the knees. Together, they were flawless. I grabbed a pair of simple, black heels that were on sale to match. I completed the look with Lyric's help picking out a pair of earrings and a necklace.

"You'll definitely have something a bit more icy before the week is out," she proclaimed as I put the necklace up to my outfit.

"He already stole my watch. He thinks I don't know."

"He doesn't care. Trust me."

We headed to the register and checked out. It felt good not worrying about a dime. I swiped my card proudly and satisfied the seventy-dollar ticket. I was handed my bags, and we headed out of the store. Seven o'clock couldn't come fast enough. I was feeling myself for once.

LUCA-EVER

I RAISED up from the bubbly water and dried my hands before checking the time on my phone. **6:15 p.m**. I'd given myself fifteen minutes to soak after stepping into the water at six. We'd gone to the mall and made it back home in under an hour. It was record time considering the fact that we were women and tended to drag out shopping trips. Not this time, and I was thankful. That gave me plenty of wiggle room.

The water level changed drastically as I lifted my 152 pound, 5'4 frame from it. It swayed from one side to the other, the dramatics sounding like waves crashing. I stepped out and grabbed the drying towel from the rack on the wall next to the tub.

Lotion was first up. I sealed in the moisture with oil of the same fragrance. I pulled the black thong that I'd never worn between my ass cheeks and situated the straps at my hips. The black lace bra that I'd planned to wear wasn't necessary. The shirt laying on my bed waiting to be worn would be all the support that my breasts needed. It was the main reason I'd chosen the top.

My hair was all over the place but luckily, it still held the heat I'd put on it the night before. With forty minutes to spare, I decided to part smaller sections to flatten and curl. The black that I would have on gave grown woman sexy, and I wanted to follow through from head to toe.

My hair swung past my shoulders when I released it from the ponytail it had to be in for work. I turned the temperature of my flat iron to 425 degrees and began parting my hair in anticipation of the beep that signaled its readiness.

Once the beeping began, I started with the first section I'd separated from the rest of them. In the same motion, I flattened and curled my hair slightly. I didn't want extremely tight curls but neither did I want super loose ones. I wanted my curls to fit somewhere in the middle of the spectrum.

I slid into the bodysuit and then the skirt after my hair was perfect and my lips were glossed. I hated to feel weighed down with makeup, so I opted for my natural skin, no matter the occasion. Some mascara, possibly eyeliner, golden bronzer sometimes, and clear lip gloss was enough.

One glance in the mirror, and I was utterly happy with the way everything had come together. I'd been trying to chase the old me, the one I was prior to my relationship ruined me but as I stood in the mirror and took a good look at my reflection, I knew that I'd never get her back. I didn't want her back either. I was slowly becoming the best version of myself and wanted to continue on that track as I evolved and evolved some more.

Just when I was about to call for Lyric, I heard a knock at the door.

"It's unlocked!" I yelled.

She stepped in, immediately snapping pictures with her phone. Lyric hadn't even given me a chance to pose.

"Can I at least get a warning next time?"

"No. Off-guards are the best. That one picture looking lonely on your feed. We need to get you some decent content."

"I made a video of my gifts that I plan to post before I leave."

"Girl, you've got a good ten minutes to spare. What are you waiting for?"

"This look has me feeling really mature. Like I'm really the thirty-year-old of my dreams right now."

"You look damn good, Ever. I can't wait to hear all about your date tomorrow. Just leave out the parts about you sucking my brother's dick and stuff. I really don't want to hear that."

"I'm not sucking dick tonight, Lyric. I'll be back home in a few hours. You can wait up if you'd like."

"Girl, I'd be up 'til morning if I waited on you. Trust me, you're not coming back home. This is how it all starts right here."

I grabbed my phone and opened my Instagram account. The video that I'd taken of my new gifts, I uploaded and tagged the person who'd gifted them. There were only five people following me so far, and they'd all know who was making me smile sooner than later. Nothing was official but neither was it a secret.

Thanks, @NoIGLuca, I added to the picture.

Just as I shut down my phone, the doorbell rang. My heart stiffened and all sound evaporated in thin air. I could only hear the ringing of my ears and my heart as it galloped in my chest. The thickness of my throat threatened to choke me as I tried taking steady, even breaths.

"Sounds like your date is here," Lyric announced.

"Can you get the door?" I asked, fanning my face as I stood from the bed to pace the floor.

"Ever, there's nothing to be nervous about, OK? You're going to have a great time."

"I know. There's no doubt about that I just... I feel like what if I'm jumping into this too early? What if I fall in love with him and fall back into the dependent role I've been in for years? What if we crash and burn and I end up at your house again? What about the girls? What if I get them involved and everything goes south?" I was in full-blown panic mode, anxiety riding my back.

"You ever heard of life?"

"Of course."

"It happens, Ever. Whether you like it or not. You had a traumatic experience and I get why you're being so cautious, but let me tell you... You can let your hair down with this one. Before he disappoints you, he'll leave. Laike is a whole other story, but this one... Luca, he's the real deal, Ever. I know you scared you'll make the wrong choice again but this time you chose wisely. I'm not just saying that because he's my brother. I'm saying that because I know the man who raised him and he's everything that our father is, only better. So, relax for once. You can let your guard down with him. You deserve to. Let this man love on you because I can't wait to watch. This has never happened for Luca."

"Me neither," I admitted.

"Then enjoy it together because I'm certain he will."

"Please go grab the door before he thinks I've stood him up."

"Okay but come right behind me."

"I am. Just want to put on some perfume. I forgot."

"Alright."

I rushed to the vanity tray on the dresser and sprayed the Zara fragrance that I'd grabbed for my children the last time I'd gone to the mall with Lyric. I didn't have the courage to spend four hundred dollars on my favorite perfume yet, so I settled for their $12.99 bottles. A mixture of two always got the job done. When I stepped out into the hallway, I felt much better.

When I reached the foyer, there stood Luca in a black Amiri shirt with black jeans to match. His chain glistened against the dark color and so did his smile. It widened as I got closer. When I was near enough, he pulled me into his arms. For once, I felt like the princess in the story who'd met her prince charming.

The embrace ended long before I wanted it to. So wrapped up in the muskiness of his cologne, I wanted time to stop until I was ready to let him go. I stepped backward with the heel of my shoes making a loud, familiar clacking noise.

Under Luca's gaze, I began playing twenty-one questions in my head. *Do I have on enough lip gloss? Wait, did I forget my lip gloss in the room? Is my hair frizzing? Can he tell I'm nervous? Where are we going? Does he like what I have on? Am I overdressed? Why is he looking at me like that? Is there something on my face? How do my curves look? Is this too revealing? What are his plans for me tonight?*

"Hi," he greeted, handing me the massive, long-stemmed roses in his hand. He silenced my thoughts and saved me before I self-destructed.

There must've been one hundred of them. The big bundle that was wrapped in craft paper was massive, and they were as heavy as they looked. I wasn't sure where I was supposed to put them or how I was supposed to keep them alive but I'd try my hardest.

"I know that's right," I heard Lyric cheering from behind. When I turned, she had her camera out, again.

As corny as it sounded, it was my very first official date. I'd never had a man ask me out or show up to my doorstep bearing gifts. I'd always been down to chill or hangout, but never properly courted. I was looking forward to our moments together starting with the night.

"Don't worry. I have footage and flicks. I'll save them for you. Luca, why you never got me a big bouquet like this?" she complained with a half-smile.

"Sounds jealous, but you could be getting the same treatment," I teased. She knew exactly what and who I was referring to.

"Bye. Not jealous. I'm happy for you, mommas. See you. Enjoy yourself."

"I plan to."

"See you later, Lyric."

"Later, Luca."

I handed the flowers off to Lyric, sure that she knew exactly what to do with them. By the time I returned, they'd be exactly where they were supposed to be. I was clueless. No one had ever bought me flowers.

I closed the door behind me and stepped off the porch. Luca was right there to hold my hand. As we walked toward his massive truck, he continued to hold my hand. Though I was trying to keep my composure, I was losing my shit on the inside. Because I was head over heels for everything about the night and the man who was making it possible.

When we made it to the truck and he opened the door, Luca spun me around to face him. He was so close that I could feel each exhale on the tip of my nose. He said nothing for the longest, simply staring back at me as I waited for him to say something – anything.

"Are you ready?" he finally asked.

"I'm ready," I confirmed with a nod, pressing my palms flat against the fabric of my skirt.

He was so perfect and so poised, yet I was becoming undone right before his very eyes. I wondered if he noticed or if I was the only one who knew just how bad I was freaking out.

"You're alright, Ever. You're in good company."

He did. He noticed, and his reassuring words were just what I needed.

"Aight?"

"Okay," I responded, swallowing the lump in my throat.

In an instant, I felt his hand on my neck as he pinned me against the truck with his body. His face was already so close to me, giving him a huge advantage. My breath hiked and chest rose as I closed my eyes, waiting for the moment his lips touched mine. After a few beats, I reopened my eyes slowly to see why they hadn't.

He reappeared as my lids separated. As soon as my eyes were open fully, Luca smiled and leaned down. His lips finally touched mine, draining my pussy of the thick white creaminess that accompanied my arousal. I could feel the throbbing between my legs. It matched my heartbeat.

I opened my mouth, welcoming him inside. As much as I'd talked myself into playing it safe, the truth was I didn't want to. I didn't think I had to, either. Not with Luca and that was exactly why I pulled him in deeper by wrapping my hands around his waist. I wanted every last drop of him, and I didn't want to have to wait for it.

"Ummmm," I moaned into his warm, open mouth.

He tasted like the finest of wines from the best grapes to ever exist. There was nothing sweet about his mix, but I welcomed the new taste. My buds quickly adjusted and adapted to his flavor and its uniqueness. And when he began to pull away, I missed it already.

"What?" I murmured, wiping the smeared gloss from my lips.

Noticing that he had some on his lips as well, I used my thumb to clean it up. He grabbed my hand and guided it toward the buckle of his jeans and then a bit further. When I felt his stiffness beneath the denim, my mouth began to water.

"I can't be out here kissing you like that, or we will never make it to my crib for dinner."

Up and down, I massaged what had to be an uncomfortably hard dick. This time, it was his eyes that closed, but only briefly. As his lids met, he gripped my wrist to stop its movement.

"Come on, let me get you out of here so that I can feed you," he finally said after composing himself.

Dick. Please feed me dick, I wanted to suggest, but remained quiet as he pecked my lips once more before lifting me into the truck. The way he handled my body so effortlessly let me know just how much of a rag doll he was capable of treating me like in the bedroom.

"Buckle up."

He patted my leg with his large hands and closed the door behind him. I watched as his long frame rounded the truck and got in. He adjusted the stereo as he pulled out of Lyric's yard and into the street. I melted in the leather seat as I rested my back against it and my arm on the armrest.

Luca's hand was near the cupholder where he could easily access the white Styrofoam cup that he'd sipped from as I settled in. Pushing my hand up slightly, I wrapped my fingers around his wrist gently. I'd learned long ago that physical touch was a large part of my love language. I'd been deprived for so long, far too long. I used to crave Dewayne's caresses, back rubs, gentle touches, hand holding, or just his closeness.

That was until I didn't want him touching me at all the last year of our relationship. It was to the point that I'd rather scratch my nails on a chalkboard than lay down with him or allow him to enter me. Before deciding to leave, we hadn't been intimate in over four months. Prior to that, it was a very rare occasion that we got along for long enough to make it to bed together. I could count on one hand how many times I'd sexed Dewayne in a calendar year.

With Luca or anyone for the matter, I didn't want to ignore my personal desires. I wanted to embrace them so that they'd be accommodated immediately. Otherwise, I'd understand that the person simply isn't for me and we could part ways sooner than later.

In my last relationship, I'd overlooked so much in the beginning, putting my personal desires on the back burner to fulfill all of my exes. When I finally realized it, things had gotten out of hand and I was the only one unfulfilled in the relationship. It was up to me to set the tone for how I wanted and deserved to be treated, and I wasn't going to let anyone off easily. It was either the best or nothing at all. I'd suffered long enough. Those days were over.

When I felt Luca reposition his hand, my heart rate sped. I could feel the breath drain from my lungs as I fought the disappointment creeping up my spine. It wasn't until I felt his fingers intertwined with mine that I settled and began to relax again. The gentle squeeze of reassurance that followed put me at ease.

I sat back as he handled the wheel, feeling like I was in a scene from one of my favorite love stories. Except I wasn't. This was my life, and Luca was as real as they came. The sense of comfort I felt in his presence proved it.

SiR's "The Recipe" serenaded our journey as we shared longing, soul-satisfying glances every minute or more. It wasn't long before we were pulling up to the gate of the home we'd dropped him off at a day prior. He stretched his right arm out of the window to enter the code, seemingly not wanting to break the connection between us, either.

TWELVE

LUCA

"I HOPE YOU DON'T MIND," I said to Ever as I pulled into the driveway of my home. "I'd rather stay in and cook for you. With my release being so fresh, a public outing for us would include constant recognition from others, and I'd rather stay centered and give you my undivided attention."

"I don't," she answered.

"If you'd rather us go elsewhere, I can arrange something with some privacy."

"No. Your place is fine," she confirmed.

Taking her word for it and finding it hard to believe she'd lie to me, I shut off the engine and released her from my grip. I stepped out of my truck and walked around to her side to help her out. She hadn't touched the door and I hadn't wanted her to either. Ever was making it clear to me she wanted the royal treatment, and I wanted to make it clear to her it was exactly what I planned to give her.

I helped her climb down from the truck. The last thing I wanted was her busting her ass in the heels she wore. That would end our night before it even got started. She slid down my body slowly, ending in my arms with her feet on the ground.

"Thank you."

"You look beautiful," I shared with her.

Leaving it up for debate or for her to wonder about wasn't an option. I wanted her to know exactly what I thought and how I felt about how she'd shown up for our date. When I first laid eyes on her in the black skirt, I couldn't determine which I liked better. The skirt and the romper were going head up in competition.

Ever only smiled, not giving a verbal response. Her right hand snaked up my chest and ended at my neck, where she caressed me. I leaned into her delicacy before pushing forward and pecking her lips. She quickly wrapped both arms around my neck and refused to let me go.

"Kiss me again," she demanded.

"Ever," I warned.

"Again," she begged, looking up at me.

I couldn't deny her anything she wanted. Saying no to Ever would hurt my feelings more than it did hers. So, I wavered. I lowered my neck and watched as she traced my lips with her tongue before slipping it into my mouth. She was playing a dangerous game and I'd be a fool not to join her.

"You're not going to make it to dinner if you keep this up, Ever," I informed her as I attempted to pull back.

"I was thinking on the way over, and I'm not opposed," she admitted, removing one hand from around my neck and placing it on my hard dick.

She rubbed it through my jeans, causing it to harden a bit more. I felt like it would bust through the fabric at any second. When I'd had enough of her antics, I pressed her back against the bottom of the passenger seat. I leaned down, following her skirt's seam until I reached the bottom. I heard the loud gasp fall from her pretty lips as I raised the skirt in one swift motion, exposing the bodysuit that was underneath it.

"Luca," she breathed rapidly and deeply.

"Too fucking late for that Luca shit. Don't call me again unless you're cumming on this dick." I explained the rules of the game that she'd chosen to play.

It had been eight years since I'd slid into some pussy and though this wasn't how I planned to slide into hers, she'd asked. I could only deliver. One thing I wouldn't do is withhold anything from Ever that I knew she truly wanted or needed, whether she vocalized it or not.

I unbuckled my belt and unbuttoned my jeans before either of us had a chance to ruin the moment with words. The twinkle in her eyes when my dick sprang from my jeans didn't go unnoticed. I conjured a glob of spit and let it fall onto my dick for lubrication.

I swooped Ever's small frame into my arms, slid everything that was blocking my entrance out of the way, and slowly slid into her. Inch by inch, I lowered her onto me. Her slipperiness was enough to get me deep inside of her pussy without assistance. She was soaking, and I planned to wring her dry before I let her in my house.

I kissed her lips again as we both groaned heavily into one another's mouth. For the first few seconds, I didn't move. I couldn't, too afraid that it would be the end of our adventure and it had just started.

Her pussy felt like everything that I'd been missing and the shit that I didn't even know my life needed. It was like the warmest of hugs on a chilly day. It was like the love you knew you needed after a long day of running the streets. It was as cozy as your favorite tee and as intoxicating as your favorite liquor.

"Fuck," I grunted, knowing that seeing her pretty face as I made love to her body was a deadly combination. So, I did something that every bone in my body advised me against. I slid out of her and forced her to turn around before sliding back into her from behind.

"Ummmmmmmmmmm." She gushed for me.

Bad. Fucking. Idea. Now, it was her ass that was swallowing her thong and bodysuit that I was forced to watch bounce as I hit her shit over and over.

SMACK.

SMACK.

SMACK.

SMACK.

Our bodies collided, thighs sounding off with each

thrust. I felt Ever's hand on my stomach as she attempted to put a halt to my stride, but I smacked it away. This was the punishment she deserved for barking up my fucking tree.

"Un. Don't run from this shit," I encouraged her. "Take this dick. You got it. You got this. Aight?"

"Umm hmmm." She moaned, nodding her head rapidly as she looked back, seemingly trying to find our point of connection or see what the hell I was doing to her.

"Shit." She felt too fucking good to be true, and I knew it wasn't only because I hadn't had pussy in a while. I knew good pussy when I slid into good pussy and her shit was spectacular. It was top fucking tier. I didn't know if it was from its snugness or the fact that I was feeling her like a motherfucker. Whatever the case, her shit was straight heat.

I reached around, pushing her clothes to the side to find the nub that would drive her to her peak. It wouldn't be much longer before I was emptying my seeds into her, but I wanted to make sure she got off first. The white thickness on my dick didn't mean shit to me. She was enjoying our time together. It was evident but I needed more from her.

I wanted her knees to buckle and her eyes to bulge. I wanted her soul to escape her body and come to Daddy, right where it belonged. I wanted her so sensitive by the time I finished with her she couldn't even stand to be touched. I wanted her to feel like a noodle that I had every intention of eating after I fed her dinner and more dick. I wanted her to say my fucking name.

Even when I slowed my strokes, I could still hear the stickiness that we created between us. I found the little switch that could take a woman from ten to one hundred in under a second. The tiny nub with over eight thousand nerves. I planned to hit every one of them before the night was out.

"LUCA!"

Her time was here and mine was to follow. I rubbed her pearl with my thumb, back and forth and I stroked her slowly, helping her reach her pinnacle. That was the goal for me. *Ever*. From the moment I'd laid eyes on her until the rest of forever, she'd always be.

"Say my shit again," I instructed, applying more pressure as she began to convulse underneath me.

"LUUUUUUUUUCA." Her body jerked forward, then backward, then forward again.

I could feel the weight of her body increase as she lost control of her movements and could no longer sustain the weight of her body.

"Ummmmmmm."

I came for what felt like an eternity, my dick constantly spitting rapid fire as Ever collapsed into my arms. My territory had been marked, and I didn't play about shit that belonged to me.

LUCA·EVER

LUCA SQUARED ANNIVERSARY EDITION

THE STEAKS WERE on the section of my stove that was created for grilling. The lobster sat beside it getting a bit pinker by the minute. The broccoli was finished and cooling. My potatoes were nearly done boiling, only needing some good seasoning, milk, butter, and mashing.

Ever sat on top of the island with a glass of Château Lafite Rothchild to her lips after taking a quick wash up in one of the guest washrooms on the first level. The heels she'd worn were off, and she'd traded flowing curls for a ponytail that showed off her beautiful features. She looked good sipping a glass from the thousand dollar bottle of wine with the bracelets I'd given her back in their rightful place. She looked expensive and that's how I liked her.

"Open the top drawer," I told her.

"What do you need?" she asked as she scooted over and opened it.

"Nothing. There's a gift in it for you," I revealed.

Her mouth slacked and eyes found mine after noticing the dark green box with Audemars Piguet written across the top. I shrugged and then nodded, encouraging her to continue. She grabbed the box from the drawer and began to open it. Once she was finally through the unnecessary obstacle course, she was face to face with the piece that would replace the watch of hers that I'd tossed.

"Please don't wear costume jewelry around me. ***Never***. If there are pieces you prefer, please let me know and I'll see that you get them."

"What is your beef with costume jewelry?" She set

her glass down again after sipping from it and then removed the watch from its casing.

Her eyes glistened in the light as she examined her new timepiece.

"Nothing really. But if I'm rocking an AP, I'll be damned if my woman is rocking a Marshalls watch. If my necklace set me back a good fifty, then I'm not letting my woman walk out of the house with one that didn't even cost her fifty dollars. I match energies, Ever. There's no I in team and neither is there a big me, little you. My woman and anyone around me will always be a direct reflection of who I am as a man. If I can't make sure they're straight, then I'm not to be trusted."

"*Your woman,*" she emphasized.

"You thought I was sliding in you raw and leaving my imprint for fun?"

"About that," she started with a smile.

"Like I was saying, my woman..." I pointed in her direction with a finger. "Is a direct reflection of me. Now, do you like the watch, woman?"

"I love the watch, Luca."

"But what?"

"I fell into my last relationship. I don't want to fall into another the same way. I want to make things official. I want to be courted and asked to be your girlfriend. I don't want to just fall into a routine and we call it a relationship." She spoke her truth, and I was happy that she had.

"Good, because that's not what I planned to do, either. I'm claiming you because I know you're mine, not because I'm trying to rob you of those feelings or desires. We won't fall into a routine and just call it a relationship. I have every intention of making it very fucking obvious when we're official."

"Thanks."

"But I'm telling you now that we're exclusive," I followed up with. There was nothing to be mistaken about that.

"I can get with exclusive. I don't want anyone being able to say they know how good you feel inside of them from this moment on, but me," she admitted. "My heart wouldn't be able to take it if they did."

She picked her glass up and sipped from it. I placed a lid on the boiling potatoes and made my way over to her. I stood in front of her and removed the watch from her hand. She placed her wineglass on the counter and handed me her left arm. I clasped the diamond-encrusted piece around her tiny wrist, satisfied to know that it fit perfectly. I'd predicted, but wasn't sure if my guess was accurate. Seeing her smile and hold her wrist in the air to get a better look was enough to swell my heart and curve the corners of my mouth.

"Mine either," I finally responded. "Tell me, what else does your heart desire? From me. From a relationship in general. What are your hard boundaries?"

"Hard boundaries?"

"Yes. Hard boundaries. The things that you will not accept or don't prefer. The things that you noticed you hate from prior situations. Shit like that."

"My hard boundaries are simple. Unless I'm married,

I'm not living with my man. I'm still wondering if I want to even after. I know it's not traditional but the thought of living with a man again brings me anxiety. Like, right now at Lyric's, I can let my hair down and be who I really am. When living with a man, I feel like I'm always on pins and needles, trying to be the whatever person he's made it up in his head that I am. It's usually an image of perfection that is exhausting trying to keep up with. I feel like the work is never ending, especially having two children.

"On top of being their mom, I have to be the cleaner, the cook, the laundry lady, the homeschooler when they're not at school, the doctor, the negotiator, and so much more. I'd rather not do all of that while trying to be the perfect partner when I would rather just relax. I won't feel like cooking every day. I won't feel like cleaning the dishes every day. I won't feel like clearing the laundry room every week or folding the clothes I wash. Some days I'll be lazy and some days I'll be fine. When I'm alone, I don't feel guilty about that."

"You shouldn't. You're not a robot, Ever."

"Well, have you met men? Tell that to them."

"Anyone who expects that much out of you is a coward. Because if you're doing all of that, what the fuck are they doing?"

"Paying all the bills," she revealed. "Which is my next hard boundary. I refuse to let a man pay all of my bills because then I feel indebted to them and that is what doesn't allow me to rest... at all. I always feel like I should be doing something to show my appreciation. Cleaning the kitchen, mopping the floors, dusting the ceiling fans... anything but sitting on my ass. For the first time, I can sit on my ass if that's what I want to do. I don't want that to stop."

"Hmmm," I responded with a nod, deciding against commenting on the damage her pussy ass nigga had done.

"No matter what it is, I want to keep a job. I never want to be jobless. Having a job actually gives me the small break I need from my children on a daily basis. I'd much rather it be my own business that claims my time instead of someone's clock, but that will come in due time. I have to stay employed. I can never and won't ever depend on a man for everything anymore. He cannot be the sole breadwinner in the house."

"Anything else?"

"My man must worship the ground I walk on. He must give me the same love that I give him. When I'm in love, I'm limitless. I'll always go above and beyond. I want that reciprocated."

"Understandable."

"Last, there must not be an intentional or obvious difference made between the children I have with them and the ones I already have. I will leave in an instant. My children's father has never been involved in their lives, although he's always been around. I don't want that for them. I want a man to be everything they've been missing, to show them what a daughter and father relationship truly consists of. They must be treated like they came from his nut sack."

"Is that something you can handle?"

"For the most part, but a few adjustments will need to be made."

"No adjustments."

"You can't hear me out like I heard you out?"

"OK. Fair is fair. Let me hear it."

"I will, after we've sat down with our food. Can I pour you another glass?"

"Yes." She handed me the glass from her hand. It was nearly empty.

I refilled her wine and handed it to her. She slid from the island and followed me over to the stove where she held her hands out for me to lift her onto the countertop that was closer.

"Physical touch and quality time. Those are two of my love languages. I'm still trying to determine whether reassurance is the third."

She continued teaching me things that I wanted to learn, but I didn't mind the lessons. It was more for her protection than mine. Ever was fresh out, just like me, and not trying to get her shit broken into pieces.

"I've noticed." I drained the potatoes of water and brought them back to the stove.

"Yours?"

She leaned in closer, watching as I added butter, milk, garlic, a pinch of dried ranch seasoning, salt, and pepper.

"Loyalty and respect. Submission, I'm trying to figure out if that's my third."

"Hmmmm. Sounds simple enough."

"'Cause I'm a simple fucking man." I shrugged.

"Have you met yourself? Far from simple, Luca," she challenged.

"How would you classify me then?"

I was genuinely interested.

"Complex."

I chuckled a bit. Not surprised by her revelation. The truth was that so many considered me the same when I was the exact opposite. However, my simplicity confused them to the point of attempting to unmask or unfold things that just weren't there. I didn't have a million layers that needed to be peeled back. Everything about me was black and white, straight to the point. Many have made the mistake of thinking I'm complex, and I didn't try to convince them otherwise. But, Ever, I wanted her to understand that I wasn't. Figuring that out was the hard part, which made everyone give up and sum it up as me being a confusing or difficult subject.

"You've only known me for like two days."

"And in that short amount of time, I still haven't figured you out. It never takes this long."

"Don't try to figure me out, Ever. Determine who I am by my actions and you'll see that I am, in fact, a very simple man. I'm straightforward, honest, respectful, and loyal. That's it."

"Sounds simple enough."

"Because it is. Taste these," I told her as I scooped a small spoonful of potatoes up and placed them at her lips. She opened and accepted it.

"Ummmm." She moaned onto the spoon as I slid it

out of her mouth. With her eyes closed, she nodded for approval.

"Are you ready to eat?"

"Umm hmmm."

"Have a seat at the table, and I'll bring your food over."

THIRTEEN

LUCA

EVER AND I sat directly across from one another in the smaller of the two dining rooms. The bigger one seated twenty and had a large table with nine chairs on each side. There was a chair at the head and the tail, totaling twenty. We'd chosen the smaller dining room that seated six. It was still far too much room but we were making it work.

"So, your hard boundaries and revisions," she mentioned as she forked a piece of the steak that I'd cut into small, uneven chunks for her.

Ever had already finished off her potatoes, broccoli, and lobster. With our mouths full, conversation was light. She'd talked mostly about her girls, one of which I'd had the pleasure of meeting, and she was everything her mother said she was.

"My boundaries are simple. Allow me to lead while you follow. Trust me, and I don't mean when it comes to cheating and dishonesty, because you'll never have to worry about that shit. I'm thirty-six. I'm ready to sit down. Build some shit. Trust me to love, protect, provide, and lead. Domestic violence or abuse of any kind; I don't play that shit. We're adults who have the power to control our emotions, words, and hands. Then, there's the loyalty and the respect. No need to explain either of those.

"As far as revisions. You've basically told me that because another man fucked up, I can't be the very man that I was raised to be. I understand living in separate spaces until marriage. I also understand wanting to remain employed so that you're always in a position to bounce if that's what you choose to do. But, you won't, so most of that shit doesn't apply to me. Coming into this with so many restrictions and preconceived notions — such as you even needing an emergency stash to leave — isn't fair to me. I'm coming to you with a clean slate.

"If I brought my past with me, then shit would look much differently, Ever. I'm not grouping you with the others. The ones who don't even know what the fuck loyalty or respect means. The ones who want your paper and will stick around as long as it's flowing. The moment it stops, they're gone with the wind. Fair is fair. Given I respect you for not giving me the chance to disappoint you but you're not giving me much of a chance to love you the way I want to, either. You've been putting your desires out there since I walked into that restroom earlier. I've listened and observed, and I will give you whatever your heart desires. But, what about me?"

She chewed another piece of steak while staring back at me, taking everything I was saying into consideration.

"What about my desires? Because if they're not met at all while yours are being met, then this simply turns into exactly what you just got out of. The only difference is, you're not the one worshipping without reciprocation. It'll be me. And instead of you taking the pain, you'll be the one dishing it. You'll always get the long end of the stick and what do I get?"

"You're right," she admitted, eyes falling to her plate as the realization sat in. "Maybe it is a little selfish."

"But, it's human. It's an honest response to the trauma you've faced over the years, so I get it. But, I won't let you do that to me."

"I won't."

"So, let's meet in the middle. Continue staying at Lyric's or even let me put you and the girls up in a secured high-rise, full-serviced so that when you don't feel like doing laundry, you don't have to. I'll pay the rent up for a year with no stipulations. If we don't work out, then we don't work out. You'll have a year to stack your paper and move wherever you want once your lease is up. All I'm asking for is a key to come and go as we both please."

"I don't know, Luca. I don't feel good about that idea."

"Fine. Then if you'd like to stay at Lyric's, then do so

but spend some of your nights here with the girls. Divide your time so that I'm not sleeping alone every night."

"I like that idea."

She needed control. She hadn't had control over her life for so long that she was desperate to control every aspect of it now. *Noted.* Strong-arming her wouldn't work. It was important to make Ever feel as if she was in total control. And I would, but only by giving her options that I was OK with and letting her choose. This way, she was still in control but I still got exactly what I wanted. It would always be a win for us both.

"I'm a provider. I understand you want to keep your job, but I also want you to understand that you won't have to spend a red cent from now on. Your expenses are now mine. This isn't a control method, Ever. Not for me. My father would kill me if I did things any differently. And you don't owe me for shit."

"Luca, I don't know."

"Would you rather keep my cards for use or me give you a set amount each month that should last you and the girls until the following month?" I gave her the options, knowing they were both favored in my head.

"Both," she replied, not choosing either.

"How much do you think you'll need in a month? Not to maintain the life that you have now, but to start living the life that you deserve?"

"Maybe a thousand dollars."

"You like the wine you've been sipping?"

With a baffled expression, she nodded.

"Good. It's a thousand dollars, Ever. A bottle of that

every week will automatically put you over the four thousand dollar mark. Please, don't insult yourself like that."

"Ten thousand dollars." She switched it up.

"Fifteen. Your wardrobe will change, and I want you to be able to afford it as you acquire the new taste."

"That's enough to get a new place," she revealed.

"If that's what you want."

"Maybe in a month or two. I have to find something close so the girls won't have to change schools."

"I have people who can make that happen. Just tell me when you're ready."

"I will."

"Every other Wednesday, I'll have the laundry service I used to use come get you and the girls' things and have them back by Thursday afternoon. Ever, if you don't want to, I don't want you to ever have to fold another piece. If you prefer being cooked for instead of the stress of cooking, we can hire a chef. With us living in separate places, let's make it a habit to eat dinner together every evening."

"OK."

"I'll talk to Lyric and convince her to let me hire a cleaning service that will come twice weekly. It won't take much because as clean as her home is, she hates the task."

"I know." Ever chuckled.

"So that won't take much convincing."

"It won't."

"My job is to make your life easier, Ever. Let me do that."

"I'm going to try my hardest."

"Compromise. It's something we both have to do if we plan to survive."

"No one has ever considered my needs or even cared to ask what I want out of a life with them."

She lowered her fork onto the plate. She'd wiped it clean. That made my heart swell. Not only was she not afraid of busting down a meal with me, but she enjoyed my cooking. I admired the way she took her time eating, not in a rush to complete her meal, but taking the time to actually enjoy every bite.

"Because they were only willing to give bare minimum. I'm trying to max you out, love," I proclaimed.

"Thank you."

"Spend the night," I pushed out, throwing caution to the wind. I wanted Ever in my arms and not just for the next hour. When I opened my eyes, I wanted her near.

"Then, Lyric will be right."

"Did you assume I'd let you go?"

"I've never done this before."

"You really don't know me."

"Obviously she does."

"Very well."

Ever nodded, not verbally responding but getting her message across. I sipped from the glass of Hennessy in front of me, combing over her body with my eyes. Her brown skin sparkled just like brown sugar. In the black attire, she looked splendid. I couldn't believe how easily I'd stumbled upon her and on my first day out. She'd been set in my path for a reason and at the perfect time. There was no doubt in my mind that she was it.

"Come 'ere."

Sliding back in my seat, I patted my lap for Ever to sit. She was making me believe that maybe physical touch was something I should consider as my love language, too, because I couldn't keep my hands off her.

Ever stood from her chair, pulled her skirt down, and tossed her dinner napkin on the table beside her plate. She grabbed her glass of wine and headed in my direction. The wine that she was drinking constantly had loosened her up a bit. Her usually timid demeanor was replaced with a confidence that looked so fucking sexy on her. Yet and still, she was delicate and graceful.

Barefoot, she tiptoed in my direction, watching me watch her along the way. When she finally made it to me, I extended an arm after longing to touch her for much more time than I'd prefer. The curves of her body contoured to my grip as I squeezed her ass and watched it take its shape again once I released it. Her arm dropped onto my shoulder and circled my neck as she lowered onto me.

"Hi," she greeted.

Her even breaths and heartbeat soothed me. She was comfortable. It was the utmost compliment for one's presence. Her hardened nipples poked through the dark fabric, causing my jaws to fill with saliva as my appetite picked back up.

"I want to explore the world," she disclosed before taking another sip from her glass.

Pushing the right side of her shirt over, I exposed her pretty, brown nipple. The pebbled nub stuck out past the rest of her breast, begging to be sucked.

"It's your world, Ever. I just live in it. Whatever you heart desires, I'm going to make happen," I assured her before gently clutching her breast in my hand and placing my mouth over it.

"Ummmmmmmmm."

She squirmed in my lap, tossing her head back and giving me full access. I pushed the other side of her shirt down and out popped her left breast. Alternating between the two, I tried giving them an equal amount of attention as Ever slowly grinded against me.

"Luca," she whimpered.

I felt her hand reach up and caress the back of my head as she straightened her posture to feed me more of her. I gladly accepted, stuffing my mouth to capacity while circling her nipples with my tongue after each trade off. Only when I felt she was primed and had enough fine tuning did I come up for air.

"Take this shit off," I lowly, but forcefully demanded as I removed her shirt from her shoulders and pulled it toward her waist.

"Stand up."

Ever stood beside me, not moving a muscle and not having to. I stripped her from head to toe and stood beside her. Her body was art. There wasn't an obvious mark in sight, not even a hint of ink. The brown, faint stretch marks that ran upward across the bottom of her stomach were direct indicators she was capable of the thing that I wanted to witness more than anything in the world. *Birth.*

I kissed them. One by one.

Muah.

Muah.

Muah.

Muah.

Muah.

My lips graced her intensely moisturized skin. I felt the tears from her eyes as they fell into my freshly cut hair. Ever was in need of some real loving and reassurance. That was all. With it, she'd be the bossiest bitch around, and I couldn't wait to make that happen for her. A man had torn her to shreds, and I couldn't wait to pick up every piece and put her back together. She was mine, now. Everything about her life was about to improve.

The only thing I wanted Ever focused on was getting better, bossier, and finer by the day. All she needed was plenty of water, plenty of love, plenty of money, plenty of opportunities, plenty of time with me, and plenty of dick. With those, she'd be untouchable in under a month.

My frame towered over hers as I leaned down to stick my tongue down her throat. I wanted to taste every last drop of the food she'd consumed. Our tongues played sweet melodies of their own, piercing the air with their wetness.

Hungrily, we devoured each other as if we hadn't just finished our meals. Judging by the roaring ache I felt within that stemmed from my vicious appetite for her, one would imagine I hadn't eaten in years. Maybe it wasn't 100 percent true. I just hadn't eaten her.

I lifted her into the air and sat her bare ass on my table. She was light as a feather. I pushed her knees upward until both of her feet were on the table. Then, I spread them.

Her pretty brown pussy lips stared back at me, glistening with its natural secretion to thank. The pinkness of her vagina made my mouth water and my dick stand. My shit rocked so hard that it felt like it would break. And the steady breathing that Ever had once displayed, disappeared.

I lubricated my index and middle finger with her juices. She flinched upon contact. Our eyes met as hers glossed over. I saw her legs trembling as she watched me, wondering what my next move was. When I inserted those same fingers inside of her, her back raised as a gasp fell from her lips. Upon her exhale, she moaned.

"Don't hurt me," she begged, voice low and sensual.

"Don't hurt me," I responded, burying my finger deeper into her pussy.

My gaze didn't waver. I continued looking her square in the eyes so that she knew I was being straight with her. My heart was on the line too. We were both in it together. Before I hurt her intentionally, I'd leave her. And for me, leaving her wasn't an option.

"Ummmmmm."

After the words came from her mouth, she seemed a bit sexier and so much more enticing. Her vulnerability was so arousing, and I imagined it was because I knew it must've been hard to become. Not only had her vulnerability been taken advantage of but it involved her putting her pride aside. For that, I wanted to reward Ever.

"Luccccccca."

I scooted my chair over until it was in front of her, still massaging her walls with my fingers with her backside pressed against my table. Once it was in the perfect position, I removed my fingers from Ever's canal and sat in it. I was ready to feast and the sweetest dessert was waiting for me. I'd eaten dinner. Now it was time to eat her.

"Open for me."

I pushed Ever's legs further apart. I didn't want restricted movement. Her pussy was to become my canvas, and I wanted to paint all over that motherfucker. Up and down, around and around, side to side. There wasn't a direction I wasn't willing to go to see her reach her climax. And even after she had, I wanted her to reach it again.

The smell of her arousal was breathtaking. It was easily my favorite fragrance now, putting all the expensive shit that I'd ever purchased to shame. The thought that pussy was supposed to taste or smell like water had always been absurd to me and possibly thinking that was reserved for the immature.

Me, however, I was a grown motherfucking man and I wanted my pussy equipped with its own unique scent I could sometimes replace my cologne with if things got wild. Or, wear it on my mustache and goatee as bird repellent for anyone who was confused about my relationship status. I wanted the joy of recognizing my pussy's arousal from feet away just in case I'd missed the signs.

Slowly, I slid my tongue from the top of her pussy to the final inch of the crack of her ass.

"Oooooooooooooh," she hissed, back arching to the point of lifting from the table.

Before revisiting her pussy, I circled her asshole, snaked my tongue upward and penetrated her. I felt her gushy walls against my tongue as I fucked her pussy slowly, while thumbing her clit.

"Luuuuuuuca!" Ever released a deep, piercing scream.

I tasted her wetness on my buds, making my dick even harder. If I didn't get it inside of her soon, I knew it would break. It was so fucking hard. I needed to be inside of her. It was the only way my shit would settle. With this conclusion at the forefront of my thoughts, I sucked Ever's pearl into my mouth and gave it my full attention. Rapid strokes, back and forward, I used my tongue to mount her.

"Fuck! Wait. Ummmmmmmmmm."

She began sliding backward on the table. I leaned forward, keeping my face buried between her legs with my tongue assaulting her clit. She tried closing her legs, but that only served in my favor. It assisted me in applying more pressure, pressure that was sure to send her to her peak. When her legs began shaking and fell to the side, I knew that moment had come.

"LUCA!" she cried. "Oh shit. Oh shit."

Letting her off that easily wasn't in my plans and would never be. I continued to suck on her pussy as she came on my tongue. Gracefully. Beautifully. Her cries to be released caused my chest to swell. I slurped everything her pussy was releasing, enjoying the fruits of my labor. She tasted divine. Only when I was ready did I stand up completely and remove my clothing, giving her time to get herself together.

Her energy had been exhausted. I was certain she'd cum in the last two hours more than she had in a single day at any point in her life. The thing was, it was only the beginning. I wanted to hit that pussy until she creamed again. And then when we woke up, I wanted to give her back shots so powerful that they left her paralyzed and relieved of another load of creaming cum.

"And what's your vendetta against beds?" she came back to life long enough to ask.

"Nothing. We've got our whole lives to fuck up the sheets. Let's start here," I guaranteed her.

"Trust me. I'm not complainnnnnnnnnnnnning," she exaggerated as I entered her.

"Then shut the fuck up, then."

I didn't stop until I'd hit rock bottom. Her pussy gripped the skin of my dick and pulled me closer to her. With her legs spread wide and my hands on her waist, I stroked her long and I stroked her meticulously. I wanted her to feel every inch of me, down to my balls. Ever deserved all the dick that I had to give her, and I would do everything in my power to make sure that she got it.

"LUCA. Oh my God."

"I love dis shit," I admitted out loud, falling victim to the spell her pussy was putting on me. I loved it. I loved every second of it.

"LUCA."

The sound of her voice as it screamed my name awakened something within me. Something that started from my toes and slowly rose with each stroke of her pussy. Something that was overcoming me. Something that I knew I couldn't avoid even though I'd try to as long as I could. Eight years without pussy was a stretch and it had me ready to cum every time I slid into Ever. So, I pulled out.

"FUCK!" This time, the grumble wasn't low. Not with the way that I was tingling all over my fucking body.

I needed a second to gather myself. Bending, I planted my face deep into her pussy and began sucking on her clit. Her legs trembled and body bounced from the table as I showed no mercy on the mission at hand. And just like that, her lava was flowing into my mouth.

"Oh God. Oh God," she panted.

Immediately, I rose and slid back into her. Her walls contracted around me, summoning my nut from my balls. Her pretty face was an accomplice, assisting her pussy in extracting everything in my nut sack. To be fair, I wanted her to cum again. I wanted us to cum together.

I placed a finger on her sensitive bulb as the contractions of her walls slowed. Her head snapped up as she tried to stop me. That shit wasn't happening.

"Please."

With my free hand, I pushed her back down on the table.

"Lay the fuck down, Ever," I demanded, refusing to stroke her if she didn't obey.

Once her back was on the table and the tears began running down the side of her face, I pulled my dick from her and then inserted it again. I pulled my dick from her a second time and then reinserted it, never removing my thumb from her clit.

"Luca, please."

"Cum."

"Please."

"Cum."

"I'm cumming!" she screamed as I followed suit.

The intensity of her climax pushed me from her pussy just after I unloaded. The sound of liquid hitting the floor beneath us was so satisfying to my ears. Ever had reached the final level.

My earth-shattering ejaculation rocked my fucking world. I fell back into the chair as my dick continued to contract, still spitting up barely noticeable cum that oozed down the sides and landed on my balls.

"Omg. What was that?" She cried from above, not understanding what she'd just done.

I, on the other hand, I fully understood.

"That's a new level of pleasure you've unlocked. Female ejaculation. It's the only way you'll climax from now on."

FOURTEEN

EVER

DISORIENTED, I stirred from my sleep. I wasn't sure what time it was and neither did I care. All I knew was that the sun hadn't risen, which meant that it was the wee hours. I'd fallen asleep shortly after a shower with Luca, where he scrubbed me from head to toe. He even massaged my scalp with his shampoo and then conditioned my dirty blonde, curly tresses.

Our shower coupled with the dick he'd given me twice and forehead kisses put me right to sleep where I'd obviously remained until now. Luca's bedroom was a dream, but without him at my side it was beginning to feel like a nightmare. His empty side of the bed left me wondering where he could've gone.

I rubbed the sleep from my eyes to see better. The sparkling lights from the city's skyline lit the room decently, giving me a better chance at finding him. Floor-to-ceiling windows surrounded me. It wasn't until I focused on the one near the edge of the balcony that wrapped around the back of Luca's home that I noticed the orange and red circle at the tip of his blunt.

I stretched my arms and removed the covers from my waist. When I stood to my feet, I noticed the feeling had returned to my legs. Luca had stripped me of all my energy and as deadly as his dick was, it was my craving for it that led me out onto the balcony in the nude.

I pulled the sliding door back until there was just enough room for me to slide through. Upon seeing me, Luca didn't budge. His tranquility remained as I closed the distance between us and eventually invaded his personal space. Our eyes smiled at one another, though our mouths remained unchanging.

I leaned forward and pulled the blunt he was burning from his hands. I clutched it between my thumb and index finger as I brought it to my mouth and inhaled. Smoke filled my lungs, introducing me to a new, dry taste that wasn't as bad as I'd always imagined.

Once.

Twice.

Three times, I pulled from his blunt, then let my hand fall to my side. I watched his dick harden through the briefs that he wore, not sure if it was the act or my body that was more enticing.

Luca was good for my system. I knew it because in

under twenty-four hours of agreeing to a date with him, the amount of confidence I felt was uncanny. In the past, I never would've even considered walking around a man's home, baring it all, but Luca was different. He wasn't just any man. The way he'd kissed every one of my stretch marks and made my body do things it had never done, he'd given me the boost I didn't know I needed to kickstart my confidence.

I also knew without a doubt just how good he was for me because my body told me so. The way that it responded to him, opened for him, was foreign but it felt so damn good. I wanted Luca. I *needed* Luca – to flush out the bullshit that I'd experienced in the past. I wanted him to get into my system with his addictiveness and never leave.

"Hi." I smiled.

"Hi," he returned, leaning forward and accepting the blunt that I handed him.

As he watched, I lowered myself onto the concrete beneath me. I pulled at the waist of his briefs and then patted his thigh. I wanted him out of them, and I didn't have time to waste. Fortunately, Luca didn't give me any push back, lifting so that I could remove them completely. Now, neither of us wore a single thread. I preferred it that way.

His dick sprang up, striking me on the side of the face and causing me to smile. I was happy to see him, too. He'd been wrecking my walls, and I wanted to repay him with my warm, waiting mouth.

Summoning every drop of spit that was in my mouth,

I spat it onto Luca's handsome tool. The long, thick, and veiny beauty glistened as my personal lubrication ran down it. I looked up at Luca, who was pulling from his blunt and staring down at me as I circled the tip with my tongue. Around and around, I got acquainted with the taste of his skin while slowly stroking him with my right hand.

"You gone suck this dick or you're going to keep playing?" he asked, the deep rasp of his voice forced me to stifle a moan. Just the sound of him made me feel good inside, so good that I wanted to vocalize it.

"I'm going to suck this dick, Luca," I admitted, creaming below.

This man has to give me his babies, I declared, gushing. He had to be my forever.

I didn't give a damn that I'd just met Luca. I wanted to rock his last name, have his babies, and suck his dick until my nose and eyes watered. The euphoria he'd introduced me to was exactly what I wanted for the rest of my life.

"Then what you waiting for?" he pulled at his blunt again after asking.

The sight of him, completely relaxed and waiting for me to please him with my mouth, made it water. Still looking him in the eyes, I lowered my head and stuffed him between my teeth and on top of my tongue.

"Big girl," he coached, never breaking eye contact.

No more words were exchanged between us as I finally closed my eyes and savored his flavor. I wanted him at the very back of my throat, so that's where I put him. I sucked his dick with pleasure, pulling him partially out of my mouth and then shoving him down my throat until my eyes watered every time.

His balls rotated between my fingers and palm as I massaged them, giving them the attention they needed as well.

"You want me to cum in your mouth?" Luca finally asked as he gripped my hair and pulled my head backward to look at my face. I was a mess. There was slob all around my mouth, running down my chin, and sitting on my chest.

"No," I admitted.

"Then, where the fuck you want it?" he bit his lips and asked. It was obvious. He was losing it. I massaged the head of his dick with my right hand and the length of it with my left, both going in different directions.

"Inside of me."

"You gone fuck around and have a nigga's baby," he warned.

I lifted from the kneeling position, finally letting his meat go. I placed one knee on side of him and then the other on the opposite side. Luca blew the smoke he'd just inhaled into my mouth and tossed the rest of his blunt on the concrete.

"That's the plan," I revealed as I slid down onto his dick.

He grabbed my neck and brought my face to his. He tongued me down as I positioned myself. With my hands on his chest and his mouth on mine, I began riding Luca. He felt so good inside of me. Way too good. I never wanted him to leave. I closed my eyes and enjoyed the founding moments of us and couldn't wait to see what we built from them.

I'd gone from thinking I wasn't ready for this man to feeling intense emotions at the mere thought of this man. My heart literally hurt as I slid up and down his pole, but not because of heartbreak. It was simply because I knew without a doubt in my mind that I'd found my soul's mate. It didn't matter how fast or how slow we got there, forever would always be our destination.

"Will you be my woman?" Luca groaned as he asked.

I nodded with teary eyes and a faint smile. His dick was lethal and even with me on top, it was about to make me cum. I could feel my orgasm rising.

Up and down.

Up and down.

Luca cupped my left breast and put it in his mouth. He circled my nipple with his tongue, pulling me closer to the point of no return. As he switched to the right nipple, I froze in place as my nerves split and small, fine bumps began rising all over my skin. I'd arrived.

"Give me forever," I requested just before my orgasm hit, wanting to make my intentions clear for the one hundredth time.

"Give me a son," he demanded as I began to cum.

"Ummmmm. Luca! Shit."

He joined me, gripping both my breasts tightly as his nut filled me.

"FUCK!"

LUCA-EVER

MAYBE LYRIC WAS RIGHT. Luca wouldn't give me up so easily, but he wasn't alone. I wasn't ready to give him up, either. So, we'd spent my day off lounging around and getting better acquainted with each other. The only time we left the house was to grab me a few pieces to stash in his closet for the days that I stayed with him.

He'd also gone as far as taking me to all the pretty little shops that I wanted to shop for the girls once my money was in order again. He bought everything and anything in their sizes that I even looked like I wanted them to have. And he'd bought them twice. One set of pieces were for his home and the other was for Lyric's. He hadn't met the girls yet, but judging from his excitement, I knew it would be heartwarming.

The more time we spent together, alone in his home, the more I fell in love with it and the easier it was to agree to allow him to put the girls and I into an apartment of our own that wasn't far from his home and had the same views. I'd been given three options and was still weighing them. I wasn't in a rush, but after witnessing the peace that the view of The Hills brought, I wanted it now more than ever.

"Baby," Luca called out to me as he nudged me, thinking I was still asleep.

"Hmmmm?" It was the second morning I'd awakened to Luca's voice, but this time I couldn't stay all day. I had work at nine and the thought of it alone made my chest ache.

"You up?"

"A little." I yawned, flipping over onto my back. I'd been awake but resting my eyes for the last few minutes.

"Where have you been?"

"On a run."

"What time is it?"

"Quit your job," he rushed out instead of answering my question.

"Huh?" I sat up in bed. "Luca, I thought we talked about this?"

"We did. I just need you to trust me on this one. I took a run to clear my head. You going back to work just isn't sitting well with me. Not because I don't want you to work. I do. But only because I know that's important to you. The thing is, if I'm here, it's my job to upgrade your entire life. Absolutely nothing is wrong with working at Baisleigh's House, but imagine how you'd feel rocking an AP and two bracelets that cost one of your customer's yearly salary? It just doesn't add up."

I hated he was making so much sense.

"So what are you suggesting, Luca?"

"You allow me to invest in your cake making business – no strings attached."

For a few seconds, I sat in silence. I wasn't sure what to say or how to feel. On one hand, I knew this was the opportunity I needed to finally get my business off the ground, but on the other hand it felt like I'd be falling into my vicious cycle that left me in the gutter.

"I know you're scared. I know you're afraid, but I can't let you allow your past to dictate your future. I'm the real fucking deal, Ever. You won't find another nigga like me, and I won't do shit to make you search, either. I'm locked in. I need you to understand that. I'm a fucking boss, baby. Nepotism makes you a boss by association."

"I've always imagined myself driving one of those Mercedes vans wrapped with my cake business info covering every side of it. And, inside, it would be built out to withstand long drives with cakes onboard. Do you know how many people ruin their cakes before they even make it to their home? Then, all of that money is gone to waste."

"What else have you imagined, Ever?"

"A space to call my own. Somewhere with a big kitchen, several ovens, and so much counter space, it makes the average person sick to their stomach. All the machines and technology the big cake makers have would line the walls and there would be a room for my girls so that they can feel at home on those days I'm working long hours."

"Anything else?"

"I haven't thought any further about it."

"Then it's time you start."

"I'm terribly scared, Luca."

"Trust me," he finalized. "Join me in the kitchen in about thirty minutes. Just as you are. I need to shower."

"What will I tell Baisleigh? She's expecting me this morning. I can't let her down."

"I hit her up yesterday. I already knew you weren't going back," he tossed over his shoulder as he made his way into the bathroom.

"LUCA! Seriously!" I chastised.

"She agreed. She was expecting the call." He shrugged, remaining too calm for my liking.

But as soon as he turned the corner, a smile curved the corners of my lips as I sat against the headboard. I grabbed a pillow from his side of the bed and screamed into it. This couldn't be my life. *Couldn't be.*

As Luca had requested, I met him in the kitchen thirty minutes later, but not without the laptop that I'd taken from his office. I'd used the desktop computer until my time was up, too invested in my google searches and google doc full of ideas, products, pricing, and potential business names.

"Turkey bacon or turkey sausage?"

"Bacon," I responded, lifting one hand in the air for Luca's assistance.

He picked me up and placed me on the countertop beside the stove. I loved being as close to him as possible, and he didn't seem to mind. The fact that he enjoyed cooking so much was the break I needed from the stove.

"What you done came up with?" he asked, taking a peek at the laptop in my hand.

"Can I have your email to share this document with you? It's full of ideas, products, and some other stuff."

"Yeah. Go to the notes. It's there. Send it to me so that I can get a head start. You thought any more about which one of those high-rises you're fucking with?"

"I did. I actually chose one."

"Aight. Which one?"

"Danridge."

"Yeah. That's the one I was hoping you chose. I'll get my people on it. Send me a copy of your ID when you get a chance."

"OK."

"Now, what am I looking at?"

He leaned closer to the screen as he rested his elbows on the counter.

"I can't decide on a name for the business."

"Ever Sinclair," he said, pointing at the first option. "Let it be your namesake."

"I thought so, too, but I didn't know if that was too in your face."

"Na. I like that. I like your name."

"Too much to change the last one?" I teased.

"Enough to change the last one."

"Then the business name would be wrong."

"Na. You'll always be Ever Sinclair. Always. Ever Eisenberg will understand that shit and act accordingly."

"Ever Eisenberg," I repeated, trying to see how well it rolled off my tongue.

"That shit sounds good, don't it?"

"It does."

Essence Eisenberg. Emorey Eisenberg, I dared to say out loud but sounded out in my head. Dewayne was a piece of shit and didn't deserve the privilege of sharing last names with the girls. I wanted them to have the same name as I did, and if that was Luca's name, then so be it.

"Once we finish eating, let's go take a look at some spaces to see if we can find the one that you imagined."

"It's still so early, Luca. I'm hungry for something, but it isn't food."

I sat the laptop beside me and spread my legs wide. Luca's brows hiked as he nodded, lifting his head slightly to see my pinkness. Without question, he stood and dropped the basketball shorts he'd thrown on after his shower. His dick was already hard, making his entry easy fucking peasy.

LUCA-EVER

AS MUCH AS Luca and I wanted to stay cooped up in his home, we knew it was impossible. So, I spent one more day with him, and as our time drew to a close, I had already begun missing him. I'd looked at so many spaces that I was having a hard time narrowing them down. Because I didn't want to be tasked with choosing, I'd give that job to Lyric.

"I feel a little sad," I admitted as Luca and I pulled into the driveway.

"I'm not far away," Luca responded as he parked his truck.

"I know. And besides, we both have so much to do. I'm sure everyone is wondering where you've been hiding these last three days."

"No one knows I'm home, Ever, and the people who do already know where I've been."

"Your mom knows we're dating?"

"Dating?" He chuckled, finding my question amusing.

"Yeah."

"We're together, Ever."

"But still, we're dating."

"Yes, baby, we're dating," he agreed with a shrug. He'd been doing it for the last three days. Anything I said, he agreed to. It was that simple. I hadn't heard the word no since he'd picked me up for dinner.

"OK. What are your plans for the rest of the day?"

"Handling some shit with Laike and then hitting the gym with Ken to shoot some hoops. After that, I'm turning it in. What's on your agenda?"

"Forcing Lyric to choose between the spaces. I'll probably use her computer to make some nice cards and flyers. I want to apply for the LLC and reserve a domain online. I'll need somewhere for them to pay for their cakes in advance. I'll probably add a new line to my T-Mobile account. I don't want anyone calling my phone. I think that's it. My girls are still at my mother's so I have a lot of free time on my hands."

"Aight. Is that your ride?" He pointed at my car that was parked on the street.

"Yes."

"Look for you a new ride while you're on the internet doing all that shit. And here. Go get your own fucking computer and all the other shit you need. 1221 is the code."

He reached in the armrest and handed me a temporary bank card. It was one of the ones they usually gave you when you lost your card. I held it up, waiting for an explanation.

"That's a temporary debit card that is linked to your new account. The official card will be here tomorrow. Keep the two separate so that you'll feel safe knowing that the money I give you isn't tied to the money that you're busting your ass to get."

"Technically, I'm busting my ass to get both."

"Well, yeah," he agreed with a shrug. "I've never paid for pussy but in this case, I'd have to agree."

"Goodbye, Luca!" I chuckled, sliding the card into my purse.

He opened his door, exited the truck, and ran around to my side. When he opened my door, I slid right into his arms. He kissed my cheeks and then my lips before placing me on the ground.

"See you later, Ever."

"Don't miss me too much."

"I will."

I headed for the door with my key in my hand but before I was able to let myself in, Lyric swung the door open. Her smile was infectious. She dragged me into the house by my shoulders, not even bothering to greet her brother.

"I told you!" she blurted.

"What? What did you tell me?"

"That you'd be sucking dick. I can smell it on your lips!"

"You cannot!" I countered.

"Okay, I can't but I know you did. Didn't you?"

"I did. Several times and it was very rewarding."

"Ugh! Lucky you. Staying out not one night, but two whole nights. Didn't you have to work today? Why are you even here right now? It's Friday."

"Luca told Baisleigh I quit." I sighed as I pressed my back against the wall in the hallway.

"And how does that make you feel?"

"Scared. Relieved. Confused. He wants me to go into business for myself."

"Is that what you want?"

"More than anything. I just never thought it would happen for me."

"Now that you have the chance to make it happen, are you going to?"

"Yes."

Lyric jumped up and down, squealing as she used her hands to cheer.

"I know that's right, friend. I was secretly hoping you invested a small portion of the money I'd given you but I understood when you didn't. You wanted a cushion for you and the girls."

"And I have one. I checked my account yesterday evening after we'd made it back to Luca's. Lyric, I've managed to save almost seven thousand dollars. Three of which is thanks to you. The other two, almost three are from my tips and the one check I've gotten from Baisleigh's. I can't remember a time when I had this much money saved. Shit. There hasn't been one. That is my security blanket. I'm making a cake for a customer of Baisleigh's who is having her brunch there, and she wants me to make cakes for her family as their birthdays roll around. She told me that if I brought up some business cards, then everyone would staple them to the customer's receipts. That'll probably bring in tons of customers."

"It will. So what are you waiting for? Let's make some cards."

"I want to go to the Apple store first."

"OK. But for what, love?"

"Luca is sending me to get a new computer and phone so that I can add a business line to my account." I removed the card from my purse and held it in her face.

"Baby, you ain't said nothing but a word. We're getting you more than that. This man gave you his card, we're getting a laptop, phone, iPad, and AirPods."

"How much will all of that cost?" I worried about the prices adding up.

"Who gives a damn? You're sucking rich dick now, babe. Let him worry about the bill."

"Your car or mine?"

"Mine," she responded, grabbing my hand and pulling me back out of the door.

The excitement that filled my bones made me feel like a little girl. I couldn't remember the last time I'd felt so giddy inside. It was as if I'd deactivated survival mode and initiated a new, more palatable mode. One that allowed me to lean into my softness without worries or fears of what was to come or the disappointment that was waiting around the corner for me.

Lyric and I climbed into her truck and hit the expressway. We made it to the Apple store in just a few minutes. I left the store with a large Apple bag in my hand that contained anything that I thought I'd need to help make starting my business easier. My total had come to less than four thousand dollars meaning that I still had six to spend before the month ended. Even the thought of having so much at my fingertips sent my thoughts spiraling.

When I made it back to the comfort of Lyric's home, I bathed and talked to the man above while resting beneath the bubbles. I was walking into foreign territory and wanted to make sure that I was fully covered. My faith led me to believe that everything would be okay, lifting a huge burden off my shoulders by the time I was dressed in my night clothes and in bed. It was still mid-day, but I knew I had a lot of work to do, and I wouldn't be going anywhere, anytime soon.

Two hours into my work session, and I was surrounded by gadgets, paper, and almonds. I wasn't 100 percent sure what I was getting myself into but it felt good. That was pretty much all that mattered.

I'd linked a new cell to my T-Mobile account and had received a secondary line. It was the number that I placed on the business cards and flyers. I'd reserved the domain and anything close to it in case I ever wanted to branch out.

This is all going to move so fast, I thought to myself as my chest tightened.

Luca had made it very clear that he was willing to do whatever to kick off a successful business of mine. I knew he would; I just wanted to be prepared for it all.

Luca. I missed his face and his smile. Though I didn't see it often, when I did, it was a treat. It had been hours since he'd dropped me off, and I couldn't help but wonder what he was doing. I pulled out my cell phone and punched his name into my contacts. It wasn't until it didn't come up that it registered in my head. We never exchanged numbers.

As much as I wanted to laugh at the irony of it, I felt pathetic. The man had been inside me, not a few times, but so many times that I lost track over the last three days. He'd cooked and cleaned for me. He'd washed me from head to toe. He'd showered me with tenderness and adoration, but I didn't even have his number.

It wasn't hard to come by, but still. The fact remained. I gathered my thoughts and decided that I'd take the walk of shame to ask Lyric for the number, but before I could get off the bed, she came bursting through the door.

"I've made my decision," she blurted with the small stack of papers in her hand.

"Okay, but first, can you give me your brother's—" I started but she interrupted.

"Y'all are pathetic. I just gave him your number. He'll be calling soon."

"Shut up," I warned her. Yes, we were pathetic, but I didn't want anyone else knowing just how much.

"Hey. I'm not saying nothing."

"Which did you choose?"

"The lakefront location and here's why…" She trailed off as my phone chimed.

The text was from an unsaved number, but I knew exactly who it was.

I'm coming to get you when I'm done moving around. Be ready in three hours, he texted, elevating my body temperature and making my mouth water at the thought of tasting him again.

FIFTEEN

LUCA

GETTING READJUSTED with the ins and outs of my business had been more consuming than I'd expected. It wasn't until I made it into my home that I realized just how much I'd been on the go and just how much I missed Ever. It had been three days since I'd seen her beautiful face, and I refused to go another.

"Hello?" Her sultry voice appeared on my line.

"What are you doing?" I wanted to know.

"Just finished eating dinner and got the girls in their pajamas."

"It's still early," I told her as I checked the time. It was only seven-thirty.

"I know. I like to clean them up right after dinner so that we have the rest of the night to do nothing."

"Or y'all could come over. I want to eat dinner, too."

I knew we'd agreed to eat dinner together as much as possible, but the time for it hadn't come. We were both extremely busy trying to figure out business.

"You sure?"

"If you're asking me if I'm ready to meet the girls, I am. Everybody get ready. I'm about to come scoop y'all up."

"No. You don't have to come get us. I can drive to your place. I have to take them to school in the morning. Essence starts daycare with Emorey."

"That's cool, too, but I can drop them off in the morning if you'd like. I need to holler at my moms, anyway. I ain't seen her in a week."

"We can take them together. We're about to head over."

"Aight."

I ended the call with Ever and cut the oven off. The chicken that I was planning to cook could wait. My dinner was on the way and it included Ever and whatever she'd cooked.

I ran upstairs for a quick, five-minute shower. It was all I'd have time for before Ever was at the door with her girls. The last thing I wanted was to smell like outdoors when they approached.

I adjusted the temperature of the water and stepped into the shower the second it was warm enough. The large beads of water massaged my shoulders as I allowed the deeds of the day to roll off my back while trying to figure out how to convince Ever that she belonged in my space more than anywhere else.

I knew she was on her *independent, don't want to live with a man shit*, but she didn't have to. I understood what her healing process required, and I refused to interfere but coming home to an empty house every night when there could easily be two giggling girls waiting at the door for me was absurd.

It didn't have to be every day or every night, but a few out of the week wouldn't hurt. If she didn't want it to be my home so soon, then I was definitely going to get her apartment situation squared away before the week was out. Shit, within the next forty-eight hours because I knew it was possible.

I'd gotten so comfortable sleeping next to her for four days straight that I wasn't getting much shut eye now that she wasn't around. I was exhausted, which is why I called them over. If they didn't come to me, then I was taking my ass to Lyric's.

When the doorbell sounded a few minutes after my shower, my stomach growled. It was as if my body understood who and what was at the door waiting for me. I turned on the lights that led to the door to lighten the place a bit. Aside from the small traces of light from the setting sun, the place was black.

Anxious to see the people behind the door, I opened it. The sight behind the door was one that I could never get tired of. There was little Emorey, whom I'd had the pleasure of meeting already. Then there was a slightly taller, slightly bigger version of Emorey who happened to be another mini Ever. Essence. She was the prettiest. So was Emorey. And, Ever. Shit, I was starting to wonder if I really wanted a boy or another one of the three people standing in front of me.

"Emorey, Essence. This is Luca, Mommy's boyfriend."

I appreciated Ever's honesty. She'd told me that lying was something she despised and chose not to do it herself. I figured that meant when it came to her children as well.

"Luca, these are the girls."

"I've met this one," I shared with Ever who was puzzled by the revelation. "At my mom's center."

I bent down and scooped Emorey into my arms. Then, I turned to Essence and watched her twiddle her thumbs in front of her. Knowing how important it was to ask permission to invade a child's personal space because there were so many adults who didn't think they had the right to have personal space, I began speaking to Essence.

"Would you like to take the express ride to the movie theater?"

She nodded, granting me access. I got a bit closer, turned around, and patted my back for her to climb on. When she was finally situated and comfortable, I stood and shifted Emorey in front of me. With both girls, I began tugging down the hallway.

"Chooooo. Chooooooo."

In a fit of laughter, the girls were delivered safely to the couch where I had the lights off and the television turned on, waiting for them to make a selection so that I could make it happen.

"Do you have popcorn, Luca?" Essence asked.

"As a matter of fact, I've got plenty."

"Caramel?"

"Caramel. Sweet. Buttery. Plain. Whatever you want. And if I don't have it, I can always get it."

"Always?" Essence followed up with.

"Always," I confirmed.

"I'll take caramel. Emorey will, too."

"OK. You know how to work this television, Essence?"

"Ummm hmmm." She nodded.

"Good. Your mom and I will get the popcorn ready while you two choose a movie. That's alright with y'all?"

"Yes, sir."

"Yes, sir!" Emorey repeated after Essence.

I handed her the remote and looked up to see where Ever had gone. I found her over in the corner against the wall observing with contentment on her face that couldn't be mistaken for anything else. Using my head, I signaled toward the kitchen where I wanted her to meet me. She nodded in return, letting me know she understood. She took off immediately.

"Be right back," I told the girls before following behind her.

"Hi, Mommy," I finally spoke to Ever once we were alone in the kitchen.

"Hi, Daddy," she returned with a smile. That unleashed the beast within me.

My hands slid up her shoulders. The right one wrapped around her neck as the left lowered until her ass was in my palms. I stuck my tongue down her throat as she moaned into my mouth. My dick hardened on contact with her skin. I cupped her ass in the black pajama pants that hugged her body just like I wanted to.

"I missed the fuck outta you," I admitted. "Come in here."

"Come where, Luca?" She looked around.

"Right here." I pointed to the pantry.

"We can't."

"Yes the fuck we can." I pushed her forward as she began to chuckle.

We made it inside of the walk-in pantry and closed the door behind us.

"Bend that shit over," I instructed as I lowered my shorts.

Once she was bent over the rack in front of her, I pulled her pants and panties to her ankles. I wanted so badly to eat her box from behind but we didn't have time for that shit. So, instead, I spat into my hand and rubbed the head of my dick. Less than two seconds later, I was sliding into her.

It had been three... whole... days.

We both sighed in harmony.

"I missed you so much," Ever whimpered as she began to throw her ass backward.

She knew what the fuck she was doing, and she knew I wouldn't last long if she continued doing it. I wasn't mad at her. Not only did the shit feel good, but it would lessen our chances of getting caught by the girls. Time wasn't on our side, and we needed to make this quickie really fucking quick.

"Shiiiiiiiiit," I barked. "That's it, Ever. Put that pussy on a nigga."

"Ummmmmmmmmmm. Feels so good."

She wasn't playing fair. The sound of our skin smacking and her moaning was driving me insane. At any second, I was going to blow.

"That pussy gone make a nigga nut. Where you want this shit?" I already knew the answer, but I wanted to hear her say it — every fucking time.

"Inside of me," she begged and that's exactly where she got it. Inside of her.

I let loose inside of her as she'd requested. My entire body stiffened and locked until my balls were empty. Exhaustion hit me heavy at that moment, and I knew for a fact that I probably wouldn't be making it through the entire movie. I leaned forward and kissed Ever's neck before pulling out of her.

"I'm not leaving you hanging. I got you whenever we get a minute to ourselves."

"I'm happy you're eager to make me cum but that was more than enough. That one was for you. Some will be for me. Others will be for us both. But don't feel any type of way because I'm still trying to catch up to your lead, so don't sweat it."

"Kiss me."

She wrapped her hands around my body and connected them behind my back as she looked up and got on the tips of her toes. She still wasn't tall enough to meet my lips, so I assisted her by lowering my head. Ever quickly pecked my lips and then lowered to pull her pants up.

"I'm going to go clean up and change my panties. Can you handle making the popcorn?"

"Yeah. I got it. Go ahead. I'll meet you back in there in a few."

One more peck of the lips, and she was gone. As soon as she disappeared around the corner, my cell rang. I didn't recognize the number on the screen, but that had been happening a lot in the last few days. They were usually connected to people who Laike saw fit to have my contact information.

"Who is this?" I answered, cutting straight to the chase.

"Wow. Is that really how you answer your phone?" the female asked.

"Either you're answering the question or I'm hanging up."

"OK. OK. So grumpy. It's Kasey. We met at Oat + Olive."

"Yeah, I remember. You're a little too late. Go ahead and delete the number, Kasey."

"Wow. You move fast." She chuckled.

I didn't bother responding. There weren't any time restrictions when it came to Ever and I. I'd never try to explain that shit to anyone, either. Whatever happened between us and whenever that shit happened was our business.

I lifted the lid on the plate that Ever had brought over. Greens, cabbage, and baked chicken were underneath. I placed it in the microwave before washing my hands and heading for the pantry again. I grabbed the bag of caramel popcorn and poured it into a large bowl. I also grabbed the cheese and caramel popcorn mix and tossed it into another bowl. With them both in-hand, I headed to the girls.

"We found a movie. It costs dollars," Essence told me as soon as she saw me.

"Well, I'm glad we've got dollars to spend. Go ahead and order it."

"OK!"

They'd chosen a minion movie. Though I was utterly uninterested, I would watch every second of the movie with them. I hadn't watched a kids' movie since I was a kid. Even then, I wasn't interested in many of them.

I sat the bowls down on the table and headed for the guest bathroom right down the hall. Before getting all up in their space, I wanted to wash their mother's scent from my body. As much as I loved it, I found it disrespectful to Essence and Emorey.

When I returned, everyone was already laying down and ready to start the movie. I hopped over the couch and landed right beside Ever. Emorey got down and ran over to my side once she noticed me.

"Can I lay on you side?" she asked before climbing up.

Kids never respected adults' boundaries, so seeing her restrain from what came naturally to her made my heart ache. I knew it was because there was once a sucker in her presence that didn't allow her in his space or possibly made her scared to even desire to be in his space. In return, she felt the need to suppress her true desire for human touch when it was the very thing that kept kids learning and growing rapidly.

"Yes. You can lay on my side, Emorey." I pulled her up and sat her beside me.

She leaned into my side and pulled my arm over her little body. I warmed inside as I wrapped my other arm around Ever. Essence was already laying in her lap.

LUCA·EVER

I TAPPED the screen on my phone once my eyes had adjusted to the dark. The movie credits were rolling and everyone around me was asleep. Emorey laid in my lap, now, and Essence remained in Ever's lap. It was just after ten but it felt like it must've been midnight.

The big yawn that followed a smaller one let me know I was due for a goodnight's rest. I took a look around me and admittedly, there was no feeling in the world I'd experienced that was better than the one I was experiencing at the moment. Pure bliss was the only way to explain what I was feeling.

I thought I loved seeing Ever sleeping but seeing her and the girls resting around me was the real fucking highlight of my week. As much as I hated to wake them, I wanted everyone comfortable and in bed. Ever was the first I nudged.

"Hmmm?" She stirred in her sleep.

"Let's get them to bed."

The room next to mine was their destination. We'd already filled the drawers with their clothes and added the necessary items to the bathroom to make their time at my home easier. The kid toothpaste, small toothbrushes, and pink towels were small additions, but meant a great deal.

"OK. Take Emorey. I'll get Essence."

"You sure? Essence is heavier. We have to go upstairs."

"You're right." She yawned. "Let me grab Emorey and you can grab Essence."

She reached over me and grabbed Emorey from my lap. I slid Essence toward me and then lifted her into my arms. Ever and Emorey took off for the stairs and we followed. As Ever grew tired as we ascended, I felt the need to relieve her of Emorey, too.

"Here, let me take her, too."

"You sure?"

"There's enough room in my arms for them both. Go ahead to bed. I can handle them."

"I can help."

"I got it," I assured her as I pulled Emorey into my arm.

"OK."

Ever waited on the same step as I continued. I cut on the light in the hallway before entering their room so that I could keep the light off when I laid them down. However, I wasn't familiar with my surroundings, so I needed to be able to see where I was going. Once I had Emorey down, I laid Essence down next. Neither even stirred a little. Hard ass sleepers, I concluded as I backed out of the room. When I made it to my bedroom, Ever was already in bed underneath the covers. I climbed in after her and pulled her closer to me. And just as we were, we both fell into a deep sleep.

LUCA-EVER

"WAKE UP, guys. It's morning time." Emorey's little voice woke me from my sleep.

I opened my eyes to find her bouncing on the bed beside us. Essence sat at the edge, swinging her feet and looking up toward our direction. Ever's eyes were open, but she still hadn't said a word. It seemed as if she'd rather be sleeping than watching her toddler jump around in bed.

"It's morning time. It's morning time," Emorey repeated over and over again.

It was apparent that no one was getting any more sleep. Emorey wasn't having that shit. Essence hadn't said much, but I could tell that she wasn't having that shit either. The sun was up, and they were both ready to get their day started.

"Alright." I laughed, finally realizing how my parents must've felt.

Emorey and Essence were my first glimpse into fatherhood, and though it had only been a few hours, I was loving the shit. Down to the squeaky voice of the little girl who refused to let anyone be.

"You get up?"

"Yes. I'm going to get up. You want some breakfast?"

"I do!" Essence yelled, raising her hand in the air.

"Me too," Ever agreed.

"Then, let's get washed up and go grab something to eat."

"They're supposed to be headed to school."

"Unfortunately, they aren't," I informed Ever. "They're taking the day off to hang with us."

"Luca," Ever warned. "I don't think you're ready for Thing One and Thing Two."

"Then I'd better start getting ready. What better day than today?"

"I have missed them so much since they've been away. Maybe I need this day with them, too."

"See." I shrugged.

"Come on, girls. Let's get you guys dressed and your teeth brushed, and I'm going to see what I can do about these heads." Ever touched Emorey's brownish blonde hair and shook her head from side to side.

Essence was already at the door waiting. I'd been around them for enough hours to determine their personalities. Emorey was the outgoing one, and Essence was the chillest. I could rock with Essence. That's exactly how I lived my life, observing instead of engaging.

The three of them disappeared, leaving me to do something with myself. Before I began, I wanted to clear my head and have a few drags of my blunt. I stepped out onto the balcony and lit fire to my spliff. Channing was the most beautiful city with an undefeated skyline. My view from the hillside allowed me to see almost 80 percent of the city from my balcony. The view was one of a kind.

I peered into the distance with the blunt to my lips. If my life for the last week was any indication of how my life would be outside of the FEDs, then I was in love with this motherfucker already. Not only did I have more money than I did when I went in, but I had the most beautiful soul at my side, and she came with two children that looked just like her ass. I was winning in every realm that I considered priorities. My family was good. Neither of them were stressed or worried about a fucking thing.

My only goal as far as they stood was releasing the guilt Lyric felt for my incarceration. By breaking those chains and releasing that hold on her, she could finally fall in love again. I wanted that for her. She was a good woman. She deserved it.

After a few puffs, I smashed the blunt into the concrete and headed inside. I needed to shower and get myself together before the girls started to get impatient. It was going to be a simple day, so I opted for a Nike shorts combination with a pair of black and white Ones to match. Once my clothing was chosen, I headed for the shower.

Just as I emerged, Ever appeared in the bathroom, naked and ready for her shower as well. It took everything in me not to bend her ass over the counter and fuck her until she came, but I knew that would only cause me to have to shower again and keep the girls waiting longer.

"I just need two minutes in here, and I'll be out."

"Aight," I responded, pulling my briefs over my ass.

With children present, I knew that there were some precautions I had to take to protect us all. Like, making sure I was decent before leaving the bathroom in the event they were in my room when I exited. And fucking Ever any and everywhere I could, would have to be cut to a minimum. When the children were around, I'd try to limit it to spaces with doors and locks so that we could have total privacy.

By the time Ever put on her clothes and met us downstairs, we were all waiting by the door and ready to roll. We stepped out as a unit, the girls in some of the new pieces I'd bought them and Ever looking as fly as ever in the gray two-piece short set that matched mine. She wore slides to match. I imagined her wobbling beside me in a few short months as she carried my seed everywhere we went until I could hold him in my arms myself. Even the thought got me excited.

"The truck is this way," she redirected me, but I still managed to pull her in the opposite direction.

"I got something to show you right quick."

She followed me around the driveway and toward the back of the house where the garage was. I'd already let it up while we were inside waiting. When we rounded the corner and she saw the wrapped Mercedes Sprinter, her eyes widened with joy. Ever's forward movement halted as she turned back to look at me. I couldn't hide my own joy even if I wanted to.

"Baby?" Her voice cracked as she tried hiding her face.

"Cry baby." I chuckled, mocking her. "Baby."

She took off in the opposite direction so that I couldn't see her emotional battle, but I was right behind her. The girls were already checking out the van, leaving us to ourselves. I ran behind Ever, only stopping when she did. And when she turned and fell into my arms, my chest sank. Her face was buried in my chest as she cried body-rocking tears. There was more sadness to her moment than joy, and I couldn't help but pick up on it.

"Hey. Hey. What's the matter?"

I brought her face up, lifting her chin from my shirt with a finger.

"Any time something good happens to me, something bad always follows. I want to be so happy right now, but I can't help but wonder what is about to happen to shake up my world."

"Nothing is going to happen to any of us. And if it does, we will worry about that when we get to it. For now, you are going to get every-fucking-thing you deserve. I'll damn near empty the bank to make sure you do. Don't cry. Celebrate! You imagined your Sprinter and now it's reality for you. Go check that motherfucker out because my stomach is touching my back right now."

I kissed her forehead and then her lips. We turned toward the van and headed back in that direction. For the next ten minutes, we checked out all the gadgets, the wrapping, and the interior. It wasn't complete on the inside, but I wanted her to be the one to give instructions on that. I didn't know what the fuck I was doing.

"Thank you, baby."

"Always," I responded to another woman other than my sister for the first time.

"I'm ready now."

"Look at you, eyes puffy, nose red, and shit."

"Shut up. Let me get Emorey's seat."

While I put the girls in the truck, she grabbed Emorey's car seat from her car. I made a mental note to ask if she'd chosen her ride yet. The building and apartment she'd already selected, and I was working on the building already. I was digging her independence but that car had to go.

"Come on, Emorey," Ever called out to Em, who was up in the front with me, playing like she was driving.

When she heard her mother call out to her, she climbed to the back and allowed Ever to strap her down. I leaned over and opened the passenger door as she rounded the truck. I held out my arm to assist with her entry. Once she was strapped in, we took off and headed for Maple Berries Brunch House, a spot that I frequented before I went in.

Ever remained silent until we reached our destination. Her desire for physical contact remained as she kept her hand wrapped around my arm the entire ride. I didn't take offense to her silence. I knew that there was some processing that had to be done.

Shit, I was even wondering if I was taking her too fast

and if I needed to scale back on the purchases I was making until she was a bit more comfortable. My intentions would never be to overwhelm her, no matter how bad I wanted her to have the world. It wasn't until we were seated and had ordered our drinks that she finally spoke again.

"I'm ready," she proclaimed.

"Ready for what, Ever?" I wanted more details.

"For whatever your heart desires for me that don't directly disregard my boundaries or at least take them into consideration."

"Today, I'd like to go to the dealership and get you in a new whip."

"Okay," she agreed, plain and simple.

"I'd also like to get you in your new apartment by the end of the week."

"Okay."

"Within the next six weeks, I want to have your space functional but in the meantime, I want to bring you some customers."

"OK."

"Did you make the business cards and shit?"

"I did. I just have to go pick them up."

"We can do that before we go to the lot and pass them motherfuckers out everywhere we go."

"Anything else?"

"I want you to relax. You're fucking with a man, now. I got you."

"It's easier said than done." She sighed, finally sitting back in her seat.

"It'll take some time but you'll get there. Trust me on it."

"I do. I do trust you. That's what scares me." Ever shook her head, visibly shaken by her own revelation.

When we walked through the doors of the same Mercedes dealership that I'd purchased her Sprinter from with a sleeping Emorey and Essence in my arms, my day had been made. Ever was willing to release the hold her past had on her and allow me to do as I pleased to upgrade her life in ways that the average woman only witnessed on the television screen.

But this wasn't fiction for her. It was real fucking life and for the rest of her life. She knew it and so did I. That's why I didn't mind spending money on her. The shit that I wanted to do for her didn't even put a small dent in my pocket. I'd spend the rest of my days showering her with love, compassion, support, and anything our hearts desired for her to have.

"You see something you like?"

"Ummm. Hmmm."

"What?"

"The GLE." She pointed with a smile.

She had splendid taste. It was the perfect sophisticated mom truck, with all the bells and whistles she'd need to feel like the fucking boss she was about to be.

"Good fucking choice, baby."

SIXTEEN

EVER

I STARED at the clock for the hundredth time as I listened for the lock on my front door to turn. The apartment was dead silent, just the way I liked it on the nights that Luca told me he was coming over. I wanted to hear him the very moment he approached so that I could pounce on him the moment he came in. It didn't matter how much time we spent together, it was the time apart that got to me the most. Some days we didn't see each other at all and those were the hardest. Our time together was split between his home and mine, and it had been that way since I'd moved in almost two months ago.

In those two months, Luca had made me smile so much that I'd cracked the sides of my lips at least once a week. I had finally gotten used to my new car, and the girls were enjoying their summer. Sundays were reserved for quality time without the girls. They were always with my mother from Saturday night until Sunday night.

During that time, we sexed in every position and in every corner of the house. He fucked me and he fed me and sometimes, we took a day trip to a near city and enjoyed a new scenery. There was always something up Luca's sleeve on Saturday night or Sunday. It was always thrilling to see what he had in store for us next.

Life for me was evolving so beautifully. My space wasn't quite finished yet, but my van was, and I received a new cake order every day. Some days, I'd get two calls and those days always led me to celebrate. Though the front of my space was still being prepared for customers, the kitchen was complete. It's where I'd made my last eight cakes, and I loved every moment of it. I'd gotten my license to produce food from my bakery that others could consume and was waiting for Code Enforcers to come check out the place. Once they approved everything, I'd be ready to hit the ground rolling. Renovations would only take another two weeks.

He's here, I thought as I heard his key enter the door and turn the lock. The top lock was always left unlocked for that particular reason. He was always welcomed. Not locking the top so that he could get in was my invitation.

My brows hiked and heart rate sped as I pulled myself from beneath the sheets and pressed my back against the wall. His footsteps grew louder with each second. My heart threatened to burst when I heard his keys hit the kitchen counter. I loved that sound so much. It had become my favorite.

The smile that I wore when he rounded the corner quickly faded when he entered my lowly lit bedroom. The city's lights served as my bedroom's backdrop, my floor-to-ceiling windows mimicking the ones at Luca's place.

"Has it come yet?" Luca asked as soon as he walked in the door.

"What? Why is there a dog in my house?"

"Has it come yet?"

"No. But, why, Luca?"

"Because I thought the girls might like him. They've been saying they want a pet."

"You've been saying they need a pet. They haven't been saying anything."

"You think they'll like him?"

"Luca. Can you get that thing out of my house?"

"Why? You don't like him?"

"I don't like dogs, period. End of story."

"He staying at my house, anyway. He goes to training camp Monday and won't be back for three weeks."

"Good."

"But your shit hasn't came?"

"No."

He was referring to my cycle. He'd been on a mission to get a little Luca out of me since the first time he'd entered me. I'd be lying if I said I wasn't onboard. I loved the idea of sharing a child with him. He was so good with the girls that I knew he'd be great with a new addition. I'd met his father, and he'd had a great role model coming up. I understood why becoming the girls' father figure was like second nature to him.

"What day is this?"

"Day two. I'm only two days late."

"You think you're pregnant yet? Or just late?" He was all nerves and it was the cutest thing ever.

"I was late last month so it could be another one of those or maybe I am. I wouldn't doubt it, Luca. All of your cum goes right into my vagina."

"You don't be complaining when I'm letting off in you," he sassed.

"And I'm not complaining now."

"You want to make a doctor's appointment?"

"No. I really don't. If I am pregnant, I don't want to see the inside of a doctor's office. I want a doula, and I want a midwife. I want a home birth and all that jazz. If I'm pregnant, we will know after my period doesn't come for a month or so. Then we can move accordingly."

"I think you're pregnant, baby. There's just something different about you, and I know it's because you're carrying my seed. You even feel different when I slide up in you."

"I'm not disagreeing, Luca. I think I am, too."

"Can he stay the night? I bought him a little pin to stay in and some puppy pads. They're out in the hallway. I knew you'd be tripping, and I thought you'd put our asses out."

"Oh, I definitely want to, but I missed you today, and

I know the girls will be so happy to see whatever he is when they wake up."

"He's a tri-color French Bulldog."

"I'd be lying if I said I cared or if I said I know what you mean. Just go get his stuff set up and come lay down with me. I want to touch your skin."

Cuddling with Luca was everything. His large frame always felt so good against my petite one. His protective nature made it even more enjoyable because I felt like while in his arms I could conquer the world.

"Give me five minutes, and I'll be back. Don't fall asleep on me."

"Have you showered?"

"Yeah. At the house before I came."

"OK."

Getting in my bed before showering was off limits. I didn't care if it was Luca's money that purchased it. I hated the stench of outside and hated clothing that had caught every particle the wind had blown to be near my sheets.

I waited impatiently and silently for Luca to return. I listened to every move he made as he got the pup settled into his home for the night. As much as I wanted to turn the little fella around and send him away, I couldn't deny the fact that he was so stinking cute.

"What if I am pregnant, Luca? You just bought a dog. That just feels overwhelming already, and we don't even know if we are yet."

"If so, he'll be damn near a year when the baby comes. He will be well-behaved. That's why he's going to school. If it ends up being too much for you to handle, I'll keep him at my parents' house. That's where my last dog lived most of his life."

"What happened to him?" I remembered it being the only picture on his Instagram profile. Now there were only pictures of the girls and me he shared with his eighty-three followers.

"Cancer."

"Wow. That's insane. I've heard it could happen, but never knew an owner with a pet that actually died from cancer."

"Yeah. He lived a good life though so I wasn't tripping. I just hate it happened while I was away."

"Is this why you've decided to get another dog?"

"Yeah. I'm a dog lover, Ever. You won't ever see me go too long without one."

"Well, you'd better train this one really good, or he will be packing his things and moving to your parents' home. I can live my entire life without an animal and I'd be just fine. Now come on. Let me touch you."

He was too far away. I wanted him close so that I could finally close my eyes and drift into a deep sleep. As he made his way to the bed, he undressed in stride. I watched as he unclothed himself, stripping down to his briefs before climbing in bed and on top of me.

"I'm tired, Ever," he admitted, leaning down and kissing my lips.

"Then let's get some rest," I advised, pulling him in for another kiss.

I turned on my side as he got comfortable behind me.

When his hand went around my waist and he pulled me even closer, I knew he was at peace. Bringing peace to Luca's world was one of my top priorities because he brought so much to mine. I closed my eyes and waited for the lovely sounds that came from his mouth once he drifted off.

LUCA⋅EVER

"IS THAT TOO HOT?" I asked as I watched Luca lower his feet into the tub of water that sat in front of him.

"Na. It's good," he assured me.

"Me first!" Emorey screamed.

"We can both just do one foot at a time, Emorey. Mommy will help you with yours."

"No. I want do it," Emorey sassed, snatching the toenail clippers away from me.

Her little attitude seemed to get a bit fiercer by the day and the fact that Luca had her back every time was making things even worse.

"Hand me the clippers, Emorey. You'll cut yourself if you do it alone."

"Emorey, I don't think you can handle those alone. Let your mom do this part and then you can do everything else by yourself. I'll make sure. Aight?"

"OK." Even with sad eyes, you could still see the fight in Em. She wanted to protest, but whatever Luca said she listened to. Hell, he was the only one she'd been listening to for almost three months.

The girls and I had decided to give Luca a pedicure. We all thought he could use one. His toenails had grown much too long, and the bottom of his feet could use a good scrubbing. When he rubbed them against me some nights, I cringed. My baby's heels were so rough and flakey that they left crumbs on my sheets sometimes.

The most hilarious thing about it all was that he remembered to lotion his feet more than I did for the most part. I got regular pedicures and thought to invite him but then the personal pedicure idea surfaced. He was excited about it, too. We'd been reminding him all week and it was finally time.

"How far down would you like me to cut them?" I asked, wanting to be sure I didn't cut them too low.

"Cut them motherfuckers off. All the way off. They got me going up a size in my shoes so that my feet are comfortable."

Though I laughed, I didn't find a damn thing funny. Had Luca mentioned the issue beforehand, I would've clipped his toenails a long time ago. They were so long that it looked as if they hurt.

"Why haven't you said anything?"

"I'm saying something now."

"You can be a real a-hole sometimes," I sneered.

"You love it, Ever."

"I do."

There wasn't any denying it. Though we hadn't actually said the words to one another, we both knew exactly what it was between us. I was waiting for the perfect moment though I wasn't exactly sure what Luca was waiting for, but he showed me way better than his words ever could vocalize. It shined through his actions when it came to me and *our* girls.

I hadn't given it much thought but when I did, I was reminded that it was Lyric who always told him and Laike that she loved them. They always replied the same thing. It was never changing.

"Always," they'd shout back at her after she'd admitted to loving them dearly.

I thought it was the cutest thing. One by one, I clipped his toenails so that he could finally get some relief. I instructed Essence on how to do the same. We then cut his cuticles and removed the buildup around them. Once we'd used all the sharp utensils, it was Emorey's turn to join the party.

After, I sat next to Luca while watching the girls make a mess of his at-home pedicure station. We'd brought the works, and they used every single product on his feet. I could admit that he probably needed it. He hadn't had any foot care for over eight years. His toes were in need of some love and care.

When it was finally time to empty the water, all I could do was laugh. It was full of lotions, scrubs, oils, and everything in between. The gunky, discolored mixture looked like it would've stunk but it smelled pretty good. Luca had been forced to lay back while the girls started his facial while I handled emptying the bowl.

He's a good one, I thought as I left them to their madness. Though facials were supposed to be a relaxing time, his would be everything but. With Emorey and

Essence fighting over his head, I was certain the cucumbers they'd put on his eyes would be coming off soon for him to fuss a tad bit to get the girls to cooperate.

I made my way to the kitchen sink and emptied the water from the new pedicure bowl we'd purchased. As I stood there, looking around Luca's kitchen, I couldn't help but consider just how blessed my girls and I were. In a month's time, we'd gone from scarcity to abundance.

And in the last nearly three months of being with Luca, we'd been showered with so much love from him that my only real job in our relationship was reciprocating what he was producing. I'd dreamed of a better situation for Emorey and Essence, and we'd been placed in one the minute we touched down in Channing. From Lyric to my mother to Mrs. Eisenberg to Luca, everyone had our best interest at heart and worked together to make our lives a breeze.

"Thank you, God." My emotions led me to say.

Because my deed was done and I hadn't approved the facial the girls were giving Luca, I made my way upstairs. While on my way, I ended up passing by the new set of supplies Luca had bought for the dog's room. I still wasn't convinced that a dog was a good idea, but I wouldn't have to deal with it much so I wasn't complaining. In three weeks, he'd be leaving training and coming to live with Luca. The only time I'd see him was when I came over, and I was already considering how much less I'd visit.

Decompressing was heavy on my heart as I made it to Luca's bedroom and laid across his bed. Naturally, my hand went to my belly and began making circular movements. We hadn't confirmed my pregnancy but my cycle still hadn't shown up to the party. I found myself a little more tired than usual, and my irritability was at an all-time high. It was obvious to both Luca and me. But until we knew for sure, we weren't sharing the news with anyone.

"Hey," I heard Luca call out as I batted my eyes, trying to adjust to the darkness that surrounded me. Exhaustion had worn me down, and I'd fallen asleep in the same position.

"Hey," I stirred, wiping my eyes as I sat up, "what time is it?"

"It's after ten."

"Oh wow. I need to get the girls ready for bed. Essence has her first day of school tomorrow."

"I know. They're already in bed and resting. We even picked out her first day of school fit. If you ask me, my baby is about to be the flyest first grader in that bitch."

My baby. Hearing him constantly refer to the girls as his tore away at my emotions every time. I'd longed for this type of love for my girls. Though I gave them plenty, they needed a father, and Luca had been stepping up to the plate since before he even got to meet them.

"Let you tell it, your baby is the flyest first grader of all the lands."

"Do we have a hater in the house?" Luca asked, pulling the covers back for us to lie underneath.

"No. Just stating facts. For the record, I think she's the flyest first grader, too."

"Then we can agree on something."

"Ummm hmmmm."

"How are you feeling, mommas?" Luca's tone changed, making it obvious that he was referring to my possible pregnancy. He was aware of the loss of Dylan and wanted to make sure that it didn't happen again, although I'd had two healthy children since.

"I'm fine. I was tired earlier when I came upstairs but now I'm fine."

"Come 'ere," he demanded after he'd slid into bed.

I'd rubbed off on him something awful. Just like me, he wanted to feel my skin against his every chance that he got. At the most random moments, I'd feel his hands caressing me or his skin brushing against mine.

Instead of getting in bed beside Luca, I climbed on top of him. My hormones were raging, and I wanted him inside of me immediately. The bulge in his briefs wasn't a surprise and neither was his hard dick when I removed it and it sprang to life. It popped me right on the stomach.

"He misses me."

"We both do," Luca responded.

I leaned forward and allowed the spit to fall from my mouth and onto the head of his dick. My precision was always commendable when lubricating his rigidness. I lifted the big t-shirt that I wore of his and clutched the extra fabric in my hand. Luca's dick penetrated my pussy with ease, proving what I'd said time and time again. He was made for me. My body was carved and contoured to match his perfectly.

"Ummmmmmmmmm."

Simultaneously, we sighed as I rested on my throne.

My pussy was dripping and ready to milk Luca for every drop of nut that he had. I wouldn't cut him loose until he begged me to and, being that he could go at least two rounds, I knew I had to work my ass off to make that happen.

Luca removed the shirt from over my head, leaving me in the nude as he massaged my tender breasts. I'd always loved them but it seemed as if Luca loved them even more. There wasn't a part of my body that he didn't love. He reminded me of that every day when he slid into me, showered with me, or volunteered to oil my body from head to toe.

"Ride this dick, Ever," Luca encouraged, knowing it was exactly what I planned to do.

LUCA·EVER

"LEMONADE OR WATER?" Luca entered the kitchen with a bottle of water in one hand and lemonade in the other.

"Water." The choice was easy.

We'd dropped the children off at school and had come to the bakery for me to put the final touches on a client's cake. It was Essence's first day so we were all on a natural high. I wanted to head to the bakery to finish up while I had the energy and time. There were a few minor details that still needed to be addressed, but for the most part, everything was complete. I couldn't be happier with the results. When my customer picked up her cake in a few minutes, she'd be the first to visit the storefront.

"You need any help back here?"

"Of course I don't, Luca. But thanks for asking, babe."

Making my cakes was the one thing that required solitude. It was my thing. The thing that I didn't need help with. The thing that truly allowed me to swim in my independence. So, it was therapy for me watching the cake transform from simple batter into a masterpiece.

"You think I'ma fuck your shit up, huh?"

"Never really even thought about it. This is just my sweet spot. It's the only place I can practice my independence, which has been a huge part of my healing. I'm at peace when I'm here, which really has nothing to do with you messing up my cakes. I'm sure you would, though."

"Whatever. I'm about to be in the girls' room watching some shit on TV. If you need me, just holler."

Before he could step out, the bell out front rang. Both of our brows furrowed in confusion. Neither of us was expecting anyone just yet. My customer wasn't coming for another few minutes. Without hesitation, he removed his gun from his waist and held his hand up for me to stay put.

"We have cameras, baby." I reminded him of the system he'd had installed.

Relief washed over his face completely as we both turned toward the split screens that were in the kitchen where I'd always be able to see them. Seeing the skinny middle finger with the long, elegantly designed nail attached made me chuckle a bit.

"Of course." I sighed with a shake of my head.

"Only Lyric's ass," Luca said even though we were both thinking the same thing.

"Please go let your sister in before she has both of our heads."

Luca didn't protest. He headed up front to open the door for Lyric. She'd been complaining about not seeing the girls and me as often, so she popped up on us whenever she got the chance. I missed her too. The four weeks that we'd lived together were unforgettable.

"OK. OK. I like. I like," Lyric praised as she removed the designer shades from her eyes and looked around the bakery.

"Hi, love."

"I'm tired of having to pop up on you. When are we going to hang out? Don't you miss me, too?"

"I really do. You have no idea just how much. But I've been so busy with the girls being out for summer, trying to get this place up and running, being somebody's girlfriend, and making cakes every day. I'm very thankful, but honey, it is a lot."

"Meanwhile, I be at home so bored that I've started knitting. Maybe I'm really getting old."

"Or maybe you need to take your ass outside and find you a nigga!" Luca yelled over his shoulder.

"Oh, shut up. If a nigga wants me, then a nigga will find me. OK!"

"How if you're always in the house?" I asked, genuinely interested in her theory.

"The same way your nigga found you."

"Technically, I was outside when he found me."

"I'm outside right now. Aren't I? I give them a chance, they just don't swing my way."

"Lyric, you probably turning your nose up at every nigga that looks your way," Luca butted.

"And, your point?"

"Not everybody," I whispered, catching Lyric's eye.

"Don't even start," she whispered back.

"My point is, it's time for you to let that shit go and find you a nigga to spend the rest of your days with. I'm trying to have nieces and nephews running around, and Laike ain't no hope."

"He really isn't, huh? He's always in last place."

"Always," Luca agreed. "But on a serious note, it's time."

"I knooooow," Lyric whined. "I just don't feel like going through ten men before the right one comes along. I want to get it right on the first try."

"It might happen that way. Just follow your gut. It'll steer you in the right direction every time. Don't ignore it when it's giving you a warning, either. Or else, you'll end up disappointed. Trust me, I know," I told her.

"I did not come here for an intervention."

"Well, too fucking bad."

"Luca." Shaking my head, I chuckled.

"I'm gone to the back."

"Bye!" Lyric shouted behind him.

Once he was out of earshot, I put down the strawberries that were going on the cake and really looked at her.

"He's right, Lyric."

"I know, but he doesn't have to know that."

"Well, I know and I'm telling you that there is a really great man just waiting for you to be the woman of his dreams, and I'm not a fool. I saw the way you reacted to that guy Ken at the mall a few months back."

"Yeah, but that would never happen. He's their best friend. He's known me since I was a kid."

"And?"

"Have you met Laike and Luca?"

"I have."

"Then that's the end of that. Besides, he doesn't look at me that way. He sees me as a sister."

"Lyric. I saw the way he looks at you and it ain't like no damn sister."

"I didn't see it."

"Because you didn't want to."

"Whatever. What are y'all eating? It smells good."

"Leftovers. Luca made fish and spaghetti last night. We have plenty if you want to heat up some."

"Sure do. And, look at y'all. All in love and stuff. I love this for you."

"I'd love it for you, too. What's been up?"

"Nothing. I put in my two weeks' notice. It's time to kiss that $100k a year goodbye. It funded my shopping habits but with Luca home, the family needs me a little bit more."

"I might be needing you, too. It seems like this business will blow up before I can truly wrap my head around the concept. I need to know where my money is going and how to reinvest it back into the business. I also need help pricing my cakes so that I'm getting my energy's worth in addition to production cost."

"You know I'm the girl for all things numbers. Do you have a list of the cakes you've already made and their prices?"

"Yeah. I have a picture beside them too so that it's easy to remember what I charge."

"What about how much time it takes?"

"I document that too."

"Good. How much money do you want to make per hour? Like, if you were at your dream job, how much would you be compensated for your time?"

"Fifty to sixty dollars an hour."

"Good, we'll go with seventy-five. Send me the list, and I will create a spreadsheet for you. Have you finished the website yet?"

"Not yet. I wanted to finalize the pricing before I did so that I didn't have to go back and change them. I have all the photos and everything else ready to go. Luca bought me a new camera."

"What about the business Instagram?"

"I'm still not ready for that. Not with the whole Dewayne situation still lingering."

"Don't let him stop your money."

"I don't plan to, but using my whole name for an account is like handing him my information myself. The page would have all the bakery's details."

"Have you talked to Luca about this?"

"No."

"Well, I think you should. He could tell you how to

move forward, but I'm sure it'll be with the social media accounts. That's how most people find services these days, hashtags."

"Yeah. I know."

"I'm going to grab me some food. I'm starving. Where is it?"

"Already in the microwave. Just grab a plate and fill it. You'll have to warm it up."

"OK."

I picked up the strawberries to resume my cake decorating, but kept Lyric's words circling in my head. Luca and I had tiptoed around the Dewayne topic, mostly because I wasn't ready to have the real conversation yet. But as more time passed and my mental and emotional scars began to fade, I knew it was coming.

SEVENTEEN

EVER

BAISLEIGH'S HOUSE was like home to me. I was there dropping off a new cake at least once a week. True to her word, she'd passed out my cards to her customers and was continuing to do so even months later. Because of her, I'd gotten most of my clientele. My bakery was ready for pickups, but I'd already scheduled the delivery for a customer who was having a birthday brunch at Baisleigh's weeks in advance.

"Oh, this is nice." She admired the two-tier gold cake with speckles of white. The simple design was so eye-catching.

"She's going to love this."

"What time is her brunch?"

"It's in an hour. We're about to close the section now and get the balloon arches brought out. What's been going on with you this week?" Baisleigh was forever doing a wellness check, and I appreciated her for that.

"The bakery is ready. I'm not ready for a grand opening or anything, yet, but I can finally service customers in the shop and have them pickup if they'd like. I'm almost ready to hire a delivery driver, but I'm not quite there yet."

"With the amount of brunches I have coming this fall you will be soon. People are going to be ready to come inside instead of being outside once that Channing cold hits."

"With the Channing heat, I don't understand how they're outside anyway."

"Me either," she agreed.

"I have another brunch happening on the twenty-eighth of next month. She ordered the package that includes a cake, too. I haven't gotten the details."

Baisleigh was all about business and collaboration over competition. She added a custom cake option to her brunch options that her customers could choose. And for the ones who said they'd just get their own cake, she referred a cake lady who happened to be me. Either way, it was me who was responsible for the cakes in the end. It was a win-win for me.

"When you get them, just let me know. I'm going to get out of your hair. I have some work to do."

"Let me walk you out," she insisted, coming from around her desk.

We both stepped out onto the main floor and headed for the door. The smell of freshly cooked bacon usually made my stomach growl, but I was trying my hardest not to barf. I rushed toward the exit so that I could free myself from the fumes, leaving Baisleigh in the dust.

"Call me!" I turned around and shouted as I opened the door. Before I could get the breath of fresh air I craved, I walked straight into someone's chest.

"My bad, baby girl," the familiar voice spoke.

I tried to place it but nothing came to me immediately. It wasn't until I looked up and saw the dark line across his handsome face that I recognized Scar. It had been months since I'd seen him, but his voice was unforgettable. It was as dark and cold as he was.

"Ever?" he asked, already knowing the answer.

"Uh. Hi."

"What's good?"

"I'd love to stay and chat, but my flight leaves in an hour. It was nice seeing you, Scar."

I didn't stick around to listen to his reply. Neither did I care to hear it. I was too focused on my visibly trembling body from the lie I'd just told and running into someone that was so well-connected to my past. He and Dewayne had always been thick as thieves, and at one point, they were thieves.

Scar had always shown me nothing but respect, even more than Dewayne, and he wasn't the man I was in a relationship with. Yet, that didn't stop me from believing that within the next ten minutes, Dewayne would know my location. That was the point of the lie I'd told, and I hoped it stuck with him. Visiting Channing wouldn't be unlikely for me in the event that Dewayne did hear that I was in town. I just prayed that Scar didn't leave out the little detail about my flight.

FUCK! I thought as I rushed through the sun's heat to my Sprinter. Baisleigh had finally gotten some trees on the edges of the parking lot. It didn't matter how far away they were, for once I was thankful for the walk. With the parking lot being so big and full all the time, it made it hard to see exactly where I was headed. That meant it was highly unlikely that Scar saw the van when I got inside.

Calm down, Ever. Calm down. Luca was the first person who came to mind, but before I called him, I wanted to make sure that I had a leveled head and my emotions were in check. When I felt the fresh hot tears on my face, I knew it wasn't smart to dial his number. I would only scare him about something that was practically out of either of our control at this point. All we could do was wait it out.

You're okay, I coached. Seeing just how shaken I was by encountering someone from my past let me know I wasn't healing as well as I'd imagined. I was living and thriving, which kept me from dealing with the trauma of my past instead of healing from it. I felt like I was back at square one, only this time I wasn't afraid. This time, I had someone beside me who would make sure that I was safe at the end of the day.

Yet and still, I wanted to continue the peaceful run I'd been on for the last three and a half months. My girls hadn't heard an argument since the day I left their father. The toxicity that he brought to their world ended when we made it to Channing. They were living in peace and harmony. Dewayne would only fuck that up for us all.

As much as I wanted to act like he didn't exist, he shared their blood. I hated that for them and for me. He didn't deserve such perfection. Luca had loved those little girls enough for a lifetime in the short time he'd been in their lives. *He* was their father. Not Dewayne. It didn't matter what the DNA said.

I rubbed my sweaty palms against my black leggings, trying to find relief from the elevation of my body's temperature. My world felt like it was spinning. Hyperventilating with tears running down my cheeks, I counted down from twenty.

Nineteen.

Eighteen.

Seventeen.

Sixteen.

Before I reached fifteen, my cell rang, scaring me to the point of leaping from my seat.

Boop!

My head hit the ceiling of the van and began throbbing immediately. Slightly confused, I removed my cell from my bag and checked the caller ID. Eisenberg's Smiles was calling. I felt my mouth drain of all its fluids as I answered the call in haste.

"Hello?" I wiped the tears from my face as I tried focusing on what was being said to me on the call.

"Emorey had an accident on the playground. She

scraped up her knee pretty badly, and we can't get her to calm down. We thought maybe we should call you to come pick her up."

"I'm on my way."

Without hesitation, I started the engine of my Sprinter and pulled out of Baisleigh's parking lot. Of course, I was going to get my Emorey. She needed me, and I definitely needed her. I wished that Essence wasn't at school because I'd be going to get her as well. Though I didn't want to overwhelm or scare the girls by projecting my fears onto them, I felt like I needed them more than ever at the moment.

The twenty-minute drive to Emorey's school only took me fifteen minutes. I used that time to calm my nerves and try to piece myself back together. For five minutes, I'd fallen completely apart.

I'd barely parked the van when I pulled into the parking lot of Emorey's school and jumped out. I left the engine running because I wouldn't be long. The closer I got to Emorey, the better I felt. I marched right past the receptionist's desk and headed for her classroom. When I entered and found over ten smiling faces and none of them belonging to my baby, panic set in.

"Where is she?"

"Her dad got her already."

The blood drained from my body as the words left her teacher's mouth. My chest tightened, and my legs weakened as I tried to form the correct words to convey my message. I couldn't. The aching of my heart and losing my breath didn't allow me to.

He's here. My thoughts crippled me. As Dewayne's face flashed before my eyes, I became immobile. I could not move and neither could I say a word. As much as I wanted to scream, I just couldn't. Nothing would come out.

"Is everything OK?" Ms. Debra, her teacher, asked after I'd stared at her for a few seconds, trying to gather myself. Trying to regain my composure. Trying to regain movement in my limbs. Once I was able to, I sprinted out the door and headed to the van where my cell phone was. I had a call to make and it was one I should've made the minute I saw Scar at Baisleigh's, but I was too shaken up to do so.

I was out of the door and headed down the stairs with one person on my mind other than my Emorey. But before I could make it to the truck to grab my phone and call him, I heard his voice in the distance. There was no other explanation for his precision other than the fact that he was my soulmate. I didn't need to call him because he was already near.

"Ever!"

"LUCA!" I cried, turning away from the van and searching for him.

I could hear him calling my name, but I wasn't sure where he was. When I closed the door, I finally saw him, and he wasn't the only person I saw.

"Mommy," Emorey's little voice cracked as she ran toward me. "I hurt my weg."

"Come here, baby," I begged Emorey, kneeling with my arms stretched so that she could limp into them.

Seeing her immediately released me from the shackles. *Her daddy*, I replayed her teacher's words when I walked into the room and didn't see her face on the carpet. Luca. He hadn't crossed my mind, but that should've been the first person I thought of. Had it been any other day it would've been the case, but after seeing Scar, I wasn't sure what to think about anything. I wasn't sure if Dewayne was somewhere lurking or if he was just in town himself.

"Ever," Luca called out to me.

"What?" I snapped my neck in his direction, fuming.

"What you mean what?" he questioned, not understanding where the strife was coming from.

"Why would you take her from school without my permission?"

"I need your permission to take Emorey for ice cream to make her feel better? Since when?"

"At least you could've called and told me!"

"She was having a fit about her knee when I walked in to holler at my mother so I took her with me. I didn't think it would be a big fucking deal."

"Well, it is."

"To who though?"

"To me!"

"Ever, you've got to figure your shit out. One minute you want me in their mix and the next you're telling me I can't take my baby to get ice cream to help her feel better? Come on, now. What sense are you making? This is me you're talking to."

"We're leaving, Luca. Next time, ask before just

taking off with her. I almost had a fucking heart attack when the teacher told me someone had taken her. You'll never understand!"

I couldn't control my emotions. My hormones were kicking my ass. Before I was able to close the door in Luca's face, he caught it with his hand.

"Ayo, you need to chill the fuck out."

"No, you chill the fuck out. You're wrong. That's the end of the story."

"I ain't even did shit, but aight. And get ready because I'm taking you to the fucking doctor tomorrow. The only reason I'm letting this shit slide is because this shit got to have something to do with pregnancy. 'Cause right now, you're fucking tripping and I ain't feeling it."

"Let go of my door, Luca."

"Don't play with me, Ever. I'll break this motherfucker and make you ride home with me until you cool the fuck down."

"Goodbye!" I yelled in his direction.

The sadness in his eyes left my heart aching. When he slammed the door and walked toward his truck, I used the opportunity to get out of dodge. I didn't want to chance him changing his mind and turning around.

Checking the clock on my phone, I noted the time. There were two more hours left before Essence would be let out of school, but I couldn't wait that long. I needed her in my sight immediately. Waiting would only cause me more stress.

I headed to my bakery to switch vehicles. Emorey and I made the exchange as quickly as possible. She'd finished the cone just before we hopped in because she knew that there was no eating allowed. I double-checked to make sure everything was locked up from the app. There was not even a possibility that I'd be returning before the day ended. I pulled off with Essence as my destination.

EIGHTEEN

EVER

"YOU SURE YOU don't want me to lay her down?" my mother asked me for the third time.

"No. She's fine."

I didn't want to let Emorey out of my sight. Her presence was bringing me the small amount of peace that I'd be getting for a while. I'd experienced so much in the last few months that something deep in my bones was telling me it had come to an end. It wouldn't be much longer before all hell broke loose.

My thoughts drifted toward Luca. The disappointment that flashed across his face as I spoke to him stuck with me. I'd been rude and disrespectful to the man who had been nothing but a blessing to me. Instead of running into his arms for the safety and protection I knew he could provide, I lashed out at him and ran in the opposite direction.

"Okay, well can you at least tell me what's going on?"

"A lot, Mom. A lot."

"Okay, well you're here so you must feel like I should know."

She was right. That's exactly how I felt. When there was no place else I felt welcomed, it was in my mother's arms. It was her I ran to, which was why I'd come as soon as I picked up Essence from school.

"I saw Scar."

"Okay, who is Scar and why is seeing him important?"

"Scar is Dewayne's best friend."

There was a brief moment of silence before she continued.

"And what did he say?"

"Nothing really. I rushed past him and told him that my flight would be leaving in an hour. You know how much I hate lying, but I had to think of something in case he goes back to tell Dewayne. I know he will."

"Is he here alone?"

"That's something I don't know either and what's killing me. Because what if it's actually Dewayne that he's in Channing with? He travels often so his presence in another city isn't unusual but Channing of all places? What are the odds?"

"Have you talked to Luca about this?"

My mother was in love with Luca. She'd met him on

several occasions and even managed drop-offs and pickups for the girls with him. She had never seen a man treat her daughter with so much respect and love me so openly until she met Luca. While she was praying for our union, I was making a mess of it.

"That's another thing. I fought with him instead of confiding in him. Now, I'm hurt that I probably hurt him."

"How? Ever, what have you done?"

My eyes pricked as I leaned my head back on the pillow of the couch. I was so ashamed of my actions that I didn't even want to share what I'd done with my mother. However, I knew she wouldn't judge me. She'd only tell me how to move forward and learn from my mistakes.

"I yelled at him and was really rude."

"What? *YOU?*" appalled, she asked. It was so out of character for me, but I only had my misplaced emotions to blame.

"Yes, and outside of Emorey's school at that."

"Ever. Come on now, baby."

"Mom, I know."

"Tell me what happened?"

"It was right around the time I'd seen Scar that I got the call from the school saying that Emorey had fallen. I rushed over to get her and when I got in her class, I didn't see her. I asked her teacher where she was and she said that her daddy had already gotten her. The first person that came to mind was Dewayne! Luca never even crossed my mind."

"But, don't you have it in the paperwork to not let him get either of them?"

"Yes, but that didn't cross my mind either. All I was thinking was that Dewayne had come and took my baby. I was paralyzed immediately. I couldn't speak and I couldn't move. When I finally came to, I rushed back outside to get my cell and call Luca. Before I could, he was calling my name in the parking lot. When I turned around to tell him what was happening, I saw Emorey beside him, and I just flipped out."

"What did you say?"

"He needed my permission to take her anywhere and some other stuff I don't even remember. All I know is that I was mean to him, and I can't stop thinking about it."

"Well, it's a good thing that Emorey is OK. I know you are going through it right now but before the night is over, you have to apologize to that man and tell him what's going on. He will understand why you reacted that way. Hell, even I understand but he won't know unless you tell him. Now, I have to go put my cornbread in the oven."

My mother stood from the other end of the couch and stretched. There was something else I had to share with her, though. I didn't want her to leave so soon.

"But, there's more."

"More?" She sighed, sitting back down. "What else is it, Ever?"

"I'm pregnant," I revealed.

"You're what?"

"Pregnant."

"I'd say you move fast, but I've seen Luca and I don't blame you, honey. I would've been pregnant day one. That man is a gift from God, him and that brother of his. I'd swear they were twins if I didn't know any better."

"No. Seriously. They're two years apart and look identical. It's insane."

"No, it's not. Have you seen your children?"

"Well, you do have a point there."

"Does Luca know about the pregnancy?"

"Yes. Well, we've both suspected it for some time now we just haven't confirmed it. But I know my body and there's nothing a test can tell me I don't already know."

"How far along are you?"

"I've only missed one period so somewhere between six and eight weeks I'm assuming. Last month, my period was extremely light and late. It only lasted two and a half days, which could've been my first sign of pregnancy. I don't know."

"Well, again, I don't blame you. Not one bit. And, I'm very, very happy for you, Ever."

"Thanks, Mom."

"Try having a boy this time. I love my girls, but James needs a buddy now. He's tired of us women crowding his space. He's been secretly wishing for a boy from you for years."

"Tell him he might just get his wish, then, because I have a strong feeling that this one is indeed a boy. Luca wants a son, too."

"I'm sure going to pray on it. You staying for dinner?"

"Yes. I'm staying until I feel a little better. Right now I'm a wreck. I don't want to be home alone."

"You don't have to be but you're being stubborn right now."

"I know, but we both need time to cool off right now. Things got a little heated earlier."

"Alright. Whatever you say. Dinner will be ready in a few minutes. I'll be in the kitchen if you need me."

This time, I allowed my mother to leave my presence and head into the kitchen. The smell of her smothered liver, brown rice, and corn on the cob made my stomach growl. I was hungry just thinking about the food I was going to pile on my plate. It had been years since I'd eaten liver, but I had every intention of making up for lost time. It used to be one of my favorites.

LUCA·EVER

BETWEEN DINNER AND COMFORT, I was unable to fight the sleep that kept knocking for me to answer. I laid out on the couch in the living room watching television with James and the next thing I knew, I was waking up to a chiming phone and darkness surrounding me.

"Hello?" I answered, recognizing Luca's contact almost instantly.

"What you doing?" My heart ached as I heard the sadness in his voice. Just like I missed him, he missed me too.

"Laying down."

"Where? Because I'm at your apartment and you're not here."

I melted. Luca was at my place, and I was miles away on my mother's couch. He'd come to me even after our spat, ready to love me through my bullshit. My eyes blurred as I thought of the words to say to him.

"I'm on my mother's couch."

"And I'm in your bed. Get the girls ready. I'm coming to get y'all."

"No. It's fine. I can drive."

"You're crying and it's late."

"Because I'm pregnant," I confessed.

"I know, baby." Luca responded in his usual, calm manner.

"And I was so mean to you."

"It's aight. I'm not laying down, pissed, so you're not allowed to either. Bring your ass home so that we can talk about this shit. There's more to the story than you being pissed about me taking my baby to get ice cream, Ever."

"There is."

"Okay and you've got all night to explain that. Come 'ere."

"I love you, Luca," I admitted for the very first time, wiping the tears that constantly fell from my eyes.

"Forever," he responded before hanging up the phone.

I lifted my shirt from around my waist and wiped my face with it. Before I hit the road, it was imperative that I cleaned up my act. Otherwise, I'd be putting the girls' lives in danger as well as my own. I couldn't have that. Luca would not approve and neither did I.

"Essence. Emorey?"

Though I couldn't see them, I could hear their little voices coming from the kitchen. I followed them until I reached my unofficial twins. They were up eating ice cream with my mom and James.

"Really? It's nine o'clock. Why does everyone have ice cream in their hands?"

No one said anything. They all just looked at me like I was the crazy one. With a shake of my head, I opened the fridge and grabbed a dipped cone, too. I wasn't going to be the only one missing out on the fun.

"Alright, girls. It's time to go home. Go grab your things and let's get out of here."

They both took off down the hallway laughing.

"Hey, Ever. Your mom tells me it's a possibility that clown might be aware of your whereabouts," James said to me, the concern obvious on his aging skin.

"It's possible, but I'm not sure yet. If he does, he will surface soon. I just hope that isn't the case."

"Me either but if he come fucking with us, I'm going to gladly put a bullet in his ass like I've always wanted to."

"I don't condone violence, but please do. He has no business even near y'all's house."

"I was thinking that we should all get restraining orders against him."

"That ain't shit but a piece of paper. I got something to restrain his ass."

"Oh Lord," my mother complained.

"What? I'm just telling it like it is."

"He's right," I agreed. "I'm going to talk to Luca about everything tonight and we will go from there. I'll call you guys in the morning before you're off to work, James."

"You ain't got to call me. I know what I'm gone do to his ass. Ole ain't shit ass nigga. Ain't worth a damn. God probably ashamed of niggas like him. Just running around causing hell like it's nobody's business, but now it's my business. It's mine, now."

I'd known James long enough to know that he'd be at it for a minute. I wouldn't wait around for him to finish his tantrum. The girls and I were going to head to the door as soon as they returned. I nibbled at my ice cream until they did.

By the time we made it to the truck, I was almost finished with it. Though I hated eating in the car, I couldn't stand the thought of tossing it so I didn't. Both Emorey and Essence had finished theirs before coming outside. For that, I was thankful.

"You girls buckled in and ready to go?" I looked in my rearview mirror at their smiling faces and asked.

"Yes, ma'am," Essence responded.

"Yup," Emorey replied.

Of course, she was the ruthless one. She didn't care what came out of her little mouth. Though I wanted to let her have it sometimes, I loved her spunk. She was the feistiest of the two, and I lived for her shenanigans sometimes. Tonight was one of those times.

"Alright. Let's go."

I'd always loved my mother's neighborhood. It wasn't the one I'd grown up in, but it still felt like home. Years before I moved away from Channing, she and James had purchased their home. Their block was extremely quiet and had some of the most beautiful, middle-class dwellings in all of Channing.

How you ain't say you was moving forward?
Honesty hurts when you're getting older.
I gotta say I'll miss the way you need me
Yeaaaaaa

I sang along to SZA's "20 Something" as I tried clearing my head of the millions of thoughts that were flowing through it. I felt like I'd had the day from hell, and I honestly just wanted it to be over already. Luca was at my home ready to make amends, and I couldn't wait until he swallowed me with his warm embrace and love.

I'd apologize until I turned blue in the face to show him just how sorry I really was. I had projected my bullshit onto him without warning, which was so unfair. Seeing Scar had thrown me completely off my square, and I had yet to recover when everything with Emorey went down. I needed to explain that to Luca. That and everything else that was happening in my world at the moment.

How you ain't say you were getting bored?
Beep.

The familiar beeping sounded in the background, causing me to look up on my dashboard and at my gas hand. I cringed at the thought of stopping by the gas station, but I refused to chance the twenty miles that were left in my tank. My apartment was sixteen miles away. There was no way I was testing the mileage or playing so closely to a disastrous end. I'd needed gas on the way to my mother's, but assumed I'd leave early enough to stop sooner.

We were nearing the expressway and almost out of the neighborhood, which meant there would be gas stations galore. Turn for turn, my eyes darted between the road and the gas mileage. Though it had barely changed because we hadn't even made it far enough, I still kept an eye on it. I didn't want any surprises.

Finally, out of the neighborhood, we stumbled upon three gas stations. The task wasn't finding one. It was choosing one. I decided on the closest and on the same side that we were on and pulled into the parking lot. I pulled up to one of the pumps closest to the gas station entrance and slid out with my card already in my hand.

"Stay put girls. I'm just going to step out and pump the gas, alright?"

"OK."

Emorey couldn't respond because she'd already fallen asleep. My little baby was out for the count. She could never hang. The princess definitely needed her beauty rest. My Essence, however, was always up for the adventure.

"Be right back, Es."

"Yes, ma'am."

I circled the truck and made my way to the pump. My card slid into the small slot with ease. I waited for the screen to request its details, but instead, it insisted I went inside to see the cashier. I felt like my day was still doomed as I knocked on the window that Essence was closest to. She rolled it down and waited for me to give her instructions.

"Lock the doors. I need to go in and pay for the gas. Is there anything you want out of here?"

"A bag of hot chips. Can I have that?"

"Of course you can."

Essence was the sweetest and always had been. She reminded me much of the present me. She was the chillest kid one would ever meet. Essence didn't give me any issues. She did what she knew she was supposed to and kept out of trouble.

"Make sure you get Em something. Or else she'll be upset when she wakes up."

Just like me, she was always putting other's feelings before her own. Emorey would definitely fuss if she didn't get anything out of the store but I didn't need Essence worried about that. I'd worry about Little Miss Feisty.

"Don't I know." I laughed. "Roll up the window and lock the door. Stay away from the front seat."

I absolutely hated going inside of the gas station when I didn't have to, and I hated it even more when the broken card system on the pump was the reason. *See Cashier* were two words that made me cringe when they popped up on the screen because I'd use the same card in the store to get the gas that I was trying to get outside. It made no sense.

Ding. Dong.

The bell sounded to alert the cashier that a new customer had walked in. My first stop was the chip aisle where I grabbed Essence a bag of hot chips and Emorey a bag of Cheetos Puffs. When I made it to the counter, the cashier had his face planted in his phone.

"Uh. Um." I cleared my throat to get his attention.

"My bad. Will this be all for you?" He grabbed the chips from my hand and started ringing them up.

"Uh, no. Actually, I need eighty on pump..." I started, but then stopped to look back at the pump to find out exactly what pump I was on.

Because I couldn't see over the large racks, I was forced to get a little closer to the door. The swift movement near my truck caught my attention. My brows furrowed as my eyes squinted, trying to figure out what was happening. When I saw both Emorey and Essence's tiny figures being loaded into the black Yukon that I was far too familiar with, my heart sank.

I pushed the door to the store open as my vocal cords completely shut down on me. The screams that were in my head simply didn't come through my mouth. As fast as I could, I put one foot in front of the other, speeding through the parking lot to get to my girls. By the time I'd made it to my vehicle, they'd already been stuffed into the other truck.

"HELP!" I found my voice. "HELP!"

WHAM! Dewayne's fist slammed into my face, dazing me upon impact. I could feel the blood rush from my nose and mouth instantly as my world began to spin.

Still managing to keep my balance, I ran toward his truck where my girls were.

I didn't make it far. His hands wrapped around my hair. I could feel strand by strand being torn from my head as he pulled me backward and in his direction. Once I was close enough, his arm went around my neck, and he began to squeeze the life out of me. My airway was almost completely restricted. I clawed at his arms, face, and head, trying anything to get him to let me go. He wouldn't. Killing me was his intention.

"If I can't have you, nobody else will. You stupid bitch!"

Those were the only words that came from his mouth before he squeezed even tighter. I managed to shove my thumb into his right eye, forcing him to let me go. Before I could make it to my girls, I felt him grab me by the hair again. This time, he didn't wrap his arm around my neck; he punched me square in the face while holding my hair in his left hand.

WHAM.
WHAM.
WHAM.
WHAM.

With each blow, I could feel my body growing weaker and weaker. My strength was depleted by the time the fifth blow came. My legs turned into mush. As soon as he released my hair, I hit the ground.

Showing no remorse, Dewayne lifted his size twelve shoes and kicked me in the chest. Seeing that there was no stopping him, my motherly instincts kicked in and my only goal was to save the baby growing inside of me. Naturally, I balled up, locking my hands against my stomach so that his blows would not carry as much weight on my abdomen area.

WHAM. Another to the chest.

WHAM. One to the side.

WHAM. One to the back.

WHAM. One to the face.

A kick to the face disabled all my efforts to protect myself or my child. My world began to spin as my sight blurred. Frozen in place, I no longer had the energy to do anything. Tears fell from my eyes as I thought of my children, all three of them. The thought of losing another child pained me. As Dewayne continued to assault my body, I began to slowly lose consciousness. My eyelids were swollen shut, forcing me into darkness. I could hear and feel everything, but I couldn't see anything. My end was near. And with the pain I was feeling, I hoped it was quick.

"Aye, dog! Back the fuck up!" I heard a voice yell as it got closer.

"This ain't yo' fucking business," Dewayne responded.

"It is now!" The sound of a gun being cocked could be heard just a few feet away.

I waited for another blow to the body from Dewayne but I felt nothing. Instead, I heard his steps backpedal as he retreated. Seconds later, I heard screeching tires.

"My... my ki—" was all I made out before everything faded into black.

NINETEEN

LUCA

I LIED awake in Ever's bed, fully clothed with my eyes trained on the circular motion of the ceiling fan. There was only one question on my mind, and I couldn't wait until Ever came home to answer it.

Why did she flip like that? I'd been asking myself all day.

The woman I'd seen in front of my mother's daycare was not the woman I'd been falling in love with over the last three months. She was kind, sweet, and ambitious. The woman I saw earlier looked identical to her but wasn't her. This woman was mean and disrespectful. She'd disrespected my character and the relationship I had with one of the people that meant the most to me in this world.

To say that I was offended would be an understatement. However, I wanted to give Ever some credit. The tear residue on her cheeks and red eyes let me know that something more was going on. I simply needed her to tell me what so that I could help make the situation better.

I checked the time on my phone for the third time. It seemed to fly by, but still no Ever. With it being well after ten and me knowing that it only took twenty minutes to get to her place from her mother's, I decided to try her line.

Brrrrrrrrr.
Brrrrrrrrr.
Brrrrrrrrr.
Brrrrrrrrr.
Brrrrrrrrr.

"Hi, it's Ever. Leave a message, and I'll return your call when I'm free. Peace and blessings."

My chest tightened as my gut began sending signals of distress. There hadn't been a time I'd called Ever and gotten her voicemail. In fact, it was the first time I'd ever heard her voicemail. I didn't know she had one.

Brrrrrrrrr.
Brrrrrrrrr.
Brrrrrrrrr.
Brrrrrrrrr.
Brrrrrrrrr.

"Hi, it's Ever. Leave a message, and I'll return your call when I'm free. Peace and blessings."

Sickness quickly overcame me as I stood to my feet and began pacing the floor. With a hand over my forehead, I tried her phone again. *Maybe she... Maybe it's dead.* I couldn't form a logical thought because the truth was that the sudden aches of my body told me exactly what I needed to know. Something was wrong. I could feel it. I could feel *her*. Feel *them*.

Brrrrrrrrr.

Brrrrrrrrr.

Brrrrrrrrr.

"Yo?"

All hell broke loose in my head the second a nigga's voice appeared on the line.

"Nigga, who the fuck is this?" I barked into my cell.

"Nigga, this Cane."

"Okay, and what the fuck you doing with my bitc— my woman's phone?" I asked, spit particles flying from my mouth as I searched the room for my shoes. Wherever the fuck this nigga was in the city, I'd be there in under ten minutes and that was a promise. I could feel his bones breaking between my fingers as he began to answer my question.

"CANE. I know you're seeing red right now, nigga, but I'm not a fucking opp."

Slowing down once I located my shoes to put them on allowed me to really capture the voice on the other side of the line. Cane wasn't a dummy and would never test me. I'd been feeding Cane since he was sixteen. He was as loyal as they came. His only goal was getting to the money. Everything else was bullshit to him. He had a bright future ahead of him if he continued moving the way he was.

"Fuck! Cane. What the fuck is going on? Where is Ever? Is she aight?"

"I don't know, big homie. I pulled up on a nigga rocking her shit. She fucked up, bro. I hopped in her truck, and I'm on my way to the hospital with her."

"FUCK! FUCK! FUCK!"

Red, thick blood trickled down my knuckles as a result of the hole I'd punched into Ever's bedroom wall. My heart felt like it had been ripped from my fucking chest as I began to struggle to breathe.

"Is she good?"

"Nah, big homie. I can't even hold you."

"FUCK!"

"I'm going as fast as I can. I'm taking her to Huffington Medical. That shit like three minutes away.

"Are the kids alright?"

"The kids?" he questioned. "What kids?"

"Two little girls. Are they not in the truck?"

"Nah. Wasn't no kids in this bitch when I put her in. What kids, fam?" Cane began to panic as he continued to ask. "Kids, Luca? What kids?"

The revelation that my children had been snatched from Ever's care had my blood boiling. I was halfway down the street on foot before I realized my truck would help me get to my destination a lot fucking faster. I doubled back into the parking lot and hopped in. As I started the truck, I explained.

"We have two daughters. They were on the way home with her."

"I swear I didn't see no fucking kids, man. That nigga wouldn't have been able to pull off if I did. Kids, fam? This nigga got your fucking kids? Who is this nigga? Let me put this bitch to bed myself."

"Biologically, they're his," I admitted, cringing at the thought. "Drop her off and put word out on the street. Dewayne Starks is his name. I got a million on his head. Bring him to me alive. This one is mine."

"Say no more." I heard the engine of Ever's GLE roaring as Cane tried getting her to the emergency room. It wasn't surprising that Cane had noticed her in distress. Her license plates read LUCA. I wanted everyone in the city to know that she was off limits, no matter where she was. I also wanted them to know what they'd be getting themselves into if they ever laid a hand on her. Obviously, Dewayne hadn't gotten the message. He would, though. Soon enough.

"Wait. One more thing." I choked off my own words.

"What's up? Talk to me."

"She's pregnant, fam. Tell them she's pregnant." My voice hardened as it cracked from the overflow of emotions following the thought of losing my unborn child.

"Aight."

I ended the call on the way to Huffington Medical. There wasn't a stoplight or stop sign I gave a second thought. Everything was getting run to get to my baby. With blurry, tearful eyes, I dialed Lyric's cell.

"Hello?" I could hear the sleep in her voice as she answered.

"Baby girl." I wept, wiping tears from my eyes with my arm as I tried to steer carefully.

"LUCA?" I could hear ruffling in the background while I tried my hardest to get my shit together.

"I'm going back to jail, baby girl. I'm going to kill this nigga."

"Luca. What's going on?"

"He got my fucking kids, and he beat the shit out of Ever. I'm going to bend this nigga's top the fuck back."

"Luca. Where is Ever? Where are the girls?"

"Ever is on the way to Medical. I don't know where they are, Lyric. This nigga got them!"

"I'm going to meet you at Medical, and I'm calling Laike. Stay on the phone."

There was a brief silence before she returned to the line.

"Big bro!" Laike hollered. "What's up?"

"This nigga has to die, Laike." I couldn't control the parade of wet tears that hit my face each time I wiped them.

In my thirty-six years of living, I couldn't recall a time where I'd shed one. Not even as a kid. Nothing, and I mean nothing, ever bothered my spirit enough to bring me to tears. Life was going to happen regardless and that's how I'd always lived mine. For every action, there would be a reaction. For every issue, there was a solution. For every move, there would be a consequence.

It was plain and simple, black and white with me. Always had been. Not even cuffs locked on my wrist after I'd pushed Chauncey's top back affected me enough. I sat and waited on the police's arrival and made sure that nigga was dead a few times before I called them to come pick his stupid ass up off the ground. When I was sentenced to ten years, I didn't bat an eye. I'd done my dirt and was ready to lie down to get my shit over with.

"Yes. Yes he motherfucking does!" Laike agreed, pure emotion evident in his tone as well.

"Find my girls, Laike."

"I'm already on it. Cane just hollered at me. He's on the way to me."

"Tell that nigga I got him."

"No payment necessary. This nigga heated he let the nigga leave with the kids. He said this one is on the house."

"I'm pulling up. Lyric, get up with her moms. Tell her no police."

"I'm on my way. Be there in five minutes."

We ended the call simultaneously as I exited my truck. I cleaned my face with the bottom of my shirt as I rushed into the emergency exit. Beds lined the walls of the hall that I walked down. I searched every bed that was out in the hallway but came up empty-handed. They'd all been brought in by paramedics.

"Ever Sinclair," I told the receptionist before she could even ask if she could help me.

She began pecking on the computer at her desk. "I'm not sure what the last name is but there was someone just brought in by that name. She was just rushed to the back. There's a team working with her now, but she can't have a visitor just yet. You'll need to give them at least thirty minutes and then I'll give you the room number to the one they're going to put her in.

"Appreciate that."

As much as I wanted to protest and demand to see her immediately, I knew that the more attention the staff put on me the less they'd be able to give to Ever. I wanted all hands on deck when it came to her care. I could wait thirty minutes and I would wait. I took a seat in the area designated for seating and released a sigh.

Dear God. It's been a while, but I need You, my nigga. I began to pray with my hands clasped together in front of me.

LUCA·EVER

LYRIC, Ever's mother, and her stepfather sat next to me as we waited patiently for the thirty-minute minimum to elapse. Silence surrounded us all, everyone in complete disbelief of the situation. Aside from checking in with Laike, I hadn't said a single word. For what? I didn't have shit to talk about. If it wasn't Ever that I was talking to, I wouldn't be talking.

Thirty-one minutes. I looked at my clock and calculated how much time had passed. I marched to the same desk that I had come from after walking in. The same receptionist was seated at the computer.

"Ever Sinclair."

"Room twenty-six," she shared.

Without hesitation, I headed down the hallway. Lyric was right on my heels. I could hear her footsteps trying to keep up with my speed. Ever's mother and stepfather were in last place and I'd be damned if I waited for them to catch up.

Twenty-four.

Twenty-Five.

Right here. I approached the door and pushed it open. The curtain concealed Ever's frame but I felt her presence. When I rounded it, my stomach turned. Completely unrecognizable, Ever laid in bed with bands strapped to her belly. Too overcome by emotions, I rushed out of her room and into the hallway.

"FUUUUUCK!" An unrecognizable growl started in my belly and rushed out of my mouth.

Combing over my face with my hand over and over, I tried settling myself. Seeing Ever in that position had me tight in the chest with steam coming from my ears. My baby's beautiful face was completely ravished. Eyes swollen shut, lips split open, lumps and bumps on her forehead and cheeks, as blood stained her nose and chin.

"Luca," Lyric softened as she approached me.

"You see that shit, Lyric? You see what that nigga did to my fucking baby?"

"She's asking for you."

"It's my job to protect her and I let this shit happen."

"You didn't let anything happen. It is not your fault. Please don't start blaming yourself for this man's fuck up."

"I'm so sorry to disappoint you, baby girl, but he has to go."

"I know. I know, and I understand. I want him dead but the difference between then and now is you have time to think. You're a very smart man, Luca, and I'm certain this isn't your first rodeo. I just need you to use your head and come back home to us. We all need you. Your baby…"

"Did she lose the baby?"

"No. No. They're monitoring the baby. The baby is an Eisenberg. It will be just fine. He or she just needs their father. We all do. Now, go in and see what she wants. You don't have to stay long. Just let her know you're here."

"He. It's going to be a boy."

"Well then, he."

"Are you strapped?"

"I'm always strapped, Luca. Don't insult me."

"Good. If that nigga comes through that door, you lay his ass out."

"With pleasure."

Without haste, I walked into the room where Ever's mom and stepfather were at her bedside. Lyric was right behind me, but stayed close to the door. For once, she was my protection. I needed this moment, and she was going to make sure I had it. As I neared the bed, her mother and father headed toward the door to give us some privacy.

"Whatever I can do, tell me," James whispered as we passed each other up.

I nodded as I continued in Ever's direction. Though I didn't want to see Ever in her current condition, she wanted me. And, honestly, I wanted her. I grabbed her right hand and pulled the chair from the wall to take a seat.

At the moment, I hated I paid so much attention to detail. The skin on her hands were severely burned from what I assumed was the concrete. Two of her nails were broken so badly that they bled. Closing my eyes, I tried to even my breaths. It proved to be very difficult. I was seething on the inside.

"We're having a baby." She cried.

"We are."

"I thought I'd loss him."

"You can't. He's an Eisenberg."

"He's an Eisenberg," she agreed, taking a big swallow.

Silence circulated.

"Luca." Slowly, she breathed out.

"I'm sorry I wasn't there for you."

"I'm sorry to... bring you into my... into my mess."

"Don't apologize and stop trying to talk, Ever. You're doing more harm than good."

"I'm sorry," she whimpered, tears falling on the side of her face.

"Shhhhh."

"Everything hurts," Ever complained. "Every-everything."

"I know, baby. I know."

"He... He took the girls."

"Shhhhhhh. We're going to get them back. I'm going to get them back. I just need you to focus on getting better and bringing a healthy boy into this world, aight? I'm bringing our girls home," I assured her, placing my hand on her belly.

When it was quiet again, I could finally hear the rhythmic beat on the machine that wasn't far away.

"What's that?"

"What's what?"

"That sound."

"The beeping?"

"Yeah."

"His heartbeat."

"He has a heartbeat?"

"Yes."

Silence followed. I listened intently to the sound of my son. Even through the brutal beating his mother had taken, he was alive with a heartbeat as strong as mine. He was, in fact an Eisenberg. He was, in fact a boy.

"I want my girls."

"Me, too. Laike has his boots on the ground searching for them as we speak. Aside from the bullshit, how are you feeling?"

"My heart hurts."

"Mine, too."

"I know... I know you want to leave."

"I have to go find our girls."

"Then go," she told me. Her eyes never opened. They

were swollen shut, but she turned her head in my direction.

"I love you." The urge to say those words wouldn't allow me to keep quiet or leave without her knowing exactly how I felt.

"Forever."

TWENTY

EVER

10 HOURS LATER...

THE SOUND of my unborn's heartbeat had lulled me to sleep and woke me by sunrise. It was the sweetest sound God had ever created. As I tried opening my eyes for what felt like the millionth time, I managed to progress. I didn't recall being moved, but I could feel the difference between the one I was in now and the one I'd left. The curtain that I'd kept hearing being pulled backward was nowhere to be found and the hundreds of noises and voices weren't either.

"Hey, you're awake," Lyric cheered.

Immediately, I felt her arms around my neck, hugging me with her lips against my ear. Careful not to apply too much pressure with her body, she refrained from touching areas where I was obviously in pain.

"Don't tell them anything. You were mugged. End of story," she whispered.

"My neck," I warned, reminding her it hurt a little, too.

"Sorry, just so happy to see your eyes open again."

"Glad you're awake, Ms. Sinclair. I was wondering if we could have a word with you."

"Hi."

"I'm Detective Gaines and this is Detective Cypress. We're here to ask a few questions about your attack. Do you happen to remember anything at all?"

"No. I was hit in the head."

"We've learned that you suffered a concussion, but we were wondering if you remember anything leading up to the incident. Any suspicious vehicles or anyone following you?"

"No."

"Nothing?"

"Nothing," I repeated, lifting my hand to place it on my forehead. I wanted them out of my sight as soon as possible and if that meant being a little dramatic, then I didn't mind.

"She's not feeling very well. I think you should leave your card with us, and we will give you a call if she remembers anything," I heard my mother say.

"Sure. Here's my card and here's Gaines' card. Make

sure you keep in touch. We want to catch whoever might've done this."

"Of course," Lyric agreed, grabbing my hand to hold.

I heard as their footsteps retreated and then headed for the door. It wasn't until they were gone that I released a sigh. There was only one thing on my mind and it wasn't the pain I was in.

"Where's Luca? Has he located the girls?"

Though I'd just awakened, the exhaustion I felt was so rough on my body and my spirit that I wanted to do nothing but cry. Everything on my body hurt. It felt like I'd been hit by a moving vehicle. It even hurt to breathe.

"Not yet, babe. He's working on it, though."

"I feel so much pain right now. It even hurts to breathe," I explained.

"You have bruised ribs on both sides, Ever. I'm so sorry that everything hurts. Would you like me to have the nurse up the pain meds she's giving you?"

"Only if it won't harm the baby."

"It won't. We've talked about it already."

"I want my girls."

My chest ached at the thought of them. I wanted to know what they were doing and if they were OK. There was no doubt in my mind that Dewayne wouldn't harm them intentionally, but he would keep them away from me as long as he could to hurt me. He knew they were my world. When he fought me like I was a dog in the streets, he never mentioned the girls. His only words pertained to me moving on with my life. He didn't give a damn about my babies. I was his only concern. Keeping me in check and keeping me at arm's length was his only concern.

Though it hurt, I couldn't resist the urge to inhale deeply as my emotions ran high. The exhale brought me to tears. Emorey's little voice rang in my ears as visions of Essence flashed before my eyes. I needed my girls. I needed them immediately.

"I *need* my girls," I emphasized.

"The police is how we'll find them, Ever. Telling them you don't remember or know anything about your attack is bullshit. My grandbabies are out there with a lunatic right now, and I'm going crazy thinking about it. And the people who can actually help us, you've shut them out and lied to them, which is not like you."

"As much as I respect your opinion, Mom, my faith in Luca to right this situation surpasses that of the police substantially. The police don't know my babies. They've never held them after a nightmare but Luca has. They've never made ice cream with my girls from scratch just to see their reactions and excitement but Luca has. They've never carried my two sleeping girls for twenty minutes after they pooped out on a family hike but Luca has. They've never read the girls four nighttime stories in one night with sleepy eyes due to the day's activities but Luca has. They've never built the girls a custom dollhouse just because but Luca has.

"My point is that Luca is invested. His mind, body, and his heart. And that's what he'll lead with. His heart. Because he loves those girls more than Dewayne, me, or you could ever even imagine. And that's the difference between him, police, and any other authorities that want to get involved. Dewayne is their father."

"Proving that he *kidnapped* his own kids isn't going to be easy and it might not stick. The only thing they'd do is slap cuffs on his wrist for what he's done to me. Domestic assault? He probably won't see a day in jail and be right back out to cause damage, try to demolish what I'm trying to build. I can't have that, so no. I'm not giving them any details and yes I did lie to them. And for my children, I'd lie again. And, again. And, again.

"This would be labeled as another domestic dispute and it's far beyond that at this point. Dewayne has involved two innocent children who he doesn't give two shits about but they won't see it that way. They lived with him their entire lives. There has never been a report made of his abuse. This would literally be a case of my word against his. In the system's eyes, they're just as much of his as they are mine. He took care of us since before they were even born. I haven't had to work since my first pregnancy. In black and white, he seems like the ideal partner. The only issue with that is... he's not.

"He's the menace the system wants to make Luca out to be with his past documented for all to see. Cuffs and a few hours in jail isn't enough for me. I want him to hurt just like I'm hurting. I've let his shit bury the person I once was. I don't even know her anymore. He destroyed me, but what I won't allow is for him to destroy my children or the family we're building. He's gone too far, and he needs a wake-up call. If there's no one else who understands my sentiments, it's Luca."

I felt like I'd run a marathon as my final words rushed from my mouth.

"Lyric, I need some water, please," I begged.

She wiped the fallen tears from my face gently, yet it still hurt. My mother nodded and stepped away from my bed. I'd never been in a situation to have to remind my mother of the facts and why I was choosing one thing over the other and it pained me to talk to her in the tone that I had. But, at the same time, she had to hear it and it was best that it came from me.

I felt the straw that she placed in my mouth. There was no way I'd be able to lift and sip from a bottle. Both of my lips hurt to the touch, and my back felt like it had been broken in half. The cool sensation brought so much relief to my mouth and throat that I didn't stop sucking until I heard the emptiness of the cup sound loudly.

"Knock. Knock."

My eyes darted toward the door as I heard an unfamiliar voice. From around the corner came a middle-aged white man in scrubs that were topped with a white coat. My assumption was that he must've been my doctor.

"Ms. Sinclair, I'm Doctor Bryan, and I've been monitoring your baby's health since they brought you in and informed us you're pregnant. I'll start by saying that I'm pretty impressed. Under the circumstances, babies don't unusually survive. I'm just going to be honest here. With so much trauma to your body, especially your abdomen area, we're looking at a miracle child. A fighter. Bruised, nearly broken ribs. Blunt force trauma to the chest, back, sides. You're blessed. We have a healthy heartbeat and were able to see in the ultrasounds that everything is in perfect condition. Not a complication in sight."

It was so refreshing hearing my pregnancy confirmed, although I'd already known it to be true. With every blow to my body that Dewayne made, I lost a little more faith that my baby would make it through. As I listened to the heart monitor continue to sound off, I knew everything would be fine.

"How far along am I?"

"According to your ultrasound, you're right at eight weeks. We're going to keep our eyes on your little one during the duration of your stay, but I have a good feeling that we won't have to worry about this one. Let me or one of the staff members know if you need anything. We're here to help. Feel better soon."

"Thank you."

"No problem. Y'all have a good day now."

"More water," I told Lyric as soon as the doctor left the room. "Mom, check on the pain meds. I'm hurting all over."

LUCA·EVER

I'D DOZED off sometime between when the OB/GYN left and when the cafeteria staff tried serving me the nasty breakfast they'd prepared for the patients. Besides the applesauce that came with the meal, I wanted no parts. Everything on the plate looked over-processed, undercooked, or too artificial.

"Lyric?" I couldn't see her, but I could feel her near.

"Yeah?"

"Have you heard from Luca?"

"He's called twice since you've been asleep to check in. What's the matter?"

"Nothing. I just miss them all. Have you gotten an update?"

"He said that he's put a word out and they've been combing the streets, checking everywhere that he could possibly be. He hasn't used his name for anything so it's taking longer than expected but nearly the entire Channing is on the case, even my father."

"Sergio Thomas. Tell them to look into Sergio Thomas. That's most likely who he's with. I saw him yesterday. I didn't get a chance to tell Luca before everything happened. I was on my way to but–"

"It's OK. It's OK. I will call and share this new bit of information with him. Anything else you can think of that might help, let me know as it comes to you."

Lyric unlocked her cell and dialed Luca's number. While we waited for an answer, she put it on speakerphone. It rang out until the automated voicemail was activated, prompting us to hang up.

"He'll call us back," she told me as if I didn't already know.

Before I could open my mouth to respond, there was another knock at the door as it opened. This time, the voice behind it I recognized.

"Hey, babe. It's me," Baisleigh stated as she entered the room.

She rounded the corner, and with sad eyes, made her

way to my bedside. Lyric made room, leaving me only for a brief second to allow Baisleigh to air hug me from close range. She repositioned herself right after.

"I hear a heartbeat," she cheered. "We're expecting a bundle of joy soon."

"We are," I agreed.

"How have you been, Lyric?" she turned and asked.

"I've been well. What about you?"

"Crazy busy. And thanks to this woman, my brunches are picking up. Everybody wants the brunch cakes at Baisleigh's."

The mention of cakes brought Scar's face back to the forefront of my thoughts. It was when I was dropping off a cake to Baisleigh's House that I'd seen him. That's what had set everything off. It was the very moment things began to spiral out of control.

"That's where I saw him," I shared with Lyric.

"Huh?"

"That's where I saw Scar. That's where I saw Sergio. Dropping off the cake yesterday."

"Who is Sergio and where does he fit in this equation?" Baisleigh wanted to know.

"He's Dewayne's best friend, and I passed him up on the way out."

"Oh, wow," she responded.

"Try calling Luca again. He has my girls, Baisleigh. Anything helps. Do you recall a guy with a large scar from one side of his face to the other?"

"I do. He was a gentleman and wanted my number, but I took his instead because I don't date customers."

"Do you still have it?"

"No, but I have camera footage of the parking lot that'll probably reveal the car he was in and the tag number."

"A black Yukon," I said to Lyric. The details were coming to me so vividly now. The previous night, everything was a big fog.

"A black Yukon?" she repeated as a question.

"Yes. That's what Dewayne was in. His black Yukon. It's registered in his name."

"Let Luca know I can give him access to my cameras. The man with the scar didn't eat alone. About fifteen minutes after he sat down, another man joined him."

"Brown-skinned? A thicker build? Hairline pushed back two inches or so?"

"He wore a hat, but definitely brown-skinned and a bit on the thick side. Not big at all though."

"It was Dewayne. Call Luca back."

This time, Luca picked up on the second ring. Hearing his voice sent me spiraling, but I knew I had to keep it together. There were a few important things that he needed to know. I missed him and my girls so much it hurt even worse than my physical scars.

"What's up, Lyric?"

"It's me," I responded.

"Hey. How are you feeling?"

"Far from good. Yesterday, I saw Scar, Dewayne's best friend, when I was leaving from Baisleigh's House. That was right before I got the call about Em and the reason I freaked out about the ice cream situation. I was on my way to tell you that last night before everything happened. He must've followed me from my mother's house. It's the only location in Channing he knows for me. He's driving his Yukon. It's registered in his name. That's all I remember."

"That's good, baby. That's good enough. Any other details you come up with, let me know."

"You can go to my office and review the footage if that helps."

"Baisleigh?" he questioned.

"Yes. I came as soon as I heard."

"Appreciate that. I'm about to head to your shit now. Anybody there to let me in your office?"

"No. But I can let you in from where I'm standing. Just let me know when you're there."

"Bet. Stay by the phone, on my way now."

"Alright."

Luca ended the call, leaving us all silent. Everyone was processing the progress we'd just seemed to have made in getting my girls back. My growling stomach broke through the quietness, making us all shake our heads. Me, not so much because it hurt to move at all.

"I think I'm hungry," I admitted.

"We know." Lyric chuckled.

"I don't want anything they give me."

"Don't worry. I'm going downstairs to the cafeteria on my own and grab you something to eat. Anything in particular?"

"French fries with ketchup. No salt. It'll only burn my lips."

"You sure you want chewable foods and not any type of soup?"

"Right now, soup would only tease me and the thought of it has me ready to barf."

"Please don't."

"Bring me some soup while I'm starving, and I promise I will."

"Baisleeeeeeeeeigh?"

Her speech slurred as she turned in my direction and bucked her pretty brown eyes. She motioned toward the door with her head, prompting me to look in the same direction. When I saw the dark-skinned man I'd learned to be Ken come from around the corner, confusion sank in. I wasn't sure why he was in my room or how he'd slid through the door without either of us hearing him. Of course, he was Luca's best friend, but his presence was still baffling.

"Ken." Lyric greeted him with a hug when he joined her at my side.

"What's good, Lyric?"

"What are you doing here?" She asked that was at the tip of my tongue.

"I'm here on uncle duty and the little nigga ain't even got here yet. I'm just here to make sure nothing and no one interferes with his debut or they'll meet their end. Expeditiously."

His presence made more sense now. Luca had sent him to the hospital in case Dewayne was dumb enough to come up."

"Thank you," I spoke, finally.

"Na. No thanks needed."

"Well, uh. I'm, uh... I'm going to head to the uh, cafeteria," Lyric struggled to get out.

"French fries. No salt. Ketchup."

"Got it. Baisleigh, you running downstairs with me or are you staying?"

"I'm going to join you just in case Luca calls you and needs me to let him in."

"OK. I'm ready."

The two filed out quickly, leaving Ken and me alone.

"Is there anything you need?" he asked.

"No."

"Aight. Let me know if that changes. I'm here until you leave this motherfucker," he informed me as he slid the chair that was on the side of my bed to the opposite side of the room where he had a clear visual of the door.

"You don't want to watch television or anything?" I asked, noting his awkward position. He was against the wall with the television. There was no way he'd be able to see it. The only thing he could see was the door and me, of course.

"I'm not here to watch television," he responded.

"Well, I'm sure it would make your stay much better."

"A pleasant stay isn't the goal, Ever. A meaningful one is. Again, if you need me, I'll be right here... watching the door. That's all the entertainment I need."

I understood why Luca and Ken were friends, and I also understood why Lyric was smitten by the deep-tenured, midnight black fella. Just like Luca's, Ken's focus was always intact. And just like his brothers, Ken seemed to have a protective nature. He was possibly the only man she could actually trust to have her best interest at heart.

"Maybe there is one thing that I need," I cleared my throat to say.

"What is it?"

"Luca."

"Luca is working on finding y'all's children. I don't think he can or even wants to put a pause on that for nothing – *not even you*."

His brutal honesty was refreshing. I was going to be fine. I knew it. Luca knew it. And so did everyone around us. His head was in the right place. He wanted our girls home as much as I did and didn't want anything interfering with his search, but I needed to see his face. I needed to hear his voice, and I needed him to look me in the eye as he told me that everything would be OK. Hearing it from anyone else just didn't mean to me what hearing it from him did. And, at the moment, I needed that.

LUCA·EVER

I WAS in and then I was out. In and then out again. My body only allowed me to stay awake for an hour or less at a time before I went to sleep again. I'd never felt so tired in my life. But as much as I wanted to stay asleep, I couldn't with the familiar scent lingering in the air. There was nothing else like it. I recognized it so easily and so vividly each time it was in my presence.

"Luca?" I stirred.

There was movement immediately and then his hand slid into mine as he stood over me. His hand rested on my head as he began to stroke my messy head of hair.

"Hey," he responded.

"Hey," I managed, while my nose flared and eyes suffered from a burning sensation.

"Shhhhhhh," he coaxed, but it was a little too late and a little too much to ask of me at the moment.

My chest rattled as I inhaled loudly, tears crowding my eyes before falling down my cheeks. My heart was broken. Broken for me. Broken for my girls. Broken for Luca. Broken for my unborn child. Broken for my mother. Broken for Lyric. Broken for James. Broken for Baisleigh. Broken for everyone in my life that I'd plagued with Dewayne's presence. I was sorry. So sorry. Sorry for me. Sorry for my girls. Sorry for Luca. Sorry for my unborn child. Sorry for my mother. Sorry for Lyric. Sorry for James. Sorry for Baisleigh. Sorry for everyone whose lives my poor decision had affected in any way.

With every ounce of strength in me, I lifted my right arm and hooked it around his neck. I pulled him closer until his face was flushed against mine. My safe haven. He was exactly that.

"I love you," he whispered in my ear. "We're going to get through this shit, baby. Just stay strong for a nigga, aight?"

"Okay," I rushed out through the tears. "Okay."

"You've got this. Everything is going to be okay."

"Can you stay a while longer?" I requested, although

I knew that he'd much rather be out searching for our girls.

"I can do that for you, Ever. I have everybody onboard and looking for the girls. It's only a matter of time before I get the call."

"Okay."

"You need anything, baby?"

"Just you."

He lifted, gently kissed my swollen and busted lips, and stood tall at my side. When I felt his hand on my stomach, I closed my eyes and savored the feeling.

"What we gone do with three of these things and a fucking dog?"

"The same thing we're going to do with four and five and six," I told him.

Luca and I had the conversation often. Both of us wanted as many kids as I could deliver before I became too exhausted and ready to give up my childbearing days. Because I'd always been the only child, I'd known for a very long time that I would have a big bunch so that none of my children ever felt the loneliness I did growing up.

"Where is everyone?"

I noticed the room was dark and eerily quiet.

"Ken is right outside, and Lyric went home to get some rest. She'll be back up here in a few hours. For now, it's just you and me. Is that alright with you?"

"That's perfect."

We're just missing our girls, I thought, but didn't voice.

"How are you doing, Luca?" I wanted to know.

Since I'd known him, he'd always managed to compose himself well. Nonchalantly, almost as if nothing in the world had the power to sway his mood. For once, I knew that his composure was masking something deeper.

"I'm feeling like any man whose children have been ripped from his arms would feel. I'm sick to my fucking stomach, Ever," he admitted.

Swallowing the painful lump in my throat, I tried nodding. It only resulted in pain.

"But, they'll be home before the night ends. I'll bet my last dollar on it."

"I know they will be."

We fell into a comfortable silence, both of us preoccupied with our thoughts. Visions of the girls being loaded into Dewayne's Yukon continued playing in my head, making me feel ill. I wanted to blame myself for leaving them alone in the car, but I knew it wasn't me to blame for Dewayne's actions.

He was a coward, and he'd wait in the shadows for however long he needed for the opportunity to take them so it was only a matter of time, regardless of what I wanted to believe. He'd come to Channing for one reason. He wanted to hurt me and hurt me badly. Without a doubt, he'd succeeded, but unfortunately, I wasn't the only one he'd hurt.

"I can't risk losing you, Luca. I can't risk you going back to prison. I just want the girls back," I broke through the silence to tell Luca. The last thing I wanted was him leaving his family again because of my bullshit, neither did I want him leaving us. Our little family needed him, too.

The thought of raising our children without him was repulsive. He deserved his freedom, and I refused to believe that Dewayne was worth losing it. He was a peasant that didn't deserve anything, not even my daughters to call his own.

"I can't overlook it, Ever, and I'm not going to explain myself to you. Whatever happens, happens. He'd already signed his death certificate when he crossed my city's limits with hurting the ones I loved on his agenda."

As he concluded, his cell rang. Without even answering it, he looked over at me and smiled. It was the first time I'd seen him smile since the day prior when we parted ways in the early hours before taking the girls to school.

"It's time to go get our girls. Get some rest," he told me.

TWENTY-ONE

LUCA

THE STILLNESS of my home was revealing. Too much, almost. There weren't any children running around intending to drive me insane. There was no Ever walking around making my dick hard at just the sight of her, no matter what she was doing or what she was wearing. The tightening of my chest as I pulled from the blunt in my hand as I sat on the balcony was the only sign that I was still among the living because since Cane had answered Ever's phone, I'd been numb.

Dressed in all black, I blended with the darkness of the night. The sun had finally settled and it was time to hunt. I had no plans of returning home or to the hospital if my children weren't in my arms. There was no way I could look into Ever's hazel eyes and tell her I hadn't found Emorey and Essence. I couldn't and I wouldn't.

An hour ago, I'd gotten the call that they'd been located and there was a team sitting and trying to wait Dewayne out. We wanted him lured off the hotel premises he was on so that there was less of a mess to clean up after ourselves, but he hadn't left the room. As much as I wanted to continue to wait, every second that my girls were in his presence fucked with me a little more. It was understood among everyone that if he hadn't left by the nine o'clock hour, we were moving in. I didn't give a damn about how much cleaning up we'd have to do. It was time to bring my girls home.

My clock read **8:42 p.m.**

I dropped the remainder of the blunt on the ground and stepped on it. Seeing my girls' faces would be the only elevation I needed for the rest of the night. I slid through the glass door and closed it behind me. My perfectly made bed hit a nerve for me. Not seeing Ever waiting for me to return from a quick smoke break was like a dagger to the chest. Instead of obsessing over the pain, I laid my cell down on the throw and headed out of the door.

When I made it outside, I almost circled the entire property before discovering the small parting in the fence that Laike had designed for moments, just like this one. I lifted the latch that was near the ground until I'd let the gate up high enough for me to slide under. The flickering headlights on the car a few feet up the road signaled that it was my ride. I walked the short distance until I reached the black Malibu with out-of-state tags.

No words were exchanged between Laike, Cane, and me as I slid in and laid my head against the passenger seat headrest. Closing my eyes, I began to mentally prepare myself for the task ahead. Taking a man's life for me wasn't exactly a walk in the park, but neither was it challenging. I could do it in my sleep and never think about it again. But the baggage that came with some deaths stuck with you for the rest of your life. And, for Dewayne, it was the case. Not for me, necessarily. He belonged in the dirt.

However, there were two little girls involved. One of whom would remember him, no matter how much he lacked as a father. Essence knew him as just that, and there was no way that I'd ever be able to look her in the eyes and admit to ending his life.

There was also a woman who wouldn't harm a fly in the equation. The guilt she'd feel from his death was heavy on my heart. An empath by nature, she would always worry more about others than herself, the bum ass baby daddy she had included. Knowing that it was my hands that was responsible for his death could easily backfire and cause tension in our relationship. I didn't want that. But, even more, I didn't want this nigga breathing a second longer than it was necessary. He deserved every bullet I was going to put through him and with the extended clip on my waist, there was a total of thirty-one.

Ever. I thought of the woman I'd grown to love in such a short amount of time.

She was an angel, and she didn't mind dancing with a demon. That's why I'd move mountains, dry seas, and hydrate the desert if it made her happy. She brought goodness to the world. To my world. It was only right that I made it hers, along with the two tiny beauties that shared her hazel eyes and perfect smile. For them, I'd do whatever. For them, I'd become whoever. For them, I'd lay down whoever. That included the man whose nut sack the girls had come from. Because, as far as I was concerned, Ever and I had created them together. The nigga never existed in my book.

The fact that she was carrying my seed complicated this situation even more. For us, it was simple but only because the baby had survived the brutal beating. Hadn't my child survived, there wouldn't even be a place in hell for Dewayne's burdened soul or the number of pieces that I sent him down there in.

Fortunately for us all, my baby was a fighter. Barely a nub in the womb, and he was holding his own. Eisenberg was written all over him.

We pulled up to the two-story motel with only half the letters lighting up, making it hard to read the name. The sight of Emorey and Essence's location had my nostrils flaring and my blood boiling. Without a doubt, I knew they were terrified and uncomfortable. I had my babies laying on sheets with six-hundred thread counts and adjustable mattresses for their comfort and a good night's rest. The hellhole that we pulled up to was far from either.

"You ready?" Laike looked at me and asked.

"Born that way."

I hopped out of the car with my gun aimed at the door, ready for anything to move that wasn't supposed to. My trigger finger was itching and my blood was boiling. Laike used the key that he'd swiped from the front desk before coming to get me. It had only cost him five hundred measly dollars.

Masked-up and trained to go, we entered the motel room and immediately spotted the girls. Laike was the first inside, grabbing them both and pulling them toward the door. He placed a finger over his mouth, instructing them to both be quiet. Once the girls were safely on the other side of the door, I proceeded.

"What the fuck?" Dewayne rushed out when he noticed he was not alone.

As much as I wanted to honor Ever and not put the pussy on his ass that emerged from the bathroom, just seeing his sorry ass face sent me into overdrive.

Doot. Doot. The silencer on my gun made his assault a quiet one. He'd made enough noise in the last two nights.

Left leg. Right leg.

They were both hit, one after the other, disabling him momentarily. Before his body could even hit the floor, I was out of the door and scooping my girls into my hand.

"Arghhhhhhhh!"

"Have them bring that nigga to the warehouse," I instructed Cane.

"Big Homie," he grunted, "Let me save us all the trip."

"Nah. I told you, this one is mine. Make sure he gets there. *ALIVE*."

"Alright."

Emorey's arms were wrapped around my neck so tightly as if she was afraid that I'd let her go. I didn't have any intention to, not even when I climbed in the backseat with her and Essence. Having them in my arms felt like a dream, and I'd be damned if I ever wanted to wake up from it. Their molly faces and dirty pajamas let me know they hadn't been properly cared for. Seeing them in what was possibly the same clothes they'd been taken in, had me wanting to go put two more in that nigga.

"Slide over, Es."

In her pink pajamas, she said nothing but followed directions immediately. Though she was always quiet, I knew that this silence was a different kind of silence. She was terrified. She hadn't blinked since I'd walked into the room as if she was in a dream and afraid that if she blinked, I would disappear.

"I wan' go with you." Emorey cried into my chest as I got situated with both girls in the back of the Malibu.

"You are, baby girl. You are."

I felt Essence's head against my arm moments shy of feeling the wetness. Silently, she cried against me, never mumbling a word. It felt as if I'd been stabbed in the chest with three knives as both girls clung to me as if it was the last time they'd ever see me again.

I waited impatiently for Laike and Cane to rejoin me, this time with rearranged seating. As I held the girls close, I watched the door like a hawk for the moment the two emerged. And when they did, I sighed in relief. Within seconds, we were burning rubber off the parking lot and on our way to my crib.

With Emorey and Essence in my sight, everything seemed to get clearer. Aside from light sniffles from both girls, the car was utterly silent. It felt like the longest ride of my life but in about twenty minutes we were pulling up to the same area I'd exited. It was imperative that I entered the same way I'd left.

"See you in a few," I told Laike while gathering the girls so that we were able to get out.

"Bet. Don't forget to handle that other business."

We knew Dewayne hadn't come alone and neither was he acting alone. He'd come with the same nigga that Ever had seen at Baisleigh's the day before. Her suspicions were right. Dewayne knew exactly where she was, especially after she'd run into his homie.

Unfortunately, he'd chose the wrong motherfucking city to pull up in. There was no way he was leaving. Just like Dewayne, he had that coming to him. They'd made their beds. It was time to lie in them.

"I won't. No loose ends," Laike confirmed.

"Burn the motel room down and compensate the owner."

"On it."

The headlights of the car helped me identify the section of the gate that could be lifted from the outside if the latch wasn't hooked. I lifted it and then put Emorey on the ground. There was no way we'd both make it under without me breaking something.

"Go ahead," I instructed them both.

When I made it under, I reattached the latch so that entry was forbidden from the outside. Emorey's outstretched arms reminded me she was still in distress. I pulled her into my chest and stood my full length with her in my arms. Essence's little fingers wrapped around mine, and we all proceeded toward the house.

Entering the house with both girls at my side was easily the best feeling I'd experienced since meeting their mother. Now, she was the only missing piece to our puzzle. As soon as she was released, she'd be right beside us, though. It was only a matter of time before we were all reunited and smiling again.

"Can I sleep with you?" Emorey asked just as I closed the door behind us.

"Me, too?" Essence's words penetrated the air.

"We're not going to sleep, we're going to see Mommy. But, when we do go to sleep, you'll both be right beside me."

I reached down and pulled Essence into my arms and started to climb the stairs. We entered their bedroom where the coziness of it made my eyelids heavy and my heart light. This was where they belonged. In the last three months, their bedroom had been transformed into their personal palace.

"What color pajamas do you want, Emorey?"

Before taking them to the hospital to visit Ever, it was imperative that I cleaned them up. The last thing I wanted to do was bring her the girls looking as if they'd been in the hellhole I'd found them in. I wanted her to see the girls she remembered and knew better than she knew herself.

"Blue."

"What about you, Essence?"

"Blue."

"Then blue it is."

I lowered them to their feet but neither of them moved. They stood at my side, watching as I pulled their drawers open, searching for a pair of matching pajamas in the color blue. I'd seen them in several so I knew there was something in the drawers for them to wear.

"Essence, you want to go start you guys some bath water while I look for your pajamas?"

"No," she admitted.

Accepting her honesty for what it was, I continued picking through their pajamas.

"OK. Give me a second, and we can all go in at once."

Leaving my side was something they weren't ready to do, obviously. So, I wouldn't force them to. I hoped that after a warm bath, they'd feel a little better. If not, I would reconsider taking them up to see Ever. I refused to traumatize them anymore and seeing their mother in her current condition would only heighten their emotions and deepen their wounds.

My cell phone rang as I pulled matching sets out for

the girls. There were only a handful of people that could be calling me so I didn't bother checking to see who it was. I answered.

"Yeah?"

"Hey. Is everyone OK?" My mother's voice was on the other end of the line, stopping me in my tracks.

"Yes."

There was a brief, revealing silence that forced me from my knees and onto my butt, with my head against the dresser.

"It's me, Luca. It's okay," she encouraged.

Heaving, I released the tension that had been building over the last twenty-four hours. The anger, frustration, bitterness, and everything else I was feeling deep on the inside surfaced and fell from my eyes as my mother sat quietly, listening to her oldest unravel. My entire life, I'd held my shit together, but this time it was different.

This time, my heart had been twisted and turned in every direction. This time, there were two little girls that I loved more than anyone around me who had been harmed. This time, the woman who'd brought them into my world and was carrying our child had been hurt. This time, everything was different. This time, I could feel it everywhere, the pain and the relief.

Feeling Emorey's and Essence's little hands on my face, trying to clear my tears and their bodies resting on my legs felt surreal. Each hour that I spent away from them over the last twenty-four hours ate away at my core a little more, but that feeling was nothing compared to the wholesomeness I felt as they comforted me.

"It's okay," Essence assured me.

"Don't cwry," Emorey added. "Don't be so sad."

"Okay." I nodded my head, taking their words of encouragement in stride and forcing myself to pull it together, not only for their sake but for mine as well.

"Mom?"

"I'm still here, Luca."

"I need to get them bathed so that we can get up to the hospital."

"I don't think that's a good idea. They've been through enough, baby. Seeing their mother laid up in the bed all battered and bruised will only hurt them worse. No one wins in that situation. Let's think about their mental and emotional health right now. I don't suggest taking them to see her at all. They won't keep her for too much longer. Give them a few days to readjust, and she'll be home before they know it. Tonight, you three need to get some rest. You've done your part, Luca. Rest."

"Easier said than done."

"It'll happen. You have the girls back. Trust me, falling asleep will come easy for you tonight."

"I just need her." I coughed back the new wave of emotions that threatened to come up.

"She'll be there soon. I heard I have a grandchild on the way."

Sniffling, I responded, "Yeah." Emorey used her shirt to dry my face of what their hands couldn't.

"Thanks, baby."

"Are you still sad?" she asked, obviously concerned.

"A little."

"Why but?"

Her twist on words made me smile through the aching.

"I miss Mommy," I admitted.

"I miss Mommy, too."

"Me, too," Essence confessed.

"I know."

I urged them both to rest on my chest. As they laid, my conversation with my mother resumed.

"You're a great father, Luca."

"Appreciate that, Mom."

"Can you get your brother onboard?"

"I think I have a better chance with Lyric."

"You're right. I'm not even ready for a little Laike. I don't even want to imagine what kind of torture that looks like."

Chuckling, I nodded. When Laike was ready, I just hoped we all were around to see his minis roaming earth. Lyric, I was ready for her to fall head over heels with someone worthy of her energy and love before giving us the children she'd always promised herself in her thirties.

"Thank you, Luca."

"No problem."

"I love you, son."

"Always," I declared.

"I'm going to let you go so that you can get the girls to bed. If you need me, call me. My phone will be near."

"OK. Can you do me a favor?"

"Anything."

"Tell Pops to meet me at the warehouse in the next two hours."

"He's already on it."

"That wasn't the favor."

"I'll be there. Just get them to bed."

"Thanks."

"Anything for y'all, Luca. You know this already."

I ended the call and rested my head on the dresser behind me. Both girls were still resting on my chest. I considered staying right on the floor and falling asleep with them right where they were, but I knew they needed a good scrubbing and to be in their beds. Me, on the other hand, I had business to tend to.

"Come on, girls. Let's get you cleaned and in your pajamas."

LUCA·EVER

BECAUSE I KNEW that Essence could handle her own, I gave her a little privacy by choosing a bath for Emorey while she showered a few feet away. She asked if I could keep the door open so that I could see her, still afraid that I'd disappear at any moment.

"I'm not going anywhere," I reminded them every few minutes.

Emorey's lack of independence was a clear sign she was fighting some tough emotions internally. She was always trying to wipe herself down without assistance. It didn't matter if it was me or Ever bathing her, there was always a twenty-minute-long protest in the bathroom at night. Not this time, though. My Em stood still and straight while I cleaned her twice.

"Did anyone do anything bad to you, Em?" I was led to ask.

"Daddy bad."

"I know. But, did anyone touch you? Hurt you? Hit you?"

With bated breath, I waited for her response. If she had given me any answer other than no, then I wasn't going to be able to see them to bed. I'd be on my way to the warehouse to end this nigga, but not before making him suffer for the shit he'd done to my family.

"No." She shook her head.

"What about Essence?"

"Daddy hit Essence. She cry."

"OK. If anyone ever hurts you, then you have to tell me, OK?"

"Daddy hit Mommy, too."

"I know."

"Daddy bad."

"Yeah," I agreed.

"Can you be me Daddy?"

Though I was honored, I knew that her line of questioning wasn't farfetched. She'd seen what type of person her biological father was and didn't want anything to do with him. I didn't blame her. What she didn't understand was that I'd claimed her as mine the day I met her. Just like her mother, she had me mesmerized. I was so intrigued by her personality that I wanted to make her part of my world that same day, but I knew I had to practice patience. It was so worth the wait.

"I'm already your daddy, baby."

"Can I call you daddy?"

"Yes. I'd love that... a lot."

Her curiosity and intelligence was mind-blowing. She was always trying to figure shit out, always trying to get to the bottom of things.

"Are you Essence, too, Daddy?"

Her and those twisted words would get a smile out of me every time.

"Yes, baby. I'm Essence's daddy, too."

"You call me baby. You call Essence baby?"

"Yes, Emorey. I'll call you both baby. Any more questions?"

"Can you cook me food?"

"If you're hungry, sure. What do you want?"

"ABC."

I knew from experience that she was referring to the meatballs and sauce cups she loved so much. Essence hated them. She preferred macaroni and cheese bowls or noodles.

"OK. Now arms up."

I wrapped the towel around her when she lifted her arms up and then lifted her into my arms. Essence was finishing up her shower and wrapping herself in a towel, too. I grabbed her hand on the way out of the bathroom, and we all headed back into their bedroom.

Essence was the first to get dressed with Emorey and me coming in second place. With matching pajamas on, they marched down to the kitchen with me. It was pitch black when we entered, but I quickly flipped the light switch and illuminated the space.

"ABCs. I wan' ABCs!" Emorey continued to shout.

"What do you want, Essence?"

"Noodles. The chicken kind."

"Spaghetti-Os and noodles. Y'all staying in here or y'all going in there to sit down?"

"Staying here," they answered simultaneously. I should've known not to even ask.

"Aight."

One by one, I sat them on the counter so that I could fix their food. Essence was up first since it took her dish longer in the microwave. When her noodles were finished, I'd pop Emorey's ABCs in while I fixed Essence's food up. She liked seasoning in addition to half of the sauce pack in hers. According to her and Ever, they were eating Ramen. Most times she'd hook it up with shrimp, eggs, and a bunch of other shit that Essence wouldn't be getting tonight. Tonight, she was eating noodles... straight out the pack.

As we waited for their food to cool, I could hardly contain the secret that Ever and I was now withholding. The girls would be welcoming a baby in some months, and I wanted to share it with them to bring some joy to their worlds after the turmoil, but I knew I had to wait. Ever was more than likely planning something special for them, so I forced my mouth shut and tried not to think about it. The task was nearly impossible.

Once both of their dishes were ready, I sat them on

the counter next to them. I didn't bother taking them to the table because they were already seated. Emorey laid down in front of her food and ate it just like that. Essence placed her bowl in her lap and ate her noodles from there, eventually ending up sharing them with Emorey who'd eaten her food as quickly as I'd set it down.

"Everybody ready?"

I'd cleaned faces, wiped hands, and washed the dishes they'd used. They were clean, and they were fed. It was officially bedtime for everyone, including me. I only needed an hour. Now that they were home, I could get a little shuteye. It had been a long day.

"I sleep with you?" Emorey asked as she jumped into my arms.

"Woah." I laughed because the impact of her little move was a bit more than expected.

"I sleep with you?"

"Yes, baby. You can sleep with me."

"In you bed?"

"Yes. In my bed, Emorey."

"Me, too," Essence added.

"Aight. I got to take a quick shower before I lay down with y'all. Can y'all wait on me?"

"We took a bath," the little one informed me as if I didn't know already.

"I know, Em. Come on, Essence."

With both girls in my arms, I hurried toward the stairs and then up them. Emorey was a big ball of laughter the entire way. I got them settled in my bed in no time.

"OK. I'm about to shower."

"No. Pwease stay."

"Emorey, we talked about this. I need to bathe, too. I'm dirty."

"No you not. Pwease," she repeated, her hands in front of her clasped together.

I looked to Essence for some type of help, but she was useless. She had the same look on her face as Emorey. Neither one of them wanted me to leave them for long.

"Aight. Let me use the bathroom, then, and I'll be right back."

The fact that they were about to make me take a wash up was insane, but it was whatever when it came to them, and they knew it. I rushed into the bathroom and grabbed the closest towel I could find. It was one of the decorative ones that Ever had put there, so I knew she'd have my ass for it. But under the circumstances, I didn't give a damn. I soaped it up and hit all the important spots before moving on to my arms, legs, and chest. With the same rag, I rinsed my body of the soap. I grabbed one of the larger towels and wrapped it around me before stepping out of the door.

"You all clean now?" Emorey wasn't missing a beat.

"I'm clean now, baby."

"Come sleep with me." She patted the bed beside her.

"OK. Let me grab some clothes out of the closet right quick."

"OK."

I grabbed the first pair of shorts that I saw, which

happened to be blue. Along with a pair of briefs, I pulled them on. When I made it back into the room, the same two sets of eyes were staring at me. Shaking my head at their commitment, I climbed between them. To my right was Essence, laying on my chest. To my left was Emorey, laying on my chest.

I ran my hands through both of their hair to relax them a bit. I knew it wouldn't be long before they were asleep. They just needed some comfort and to feel protected. Not long after I laid down, I heard Essence's light snores. Emorey was next to go down. I was in last place, but having the girls in my arms put me to sleep with ease.

LUCA-EVER

I STIRRED AWAKE, checking the time on my phone. An hour and a half had passed since I'd fallen asleep with the girls in my arm. As if on cue, my phone buzzed in my hand. My father was calling.

"Pops?" I yawned.

"I'm outside."

"Outside of my house?"

"Yeah, Luca. Where else?"

"For what? I told Moms to have you meet me at the warehouse."

"I'm taking you and I brought your mother to stay with the girls. I don't want you driving right now, son. Come outside when you're ready."

"Appreciate you. I'll be out in a few minutes. I need to get dressed."

"Alright. I'm sending your mother on inside."

Our call ended and I was up on my feet instantly. Inside my closet, I pulled out a few pieces that reflected my mood. The black pants, shirt, and hat were on my body and I was on my way downstairs before my mother could make it in the door good. In passing, she grabbed me, pulling me into her chest for a hug.

"Be safe, Luca."

"I will."

"I love you, son."

"Always."

"Where are they?"

"In my bed. I'm sorry to have you out so late."

"I wouldn't have it any other way. I'm going to lay down with them until you two get back. I doubt I'll be able to get any sleep."

"Try... for me."

"I will."

I kissed her cheek and was out of the door in a split second. My father was waiting in the driveway in a vehicle that I was unfamiliar with, but knew better than to question when I finally sat next to him in the passenger seat.

"Bare hands, huh?"

He knew me well. Very fucking well.

"Getting hit with a few bullets would be too easy of a death for this pussy. I'm going to beat this bitch the same way he beat my Ever and then I'm going to break his fucking neck."

"Luca." My father sighed.

"It's personal, Pops. Very fucking personal."

"I understand."

Nothing else was said as we made the thirty-minute drive to the warehouse where I noticed a few whips at the dock. Before I could ask, my father was informing me.

"The clean-up crew, your brother, that boy Cane, and Mook."

Nodding, I waited until the vehicle came to a complete stop before slowly exiting. Without haste, I made my way up the dock and through the side door. Laike was waiting in the front for me, massaging his fist as he stood to greet me. I pointed at his swollen fingers as I squinted in his direction. He tossed both his hands in the air, shrugging as he warned me about what I was walking into.

"I couldn't help myself."

Deciding against chastising him and respecting his stance in protecting my family, I pushed through the door and entered the large, empty space where Dewayne sat in a chair. As I approached, I called out to him, needing his full attention. Recalling the days that I'd laid niggas flat on their backs, I removed my shirt from my body, refusing to stain it with his blood.

"Aye, pussy."

His head lifted as he searched for my voice. Evidence of Laike's presence was left on his face. His right eye was swollen and there was a gash in his lip that leaked profusely.

"Stand up," I instructed, knowing that the two bullets I'd put in him had gone straight in and out, leaving little to no damage. He was able to stand and he was able to walk.

"Man, listen," he begged. "Listen."

"Stand the fuck up!" I barked a second time.

His feet shuffled as he rose, slowly.

"Listen, man. Ever—"

WHAM! With enough force to do damage but not knock his lights out, I cocked back and landed the first blow. His head jerked as his body shifted, making it hard to maintain his balance.

"Keep her name out your fucking mouth," I warned. "Now, beat my ass like you did hers. Show me how tough you really are, nigga. Beat my ass, nigga."

Pride forced his fists in the air as he joined a losing battle. I paced myself. Though I was ready to rock this nigga to sleep, I wanted him to feel the same pain as Ever and Essence. He'd put his hands on them both, so dying wasn't optional tonight. However, I wasn't in a rush to end his world. Not until he felt some degree of the pain he'd caused in mine.

"Luca, kill this nigga," Laike suggested. "Shoot him in the center of his fucking forehead."

Ignoring him, I struck again.

WHAM.

And, again.

WHAM.

And, again.

WHAM.

Images of Ever's bruised skin flashed before my eyes.

WHAM.

The painful kisses she suffered through made my nostrils widened as the next blow was thrown.

WHAM.

I moved to his ribs, hearing them crack upon impact.

WHAM.

I followed up, wanting to crush his shit until his lungs and oxygen levels suffered.

WHAM.

I stayed on him, not allowing him the break I knew he desperately wanted.

WHAM.

He stumbled.

WHAM!

Fist to face, I tried to reconstruct every feature on his shit. He fell backward, unconscious. Before his body could drop, my hands were at the top and bottom of his head. Together, we hit the concrete beneath us. Twisting, I tried my best to remove his head from his shoulders. Even the cracking of his neck wasn't enough to halt my attempts.

"Umph," Laike grunted at the sound of it.

I blacked out, unable to control myself, my thoughts, or my actions. Still, I clung to his lifeless body, forcing his spine to bend in ways that was unnatural and scientifically impossible.

"Luca."

I heard my father calling my name but I couldn't see him. I couldn't see anyone or anything but Ever's pretty face that had been destroyed.

"LUCA." My father called again.

I tightened my grip, biting into my bottom lip while mustering every ounce of strength I had stored.

"Son!"

"Let him get that out of him, Pops," Laike advised.

His voice was faint, but I'd heard every word.

"Luca. Come on, son. It's done. It's over."

Unable to collect myself, I remained in position. Blood filled my mouth. I'd broken skin, piercing my flesh.

"Luca. Come on, son. Emorey and Essence are waiting for you."

It wasn't until their names fell from his lips that I snapped back into reality. Slowly, I loosened my grip, allowing Dewayne's lifeless body to hit the ground. At that moment, I felt vindicated, not only for me but for the three girls that owned my whole heart.

"Bitch," I grunted, stepping over him and heading out.

LUCA·EVER

MY PHONE VIBRATED CONSTANTLY, waking me up from my sleep. I opened my eyes and took a look out of the window to find that the sun was just beginning to rise. It could be no later than seven.

"Yeah?" I answered, groaning at the sudden movement I'd made.

It was then that I realized I had Emorey's feet in my side and Essence's feet on my chest. They were still sound asleep, unaware of anything going on around them. My back was aching and so was my side. I'd slept horribly wrong.

"Hey," Ever's voice sounded clearer and her spirit seemed lighter.

"Hey," I responded.

"How are they?"

I hadn't told her I'd brought the girls home, and I was sure no one else had. She just knew.

"Sleeping and breaking my back in the process."

"They're in bed with you?" Ever chuckled. "Owwww."

She was still in pain, and I couldn't wait for her to get better.

"Yeah. We're in my room. They didn't want to sleep alone."

"How are they? Really?" The seriousness in her tone let me know she wanted to know more about their mental, physical, and emotional states due to the tragedy they'd faced.

"They're scared. Terrified. I can't leave their sight for more than a minute or two. They don't want to be alone at all. Emorey said that she wasn't hurt but that her dad hit Essence. I'm sitting here wondering if it's possible to do a motherfucker twice."

"Luca."

"It is what it is."

"Let's just leave it at that, OK? Does Essence have any bruising?"

"Na, but she's not saying anything. And, I don't mean the normal silence. I mean, not saying anything but 'Me, too,' to everything that Emorey says."

"My poor baby."

"I hope she feels better when she wakes up. Emorey is a tough cookie. She's going to be alright. It's my Essence that I'm worried about most."

"I know. I'm going to look into some therapy for her. Or, maybe you know someone who won't share whatever she tells them with anyone else."

"My mother is a licensed pediatric therapist. She can help, and if Essence doesn't feel comfortable talking to her, then she can put us on to one of her friends. The network is extensive. Just tell me what she needs, and I'll make it happen."

"How are you?" She was always worried about everyone else.

"I'm better."

"I miss you."

"I miss you, too, Mommy," I toyed, trying to get her to smile at least. I knew her heart was still heavy and so was mine, but we'd get through it together.

"I can't wait to get out of here."

"How are you feeling?"

"I'm still hurting, but that's expected. My swelling is almost gone but there's bruising. Lots of bruising. A blood clot has formed in my eye. The doctor says everything is fine, however, and it's nothing to worry about."

"Mentally?"

"Better knowing my girls are home. Sad because I miss them so much, but don't want to see them while I'm in the shape that I'm in."

"They saw what happened."

There was a gasp before the line fell silent.

"I hate him." Ever cried to me. "I hate him for doing this to us."

"Hey. Hey. Heeeeey. Everything is okay, baby. Don't upset yourself."

"I should've fought harder. I should've fought back harder, but I was so afraid of losing the baby. My only goal was to protect the baby."

"And you did. That's what's important. You left that nigga for me to deal with, which is what you were supposed to do. Our baby survived. You succeeded. That's all that matters."

"I feel like I saved one kid and failed the other two."

"Ever, you're talking crazy, baby. Have you eaten this morning?"

"No."

"Lyric there?"

"Yes.

"Tell her to come to the crib. I'm going to bring breakfast, and we can eat together, aight? Hopefully, that'll make you feel a little better. Anything you want in particular?"

"You."

"I'm coming, baby."

With the girls asleep, I knew it was the perfect time

to shower. It had been a long fucking night, and I wanted to clear my head before I went to the hospital to see Ever. It had been two nights too long without her at my side.

I slid from between the girls with ease, knowing that neither of them would wake up. They slept hard, and they slept well each night. Ever was the same. While the slightest noise would wake me, the three of them could sleep through a tsunami. It was baffling to me. I'd never aspired to get that type of rest. It was insane.

LUCA-EVER

IT WAS ONLY eight in the morning, and my home was jumping with cartoons playing in the background as I finished a batch of pancakes for Emorey and Essence. They'd loosened the rope on me and allowed me to cook while they watched television on the couch. Pancakes, eggs, and fresh fruit were their choices.

The duo were still in their pajamas. I, on the other hand, was fully dressed and ready to walk out of the door whenever Lyric decided to make an appearance. It felt like she was taking her precious time, but I knew it wasn't the case. She'd been thugging it out with us, too. I knew that before she came to my rescue, she wanted to clean herself up. It had been a long two nights for us all.

"Breakfast is ready!" I yelled to the girls.

A second later, I heard tiny footsteps trampling through the living room and heading for the dining room. I followed behind them, happy that they were gaining their independence so quickly. For a moment, they had me spooked. This morning, they were almost back to the little girls I'd seen off to school the day that everything happened.

"You not eat with me?" Emorey was the first to inquire.

"No. Not today. TT Lyric is on her way over to eat with you. Is that OK?"

"Umm hmmm. You not eat?"

"Yeah. I'm going to grab something to eat on the way to see Mommy."

"I want to see Mommy," Essence told me as she sat down at the table.

"Me, too, Daddy."

All movement in my limbs ceased as I turned in Emorey's direction. Though the smile didn't reach my face, it was surely on my heart. There'd never been a child to refer to me as Daddy and only three months out of the FEDs, I wasn't expecting it to happen so soon.

I assumed it would be a few years before I found the perfect wife, married her, and then filled her with my babies. Ever stumbling into my life unexpectedly had put my aspirations of fatherhood on the fast track and made it happen within a week. Now, as I stared back at Emorey as she smiled at me, I couldn't help but thank her mother for that.

"Mommy wants you to stay home until she feels better so that she won't get you sick, too," I regained my composure and responded. My mind was still blown, and my heart was still racing.

Me, too, Daddy. Her little voice rang in my ears.

"OK. Her feel better soon."

"Yes. She'll feel better soon."

Emorey and Essence both had two separate plates to keep their hot food away from their fruit.

"Anybody want syrup?"

"Me, too!" Emorey screamed.

"I do," Essence said.

"Alright. Not much, or your mother will kill me."

Ever hated the idea of too much sugar being given to the girls. She tried her hardest to keep them away from candy and even snacks that were loaded with sugar. As I poured a reasonable amount of syrup on both of their pancakes, I heard bags rattling and footsteps nearing.

"It smells good in here!" Lyric rounded the corner. "Hey, Essence. Hey, Emorey."

"TT Lyric, you wan' eat wit' me?"

"Sure, baby. If Luca made enough for me."

"He name Daddy, TT Lyric."

Her eyes bloomed just like mine had a few minutes ago before she walked in. It took her a second to adjust to the new piece of information she'd received but when she finally did, she agreed.

"Yes. His name is Daddy for you and Essence, but I have a different daddy. His name is Liam. You've met him, right?"

"Umm hmmm."

"Luca, how about you come fix me a plate, too?" She tilted her head toward the kitchen with hiked brows and urgency in her eyes.

"Aight."

I followed her out of the dining room and into the kitchen. There was plenty of food left. I'd cooked extra just in case she hadn't eaten.

"Daddy?" She blew out, fanning her face. Between her and Laike, I wasn't sure who was the most dramatic.

"Same thing I said. Blew my fucking mind right before you walked in the door."

"Wow."

"She asked if she could call me daddy last night, and I told her yeah."

"She wasted no time."

"I like that shit, too." I chuckled. "Shit kind of has a kick to it. Don't it?"

"It does." Lyric nodded with a smile. "So that means I'm like officially a TT now and not just Mommy's best friend who I call TT?"

"No longer just Mommy's best friend who they call TT."

"How have they been since they've been home?"

"Last night was a little rough but this morning they're better."

"Good. They weren't harmed, were they?"

"Aside from Emorey telling me he hit Essence, nothing else has come up."

"OK. I'm just glad they're both OK."

"Yeah. They're straight. Now fix your own fucking food. I'm heading out."

"Meany," I heard her say as I left the kitchen and headed out of the door.

The sun was beaming, providing me with a healthy

dose of light as I slid into my truck. Unlike the last few times I'd climbed in my ride, this time I wasn't filled with gloom. A huge weight had been lifted from my shoulders. My girls were home and their mother wouldn't be too much longer getting there.

I pulled out of my driveway with that on the forefront of my mind. That was enough to keep me pushing and help me get through the day. Because, in the end, my family would be reunited, and I couldn't wait for the day. Until then, we'd make the best of our current situation.

Ever. The thought of her brought a smile to my face. It always had. With the blunt from my ashtray at my lips, I came to the conclusion that there wasn't anyone else in the world I'd rather call mine. There wasn't anyone else's arms I'd rather be wrapped in when I slept like a baby at night. It was her. She was it for me. Before lighting the blunt that was at my lips, I picked up my phone and dialed the number that I was all too familiar with.

"Yeah?" My father answered the phone. It was our signature. Those wondering why I answered the phone the way I did, I assumed had never called my father.

"Old man."

"Boy, stop playing on my fucking phone. What is it? I'm golfing."

"You ain't hitting nothing. Missing every hole."

"I ain't missing shit. How do you think I got you three? I have perfect aim. Better ask your mother. And, according to sources, you don't miss, either."

"Like father, like son. I told you I got you. You thought I was bullshitting?"

"Ummm hmmm. Did you tie up that loose end?" He cut to the chase.

"Laike is making sure it's tied, burned, and disposed of."

"Good. Now what you want, Luca? I've got things to do." He swore he was so busy, but his days mostly consisted of golf, television, dinner dates with my mother, and yard work that he never seemed to complete.

"I'm going to marry her," I revealed, lighting the blunt in my hands.

"Hell, you'd better or don't call me or your mother anymore."

"You're choosing a stranger over your own son? You've only known her for three months."

"I like her better," he admitted. "She's good for you, son. Only one of those kinds swings by in a lifetime. Don't let the opportunity pass you by."

"I won't."

"Is that all?"

"Nah. Not really."

"Ooooooh. I see. Mr. Big Shot is scared." He tittered, having a field day with that piece of information.

"Not really."

"Oh, yes, you are. That's why you called me. What you want some advice, son?"

"It would help."

"Ask her in private. She's the type of person who doesn't like attention or the pressure other's presence would cause. Don't put her on the spot like that. Make it simple. She'll love that. Don't involve the kids. Make this moment about her and her only. Kids can be difficult when the attention is not solely on them."

Emorey, I thought immediately.

"Make it part of your normal routine. She'll notice. They always notice when something is different. Don't weigh her finger down, either. I know how you get. She's a graceful, elegant girl without needing the bright lights and marching band. Give her a simple, meaningful diamond that you can upgrade as the years go on, eventually getting her the chunk of a diamond that I know is on your mind right now."

"Is that all?"

"Na. Focus on the marriage and not the wedding. If I could go back in time, I wouldn't even have had a wedding. Your mother and I hated that shit. Don't assume she wants it just because most women do. Ask her how she wants to proceed and take it from there."

"Alright."

"Now, I've got to go before I have to whoop one of these crackers on the course with my club for looking upside my head like they ain't got no damn sense."

"Behave, old man."

"I love you, son. I'm proud of you."

"Always."

I ended the call with my father and immediately dialed Rico's line. He answered after a few rings, sleep still evident in his voice.

"What's up, Luca?"

"Shit, nigga, wake up."

"I'm always up when money on the other end of the line."

"Bet. I need something special from you, and I need it as soon as possible."

"Run it down to me and you know I got you."

"I need a ring for my ole lady. She's simple and classy. Give me something serious, but not too heavy for her pretty little fingers. Something that won't freak her out."

"Any specifics?"

"Nah. She's a size six."

"Bet. I got something in mind. Get back to me in a week and it'll be ready for pickup."

"Then I'm coming to pick it up. No more to talk about."

"That works, too." He chuckled.

"Appreciate you."

When we ended the call, I was finally able to boost the volume of my stereo. *Chasing Summer* was on rotation.

She's so happy when she's next to me
Thought she had me
Baby really thought that she had me
Now she's feening for the rest of me
But that isn't in the recipe

I sang along to the lyrics of "The Recipe". The drive to Original Cakes was a smooth one, making me forget my intentions of checking in with Ken. I made my third call of the morning, already tired of the amount of socializing the pleasant mood of mine had bullied me into.

"What's up, Luca?"

"Shit. You good?"

"Yeah. I'm straight. Everything good on your end?"

"All good. I'm pulling up to Original, you want anything?"

"Yeah. Load me up. Don't matter what."

"Aight. Is she awake?"

"Yeah."

"Tell her don't fall asleep. I'll be there before she knows it."

"I'll let her know."

"Appreciate you."

"Aye." He stopped me from hanging up.

"What's up?"

"Yeah, you hit the jackpot with this one. Sit her ass down, ASAP."

"Already did. Nigga, you hear the monitor. It done put your ass to sleep and woke you back up. That's all me."

"Yeah. Yeah. I've got to play catch up. How you get out and put one on the scoreboard before me?"

"You slipping. You've had an eight-year lead."

"Yeah, man. I'm in here thinking about that shit now. But, aight. I'll see you in a minute."

"Aight."

LUCA+EVER

I WALKED into Ever's room and found her sitting up. For the last two days, she'd been in too much pain to move much at all. Going to the bathroom was so painful that she'd been given a catheter but even that was gone. Doctors also wanted to monitor her urine to make sure that there wasn't any internal bleeding. So, with that being gone, I knew it was a good sign.

"Hey," she greeted me as I rounded the corner.

The smile on her face looked so familiar, even bruised and battered. It felt like forever since I'd seen it.

"You're up." I handed Ken his food and continued into the room until I was at Ever's side. Our food was separated in two bags that I set on the small table in front of her.

"I'm up."

She stretched her arms and invited me in for a hug. I gladly accepted the invitation. It felt so good seeing her using her strength again. I restrained myself, remembering not to squeeze too tight and allowing her to lead while I followed. Easing her into any movement was the best idea for everyone. There would possibly be a new ache or new bruise discovered each day for the next few days.

When she finally let me go, I gently kissed her lips. The swelling had gone down tremendously. She was looking a little more like herself now. I moved further down until I was near her flat stomach. It didn't matter if my baby wasn't visible yet. He was there and we all knew it. I made two full circles with my hands before kissing the cloth of her gown.

"Where's my food?"

"Damn, it's like that?"

"I love you, babe, I really do, but they have been

trying to feed me nursing home food, and I'm not in a nursing home."

"I see," I told her as I took a look at the contents of the plate that she had left sitting on the table.

"I got you a few things, not sure of what you wanted."

"Just feed me. I don't care what it is."

With a hiked brow, I smiled. "You sure?"

"Luca, get your mind out of the gutter."

"Just saying." I shrugged.

Ever chose the cheese eggs and sausage patties cut into small pieces. They were the easiest to chew and get into her system without burning her lips or hurting her jaws. Together, we shared the meal with random commentary from Ken. I appreciated him more than he could imagine.

Once Laike gave me the green light on the Scar situation, he could go home and get some good rest. He'd left his own operation to look over my woman and unborn child. There wasn't anyone else in the world I trusted with the task other than him or Laike. I knew that they'd save them before they saved themselves and that was the only amount of loyalty I'd accept in their presence.

TWENTY-TWO

EVER

"I GOT IT," I told Luca.

"You sure?"

"Yes," I confirmed as I gently climbed into his bed.

It felt so much better than the one I'd been sleeping in for the last few days. After a week, I was finally released and sent home to be with my family. Doctors wanted to keep a close eye on any possibility of internal bleeding or any immediate threat to my baby's life. My lungs were showing low oxygen levels after the first two days, which required round-the-clock assistance from the oxygen machine. But after the fifth day, everything was normal again and my vitals were spectacular.

"When are the girls coming?"

"You sure you got it?"

"Would you like to lay me down yourself?"

"I would," he admitted.

"I'm fine, Luca. Just taking it easy."

He acted as if I would break at any second. Coming home to his concerns was worse than staying at the hospital and having someone knock on the door every two or three hours to bother me, but I knew he meant well.

"They're on the way now. My mom is bringing them on her way home."

"Good."

"You need anything?"

"Just my girls and for you to relax."

"I'm cool. I just need you to relax."

With a shake of my head, I rested my back against the headboard. It felt so good to be home. Even the air smelled different at Luca's. It smelled fresher, better, and the city view brought me comfort that was inexplicable. I'd missed everything about Luca and his home and the girls and my apartment. I couldn't wait to get back into the swing of things.

"I know my customers are going to kill me. I'll have to cancel a few cake orders and refund them. I know I'll be down for at least another week with my ribs healing so slowly."

"We can worry about that later. Lyric has your business line and has been trying to figure out where your schedule is. I know you don't like help in the bakery, but maybe a temporary assistant until you're fully recovered is a good idea. You might actually appreciate the help more than you know. A few days a week won't hurt."

"I'm sure I'll need the help."

"Mommy!" Little hands and little feet came bursting through the bedroom door, bringing me so much joy.

Emorey was the first to climb up and get in my lap. Essence followed suit, but sat right up under me. I wrapped my arms around them both. With sweaty palms and bright eyes, I kissed them all over their small faces. The fulfillment of seeing them brought me was unmatched.

"I missed you two so much."

"Mommy, you feel better?" Emorey inquired, always the inquisitive one of the two.

"Mommy feels so much better."

"My old daddy hurt you?"

"Let's not talk about that, Emorey," I quieted her, placing a finger to my lip for emphasis.

"I got a new daddy, Mommy," she told me in a low whisper.

"Do you?"

"Me, too," Essence joined.

"Really?"

"He name Daddy." Emorey beamed with joy, looking over at Luca.

"Really?"

"Umm hmmm."

"Well, guess what, guys?"

I felt that there was no better time to tell them

about the bundle of joy their new daddy had blessed us with. I looked to Luca before focusing on the girls again.

"What, Mommy?"

"What?"

"You get to share your new daddy with a new baby soon."

"You're having a baby?" Essence lit up.

"You have a baby in you tummy?" Emorey frowned, tilting her head to try to understand how.

"Yes. Mommy has a baby in her tummy."

"You tummy little, Mommy. You not have a baby in there, silly." She laughed.

"I do. It'll get really big soon and Mommy will hardly be able to walk and then you'll have to help Mommy around the house. You think you can do that?"

"Yes, 'cause I strong, Mommy. Woook at my muscles. I stronger." Emorey balled her fists and showed me the muscles she thought she had.

"Oh wow. Big, strong muscles."

"Is it a girl or a boy?" Essence wanted to know.

"We don't know yet but your dad seems to think it's a boy. We'll just have to wait and see. What do you think?"

"I think it's a boy, too," Essence agreed with Luca.

"I don't wan' a boy!" Emorey folded her arms over her chest.

Everyone in the room burst into laughter, knowing how things could go south if we continued the conversation. Emorey had a way of believing that it was either her way or the highway. Unfortunately, in this case, she didn't get to choose. We could only take what God gave us.

"Is your mom downstairs?"

"I'm sure she is. She wants you to meet someone from the daycare who will be helping us out with the girls until you are back on your feet for good."

"You hired someone?"

Luca was always being extra cautious and always thought everything through. He executed a plan better than anyone I knew because he was such a meticulous person. In some cases, it made me love him a little more. In other cases, it made me want to chew his head off.

"Yeah. To pick the girls up from school every day and make sure they're fed. I'll do the drop-offs. She'll be gone by bedtime each day. She's on from 4:00-9:30 p.m. weekdays and 12:00-9:00 p.m. on weekends. Whether you're at my house or your apartment, she'll be there to help."

Luca knew just how much peace being at my apartment with my girls brought me. I loved his home just as much, but there was something about mine that just broke the mold. I'd carefully curated a welcoming space that kept my energy up and my spirits high. Splitting the time between our homes would still be a thing for me. I simply wanted to rest at his place for the next few days, however.

"OK. You can bring her up."

Luca disappeared and headed down the stairs. When he returned, he was followed by his mother and a familiar face from the daycare. It was Essence's summer school teacher.

"Ms. San," I greeted her with a smile.

It was good to see that Mrs. Eisenberg had chosen someone that I was already familiar with and trusted. The introductions weren't needed. I'd seen her almost every day in the summer. Essence loved her.

"Hi. Just wanted to say hello. I'll keep the babies out of your hair so that you can get some rest. I'm going to make sure everybody is fed and in bed by nine. Is there a specific schedule or meal plan you'd like me to follow for the girls?"

"We're not big on screen time. I like to have dinner done and them sitting down to start eating by seven, seven-thirty at the latest. Bath time is at eight or eight-thirty, depending on how late we stayed at the dinner table. Bedtime is between eight-thirty and nine. I like to read them at least one bedtime story each before they go to bed. Essence is working on weekly spelling words so it's important that she studies them after school and before bed," I explained.

"Sounds simple enough. Any food allergies or preferences I should know about?"

"They're open to trying new things. No one has any allergies that I'm aware of yet."

"Good. Good. Send them on down when you're ready. I'll be down here in this kitchen, trying to figure out what we're having for dinner."

San was in her fifties and still had it. She loved kids just as much as Luca's mom. I could tell how much they brightened her day from the look on her face when another one walked through her classroom door.

"OK."

"How are you feeling today?" Luca's mom stepped up to ask.

She parked it right on the edge of the bed, resting her legs but still giving me plenty of space. She was such a selfless woman. I just hoped that I had been labeled the same. I tried to add some good to everyone's lives I entered, and I hoped it didn't go unnoticed.

"I'm feeling so much better. It feels so good to be out of that hospital. I can't wait to get back into the swing of things."

"Let's not rush it. You have all the time in the world and help as long as you need it. Focus on healing. Everything else can wait."

"Everything," Luca cosigned.

"I heard her, Luca."

With a smile, he warned me with a finger. I'd missed being in his arms at night and couldn't wait until the sun fell so that I could fall asleep in them.

"You're carrying the first Eisenberg grand. Your health is top priority for us all. If there's anything I can help with or do for you, I'm a call away."

"OK."

"I'm going to get out of your hair. I have a date with this fine man tonight, and I wouldn't miss it for nothing in the world."

Her haughtiness was exactly why Lyric was the way that she was. Lyric was an exact replica of her mother, down to the dimples in her cheeks. It was funny seeing just how Lyric would be when she got older.

"Man, that nigga old and almost out of commission."

"Son, you shouldn't be such a hater. After all, without the juice from his nut sack, you wouldn't be here. Show some appreciation."

"Please leave, woman. Like, now!" Luca pointed toward the door.

"I'm just being honest."

"No one asked for your honesty."

The two bickered as I listened, utterly amused. I imagined it was what my son and I would look like when he was Luca's age. That's if I was having a boy. Luca was convinced, and I was starting to believe him. His faith had rubbed off on me something tough.

"You hear that shit?" he asked when she finally made it out of the room.

"Your family is hilarious."

"And you're guilty by association. Our family... our family is hilarious."

"Our family," I agreed.

My girls had been so silent that I forgot they were still in the room. When I looked down, I realized why. They'd both fallen asleep in my arms.

"Awwwww. They're sleeping."

"They've missed you."

"I've missed them, too. And, I'm sleepy, too." I chuckled.

"I'm going to go lay them in their beds so that you can get comfortable."

"Get the little one first. I want to hold on to my big baby a little longer."

Luca took Emorey to their room first and followed up with Essence. When he made it back to the bedroom, I'd already slid down and propped pillows underneath me so that I wouldn't wake up in pain.

"You good?" he sat at the edge of the bed next to me and asked.

"I'm great, baby."

"Aight. I'm going on the balcony for a minute to clear my head. Yell for me if you need me."

"I will."

I watched as he stood and left, leaving me with a big, silly smile on my face as I got comfortable and ready for an evening nap. As I closed my eyes, I was led to thank the only person who could've made any of this possible. *Thank you, God.*

LUCA·EVER

I WOKE to the sound of birds chirping in the distance. Opening my eyes, I tried locating Luca, but he was nowhere in sight. The sliding door to the balcony was open, so I knew he wasn't far. The sun was falling and nighttime was in the air.

To clear my vision, I rubbed the debris from my eyes. Just as I felt the burning sensation from the foreign material that brushed against my skin, I heard Luca's baritone.

"She has risen."

He walked into the room with a bouquet of the reddest roses I'd ever laid eyes on. I placed my hand in front of my face to see what had done the damage to my eye and was taken aback instantly. The pretty, sparkling diamond rested on my finger as if it truly belonged there. I looked from Luca and then to my hand and then to Luca again.

"What have you done?" I asked.

"Put a ring on it," he told me, placing the roses on the table next to the bed and getting on one knee.

I quickly sat up and tossed my legs over the bed.

"You're serious?" I asked.

"Very fucking serious," he assured me.

"Oh my God. My nails are a mess."

"Who gives a fuck? Your heart is flawless and that's all that matters to me."

"I love you."

"Nah, baby, I love you. I don't have to run this shit down for you to get my point. I'm just trying to see if you're trying to marry me?"

"Yes. Of course," I answered his question without hesitation. There wasn't a doubt in my mind that he was the man I wanted to marry. I'd known from the moment I saw his face.

"You like the ring?"

"I love the ring. Oh my God."

I wasn't sure if I wanted to jump, shout, dance, or cry at the moment, but the love that I felt as Luca looked at me in my eyes only made them water. Big, thick tears fell down my face and onto my thighs.

"Thank you for loving every piece of me, even the broken ones."

"Thank you for having faith in me, even during the

times it was hardest to. Thank you for coming into my life when I needed you the most. Thank you for giving me two little girls. Thank you for giving me a child. Thank you for always putting us first. Thank you for your selflessness. Thank you for your generosity. Thank you for that bomb ass pussy between them legs I can't wait to get to once you're healed."

"Luca." I laughed. "How did it go from all these wonderful things to my pussy?"

"Because it's a wonderful thing too, baby. I wish you could feel that motherfucker. You'd understand why it had to be included. I couldn't leave that out."

"Oh my God. You're so intolerable."

"But you love me."

"So much that it used to scare me. Now, it excites me. You are everything I prayed for in a husband and here we are."

"I don't want to wait to make you my wife. How long does the wedding shit take?"

"I don't want a wedding, Luca. I just want you. By the time we plan a wedding, I'll be big and pregnant and too irritated to walk down anybody's aisle. Just marry me. We can worry about the glitz and the glam later."

I'd never wanted to be the center of attention and never saw myself desiring it either. A wedding seemed like far too much pressure. I didn't want to put that on me or my loved ones. If I had to be honest, the courthouse suited me, but I knew Lyric would never allow that.

"It's your world, Ever. I just live in it, baby."

"Come kiss me," I pleaded.

Luca stood to his feet and leaned over me to kiss my lips. He felt so much like home. He felt so much like mine.

"Mommy!" I heard Emorey call out to me, causing me to snap my head in her direction.

"Yes, baby?"

"Are you sad?" She rushed over to my side of the bed to inspect.

"No, Mommy is happy. Daddy just asked Mommy to marry him. Mommy is very, very happy."

"I happy, too."

"Yeah? Well, that makes two of us."

"San made dinner. Do you want to eat here or downstairs?"

"Downstairs."

"Aight."

"I need to shower, first. I smell like that hospital and it's making me sick to my stomach."

"Let me get the girls settled on the couch downstairs and then I'll be back up to help you shower. I need one, too."

"OK."

As soon as Luca and Emorey left the room, I grabbed my phone from the other side of the bed. I snapped a picture of the gorgeous ring that I'd just received and sent it to Lyric.

I's a fiancée, I texted along with the picture.

The gray bubble appeared and then disappeared. My cell phone rang right after.

"Get the fuck out of here. What type of super-duper

gushy, mushy pussy are you putting on my brother? A baby and a ring in three months? Please teach me your ways, love. Oh my God. Congratulations!"

"Thank you. And, I don't have anything to teach you. Luca only asked me for two things. That was loyalty and respect. I've given him both and in return, he's given me the world."

"I know that's right, honey. My friend is getting married!" she yelled into the phone.

"Lyric. Why are you so loud?"

"Why aren't you? You're the one that just got a ring bigger than my kneecap. If you won't scream, then I'm going to do it for you. I'll pour a drink while I'm at it because you can't have one."

"Ha. Ha. Really funny. That was a very low blow."

"It was, wasn't it? My bad. But, soon. Hopefully."

"Not soon enough. This journey is just starting."

"It'll be over before you know it. My God. You're getting married. When are we going to plan the wedding for? After the baby or rush it to make it happen before the baby comes?"

"Neither."

"What do you mean, neither?"

"I'm not having a wedding, Lyric, because I'm not waiting to marry this man. You can plan something super small and intimate that must happen within the next two weeks, but nothing big. Only family. Only us. And, lots of white flowers."

"Boring, but doable. Should've known you'd say no to anything that put you in the spotlight."

"I'm happy to know that you know me so well."

"Whatever. Can we at least go pick out a dress?"

"Yes. A simple one and it'll only be you and my mother. That's all."

"OK. Fine."

"I'm not playing, Lyric. Simple. Just us and a pastor."

"Can we at least have cake?"

"Yes, one that I plan to make."

"You can hardly lift an arm."

"I'll be able to in less than two weeks."

"Well, you're right about that."

"You ready?" Luca walked in and asked.

"Yeah."

"Hey, Luca!" Lyric yelled. "Congratulations!"

"He can't hear you but I'll tell him."

"Okay, call me tomorrow."

"I will."

I ended the call and extended my arms for Luca's embrace. He obliterated the space between us, pulling me into his arms gently. He'd killed two birds with one stone, helping me from the bed while covering me with his love. Going the extra mile, Luca lifted me into his arms and carried me into the bathroom.

"Can we take a bath tonight?" I couldn't remember the last time we'd relaxed in the tub together. I needed that time with him, and my body needed to soak. The aches and pains would be less brutal if I could.

"Dinner is waiting."

"I don't care."

"Me either," he told me with a shrug.

"Sit down while I start the water."

I watched from afar as he worked his way around the bathroom to grant my request. As much as I liked to shower with him, I loved our baths together. The intimacy that it supplied was the greatest. Physical touch was unavoidable and the main reason I enjoyed the moments so much.

"You ready?" Luca asked once he'd gotten everything situated and ready for us.

"I'm ready."

TWENTY-THREE

LUCA

1:33 a.m.

Sniffles woke me from my sleep. It had only been thirty-five minutes since I'd dozed off. I vividly recalled watching the clock as it approached the one o'clock hour before succumbing to sleep.

"Ever?"

As I called out to her, I waved my hand across the lamp to illuminate the space to some degree. It was pitch black around us, not a single light in sight. Her tear-stained face was the first thing I laid eyes on. Her pretty, brown, saddened eyes began chipping away at my heart as I gathered words to share with her.

"What's the matter? Are you hurting? Do you need a doctor? The bab—"

"I'm fine, physically, Luca. I just... Mentally, emotionally, I've been destroyed. I'd love to—" She choked up. "To think this is just something I ca-can bounce back from but I don't know. I-I feel so much discomfort. So much sadness. And– I'm– I'm– Luca, I'm scared."

I pulled myself together while tossing the cover off my body. I rushed into the bathroom to retrieve a clean, warm towel. Though I hated to leave Ever alone for even a second, it was necessary. Upon my return, I watched as her body shook under distress.

The strings of my heart were tugged and pulled in twenty different directions. The time between words gave me a chance to collect myself. In any given situation, I had the solution. That was my job. I was the problem solver. I had the resolution. *Every single time.* Except this one.

If I had the ability to go inside Ever's head and rearrange her thoughts, I would. But, since I couldn't, I was left scrambling to fix things within from the outside. Blindly, I began casting aside her worries and trying my damnedest to make her feel as beautiful as she was and as beautiful as her life was about to become after this was all over.

I swiped the warm towel across her face, clearing it of tears and bringing comfort to her irritated skin. It was red and blotchy from her whirlwind of emotions, constant rubbing, and contorting. As quickly as I wiped the tears, they were replaced. I tossed the towel on the floor once satisfied and pulled my entire heart into my hands.

"Ever, baby." I sighed, unsure how to unknot her tangled heart. "I can't change what has happened. Lord knows I would in a fucking flash. I can only promise that it will never be the case again. I'll live and die on that hill. Someone hurt you.

"My world almost ended getting that call. I never want to hear anything like that again. I won't hear anything like that again. I've made sure of it. I want you to live a life you love, Ever. One where you're not looking over your shoulder. Had I known the extent of this situation, to begin with, you wouldn't have been looking over your shoulders, to begin with.

"I would've made sure you and my children were safe. That's my number one priority and that hasn't changed. It'll never change. I don't want you to be afraid of anyone as long as I'm alive and well. Your fears should be as natural as any other mother.

"Shit like Emorey falling off her bike or Essence falling in love with someone who will take advantage of her gentleness or giving birth naturally or if your new recipe will come out as perfectly as you imagined. That's it, Ever. Let me worry about the big shit.

"Your burdens, give them to me. Your battles, let me fight them. Your dragons, let me slay them. Your fears, baby, let me handle them. It's hard, Ever. I know it is, giving up and giving in to me completely, but baby, I promise I've got you. I'll leave no stone unturned."

I cupped her chin, pulling her face in my direction.

"I'm not that nigga. I'm *THAT* nigga. Your nigga. Give it all to me, Ever! I want your problems. Your faults. Your fears. Your flaws. Don't be afraid to release that shit. I'm a big boy. I can handle it. I will handle it.

"My desire is for you to live life free of the anchors, free of the hindrances, free of the baggage, free of it all. Essence, Emorey, and our little baby, I got them just like I've got you. Give it all to me, Ever. Right now. Give it to me."

"I feel responsible." She cried in my arms.

"You didn't birth that hoe ass nigga. It's not your fault, mommas. If it wasn't you, it would've been someone else. His bullshit stops at you. He chose the wrong motherfucker to push up on and now his mo–" I grimaced, stopping before I shared information with Ever that she couldn't stomach at the moment.

"I just keep feeling like I should've left so many years sooner. I should've just had the strength."

"Then there'd be no Essence. There'd be no Emorey. My heart can't stand the thought of that, Ever. Your time there served a purpose. It wasn't in vain. We got two little ones out of the deal so it wasn't all bad. In the end, we win. We always will."

She twiddled her fingers, nervous energy radiating through her frame. I picked up on the shift immediately.

"Talk to me. I'm listening, love. I promise."

"I know."

"So, don't bottle it up. Give it to me straight."

"I'm afraid you see me differently now," she blubbered, her tears casting down her face in droves.

"I do," I admitted. "I see your resilience a little better. I see your strength a little better. I see your selflessness a little better. I see your beauty a little better. I see your heart, Ever. I see you. I see our future. I see you in a white dress, walking your fine ass down the aisle on the way to make this shit official. That's what I see. I see a woman who will die in old age, happy! I'm going to make sure of that. So, yes, I do see you differently. I see you so much better. Shit is so much clearer."

"What did I ever do to deserve you, Luca?"

"I'm the only nigga you deserve. I'm the only nigga that was meant for you. I'm the only nigga you could've ended up with. Our paths didn't cross coincidentally. They were meant to. God sat you right on top of my heart and from the minute you opened your eyes, you'd penetrated that motherfucker. I've done some shit in my life, Ever. I'm not a perfect man and I'll never strive for perfection. I'm flawed. I've fucked up. So, it's me that wonders what I ever did to deserve you."

"I love you. So, so much."

"Forever, baby."

Back and forth, I rocked her body until the crying stopped completely. Minutes later, light snores erupted in the silence. Her comfort was a source of solace, but circumstances were different at the moment. My eyes remained opened as I replayed our conversation in my head. Her fears were real and I needed to dead them as soon as possible.

For an hour, I held her in my arms, rocking her fragile body, before gently laying her on the bed. I pulled the cover over her and kissed her cracked lips that were still swollen and sore. Closing my eyes, I wished I was able to kill that nigga again. He'd done damage in my home, disrupting our peace and bringing us nothing but pain.

On my way to the kitchen, I shot Laike a text.

Pull up.

Almost instantly, he read the message. Though he didn't respond, there wasn't a doubt in my mind that I'd be seeing him soon. When I called, he came and vice versa. Shit had always been that way with us and would remain the same.

I poured a glass of brown liquor from the bar and grabbed the contents to fill the blunts I planned to roll. Strolling through my home, I silently prayed for the day that it was Ever's safest space again. The place she felt secure and most like herself. It would take some time, but I'd be damned if I didn't help her along the process. She deserved the peace that I could offer her. I planned to make sure she got back to it. For the time being, I wouldn't let her out of my sight. Her nor my girls. We'd be locked in this bitch until we all felt better, no matter how long that took.

I slid the door back, stepping out into the backyard to find Laike rounding the house. His timing was impeccable. However, I couldn't help but wonder how he'd gotten to me so fast.

"How'd you get in?" I asked.

"Did you forget I designed this motherfucker?"

"Sometimes," I admitted. "Where the hell were you?"

"Up the street, really. Spinning some corners, clearing my head."

"Or watching the house?"

"That, too."

"Appreciate it, bro."

"You got my front. I got your back."

"I doubt that nigga still in Channing and I doubt he knows where we rest our heads."

"Can never be too sure. It's possible they were here long before the gas station."

"True."

I sipped from my cup and passed it to Laike. He accepted as I began rolling the blunt on the tray I'd brought out the supplies on. Before I was able to get the buds inside of the paper, I smelled some sticky that smelled just like the buds I was rolling.

"Impatient ass nigga."

"Stay ready so you never have to get ready," he responded. "What's up? What's on your mind?"

"Just got to get some shit off my chest, ya know?"

"Shoot for it."

"Ever, man." I sighed, shaking my head as my stomach turned, considering what I was about to say.

"How is Sis?"

"Scared."

My voice cracked. In efforts to conceal my emotions, I cleared my throat.

"Bro," Laike called out to me, slightly closing the gap between us.

I looked up at him, titling my head to meet his gaze.

"This me," he said, patting his chest. "Don't do that. Don't offend me, either, nigga. I'm lil bro."

As the words left his mouth, the tears fell from my eyes.

"Them tears don't make you pussy, nigga. They make you real."

"She's scared, nigga. Scared." I shook my head continuously.

"If that was my shorty and my situation, I'd be no good right now, nigga. I commend you for holding it together this long. Get your big ass up," he commanded.

I stood to my feet, dusting off the debris from the blunt I'd finished. Laike wrapped his arms around me, pulling me into a hug that I discovered was needed. He pounded my back with his fist before releasing me.

"I'm going to handle that shit. You don't have to worry. I'm on it."

"I already know."

I grabbed the blunt he was handing me.

"Now, what's on your dome?"

"Shit, getting Ever down the aisle a better woman than she was before all this shit popped off."

"You will."

"She's my life, Laike. It's like, my life was never shitty, but her presence makes it feel like I wasn't really living before she walked into my world. Like... it's so hard to explain. It's like she woke up something within me that I never want to go without again."

"I feel ya, nigga. I'm not a stranger to that feeling. I've felt that shit. Since me and B called it quits, I've felt unalive. Shit is weird because I'm having the time of my life, but a nigga ain't living."

"You need to get back right with Baisleigh, Laike. Ain't shit out here better than having a home. Not a location, but a person."

"Who you telling, my nigga?" He huffed. "But, I'm no good for B, man. She's on top of her shit. I'm poison, Luca. I don't want to fuck up her world. I know I will. I'm cool with watching from the sidelines."

"No you're not."

"I'm not afraid to pretend."

"Bullshit."

"But, we're not talking about me. We're talking about you."

"I know."

"You 'bout to be a fucking daddy, nigga. What you feeling?" He laughed. "How that shit feeling?"

"I'm already a father, Laike. I've been Daddy since I walked out of them gates, man. The only thing that changes this time is I'm here from day one. That part, I'm looking forward to. I can't lie. Seeing her belly grow. Watching her body change. I'm ready for whatever."

"Per usual."

For two hours straight, we found comfort in one another's company. The sun peaked through The Hills, bringing our gathering to a close. Intoxicated and feeling as if the weight of the world was resting on my shoulders, I stumbled to bed. Underneath the covers, I pulled Ever close, wishing I could take her pain away at once. Sleep never found me. I listened to the beat of her heart as I stared into the open space around us.

God, grant me the power to help Ever heal, I prayed.

LUCA-EVER

HIS SLUMPED POSTURE and somber appearance confirmed his identity. Sitting on the edge of the porch, he turned up the cup in his hand a final time before standing to his feet. He walked closer to the street, leaning against the fence that led to the sidewalk. The darkness that covered the sky made it slightly difficult to see his face, but I didn't need to. I was certain I'd found my mark. The last four hours I'd been sitting on him, he checked every box as described and matched the images I'd obtained over the last week.

My cellphone vibrated in my pocket. Pressing my back against the seat, I stretched my legs slightly in order to retrieve it. I glanced at the clock on the radio, noting that Ever was more than likely resting for the night already. For a fact, I knew it wasn't her calling unless there was an emergency. I prayed like hell there wasn't an emergency. Laike's name appeared on the screen, prompting me to answer.

"Yeah?"

"We're not the only ones gunning for this nigga's head." He huffed into the phone.

"Yeah?"

"It's a nigga been sitting on his ass the last two hours I've been here."

"Yeah?"

"Yes, bro. If he gets to this nigga first, I'm going to be pissed!"

"Lay low."

"Bet."

I ended the call, exiting the vehicle in pursuit of my target. Sitting like a duck, waiting for Laike to handle his business and finish off whoever he thought had witnessed his crime was not a part of my plan. I crossed the street while attaching the silencer to my piece. It locked as I approached the dark figure dressed in denim and a white shirt.

"Yo?" he asked, scrunching his features.

His delayed response to my presence assured his state of mind. He was intoxicated, mourning the loss of his homie. My condolences were not with his ass. I hoped that nigga died a couple of times on his way to the devil's playground. Though I could've laid his ass down from a far with my precise aim, my conscience wouldn't allow it. I needed further confirmation of his identity before I put an innocent person in the mud. There was no doubt that I had my guy once I was close enough. He reached for his waistline, revealing his piece as a warning.

Don't show it if you ain't gone shoot it, I thought. That was the difference between me and the rest of niggas. You wouldn't see my piece until your time had come. I was a walking threat. I didn't need a gun to enhance the fear in niggas, not when they very well understood I could end their lives with my bare hands, too.

"Tell Dewayne I'll meet him in hell."

Doot. Doot. I penetrated his brain and pierced his heart one after the other. As his body hit the pavement, I crept to the car from which I'd come. As I slid into the vehicle with the engine still running, my cell vibrated again.

"Yeah?" I answered.

"You can't be fucking serious right now, nigga!"

Silence coated the line.

"I know your wide back ass from anywhere," Laike joked. "The fuck you got me wasting my time for when you knew you'd handle the shit. I could be laying up in some pussy right now."

"I couldn't sleep."

"Nigg—"

"I haven't slept in two weeks, Laike. Two weeks. I'm fucking tired. I want to lay down, close my eyes, and rest knowing I'll see them niggas in hell when I get there. I can't do that with that nigga still roaming, gathering his thoughts and planning his retaliation. Ever expecting me to marry her at that altar in fourteen hours, bro. That couldn't happen until he was extinct."

"I was going to handle it... tonight."

"I know you were. I never doubted that. But, shit, bro. It was a little more personal than I let on."

"Understood."

"You know where to meet me. Wheels up in thirty."

"Bet."

"Put the car in the cubby closest to the hangar. Next to mine. It'll be handled."

"Say less."

Feeling three hundred pounds lighter, I hiked the volume on the stereo slightly. Stan played low as I burned the tires of the Toyota headed straight for the strip. My home, my bed, my children, my future wife, and our unborn child were the only thing on my mind. I needed them all and I needed them bad. I desperately wanted to go home, stretch my limbs on the couch as they snuggled around me, falling fast asleep as soon as their heads touched my skin.

Serenity lingered, filling me to capacity. When the plane was in sight, my nervous system was given permission to rest. I parked in one of the designated spots and laid my head against the seat. Blindly, I unscrewed the silencer while allowing exhaustion to have its way with me. The consequences of two weeks of cat naps and restless nights hit me simultaneously.

I exited the car and made my way onto the plane, which was fueled and waiting for departure. When I made it up the staircase, staff was waiting to greet me. Unfortunately, I had no words for anyone. A simple head nod or three and I was seated, waiting for my brother and little homie to arrive.

I didn't have to wait long before watching Laike swerve into the lot like the fool he was. Hopping out, he took a deep pull from the blunt in his hand. With his FN in his other hand, he pulled his pants up on his waist, walking gap-legged toward the staircase. Sighing, I rested my forehead between my index finger and thumb.

"Nigga, what you got a fucking turbo engine in that

little piece of shit?" he asked the second his feet touched the cabin.

"Laike, I'm tired and I'm not on that shit this morning."

"Fuck what you on." He scoffed. "You owe me a kill, nigga."

"Whatever."

"I'm serious."

"Aight. But, I'm off that. I'm done with that shit. Tried to be, at least."

"Them niggas had that coming, though. They brought that upon themselves," Cane interjected.

"True." Nodding, I agreed with him.

"So, feel free to go around slinging that fucking FN. I'm chilling. I have no desires to end another man's life."

"Unless he brings it upon himself," Cane added.

Agreeing again, I nodded. "Yeah. That shit right there he's saying."

"Well, we can't count on niggas to act right, so there will come a time," Laike assured us.

"I'm heading to the back, fellas. Appreciate your services."

"Services? Nigga, we didn't even touch the fucking triggers!" Laike called behind me as I slid the door of the bedroom backward and stepped inside.

I didn't bother responding, knowing just how salty he was about what had transpired and his missed opportunity. I removed my shoes and the black cap from my head as I sat down on the bed. The softness welcomed me. I laid flat on my back, feet still on the floor. Visions of a battered and bruised Ever resurfaced, tightening my chest and gripping my heart.

I lifted my phone and typed the simple code to unlock it. Ever's number was hardly in my call log because I hadn't left her side in the last two weeks. I had to scroll for ages to finally locate it. When I did, I tapped it, connecting the call. Though I knew she was, undoubtedly, asleep, I wanted her. I needed her. Her voice. Her softness. Her words. Her attention. I needed it.

"Hello?" She groaned. "Luca?"

The words came one after the other. I could hear the concern intertwined in them.

"I'm okay, Ever."

She sighed in relief before continuing.

"Baby, where are you?"

This time, I couldn't put her worries to rest. Instead of responding, I remained silent, hoping she understood my position.

"Well, when will you be home, Luca?"

"Soon, love."

"Okay."

Silence.

"I love you."

Silence.

"Luca?"

My chest burned. This woman, Ever Sinclair, was my entire world and I wondered if she knew it. Putting into words how I felt about her would be impossible, which meant the vows I'd been tasked with writing and reciting in the next fourteen hours would only be a fraction of my feelings in word form. I'd never be able to truly explain. The feeling she gave me was beyond words. Beyond me.

"Hmm?"

"Why'd you call? Are you sure you're OK?"

"I'm tired, Ever," I explained, swiping the tear that rolled down the side of my face.

Silence.

This time, it was her response that was delayed.

"The plane."

Silence. I didn't have to confirm what she already knew.

"Baby... Talk to me."

"I just want to go to sleep. I just can't do it without you."

"Get in bed," she instructed. "Rest your head on the pillow."

I followed directions, climbing up the bed and resting my head on the pillow.

"Put the phone on speaker."

I did as I was told.

"Are you laying down?"

"Yes."

"Close your eyes."

They were the last words I'd heard before tapping out.

EPILOGUE

LUCA

"FUCK FOR BETTER OR WORSE, it's forever and for Ever for us. Richer and richer. Through wealth, questionable health, disagreements, failures, struggles, and everything that comes with life, I'll continue to love you, continue to pour into you, continue to be the man for you, and continue to meet you where you are.

"Because, wherever you are, Ever, that's where I want to be. I've never felt anything like this before. That's how I know it's real. That's how I know it's true. The day I saw you in my sister's Jeep, sleeping without a care in the world, I knew then. I couldn't even see your face, but I knew. When you finally opened your eyes, I knew. When you opened your mouth, I knew.

"My heart was comforted. My thoughts were lulled to a more pleasant place. *That's my wife*. Right there was where they rested and I couldn't be happier. Or at least I thought I couldn't be, but then I discovered there were two more of you. My heart nearly exploded the day I saw those hazel eyes on Emorey. She fit so perfectly in my arms when she climbed into them. I knew then, too.

"She's mine, I thought. You were written all over her. I found myself falling in love all over again. And, then, a third time when Essence's tiny, timid soul made me want to protect her from all forms of hurt, harm, and danger.

"Ever, I don't think you'll ever comprehend how much better you've made me. How much peace you've brought me. If it means I'll meet you again in the next lifetime, I'd repeat every single thing in this one. I'd serve my sentence a hundred times if every one of them ends with you waiting at those gates. I love you. I'm in love with you. And, that'll never change. I'm yours until the day that I die."

As beautiful as Ever was in the simple white dress that resembled a slip of some kind, her face was a mess. Her small nose was red at the very tip and her eyes were swollen. She'd cried all morning. I knew because I'd answered four calls from her, each starting and ending with her in tears.

"Mine weren't that good." She sniffed.

The words were straight off the dome. I didn't need a pen and paper to confess my love for Ever. They were at the forefront of my brain always, though they weren't enough to truly convey my feelings.

"Yes they were," I assured her.

The words of the pastor blended into the background

as I listened to Ever. She was a fucking dream in that dress.

"Then kiss me."

Obliging, I leaned forward, pulling her closer to me with a hand on the back of her head. I devoured her, caring less about the people around us and more about the woman that I'd promised to love, honor, and cherish for the rest of our lives.

"That's why you—"

"Shut up!" I pulled back to silence Lyric.

"Mr. and Mrs. Eisenberg!" Laike chanted, moving closer and removing the plastic from the mountain of bills in his hands.

Keanu followed his lead, loosening his money as well. As we made our way out of the backyard and into our home, it wasn't rice that was thrown. Bills rained down on us. My father, Laike, and Keanu emptied their hands, reloaded, and emptied their hands again.

Upon approaching the house, we were greeted with a photographer who snapped pictures as we continued our journey into the large dining hall Lyric cleared out and arranged for the wedding. In a dinner-styled setting, as Ever requested, tables lined the area, topped with the finest dinnerware my father's money could buy. Because he'd forced me to allow his pockets to hurt for the recital of our vows, it was him footing the bill.

Our loved ones followed us inside, everyone taking their positions and abiding by the photographer's rules to get the family images taken. Within ten minutes, we were free of obligations and ready to get out of our clothes.

According to my watch, we were making great progress and still on schedule. Ever and I were scheduled to be on the plane in five hours flat and I'd be damned if we were late. Our mini moon would only be three days but I intended to enjoy it fully before returning to our babies.

"We're going to head upstairs to change into our reception attire. Hold this shit down until we get back."

"Just don't be trying to put another baby in her while you're away. Save that for the flight," Lyric joked.

"Nah. Not today. I don't think she's ready," I admitted.

The thought saddened me and quieted Lyric. The fact still stood that my wife had been assaulted two short weeks ago and was still recovering. Not until she told me with her own words that I could have her body to myself again, I'd wait. Those facts didn't make our day or our honeymoon any less special.

"I'm so sorry, Luca."

"Ever just agreed to be with me for a lifetime, Lyric. Sorry for what?"

"I just... I don't know."

"I don't know if I could ever thank you enough for bringing this woman into my world. You did your brother a solid one."

"I owed you a solid one, Luca. I really did."

"You owed me nothing, baby girl. I keep telling you that."

"I know but it still felt like it. Now, I feel a little better knowing I could at least make the rest of your life a fucking dream."

"Because that's exactly what she is."

"Isn't she?"

"Yes. You're next, Lyric. I can't wait to see you in a white dress. I'm sparing no expense, baby girl."

"Ugh. Go upstairs and don't start with that. Maybe one day, maybe not."

"One day," I confirmed, reaching over and snatching Ever away from her mother and stepfather. "Let me steal my wife for a second. We have to change."

"Of course," her mother yelped, fanning us off.

I pulled Ever through our home, up the stairs, and into our bedroom where I closed the door behind us and cupped her chin. My lips, with a mind of their own, rested against hers.

"I love you," I admitted, not pulling away until I was left breathless.

"Forever." She breathed life into me.

I turned toward the bed, where I'd laid our clothes out before heading downstairs to take my place at the altar, to find two paper bags sitting on the bed. I didn't remember them being there before I'd left. Slowly, I approached them. Light sniggers from Ever let me know she had everything to do with them.

"What's this?"

"It's a wedding gift from the girls."

Taking a second to allow her words to register, I let the smile rip through my face.

"Well, are you going to open them?"

Nodding, I reached into both bags and grabbed a single sheet of paper from each. The different hues of blue on both papers looked oddly familiar but it wasn't until I read the curved lettering that I realized what I was looking at.

Social Security Ca... My head whipped in Ever's direction as the tears fell from her pretty brown eyes. I tilted my head to see if she was serious and to see if I was seeing what I thought I was seeing. I looked at the two papers again, reading the line that spelled out each girl's name.

Essence Eisenberg.

Emorey Eisenberg.

Through blurred vision and teary eyes, I must've read their names twenty times before I looked up at them both. They had always been mine, but seeing Eisenberg at the end of their names made it all real. Now, we all shared the same last name. We were officially the Eisenbergs.

PLEASE NOTE:

*Luca's second edition ends here, but feel free to continue reading the **slightly revised** Ever (continuation of Luca + Ever's love story).*

UNDERSTAND THE MOOD CHANGES DRASTICALLY IN THE NEXT STORY. NONETHELESS, ENJOY.

LUCA²

ANNIVERSARY EDITION

GREYHUFFINGTON

TRIGGER WARNING

PLEASE READ THIS SECTION!

Seeing this note means the book that you are about to read could contain triggering situations or actions. This book is subject to one or more of the triggers listed below. **Please note that this a universal trigger warning page that is included in Grey Huffington books and is not specified for any paticular set of characters, book, couple, etc. This book does not contain all the warnings listed. It is simply a way to warn you that this particular book contains things/a thing that may be triggering for some.** This is simply my way of recognizing the reality and life experiences of my tribe and making sure that I properly prepare you for what is to unfold within the pages of this book.

TRIGGER WARNING

violence
sexual assualt
drug addiction
suicide
homicide
miscarriage/child loss
child abuse
emotional abuse

CONTINUED...

EVER

ONE

LUCA

The moment I slid into Ever's moist pussy would always be my favorite time of the day. As she bent over in the shower with her hands gripping the rails for support, our skin slapped against each other. It was the most glorious sound to ever be made and whenever Ever was involved, I wanted to hear it loud and clear.

"Luuuuuccccccccca!" she screamed, revealing her status.

She was at the brinks, and I was right behind her. I rounded her body and slid my hand underneath her nine-month pregnant belly to place my thumb on the nub that made her legs quiver. My time was almost up. I could feel my nut rising from my balls.

"Baby, please," she begged, but there would be no remorse.

ONE

"Open up for Daddy," I coached.

Boom.

Boom.

Boom.

Boom.

Boom.

Fuck, I thought. The banging on the door meant that we'd been gone a little too long and enjoying our shower a little too much. The girls had come to find us.

"I'm cummmmmmmming."

"Me too."

I released as she did the same, simultaneously releasing satisfying groans. We rushed out of the shower and to our towels so that we could tend to the impatient visitors at the door.

Boom.

Boom.

Boom.

I knew Emorey's knock by heart. It was the hardest and the most demanding, just like her. While Ever got herself together, I pulled on a pair of shorts, not bothering to find briefs to go beneath. My children didn't have that much fucking patience.

Boom.

Boom.

Boom.

Boom.

I opened the door to find Essence, Emorey, and even Elle waiting on the other side of it for us.

ONE

"Milk," she repeated three times as she squeezed her fingers together to sign for milk.

"Milk is coming, baby girl," I assured her before kissing her chubby cheeks.

Ever had dominated again. Our daughter was an unofficial triplet with the same hazel eyes and blonde hair as her sisters. Only her hair was much lighter and so were her eyes with green speckles that left everyone clueless.

Ever appeared from behind the door wearing a simple gray dress that only held one boob. The other was already out and waiting for Elle to latch. She had turned a year old already, but baby girl wasn't ready to give up the boob. I didn't blame her. Shit, I wasn't ready when I found out they'd be hers alone. But, over a year into our breastfeeding journey with perfect health, I'd agreed with Ever that it wasn't necessary for her to discontinue the boob. When Elle was ready, she'd let it go.

Ever positioned her over her large, round belly so that she could get a good flow going. Everyone had just finished breakfast so we knew she wouldn't be long. She simply wanted to be put to sleep and nursing helped speed the process along.

As much as I'd wanted a son, finding out Elle would be joining the other three women in my life brought me just as much joy. I could wait for my son. Ever was willing to remain barefoot and pregnant until I got him so I was winning no matter what. We'd soon have two children under the age of two, but we'd already hired San full time so that Ever wasn't overwhelmed. Her hours would

ONE

increase during Ever's final month of pregnancy so that she could rest.

Because the chances of Ever carrying a boy inside that round belly of hers was highly unlikely, we'd decided to wait until birth for the revealing of the baby's gender. If there was another little Ever in there, I didn't mind. But, if there was a little Luca, I'd lose my shit. A healthy baby was my top priority, not their gender. So far, we'd managed to keep the baby happy, healthy, and growing like wildfire.

"What's up, girls?"

The curiosity in the oldest two eyes left me with questions. There was either already a plan in place or they were still coming up with one. However, something was in motion. I knew them well enough to understand that look on their faces.

As Ever took a seat in the rocking chair, I tended to them, waiting to hear what came from their lips. With Emorey and Essence, you never quite knew what was next. Nevertheless, it was rare that we didn't agree, oblige, or cheer them on. Their ideas were always worthwhile.

"Well, Es—"

"And, you, Em."

"Well, we want to watch a movie in the front with everybody," Emorey finished, twirling in her blonde curls as she twisted her body from side to side.

"A movie, huh?" I asked, pulling her into my arms.

"Umm hmm."

"Please," Essence begged.

ONE

"What are we pleading for?" I asked. "You both know the answer is yes."

"Thank you!"

"Yesss!" Essence chanted.

"Mommy, the girls want to watch a movie. We're not going in there without you and Elle."

"We're coming. Can you give me a hand?"

Ever stretched her hand for me to grab. I pulled forward once our fingers linked, assisting her out of the chair without interrupting Elle's meal. Halted movement concerned me.

"What's wrong?"

Ever's brows raised as she began explaining. "I've been hurting all morning but I didn't want to worry you. I don't want you to panic but my water just broke. I don't have to wonder anymore, baby. I'm in labor."

"Like now?"

It didn't matter that I'd gone through this just a year and a half ago. I didn't think I'd ever get comfortable with labor, knowing I could very well gain someone special or lose someone in the process. My nerves were all over the place as I pointed to my cell on the nightstand.

"Es, grab my phone, baby girl."

"Luca." Ever chuckled. "Calm down, baby."

"Why didn't you say anything? How long have you been in pain?"

"Since last night."

"But, this morning... We just..."

"I know. I was hoping it confirmed or denied my suspicions. It confirm—Whew. Yes. Definitely labor."

ONE

She nodded, rubbing her back. "It's in my back. I can't feel much down below other than pressure."

"Ever. What the fuck?"

"Luca." She laughed, finding everything funny at the wrong time.

"Baby, what?"

"It's fine, baby. Just get our team on the line. Everything will be alright."

"Ever, why are you not panicking right now?"

"Because then that would make two of us. It's my fourth rodeo, Luca. Losing my shit won't help in this situation."

"Do you think the baby is coming now?"

"I do. Honestly. Soon, at least. I've been laboring all night. It felt different because the pain is in my back. It's not down here."

She pointed between her legs.

"Which confused me. But, the mess I've made, there's nothing to be confused about there."

"Let's get you cleaned up."

"OK."

"Here, give me Elle. Head to the shower. Can you walk?"

"Yes," she sniggered. "I can walk. I can also shower alone. I just need you there to watch me in case I get lightheaded or need your help."

"Alright, and then what?"

"And then we go to the living room and we watch the movie we planned with the girls. Nothing changes, Luca. The baby isn't coming this instant."

ONE

How she managed to remain so calm through it all left me baffled. But, as she'd instructed, I got the girls situated in the living room and rushed to aid her in the shower. We got her dried off and in a robe before slowly making our way to the living room where she labored for three hours and through two movies.

It wasn't until the second one ended that she agreed to get inside of the tub full of warm water I'd run for her. The doula, midwife, and doctor were all in attendance when Ever settled into the large jacuzzi, preparing to push.

"I can feel it." She moaned.

"Yeah?" Yoshi asked.

"Yes. I think it's time to push."

"Listen to your body. If you think it's time, then it's time," Doctor expressed. "We're here to assist. You've done this before. When your body tells you to push, then push. When you feel you need to stop and rest, stop. Alright?"

"Okay,." Ever breathed. "Baby?"

"Yes?"

"Are you ready? I'm going to push."

"I'm ready."

During the next contraction, Ever bore down and began pushing. It was such a beautiful sight, watching her bring new life into the world. She was a fucking soldier four times over. I'd be indebted to her for the rest of eternity.

"That's it, baby. Push for me," I coached.

In the three hours she'd labored, I managed to get my

ONE

shit together. Maybe it had something to do with the two shots I'd had or maybe it was the bud I'd rolled and smoked before taking a shower myself.

After several attempts, she managed to push our baby out and into the water where I waited. The sounds of a newly born baby pierced the air, bringing us all pure joy. My heart swelled, pressing against my chest cavity as it tried to escape confinement.

"You did it, baby!" I yelled, clinging to our child.

Because the baby was still connected to her by the cord, I was sure not to put too much distance between them as I lifted them into the air and examined their private parts. The small set of balls and hammer hanging between the legs summoned a smile on my face.

"It's a boy. It's a boy. I got my fucking boy, baby!"

TWO

EVER

Fresh, warm tears kissed my skin after a single blink, ran along my cheeks and ended their journey in the fresh linen beneath me. Voiceless, I'd been reduced to silent cries that I felt as if no one heard. And, as plentiful as they were, I seemed to always have more – *and more and more.*

For the last eight weeks, it was more of the same. Each day, I was a bit more rooted in my sorrows. I'd gotten so deep into the abyss that I didn't think it was humanly possible to pull myself out. I felt like it was useless to even try at this point because I'd done so for weeks, only to end up in worse shape than I'd started. It was like a never-ending cycle of sadness, tears, dissatisfaction, disappointment, and shame.

This new territory I was treading was both scary and

embarrassing. Though it was likely I wasn't, I felt like the laughingstock of my home. All jokes were on me. Sometimes, I could even hear the gentle giggles at my expense. Maybe it was all in my head but maybe it wasn't.

Rolling over in the bed that still felt foreign to me, I hugged the pillow. I missed my bed. I missed my children. I missed myself. *I missed my Luca.*

Isolation was never my preference, but lately it was the only thing that allowed me to maintain the piece of sanity I was clinging to. The second I attempted to step out of my new bedroom, the world came crashing down. I never imagined not sharing a room with the man I loved more than life itself, but it was life that had gotten in the way of that.

And no matter how hard I tried, I couldn't get back to that. I couldn't get back to him. My center no longer existed – just darkness, pain, and depression. The thought of it made the same heart I'd used to love him heavy with grief for the loss of what we'd worked so hard to build. It hurt. All of it, burdening me with an anxiousness for the unknown that I could never and would never be able to fulfill.

"Eh. Eh. Eh. Ehhhhhhhh!" Lucas wailed.

What was once the most precious sound was like fingernails on a chalkboard now. Cringing at the sound of my son's cries was the most hurtful, but I seemed to get more peeved with the sound each time I heard it. The disgust had hardly anything to do with my precious boy and everything to do with my uselessness in his world. Aside from being his source of nutrients, I had nothing more to give him. Not even the love I'd given the rest of my children – especially in the first few weeks of their lives. This time, things were different.

Luca's footsteps were the next thing I heard. Like clockwork, this was our morning routine. We'd been reduced to nearly nothing. Yet, he was still resilient and patient and beautiful and loving and so damn amazing that I was still wondering how God could make a man so perfect. And, then hand him over to me as if I deserved him. I didn't. Especially not now.

As the father and son duo closed in on me, the cries got louder, the tears got thicker, and my breast began to throb as they lactated. My body sensed my son's hunger and worked overtime to produce the milk that he needed to survive. It understood my son's need and could still produce under stress while I withered away, as if I couldn't muster the strength to do the same. Though amazed at its capabilities, I was still jealous. I, too, wanted to be everything that my son needed. I just couldn't be.

The creaking of the door as Luca pushed it open forced me to take a deep breath and hold it before releasing it. By the time I did, he was flipping on the light. My eyes burned as forced light intervened the darkness I preferred. I failed at the lousy attempt to get myself together, flopping my tired hand next to me on the bed instead of clearing my face of tears.

I had nothing to hide. Luca was well aware of all things concerning me. I had nowhere to hide, anyhow. He could feel it all. I could see the worry lines on his

TWO

handsome face as he got closer and finally sat next to me on the bed.

Still hugging the pillow, I began to weep. His presence was the gravitational pull I tried resisting because it lowered me deeper into the hole I couldn't climb out of. Feeling like the biggest disappointment in his world, I could hardly stand to look at him. I'd let him down. No longer was I the woman that he'd fallen in love with and married. I wasn't Ever Sinclair and neither was I Ever Eisenberg. I wasn't sure who I was.

Yet, he continued to master perfection and never left my side while doing so.

THREE

LUCA

The ivory sheets that bundled on the bed once kept my heart warm. Now, she was four rooms down, furthest from every indication of life outside of her head. That's the way she wanted it and deep down inside I knew it was the way she needed it.

Since our son Lucas was born, her mental health had spiraled and I was still trying to help her gain control of it. She didn't want to be in the space she was in, which only pushed her further away. The thought of not being herself and unable to perform the tasks as the mother of our children gutted her and left her with mere pieces of the woman she was prior to his birth.

Postpartum depression was new for us both and it was the toughest shit I'd ever had to deal with. Not even the eight years that I put down in the government books

THREE

compared. Seeing my wife broken and battered, mentally, without the power to help was heart wrenching. There was no amount of money in the bank that could cure her. There was no amount of pleading on either of our ends that would result in a decluttered mental space. Not even therapy had helped.

Lucas laid still on the bed as I watched his little chest rise and fall. He had fallen in line with the rest of our bunch and adopted all of his mother's features. I was sprinkled throughout, but just like the rest of our children, he was Ever's mini. His big, blue eyes and light blonde hair was the only thing that separated him from the others. We were all still trying to figure out where they'd come from. But, came to the conclusion that both Ever's and my gene was recessive in that match up, leaving him with eyes unlike any of ours.

Clearing my throat, I tried swallowing the sea of emotions that rose each morning after I got the girls out of the door and strapped into San's truck. I'd upgraded her Honda so that she could comfortably fit several car seats at once. Seeing the girls off to school with constant questions about Mommy's condition and curiosity of why she couldn't participate in their mornings was a struggle that I'd never successfully conquer. Especially not when everyone was accustomed to having their mother be part of every minute of their day at home.

I saw my chef more than ever now. Dinner wasn't prepared by Ever and I was simply too exhausted with the day's work and the girls to cook it myself. With me caring for Lucas every day, San was the girls' full-time nanny for the moment.

The clearing of my throat startled a sleeping Lucas. I stiffened, refusing to move a limb as I silently prayed that he didn't wake up. My prayer went unanswered as he began to squirm a little more, eventually stretching his tiny arms and voicing his disdain. His belly was empty and it was time to eat.

I'd grown to dislike feedings because it only meant that I'd be inflicting a little more pain on Ever. Seeing Lucas but realizing she was helpless to his cause always burdened her. But, as out of touch with reality as she was, I refused to allow her to let go of the one thing that kept her in contact with the light at the end of the long, dark tunnel. Breastfeeding was a glimmer of hope for her and the one time she was able to feel useful.

Besides, she'd hate herself if she allowed her milk to dry by the time she came out of this cycle she was in and Lucas was forced to depend on shelved milk. It would destroy her. So, for preventive measures – though very hard – I made sure she kept her milk flowing and Lucas fed.

FOUR

LUCA

"Eh. Eh. Eh. Ehhhhhhhh!" Lucas cried.

He had a healthy set of lungs on him I knew would disturb his mother so I rushed to his side and picked him up. His little eight-week-old body settled into my arms, fitting perfectly as I began my journey down the hallway where we'd find the source to his aching stomach.

As what could only be described as too soon, we arrived and I was burdened with the most unpleasant task of all. *Click*. I flipped on the light. There she was.

The sight of my thinning wife left another hole in my heart each day that I witnessed her. Eating was last on her list. Sleep was her best friend and tears had become her favorite beverage. She drank them daily as they slid down her face and reproduced them from her eyes at a moment's notice.

FOUR

I inched toward the side of the bed where I sat. As I laid Lucas beside her, Ever clenched the pillow she was hugging a little tighter. I remembered a short time ago when she hugged me like that... when I was her pillow.

"I'm sorry." She cried.

"Shhhhh."

"I just can't free myself," she admitted.

"It's OK. Come on."

After standing up, I leaned over the bed and sat her up against the headboard. Even that was too much of a task for my baby. I pushed aside the part of her shirt that was meant to be lowered for nursing to expose her beautiful breast. I missed them so much. I missed her so much.

I returned to my spot on side of her and cleaned her face of tears. When I felt she was ready, I reached over and grabbed our son. Ever closed her eyes, too consumed with her own disappointment to fully accept Lucas.

"Look at him, love," I encouraged.

"He barely even knows me." She sighed, tears streaming down her face again.

"You're all he knows, Ever," I explained.

Lucas felt the absence of his mother. At only eight weeks, she was everything to him. Her lack of presence was the main reason it was hard to get him to quiet, sleep, or get through the day without being swaddled tightly.

"I'm useless," she told me, finally opening her eyes.

"You're sick, Ever. There's a difference. Your son needs you. The girls need you. *I need you*, mommas."

"I just don't feel so good, Luca."

"I know."

FOUR

Not wanting to overwhelm her, I decided to let the topic rest. It was the same thing day after day. Instead of continuing the conversation, I allowed her to gaze at our handsome son. My heart smiled when she mustered the courage to lift a finger and move the patch of his long hair from near his eyes.

Our eyes locked when the familiar sound of discomfort erupted from his quivering lips.

"He's hungry," I explained, hoping to cancel any thoughts in her head that formed about his displeasure for her presence.

"Here, let him fill his tummy," I insisted, pulling the pillow over and positioning Lucas on it so that Ever didn't have to hold him. She rarely ate a bite of her food on a daily basis and simply didn't have the strength to manage his weight.

Right away, my greedy boy took to his mother's boob and began suckling. I watched from afar as Ever stared down at him as he guzzled the milk from her boobs. This was new for her. For us. The slight twinkle of admiration in her orbs that I witnessed, I hadn't seen since the week after his birth when she began falling into her deep depression.

Still, the painful smug on her face remained. But, that didn't stop the glimmer of hope that I clung onto when I saw her hand lift again, this time to rub our son's face and then the hair on his head. Though a small gesture, it was progress for us all.

Baby steps. Baby steps, I thought.

FIVE

EVER

I could hear his footsteps long before he entered the room. Silently, I prayed he wasn't trying to interest me in food because I didn't have an appetite. As much as I knew I should, I just couldn't bring myself to accept food. It only upset my stomach and left me feeling nauseous. Frequent trips to the bathroom weren't ideal for me at the moment. Not even opening my eyes, which was why I hoped he didn't turn the light on again.

"Ever," he whispered as he neared the bed.

I imagined he wasn't expecting an answer because we both knew that I didn't have it to give. But, I'd heard him. My heart had heard the pain and trauma my situation was causing him. We'd heard him, clearly, even the words he'd never say.

FIVE

"It's time for a bath," he revealed, making my flesh crawl at the thought.

As his large, comforting hand rubbed against my sandy bush, I could feel the chunks of hair as they gathered in his fingers and dislodged from my scalp. When it was all said and done, I wasn't sure if I'd be left with any of the hair that I once loved so much.

"Cut it," I said to Luca, finding the words to describe my most prominent feeling at the moment.

"Ever, you don't mean it."

"Please."

"Do you think it'll make you feel better?" he asked, obviously willing to do anything to help.

My hair had grown to the middle of my back. Pregnancy after pregnancy had left me with too much to maintain. For once, I wanted to be freed from whatever shackles it must've had me in.

"Yes," I admitted, clinging to the pillow that I'd discovered as my safe haven.

"If I do something for you, you have to promise you will do something for me," Luca bargained.

"I can't," I told him immediately.

"You don't even know what it is and I know you can, baby. You simply have to let me help you. OK?"

"Luca, I can't."

The truth was, I couldn't. If it didn't involve hours on end of rest, then I couldn't.

"Yes, you can, baby." Luca gritted. I could hear the frustration in his voice.

"Please don't get upset," I pleaded, emotions climbing. My eyes burned from the nonstop tears I'd cried over the weeks but I could feel the fresh ones stain my cheeks.

"I'm not upset, love. I'm just... I'm trying, Ever. I'm really trying. I'm fighting and I need you to fight with me. I can't do this without you. I'm miserable. I'm miserable every day I wake up and you're not beside me. Every time I hear our son cry out to you but you can't be there, I'm sick to my stomach. Every time the girls ask about you or Elle cries for you, my shit hurts. We're all feeling the effects of your absence and we need you back. So, understand that I'm not upset. I'm just hurting, Ever. I'm hurting because for once I can't fix what's wrong with you. But, I'm not going to stop trying. Don't punish me for that."

"I'm sorry. I'm sorry I'm letting you guys down. I just don't know how to come out of this dark, dark place I'm in. I can't find myself in there. I feel so lost."

"Let me help you," he asked. "Please."

"I don't think you can."

"If you try, too, then I know we can figure this shit out, Ever. It's us. It's me and it's you."

"My God, you're perfect." The words that haunted me fell from my lips. I was everything but. Yet, I'd been given a man that was closest to perfection as it got.

"I'm far from it. If I cut your hair for you, I need you to promise me you will join me for lunch in an hour. We don't have to leave the house. I just want you to come downstairs and sit at the dining room table with me. I'll make something simple, like sandwiches or some shit. Or, I can order whatever you want to be delivered. It's what-

FIVE

ever you want, Ever. I just want you there with me. I feel so fucking empty out here."

I carefully considered his offering, wondering if I had the strength. I quickly concluded that I didn't, but the denial I wanted to give him just wouldn't surface. Before I knew it, I was agreeing to something I knew I wasn't capable of. I just didn't know how to tell him.

"I promise."

I didn't recognize my own voice, but I did recognize the smile on Luca's face as he heard the words. And for the first time in weeks, I felt good about myself. I wasn't sure how I'd make it to the dining table or if I would, but for him I'd try. Because, without a doubt, I knew he'd do the same for me.

SIX

EVER

Luca's large hands stabilized me as he lifted me from bed. Dangling from his broad shoulders, I bounced with each step he took as he made his way into the bathroom. Walking required energy that my body didn't possess. Even emptying my bladder was too much of a task.

Before lowering me onto the toilet, he pulled down my underwear and the pajama shorts that I wore along with them. As soon as my butt brushed the toilet seat, my bladder gave in and released everything I'd been holding onto. The relief I felt was incredible.

I could hear as Luca rolled the tissue onto his hand. Shame covered me as he ripped what he'd be using from the roll. *Please, Ever,* I begged. *Come out of this.*

Once I finished, I leaned forward and allowed him to

SIX

clean my bottom. When I was ready, I lifted my arms so that he could rescue me once again from my miserable attempt to care for myself. Happily, Luca helped me up to my feet and lowered the toilet seat. He rested me on top of it and stood back for a brief moment with a hand on each hip.

"How short are we talking?"

"Can you decide?"

I couldn't. But I knew Luca wouldn't steer me in the wrong direction. I trusted him more than I did myself.

"Aight. I want your shit even so I'm going to use my clippers," he explained.

Less energy distribution was my best bet for now, so I didn't bother to respond. Besides, there wasn't anything left to be said. I wanted this all to be over quickly so that I could get back to bed. Luca had replaced the bathroom light with dimmer, less intimidating ones but after a while it still made my head throb.

As I closed my eyes to stop the room from spinning and the little flies from popping mid-air, Luca exited. Too exhausted to stay upright, I rested my head on the bathroom counter. Sleep was so easy to come by. The coolness of the counter didn't help much, either. Before I knew it, I'd drifted off to sleep.

Hearing Luca re-enter the bathroom startled me. The quick snooze couldn't have lasted any more than four or five minutes but I wasn't complaining. Rest shut my thoughts off completely and made everything feel fine for once. That's why every chance I got, I wanted more of it.

SIX

Luca got everything set up as I continued to lie on the counter, trying my hardest to catch a few more Zs. When I felt his hand on my head, I knew it would be impossible. He lifted my face from the cool counter and sat me upright. There was a small comb in his hand that I was sure he'd stolen from the girls' room.

Without hesitation, he began combing through the knots in my hair. In clumps, my hair fell onto the floor all around me. To avoid the tears that were working their way up at the sight of my beautiful hair falling so effortlessly to the floor, I closed my eyes.

It wasn't long before I heard the familiar sound of clippers. Bzzzzzzzzz.

"I need you to hold still and try not to move. If you feel yourself getting too weak, then let me know. We can finish another time."

Luca knew I understood even if I didn't have the ability to respond. As the sound of the clippers lulled me into a calm that I hadn't experienced in weeks, my eyes remained closed. I counted down from twenty over and over. I'd lost count of just how many times I'd done so by the time the sound of the clippers ended.

Then, there was the comb, again. Though my eyes were still closed, I knew every move Luca made. The buzzing started again. Then stopped. Then started. Then stopped. And, finally, there was the comb again.

Shortly after, Luca brushed hair from my shoulders. I could feel the smile on his face as he stood back and admired his work. Because, surely, he couldn't have been

SIX

admiring me. I was and had been a mess for the last six, nearly seven weeks.

When I felt his hands underneath my armpits, I knew he was ready for me to see what he'd done. Unfortunately, I was unable to assist him in his attempt. Nevertheless, it was successful just like the rest of them.

I'd forgotten how his body felt against mine until he pulled me in front of him and placed my hands on the counter. His solid chest against my back reminded me of the times when my mental health wasn't a barrier of ours. It wasn't long ago. Just eight weeks ago, we were both the happiest we'd ever been. Bringing Luas into the world felt like my redemption after losing Dylan but I'd quickly learned that it was the start of my demise.

"Open your eyes," Luca instructed. I could hear the smile in his voice.

Obliging, I unsealed my lids. Staring back at me was a woman that I didn't recognize. A saddened, unhappy version of myself that I wanted so badly to overcome. And, then there was Luca.

He was still as beautiful as I remembered. His brown skin was flawless and so was that heart of his that I heard thudding in his chest. The smile that he craved, I couldn't muster, but I did admire the work he'd done.

The very blunt cut stopped at my shoulders, lifting so much weight from them. I felt like I'd shed much more than the tears I cried had allowed in weeks. For the first time, I felt like I'd taken a step closer to the light that was too far away to even see much of any more.

"I'm going to come out of this."

SIX

I heard myself say. I wasn't sure where it came from, but it didn't feel like as much of a lie as it sounded. The tears that I expected to come were nowhere in sight. Postpartum for me was debilitating. It was a mental hell that stole my ability to move my limbs, my lips, and my mind.

"You will."

SEVEN

LUCA

Her skin was still perfect. Because bathing her was the only time I truly got to explore the flawlessness of it, I found myself enjoying bath time a lot more than Ever. She hated it. The bright lights that once made her squeal upon entry, I'd switched for dimmer ones so that coming out of the dark wasn't as difficult. Sometimes, we even opted to leave the lights off completely.

Though Ever didn't have many words during these moments, I could feel her most. I could still feel her angelic spirit and still feel the woman underneath the surface. I could still feel my baby. She was in there, just a little lost.

Because today felt extra special and Ever had given me more than I could've imagined she would on the dreadful walk to her room this morning, the tub was filled

SEVEN

with bubbles. The fizzling sound they made as they burst one by one seemed to be satisfying to us both. With her eyes closed and her head leaned back slightly, Ever enjoyed the warmth of the bath and the quiet of the moment.

"You're amazing," I told her, repeating the affirmations that I recited during bath time.

It was important for me to speak life into Ever, even when she didn't feel like hearing it. I was her voice of reasoning during this trying time. I wanted to be that center she claimed was missing. I had to be the landmark that would help her find her way. Otherwise, my baby would be lost forever, I was afraid.

"You're kind and you're loved."

I used the sponge to wet her freshly cut hair. Ever becoming more beautiful, I thought was impossible but I was sadly mistaken. The fresh cut brought about a change that I didn't know she needed but was truly happy with. And, to top it off, it was beneficial to her mental and emotional health. She'd smiled, sort of. That was a start.

Baby steps. Baby steps.

"You're special to me and Essence and Emorey and Elle and Lucas. You're the light of our lives. You make us all better. You deserve to rest. You deserve to be taken care of. You deserve to be catered to."

Ever said nothing as I poured the two-in-one shampoo and conditioner on my hands. I began working it into her sandy blonde strands, massaging her scalp in the process. The humming from her throat assured me she was enjoying the feeling of my hands on her scalp even if words weren't released.

God, I miss my wife. I felt empty inside. The physical exhaustion was nothing compared to the emotional toll that Ever's state had taken on me. Her bubbly, bright energy had fueled my somewhat dark energy for so long and now that it was missing, I, too, felt lost. She was my center. She was my landmark. She was my happy place. Without her in my world, I was devastated.

"We miss you," I admitted. "You hear me, Ever? The girls and I miss you. Essence, as sweet as she is, is missing you the most. And, Emorey, she's confused. Elle is, she's not taking the milk in the cup so well. We need you to fight, mommas."

"Please, Luca." Softly, she begged, "Please stop."

With her eyes still closed, ridges developed along the bottom line of her top lid. She didn't want to hear the mess our home was in her absence and I wanted to kick my own ass for mentioning it. But, it was hard not to when everything was going to shits while she withered away. We needed her back. It was as simple as that.

"What would you like for lunch?" I asked, changing the subject.

"Luca." She sighed, preparing to deliver bad news.

"You promised, Ever. You've never lied to me. You're not going to start today."

Another deep, long sigh slowly escaped her lips before she nodded her head.

"Okay. But please let me have a nap first. I feel so tired."

SEVEN

She did. I knew she did. The amount of work she'd done this morning was more than she had in weeks. Though excited about the progress, I knew it was exhausting for her.

"Aight. I'll think of something. But, before you go to sleep, I need you to feed Lucas."

"Okay," she agreed.

"I love you, Ever. And, I'm never going to stop. Let's get through this and put it behind us like everything else."

"Okay."

That was all she had for me and that was okay with me. As long as she was giving me something, I could work with that. If it was the last thing I did, I'd make sure that my baby came out of this an even better person. This was only a bump in the road. It was till death for us.

EIGHT

EVER

I imagined this was how heaven felt. Big, bright, and warm at the same time. It had been weeks since I'd been out of the room, into the hallway, and down the stairs. Everything was foreign. And everything was bright. Possibly a little too bright for my, now, sensitive eyes.

A heavy sigh left my lips as I forked the salad in front of me. It was delicious. I'd eaten almost half, which was a lot more than I'd eaten of anything else. I was impressed. From the look on Luca's handsome face, so was he.

I wanted to tell him how much I'd rather be in bed than at the table, but his excitement for my presence was too obvious in his brown orbs. I'd been letting him down for far too long, now, and craved satisfaction for him. So, even with burning eyes and a heavy heart, I remained for him.

EIGHT

He'd chosen the smaller dining table, but even it felt vastly larger than I'd recalled. It was still beautiful, nonetheless, but its size was a painful reminder of my circumstances. The empty chairs that surrounded it were once filled with little bottoms, booster seats, or removed to make room for high chairs. Now, there was only us.

Is Mommy still sick? Emorey's voice rang loud in my head. I missed her awfully. She was the most fearless child I'd ever seen in my life and to know that I'd birthed her was still stunning to me. Her confidence was commendable and her vocabulary was impressive. She said whatever came to mind and had no apologies for it. I admired her will and dedication to authenticity. She'd need it in the world that we lived in.

Then there was Essence, who stuck a note underneath the door at least three times since I'd been inside. *Feel better. I love you, Mommy*, she'd whisper underneath the crack between the door and flooring. Her heart was gold and to know that I couldn't bring myself to be at her side hurt me to the core.

I still hadn't brought myself to read either one that Luca had laid next to me. Though she didn't have the words to say, often, she had them to pen. Her soft nature reminded me of the version of me I loved most and that I was able to be once Luca came into my life.

She had me on my knees more than any one in my home because I knew that the world was hardly any place for softness. It hardened you and it did so quickly. Before depression crippled me mentally and physically, I prayed for my baby often. It was important to me that she

EIGHT

found someone just like her father who'd protect that softness and nurture it like he'd done mine. Otherwise, she was doomed.

Elle. My sweet baby had no idea where Mommy was and didn't know how to voice her objections to my absence all that well. *Mommy. I want Mommy.* I'd heard night after night as I laid with my sorrows heavy on my heart.

I wanted her too. I wanted her sweet kisses and her random hugs. I wanted her greedy little hands on my boobs as she disregarded my rejection for her obsession with milk straight from my boobs. She was a big girl now and I wanted her to understand that it was OK to sip from somewhere other than Mommy's fountain of milk.

And, Lucas. I'd only spent a healthy week with him before my mental health began to decline. I didn't know my son and that, most of all, kept me down in the dumps as time continued to tick away. He was as precious as his father and a very good boy.

I imagined his presence would bring me so much joy, but it killed me. It killed my spirit. And, for the life of me, I couldn't find the same joy and comfort in his birth that I had the three times before. I'd found myself asking if I truly loved him or if he truly belonged to me. He didn't feel real and neither did he feel like mine.

The questions got louder and louder in my ear each day and eventually, I began to spiral. They opened doors for new questions, doubt, and fear. Before I knew it, I was weeks in and had no contact with him or my other children unless I was feeding him.

EIGHT

"What's on your mind?" Luca spoke for the first time since we'd sat down.

We hadn't said a single word to one another, both too lost in our thoughts to even notice. I inhaled to the point of pain and then released the breath I'd taken in. I struggled to find the correct words as my eyes darted across the room. It wasn't until they landed on the assortment of rain boots that were lined up in the mudroom that they came to me.

"They must hate me so much," I shared.

Luca shook his head as he laid his fork down on his plate. "Stop telling yourself that any of us hate you. It's just your mind playing dirty, dirty tricks on you. Listen to me... listen to your husband, Ever. We love you through sickness and in health."

"Please help me," I pleaded. "Please help me get back to my family, Luca."

NINE

LUCA

She finally went down and hardly with a fight. Lunch had taken more energy from Ever than she had to give. She'd sacrificed her comfort to satisfy me and I was grateful for the effort. Though she would've rather had lunch from bed, seeing her sitting across the table from me was evidence that she was ready to break through the barriers and get better.

I stepped back from the thick sheets that I'd tucked her underneath and admired her from afar. It had been weeks since she'd stepped foot inside our bedroom and even longer since she'd last rested her head on our pillows. So, watching her chest rise and fall as she fell deeper into slumber made my heart swell in my chest.

I love you more than you'll ever know, I thought to myself as I gazed. To the point of pain, I loved my wife

NINE

and I'd do anything for her – even lay my life on the line. When it came to her, there were no limits to where I'd go or what I'd do. She and those four little people of ours were my everything. They knew it, and so did everyone else around us.

Lucas' tiny fists clenched and then unclenched as he had his helping of milk. I'd convinced Ever to kill several birds with one stone. All I needed was for her to agree to lie in our bed for her nap. As a result, she'd be able to feed Lucas, sleep in, indulge in skin-to-skin contact, and spend some much-needed time with our boy.

Please help me get back to my family. I'd heard her words loud and clear. As I made my way to the sitting area of our bedroom, I grabbed my laptop from the nightstand. I'd been waiting for the moment that she insisted on my help. I'd learned the hard way that it didn't matter how much I wanted her to get better, she wouldn't until she was ready. With the progress she'd made in the last twenty-four hours, I knew that time had come.

Belize. I wasn't sure why that destination was at the forefront of my mind but I stuck with it. Within an hour, I'd managed to book us a private flight out, a villa for five days, and some excursions. I logged out and shut down my computer screen when I was finished. My view was like nothing else. Seeing Lucas' tiny hand clinging to Ever's body as she slept peacefully beside him. Her boob sat comfortably in his mouth, serving as a pacifier as her heartbeat lulled him through his nap.

Just like that, I remained until there was movement. Ever batted her eyes as she tried to comprehend what was happening around her. She'd obviously forgotten where she was and the fact that she'd agreed to be there.

"Luca?" she whispered, confused.

"You're okay, Ever. You said it was okay for me to put you in our bed."

"I know. I just... I want you near."

Her words were like medicine on the wound her health condition had left me with. I stood to my feet and erased the distance that kept us apart. When I made it to her side, her left hand ran the length of my arm.

"I love you," she admitted for the millionth time in her life.

"I love you," I responded, placing my hand on her thigh.

A gasp left her body as her brows furrowed and breath hiked in her chest.

"What's the matter?" I asked, concerned with whatever had come over her.

"Nothing. I just..." she stuttered. "Nothing."

"What is it, Ever?"

Silence coated the air as we both held one another's gaze.

"What is it?" I asked again.

"Can you make me feel good?" She rushed out in a whisper as she closed her eyes and turned her head in the opposite direction.

I grabbed the bottom of her chin and turned her in my direction again. Her shame was not acceptable and silly at the same time. Whatever she wanted, Ever could have.

NINE

"Yes. Yes, I can make you feel good, love. All I need for you to do is tell me exactly what you want and how you want it and I got you."

"Yeah?" She nodded her head, but in question.

"Always and forever. Now, I just need you to open your mouth like a big girl and tell your husband how he can make you feel better this afternoon."

Ever swallowed long and hard before opening her mouth as she'd been instructed. But, when she did, I was all ears. I wanted to hear what she had to say. The anticipation made my dick hard.

"I want you to eat it until I cum," she admitted.

"Eat what?" I probed.

Closing her eyes, she confessed, "My pussy."

TEN

EVER

With a hand over Lucas' small body to protect him from falling off the bed – as if he could roll – I watched as Luca admired me. I wasn't sure what he saw that was so fascinating. I was a mentally ill woman who couldn't even care for her own flock. I'd spent so many days in hiding that I didn't even know how to accept the light. Everything in my home felt foreign to me now, even him.

"Get out of your head," he insisted.

As he released the words, his fingertips glided across the pink flesh of my center. He purposely initiated the bulb that was the most sensitive feature of my body. Without warning, my body submitted. My legs opened wider, giving him free rein over my glistening cave. My back arched slightly as a silent cry tried to escape my lips.

It had been far too long since Luca had touched me.

TEN

And, I didn't mean in a normal way. He did so every day. I meant really *touched me*. Like lovers. Like for-lifers. Like he used to. Like I loved for him to. Like only he could.

"Look at me," Luca demanded.

There was no doubt in my mind that I loved this man with everything in me. And, while postpartum depression was tough, he was even tougher. There was no doubt in my mind that he would be the difference maker for my condition. And, before it was all said and done, he'd be the cure, too.

He was medicine for my soul. While most deemed it idiotic to claim one as your completion, I believed it wholeheartedly. I wasn't like most. I craved companionship. Though he'd entered my life when I was dead set on my independence, deep within I knew that someday I'd search for my soul's mate again. I just needed time to heal from the damage that had been done in the previous relationship.

I didn't have to search. He found me. He was effortlessly put in my path and that's how I knew he was destined to be mine. Luca completed me. I wasn't ashamed of that truth, especially because I knew the same was for him.

I gave him my eyes as he'd requested. Just as I did, his eyes lowered until they were leveled with my pussy. I watched as he swiped his tongue across my flesh. Once. Twice. By the third time, My eyes were closed and my mouth had slacked.

"Ummmm, Lucaaaa." Lowly, I moaned.

TEN

His tongue against my flesh was divine. It had been far too long since I'd experienced his skill. He was a very calculated and confident man. He knew exactly how to make my body cream.

Luca sucked my nub into his mouth along with everything surrounding it and began flickering his tongue back and forth, mercilessly forcing me to surrender to his deepest desires. *Cum in my mouth*. His words were so vivid, as if he was speaking them through his silence.

A surge started from my toes and made its way up both of my legs until it combined at my center, doubling in intensity. To combat the pressure, I squeezed my eyelids, pressing them together, hoping I could suppress the inevitable. I wasn't ready for our moment to end because I knew that once the fireworks ended, the mental turmoil would commence.

"Cum," Luca begged, stopping momentarily and commanding my attention.

At the sound of his voice, I was undone. The universe shattered behind my lids as I reached my pinnacle. I felt as if my world finally made sense while simultaneously making no sense at all.

"Luccccccccaaa!"

My hands wandered at alarming rates. Lucas' safety was no longer my top priority. Not falling from the mountain top I'd been hoisted onto was. I found Luca's arms and slid my fingers up his body until I had his head between them. My body rocked back and forth in an effort to prolong my orgasm while holding Luca in place.

TEN

The second he disengaged, it would all be over. I wasn't ready.

"Oh God. Oh God. I'm cumming!" I breathed, rubbing my pussy against his tongue.

My fluids raced from my body and out from my spout, forcing me to release Luca from my grasp. The fountain intensified as he gave it space. And just as it slowed to a creep, my husband's girth filled me.

ELEVEN

LUCA

My God was she glorious. Her walls accepted me, hugged me, and cried to express just how much they missed me. And, I missed them. I missed her. Beneath me, she spat words from her mouth that I hardly understood. I wasn't sure if I wanted to, either.

Her nails pressed against my skin as I dug into her, softly and with as much care as I'd been taking of her over the last few weeks. I didn't have to examine my shaft to see just how much she was enjoying the long, deep strokes from her husband. I could hear the sound of her wetness in the silence, confirming what I already knew.

"I love you," she rushed out. "God, I love you."

"Forever," I responded. It was so true.

I loved my wife with every fiber of my being. She felt

ELEVEN

so close to the reason for my existence these days that I couldn't decipher the difference. I lived for her. I breathed for her. I mourned for her, too. The woman she was trying to find had died and I couldn't wait until she embraced the new woman she was becoming.

It would simply be the upgraded version of the Ever she once knew. I'd already prepared myself for her. And, I, too, would elevate with her. While it was depressing for her to even consider, it was beautiful for me. I'd loved Ever at every stage and would continue. I'd loved each version of her she'd evolved into after each child and each life-changing experience. It was understood that I'd continue to love the newer versions of her as life continued.

That's what I'd signed up for and I wasn't backing out. Love didn't work like that. Marriage didn't work like that. Ever and I… we didn't work like that, either.

I quickly realized that I wouldn't last much longer than a minute or three. It felt like forever since I'd slid into her warmth. I wasn't prepared, not mentally or emotionally.

"Come back to me," I begged my wife as I felt my nut on the horizon. "Come back to me."

"Okaaaaaaay." She cried, tears streaming down her gorgeous face.

"I'm cummin'," I announced, reluctantly removing myself from her well.

It was the first time I'd ever forced myself out of Ever and it wasn't easy. However, I understood we weren't in a position to bring another child into the world, not now.

We had to work on getting her mental health in order so that we could care for the one we'd just had – and as a team instead of alone.

My dick was completely covered in her juices, wetting the bottom of her shirt when it made contact. I watched as my semen shot from the tip of my dick and soiled her top. Her eyes widened at the sight as a tired smile curved her lips upward. This was a first for us both and until I knew she was better, it would be the standard. I owed it to her, her mind, her body, her heart, and her spirit. They all deserved the break that we were ready to give them.

"Feeling better?" I asked when I returned with the towel to clean us both up.

All by herself, Ever had managed to remove her shirt and strip down to nothing. After birthing an entire squad, she was still flawless. *To me*. The tiny lines along her stomach were reminders of her sacrifices and I appreciated her for each one of them.

"I feel like..." She struggled to verbalize her sentiments. "Like I was just given the closest thing to a cure that I could've gotten."

"Let me find out it was just some dick you needed all along," I toyed, though I knew it wasn't the case. My baby was battling something far beyond my imagination. "Sexual healing."

"That's not all I need but it really, really helped."

"That's good because you can have as much of it as you want over the next week. We're hopping on a plane

ELEVEN

and getting out of here. You deserve some time away from it all and that's exactly what you're about to get."

She perked up. The brightness in her eyes made butterflies swarm in my stomach and my heart pound against my chest. She was excited about something. That shit nearly made my head explode. However, she saddened just as quickly and then those big, watery eyes stopped the heart they'd made beat erratically.

"What about Lucas?" She worried.

Of course. It was just like her to worry, but with me around she didn't have to do that. We'd established that long ago but I guess she'd forgotten. I was going to make her remember though. I'd made sure to come up with a solid plan for the children. They'd be well taken care of while we were gone.

Between the women of my family, they wouldn't suffer a bit in our absence. Everyone was more than willing to lend a helping hand. And, when it came to Ever's health, they were ready to go the extra mile to assist with recovery. All we had to do was say the word.

"Don't worry. It's all straightened out. All of that breastmilk you've been storing in the event of an emergency is about to come in handy – for this emergency. They're going to split time between my mom and your mom's house. Then there's San. There's also Lyric. They'll be fine. I just want you to get better and I think this helps."

"Can I at least see them before we go?" she asked, stunning me into silence.

I simply nodded my head for a few seconds while I

ELEVEN

tried to find the words to respond. I wasn't in search of anything massive, but words, in general. Because this was monumental. This was a step in the right direction. This was exactly what I'd been waiting for. My baby was on her way back to me... on her way back to *us*.

TWELVE

LUCA

She's my whole world and I wonder if she knows it. From the driver's seat, I admired my wife's honey-colored skin that matched her brown eyes and blonde tresses. The sadness in her eyes and the heaviness of her emotions were written all over her beautiful face.

"What's the matter?" I asked, reaching over and placing a hand on her thigh.

Though I knew exactly what was tugging at her heart, I wanted her to voice it in order for me to assure her that things would be fine.

"I just feel so... I just..." she stuttered.

"Tell me how you feel, Ever. Tell me and don't bury it. Be upfront and honest about whatever is bothering you."

TWELVE

"Unfit." She sighed as her body rocked. "I feel so unfit."

"If ever I'm ill and can't care for you or the children properly, I expect you to pick up the slack. The people around us, I expect them to chip in, too, because that's what this shit is all about, baby. Making sure one another is straight. The village isn't there to just be there. They're ready and willing to help so we're going to let them. You're far from unfit. You're sick, Ever. Just because your sickness doesn't look like other sicknesses, it's here and we're handling it. Until you feel better, stop beating yourself up. And, even then, don't beat yourself up. Okay?"

"Okay," she answered, nodding as if it would help convince her of the things I'd just said.

"If you were unfit, I wouldn't have fucked with you." I chortled, confirming things she already knew. "Not knowing my plans for the future and the family I desired."

"The thought of you not pursuing me depletes my lungs of oxygen and I feel like I'm fighting for my life immediately. Please, don't ever mention anything remotely close. I can't handle it."

"That's *The Eisenberg Effect*, baby."

Smiling, I watched as she cringed, scrunching her pretty features while looking in my direction.

"Is that what it is?"

"Without a doubt."

"Well, it's all-consuming, overpowering, and has some magic mixed with it."

"I can't disagree with that," I replied, bringing her hand up to my face.

Muah. I kissed her pinky.

Muah. Her ring finger.

Muah. Her middle finger.

Muah. Her index finger.

Muah. Her thumb.

Muah. I ended with a kiss on the back of her hand.

"I love you."

"Forever."

Silently, we tackled the rest of our journey to the hangar where Ever followed me onto the plane. We took the second row of seats where hers faced mine. If either of us got too tired on the flight, the bedroom was just behind us. After we settled and the crew announced our departure, my eyes still hadn't left my wife's frame.

Upon noticing my gaze, Ever's cheeks flushed another shade and her nervous eyes skirted all over the plane. My heart broke at the sight of her trembling hands and the gnawing of her bottom jaw. Her breathing was erratic and far from controlled. She was unrooting before my very eyes and it was hard to watch.

"Whaaat?" she asked, forcing a smile.

"You're the prettiest thing I've ever seen in my life. It's always a treat when you cross my line of vision."

"I must look a mess," she chuckled, nervously, unable to sit still in her chair.

Through gritted teeth, I tried repairing my broken heart. This wasn't just any woman. Ever was mine and I halfway blamed myself for not taking better care of her

TWELVE

mind. Her body, I'd handled with care since the day that she entered my world. It was tangible, something I could see and feel and touch.

Her mind, I could've cared for so much better. Because it wasn't something that I had the privilege of seeing, it was a bit harder to determine when it needed a little extra attention and care until it was too late. I felt like I'd be kicking my ass for years to come, not quite forgiving myself for letting baby girl slip and not catching her.

Ever ran her hands through her hair, trying to improve her appearance as if she wasn't already perfect. She had to know it. It was impossible to think otherwise with a face like hers. It was unlike anything or anyone else. Unique in every way, I loved everything about it. *About her.*

"You look like a slice of heaven, baby. I don't think I've made a better choice in my life. Choosing you was the best decision I could've made. I'm a lucky ass nigga."

"I fear that I'm the luckiest of us both. I have you."

This time, her smile was genuine.

"I never imagined you'd lie to me, but here we are."

It was as if time had slowed. When I watched her toss her head back in laughter and show every tooth in her mouth, every crack the breaking of my heart had left was sealed together with her love. It was almost all I'd ever need in this lifetime. God had truly been on my side when He sent her my way.

"Where do we go from here, Luca?" The seriousness

in her tone let me know she wasn't referring to the lie she'd just told me.

Sighing, I reached over and grabbed her right foot. As I removed her shoe, I stared back at her. The confidence that she once sported was showcasing itself again. I could feel a shift in her demeanor. It was a shift that I wasn't opposed to because it was in the right direction.

Her bare foot against my palms was gratifying. Under her spell, I lost track of my thoughts momentarily. I watched as she found comfort in a new position, one that supported her leg that rested on mine. I massaged the middle of her foot before moving upward.

"We go wherever our love leads us. There's no roadmap for us, Ever, and I'm not looking for one. I'm committed to this rollercoaster, no matter where it takes us. I'm locked in and I'm not getting off. Postpartum ain't got shit on this love I've got for you. When we beat this, it's back to living and enjoying life together. Back to spending this fucking paper. Back to blowing your back out. Back to living out every dream you've ever had. Back to being the best fucking mother you can be. Back to us. Back to Ever and Luca. 'Cause half of me is missing right now. I'm not whole. I won't be until you shake back."

"I've taken so many parts of you through this all. I owe you."

"You don't owe me a thing, love. I just want you better. Lending pieces of me to help you get there is nothing. I'd do it a hundred times over. Just get better and we're back to it. For now, get some rest because you look like you could use it."

TWELVE

"I'm so tired all the time," she admitted, yawning in the process.

"You're exhausted, mentally. This week is your time to really rest. I know it's hard back home. Although you're asleep, having the children running wild through the house—"

"Keeps my mind going, even when my eyes are closed and I'm resting."

"I know."

I released her foot from my grasp and stood to my feet.

"Come on. Let me get you to bed. We have a few hours."

"You coming to bed with me?" she asked.

"I'm not sleepy, baby."

Her big, glossy eyes warmed every inch of me. I'd obviously disappointed her with my statement.

"Fix your face, pretty. I'm not leaving your side. Not tonight, not ever."

"Seriously? You'll stay back there with me."

"Wherever you are, that's where I want to be. Take my hand."

When I extended my arm, she placed her hand inside of mine and followed me through the aisle until we reached the door that separated the bedroom from the rest of the plane. I waited until Ever was completely inside and on the bed before closing the door behind us.

"Here, I got it."

Leaning down, I removed her other shoe.

TWELVE

"Can I undress?" she asked, looking up at me. I loved when she did that shit.

"If you're trying to give that pussy up, yeah. If you're just trying to rest, then I suggest you keep that shit on."

"What about both? I always get the best sleep af—"

"Say less."

Without hesitation, I unclothed Ever and allowed her to climb in bed. Once she settled, I removed every article of clothing I'd chosen for travel. My dick stretched after being restricted for far too long. It was happy to be free and happy to get reacquainted with its very best friend.

Ever glared from the bed. The smile on her face was comical. Baby was deprived. I could smell her magnificent arousal as I climbed in bed next, hovering over her. Her pussy would get the attention it deserved, but for now, I wanted to feast on her pebbled nipples and hope she didn't drown me in breastmilk.

THIRTEEN

EVER

The Belize morning sun had kissed my face a thousand times, or at least that's how it felt. Truthfully, it had only been fourteen times, which was a lot more times than we'd planned. But, after seven days, I wasn't ready to return to reality. Here, it was paradise.

The chains that had been locked around my brain since having Lucas were broken by day four and freedom found me. I could breathe again. I could feel, again. I could see again and the first face I saw when the blinders were removed was Lucas'. And, my, was it a beautiful sight.

From the moment we touched down in Belize, he'd been careful with my heart and my healing. He gave me the space I required and welcomed me into his space whenever I didn't need my own anymore. He cooked

THIRTEEN

each morning for me, bringing me breakfast in bed until I was ready to join him at the table. He explored the island alone until I was ready to explore it with him. He didn't force my hand on any matter, giving me exactly what I needed but only when I was ready.

I slowly, but surely, came out of the zombie-like state that I'd been stuck in for weeks and weeks on end. Everything was so much clearer and the load that sat on top of my chest began to shrink. The guilt of Dylan's death was no longer weighing me down. The hardships of my life before Luca was no longer replaying in the back of my head. The guilt of Dewayne's death didn't feel so heavy anymore.

The burden of loving all of my children equally didn't bother me like it had been. The burden of having so many children to nurture didn't seem like a burden anymore. The thought of therapy that had been suggested by Luca earlier on didn't irritate me anymore. Everything felt so much better. I felt better.

After two days of resting, I climbed out of bed alone. The physical restraints of depression were no longer handicapping me. I could move about as freely and as often as I wanted. That, within itself, was not progress that I took lightly.

By the third day, I was able to shower for nearly an hour, only taking small breaks to sit on the bench inside of the gorgeous shower. I never wanted to leave it. I found so much peace inside that it held me hostage. With each tear I cried during the shower session, I shed some more of the weight that was heavy on me. When I exited, I felt fifty pounds lighter.

By the fourth day, I began exploring the island with Luca. We'd leave for hours and only return when it was time for bed or until our feet began to cry for help. From shopping to dining to participating in the cultural happenings, we were having the time of our lives. And, on that day, I began to truly smile again.

When day seven reached us, I simply wasn't ready to go. I packed all the milk I'd pumped in the last seven days and Luca had it flown straight to Channing so that Lucas could feast on fresh milk. Day seven was the day that I felt most peaceful and more prepared to take on the rest of my life, but it didn't mean that I had to. Not right away, anyway. I wanted to spend some more time with myself and then a little with my husband before the craziness of our world got a hold of us again.

Day eight, I discovered my love for meditation and yoga. From day eight until now, I'd start my mornings with a twenty-minute meditation session and then follow up with forty-five minutes of yoga. I was feeling and looking a lot better. I promised myself those two things wouldn't change upon my return. I wanted them infused in my everyday life and be my own little *calm before the storm*.

Day twelve, a void was birthed. One that involved my children, their smiles, their love, and their innocence. I missed every little finger and every toe on their bodies. I missed hearing them laugh and play and fight. I missed

THIRTEEN

the tantrums and the hugs. I missed the long weekend days in bed for hours watching movies.

I missed Lucas and I missed nursing him. I wanted so badly to have him in my arms. I didn't know my son, not at all. I didn't know what he loved or hated. I didn't know how he slept or the hours he was awake. I didn't know his scent or how bad his poop smelled. I didn't know what his cries meant or how he liked to be held. I knew nothing.

While that reality had crippled me for weeks and weeks, that wasn't the case now. I was desperate to get to know my boy. I had to. I was his mother and I wanted to be his entire world until he was old enough to determine that there was more to life than me.

Luca was surprised to hear that I missed my babies by day thirteen. He said he knew it would come, but he was unsure of when. I missed them all. I really did. Finally, I was ready to get back home, put on my big girl panties, and face the music. I couldn't run forever and I didn't want to. Being a mother was everything to me and that was the problem this time. It became a little too much too soon. I needed the break from it all. The break had saved me.

Feel better, Mommy. The last words that Essence spoke to me were so clear and so close as I tried combating the exhaustion I felt from Luca's greed in bed. He couldn't keep his hands to himself and he was wondering why we had so many children to begin with. Though we both wanted more, we knew the time wasn't right. When it was, he'd have no trouble making it

THIRTEEN

happen. He hardly wanted to get off me. I didn't want him to, either, especially not last night.

"Feel better, Mommy?"

I opened my eyes and sprang forward in bed. The second time was much clearer and felt so much closer. When my ears stopped ringing and settled, the sound of tiny laughter and soft voices curved my lips upward into a smile. My eyes began to burn from the tears that were fighting to find the surface.

"Feel better?" my sweet girl asked again.

I turned to find Essence at the edge of the bed, sitting, watching as I unraveled. Loud and unashamed, I sobbed. This time, it wasn't tears of sadness but those of joy and completion.

"Mom," Essence spoke again.

"Yes?" I asked through tears.

"You're going to wake Lucas and he's nothing nice when he's awake."

I turned to the other side, and there he was, sound asleep, without a care in the world. He was so handsome in his onesie. Disregarding everything Essence had said, I leaned over my baby boy and tucked my hands underneath him to pick him up. He stirred until he woke completely.

"Hiiiiiiiii." I cried, staring down at him as I placed my back against the headboard of the bed. "Hiiiiiii, you."

I removed my breast from my shirt and positioned him more comfortably. The second my boob was close enough for him to smell the milk that was beginning to seep out, his lips began popping. I pushed him forward,

THIRTEEN

close enough to latch. And, when he did, tranquility swept through me.

"Somebody's awake," Luca said as he entered the room with Elle in his hands.

Immediately, she stretched her arms for me.

"Milk," she said while signaling with her hands.

Though she wasn't exactly a breast baby anymore, I wouldn't deny her. My breasts were full and overflowing. There was enough milk to feed both her and Lucas. In fact, I preferred it so the stiffness and tenderness would both subside. She climbed up onto the bed and raised my shirt, herself. When she was comfortable enough, she latched on as well. The wholeness of my heart was inexplicable.

"Mommy!" Emorey ran in behind Luca. She still had food in her mouth.

"Em!"

"Can we go swimming today?"

"Only if your dad says yes."

"So say yes, Daddy," she begged.

"Yes," Luca said without thinking twice.

"Thank you. Thank you. Thank you."

She jumped up and down, bringing a smile to my face. Luca leaned over and kissed my moist lips before wiping the tears from my face.

"I love you," he said to me.

"Thank you," I replied. "Thank you."

FOURTEEN

EVER

"How are you feeling?" Laura asked as soon as I stepped into the building with a sleeping Lucas in one hand and a very tired Elle in the other.

It had been two weeks since we'd been back, and adjusting was a lot. When I had Lucas, I dropped off the face of the earth. It was Luca who'd adapted to life with four little ones under the age of ten while I drowned in my sorrows. However, since the much-needed vacation we'd taken, I was more than happy to resume the role of their full-time caregiver with the assistance of my husband.

Today was the first day that I stepped foot outside. I'd been inside, admiring the beauty of our home and exploring the little minds of our children. I was submerged in love and didn't want to lift my head or

FOURTEEN

resurface. If I didn't think I'd have another mental breakdown, I would've stayed inside with my children and husband for the rest of my days. But, we all knew that we had to come up for air sooner or later. Now we were here.

"I'm better," I admitted.

Was I at my best? Probably not, but I was far from the woman I was a few weeks ago. I didn't even know who she was. While I still didn't recognize myself, it wasn't for the same reason that I hadn't weeks ago. This time, I was simply trying to get acquainted with the newer version of myself, the mother of five with a thriving bakery and amazing marriage. She was someone that I was desperately trying to meet and maybe have a sit down with because she mattered most to my future.

"That's so good to hear. You look good and well-fed," she joked.

"Luca is making sure I'm stuffed every day and every night. I've tried more new foods in the last couple of weeks than I have my entire life but I'm not complaining."

"I know that's right. Here, let me get him while you go lay her in my office."

She was part of the reason the children were so spoiled. Mama Eisenberg's day job consisted of carrying our babies around everywhere she went in the daycare. Now that Emorey was in pre-k, it was only Elle and Lucas. Up until the day that we went on vacation, it was only Elle. Lucas was home with us. But, now that he was part of the daycare clan, I could count on her spoiling him rotten, too. It was inevitable.

FOURTEEN

"You're going to spoil the poor thing," I warned.

"And? That sounds like my problem, not yours since I plan on having him during business hours while you and Luca do whatever you do."

"We work." I chuckled.

"That's not what that belly says every few months." She scoffed.

"I can admit that we make a lot of babies, but that's just to keep you in business. Aren't you grateful to have someone to keep you company in that big office of yours?"

We headed in that direction. She was now holding Lucas while I kept Elle attached to my hip.

"Ummm hmmm."

"We're just trying to keep the last name alive. Lyric can't do it and Laike won't do it. We're your only hope."

"You kind of have a point there." She tittered. "That boy won't even give me a damn dog if I asked him. Lord, where did I go wrong with that child?"

"Somehow, he remains your favorite," I reminded her as I sat Elle on the large bean bag so that she could rest if she wanted. She was a little tired when I woke her this morning.

"Whatever."

"And, you shouldn't be worried about a dog. We got you one of those, too."

"You two are the gifts that just keep on giving, huh?" she asked sarcastically.

"It's why you love us so much."

FOURTEEN

"Bye. Get out of here and go enjoy your day. I'll see you later when I drop them off."

"See you later," I told her as I waved. "Everything is in the bag, including frozen milk and fresh milk.

"Bye!" she screamed, forcing me out of her office.

I shook my head as I made my way down the hall and out of the door. When I finally made it to my truck, I climbed inside and sat in silence. Before starting the engine, I took a second to acknowledge the progress I'd made this morning. Luca offered to take everyone to school, but I was adamant. I knew I could make it happen and I did.

The smile that stretched across my face hurt so damn good. I felt the stinging of my eyes and tried to will myself not to cry. However, this was major for me. It meant the world. All I'd ever wanted to do was be the best mother I could be and getting back to that person – no matter how slowly – was at the top of my priority list.

I did it. I did it. He'll be so proud, I thought of my dear husband.

Speaking of him. My phone started ringing. I looked down in my lap at the screen to confirm it was Luca. It was. It always was.

"Hi," I answered.

"Hi. Everything going smooth?" He questioned.

"Yes. Everyone is at school."

"That's what's up, Ever. I'm proud of you, baby."

"I told you I had it."

"You did and I never doubted that you did, love."

FOURTEEN

"Thank you... thank you for never doubting me or giving up on me."

"I love you too much for all that and you know it."

"I know."

"You got places to be, though, so I'm going to let you go."

"See you in two hours for lunch?"

"See you in two hours for lunch," he confirmed.

I started the engine and headed for my next destination. I made it in under twenty minutes. The humongous building was something straight out of a magazine – intimidating almost. However, I found the office I was meant to be in, in only a few minutes. And, when I was face to face with the woman that was highly recommended to whip my mind back into shape, relief washed over me. Even her presence was like the calm to the storm brewing inside of me. Therapy had already started and I hadn't even introduced myself.

"Good morning, I'm ***Kirklynn Benedict***. Right this way," she greeted.

FIFTEEN

EVER

If I was tasked with describing how much better I felt, I wouldn't be able to. The solo nail appointment was everything my heart and soul needed after the emotional day I'd experienced. The first day at Kirklynn's office left me drained, completely.

After a long and late lunch with Luca, I went home alone to digest everything we'd touched on in the session. Though my eyes were tired of crying and I felt like I had no more tears left, more appeared. But, for the first time in a long time, the tears I shed made me feel so much better than I had before.

"Goodness, I feel like a new person. I think I recognize myself a little," I said aloud, talking to absolutely no one.

Naturally, my eyes landed on the large, well-lit sign

FIFTEEN

that was just across the street. *Ever Sinclair*, it read. *That's me. That's mine.*

With weights on my chest, I took a step closer to the edge of the curb. Then another. And, it wasn't until I reached the front door that I stopped. In an instant, I unlocked the door using my code and entered the building.

I looked around the place, standing right in the middle. All of my hard work had been put into the bakery and I missed it more than I could've imagined. From the formulation of sweet treats to the feeling of dough rolling underneath my palm, I missed it. Everything.

"God, please give me the strength to get back in here. Help me. I need You now."

Unable to withstand the emotional load the bakery required of me at the moment, I quickly exited. There was so much on my mind as I made my way to my vehicle. Though the moment was heavy, it was the motivation I needed to keep going until I could get back to myself – *just as Lucas said*.

I didn't bother selecting music during my ride. My thoughts were running rampant and all I wanted was to feel things, whatever they were. No matter what they were. And, to my surprise, they were much more pleasant than I'd expected.

"I'm going in tomorrow."

As I pulled into our garage, the words left my mouth. There was as much conviction as there was confidence behind them, making me smile until my lips reached my eyes almost.

FIFTEEN

"I'm going in tomorrow," I repeated, this time a bit louder and with much more enthusiasm.

Excitement grew in my belly, not only from the anticipation of what was to come the next day but from what I knew I was about to walk into. The chaos, I was prepared for it. Once, I thrived in the trenches of motherhood and I was slowly getting back to that.

I stepped into the house from the garage entry and followed the noise all the way to the living room where my girls were all enthralled in a different activity with the television running in the background. There was so much beauty in the room. Each one of them had stolen my entire face to have as their own. Had they not been years apart, they'd all get mistaken for triplets.

"Heeeeeeey, Elle." I greeted the tiniest one who noticed me first.

Her hands were stretched as her fingers wiggled. She, too, was happy to see me.

"Did you miss me, mommas?"

"Pick up. Pick up."

She bounced up and down, ignoring my question.

"Alright, alright. Just for a second. Mommy has to feed Brother, OK?"

When I pulled her into my arms and up on my hip, her little lips landed right on mine.

"Down, Mommy!"

"What? You just got up here."

"Down, Mommy."

"OK. OK. I'll put you down."

FIFTEEN

"Hi, Mom," Essence called out, not budging from her spot on the couch.

"Hey, baby. How was your day?"

I sat Elle back down and began to remove my shoes. My feet were begging to be freed.

"It was good. How are you feeling?"

"I'm feeling good, Essence. I figured I'll try to go to the bakery tomorrow. I'm actually really happy about that."

"Me, too. If you get the chance, can you make us some more snickerdoodles? I miss those a lot."

My best friends. Essence had been such a great friend to me since she was born. She didn't know it, but she helped me fight so many silent battles by just being there with a toothless smile or kisses like the one Elle had just given me. Then, Emorey came along and the two tackled the position that most parents refused to allow their children to fulfill. My children were my friends and I wouldn't trade that relationship for anything. Our friendship was deeply rooted and solved problems that many didn't have to suffer through if they'd just opened their minds to the idea of friendship with their children. It was as pleasant as it was helpful.

"I will. That'll give me something to actually do when I get there. I had no idea what I'd be doing. I just know I want to go."

"You should."

"Mommy, I painted this," Emorey said, pulling on the end of my shirt while holding a sheet of paper up as far as it would go.

FIFTEEN

"You did? Let me see, Em."

I kneeled to her height so that she could understand she had my undivided attention. It was the only kind of attention you were to give Em, or not give her any at all.

"You like it?"

"I love it. Is it for me?"

"No," she stated, snapping her neck.

"Oh. Well, uh..." I didn't exactly know how to respond, too tickled with her display of sassiness.

"It's for Daddy."

"OK. It's the second picture this week for Daddy. Does Mom get any?"

Her obsession with Luca hadn't gotten any better. It had actually gotten worse. Their father-daughter relationship was the purest, kindest, and most gentle I'd ever witnessed. During my downtime, they seemed to get even closer. I wasn't sure if that was possible but they'd proved me wrong.

"Next week."

"Alright. I'm going to hold it to you. Speaking of Daddy, where is he?"

"Making dinner."

Just as she mentioned it, the seasonings hit my nose and made my stomach growl.

"And, where's Lucas?"

"In the kitchen," Essence answered.

Emorey was over me the minute I asked about someone besides her. For her to have so many siblings, she still suffered from *only-child* syndrome. I doubted it was something she'd ever overcome.

FIFTEEN

"Thanks, Es. Get everyone washed up and ready for dinner. I'm going to check on the guys."

"OK."

I headed for the kitchen, allowing the aroma to lead the way. When I entered and saw Luca mixing the salad with Lucas not too far, chilling in his car seat, I couldn't help but take a second to savor what was before me. I'd envisioned a better life all those years ago, but I'd never imagined this level of perfection and pure satisfaction. My heart was full watching them both. My boys.

"You're home," Luca rejoiced, finally noticing me.

He was all up on me and all in my space before I could manage to respond. His lips were as soft as they'd always been when they landed on my forehead and then my lips. I kissed him hard and I kissed him deeply, only ending the connection at the sound of Lucas' whimpers.

"I've missed you," Luca whispered against my mouth.

"I've missed you."

I had. Although he was right there with me through it all, I missed the version of him that didn't carry so much weight or have double the responsibility. I missed the version of him that required my presence and my light. My heaviness had spilled over into his world and I could see it on his face each day. But, we were in such a better space that I knew it wouldn't be long before my Luca resurfaced.

"I need to feed him."

"Yeah. He's about to start tripping."

"I see."

Slowly, I reached into the car seat Luca had on the

counter and pulled Lucas into my arms. Before honoring his request for food, I pressed his body against mine and rocked from one side to the other. His birth had taken so much from me and required so much of me I once hated the thought of it. But, now, as the band aids were being ripped from my wounds, I was thankful that I had them. Lucas' birth only made them real. They'd already been present. He forced me to face them, remember they existed, acknowledge them, and begin to heal them.

"Hey, Momma's man. Hey."

As if he could hear my thoughts, Luca appeared with the wrap that I was about to search for. With Lucas in my arms, I began wrapping us properly so that I could free my hands to help Luca as he emptied my breasts.

"I'm ready. I've decided to go into the bakery tomorrow and spend some time there. Essence wants some cookies, so I'm going to make us a batch," I revealed while unhooking my bra to give Lucas access to his milk supply.

"Yeah? That's good shit, baby."

The cheer in his voice was the most rewarding thing I'd ever heard.

"You think it's a good idea?"

His opinion mattered to me. Always had, always would.

"A great idea. You'll feel a lot better, I bet."

"I think so, too. After my manicure, I went over. It was the motivation I needed."

"Glad you did that, then."

FIFTEEN

"I feel so close to whoever it is this situation forced me to become. I'm not avoiding her anymore. I'm ready."

"That makes me a very happy man, Ever, hearing that."

He stopped what he was doing to look over at me. *I love this man so much. Every part of me. Every single piece of me. I love him so much it hurts. My God. He's mine.*

"Why you looking at a nigga like that? What's on your mind?"

"Nothing. Just that I'm a blessed woman to have you by my side. With you, I feel like nothing is impossible, even my reset. Laying in that bed all those weeks, it was you that kept me going. Being unwell and seeing you handle everything so graciously and so well, that altered me. After so long, I knew I had to get back to you so that I could relieve you."

"I didn't need relief, baby. I just needed you. Now that you're making strides, I'll still carry as much of the load as I need to until you're all better."

"Thanks, baby. What are we having for dinner?"

"They begged for pasta, again. So, we're having that and salad. I made some garlic bread and salmon, too. I'm afraid I'll turn into a noodle if I eat any more pasta alone."

His lips turned up as he scoffed, shaking his head. When it came down to the kids, he was willing to suffer for their satisfaction.

"How can I help?"

"Help me get the plates fixed and to the table."

FIFTEEN

"Say no more."

I stepped up to the sink and twisted the handles on the faucet. This was it. This was exactly what I needed to end the day. Time with my husband and the children we shared. Nothing more mattered. Nothing else ever had.

The end.

LUCA'S LETTER

What a wild fucking ride, huh?
Grey tells me it's been an entire calendar since we first met. It feels like yesterday when I entered your world and you entered mine. It feels like yesterday when I walked through those gates and Lyric ran right into my arms. It feels like yesterday when I saw Ever's fine ass in that passenger seat, tired from a night out with her best friend. It feels like yesterday that I couldn't keep my fucking eyes off of her. It feels like yesterday when I realized I can't keep my fucking dick out of her.
If I told you what number we're on now, you'd swear I'm lying, but I'm not. After

LUCA'S LETTER

Ever's struggles to come back to me when Lucas was born, we chilled, but after that break she couldn't stop popping that pussy and I couldn't pull out of that motherfucker, either. I'll just say that my large family has been made possible by Ever Eisenberg. And, my God do I love that woman a little more each and every day. She's so fucking pretty.

A real dream.

A nigga is living a dream. Every time I see that face, I want to pinch myself. Every time I hear those little feet patting the floors in pursuit of me, I want to pinch myself. Every time I'm encouraging Ever to push one more time right before hearing a whaling baby, I want to pinch myself. But, I don't because I understand I've been blessed to have everything I once dreamed of.

This is my reality and I can't help but give Grey Huffington a big fucking shout out for creating this space for me to live in my truth.

Far from the average nigga, I'm THAT nigga. Nevertheless, I want to give a huge thanks to everyone who's ever opened the

LUCA'S LETTER

pages of my story and began to read this rollercoaster.

You did this.

You made me an even bigger nigga and I didn't think that was possible. Keep saying my name, keep pushing my book, keep my story alive. My time in #greynation has ended but my story continues. Appreciate everything you made me, G.

Love you... always.
Luca.

Want more of these two? Be sure to **scan the code** to get the **deleted scenes** for this book and many others.

or sign up for deleted scenes at **https://theliteraryheroine. ck.page/e2956a645b**

MORE FROM GREY HUFFINGTON

SYX + THE CITY
SYX + THE CITY 2
SYX THIRTY SEVYN
SXYTH GIVING
SYX WHOLE WEEKS

WILDE + RECKLESS
WILDE + RELENTLESS
WILDE + RESTLESS

MR. INTENTIONAL
UNEARTH ME

THE SWEETEST REVENGE
THE SWEETEST REDEMPTION

HALF + HALF

MORE FROM GREY HUFFINGTON

THE EMANCIPATION OF EMOREE

SLEIGH
SLEIGH SQUARED

THE GIFTED
MEMO
GIVE HER LOVE. GIVE HER FLOWERS.

UNBREAK ME
UNCOVER ME

AS WE LEARN
AS WE LOVE

JUST WANNA MEAN THE MOST TO YOU
SENSITIVITY
10,000 HOURS
DARKE HEARTS
MUSE.

SOFTLY
PEACE + QUIET
PRESS REWIND
JAGGED EDGES
MY PERSON
THE REALM OF
RIOT THIMBLE
WHOSE LOVE STORY IS IT ANYWAY?

MORE FROM GREY HUFFINGTON

<u>WEB EXCLUSIVES:</u>
ghuffington.com

HOME*
BLUES*
31ST*
WHAT ARE WE DOING?*
NOW THAT WE'RE HERE.*

THEN LET'S FUCK ABOUT IT*
GIVING THANKS

LUCA
LYRIC
EVER
LAIKE
BAISLEIGH
LIAM

LEDGE
HALO
LAWE

Made in the USA
Columbia, SC
26 June 2024